TO BE A KING

TO BE A KING

A Novel about Christopher Marlowe

Robert DeMaria

Vineyard Press
Port Jefferson, NY

"Is it not passing brave to be a king,
And ride in triumph through Persepolis?"

Tamburlaine the Great,
Act II, scene v.

TO BE
A
KING

I

CANTERBURY

i

THE work is done for the day in the cobbler's shop at number 57 St. George Street. John Marlowe sends his apprentices home early. Tomorrow is a special day in Canterbury. Tomorrow the Queen is arriving from Dover on her progress through Kent, and the four thousand inhabitants of this medieval town can talk of nothing else.

Lore Atkynson and Harmon Verson sweep up hastily, replace tools, stack boots, and mumble their thanks to the master cobbler, who waves them out with a rough gesture. He shutters the shop and sits for a moment in the dim light to collect his thoughts.

Through the thin wall he hears his daughters squabbling. One of them is crying—Anne, the youngest. She's only two. Joan is four and Margaret is seven. Mary May, the housekeeper, is scolding them. His wife, Katherine, has taken to her bed with an enormous belly, due within a week or two to deliver another child.

He picks up a scrap of leather, turns it this way and that in his hands, and then, satisfied that it can be of no further use, tosses it onto a waste pile in the corner. The dog, who has been asleep under the workbench, stirs and moves with him toward the door. John hesitates before plunging into the chaos of his family. His life is not easy, but he is making progress, he assures himself. He is thirty-three, a respectable member of the community and of The

Brethren of the Assumption of Our Lady, of the Crafts and Mysteries of Shoe-Makers, Coriours and Cobblers. He slips into financial calculations as poets slip into reveries.

He is shocked out of his shillings and pence by crashing crockery. Little Joan has gone over backwards in a chair with a stolen pot of honey in her hands. Mary May shrieks and drops a ladle of hot soup, which she has dipped from a kettle over the fire. The baby Anne begins to cry again, strangling the panic-eyed maid, whose white cap is awry over red hair and whose apron is a chronicle of the day's disasters. "She's been at the honey again, Father," says big sister Margaret, trying to ally herself with the master.

The inevitable explosion comes, just as the bells of St. George the Martyr ring out. Their music mingles with his curses, and he seems to be singing like a madman as he flings his cap across the room and kicks at the fallen chair. "Peace and order!" he shouts. "Why can't a man have a little peace and order in his own house? What in God's heaven is going on here?"

Mary May clutches the child in her arms, a hint of assaulted youth showing through her thirty-year-old middle-aged face. The bells stop ringing. Silence grips the kitchen. The dog slinks for cover behind the woodpile. He begins again, but somewhat calmer: "I've been working like a fool these past few weeks, trying to satisfy everyone, and I do not want all this whining and squabbling. Do you understand?"

"Yes, sir," says Mary May. "I'm sorry, sir. But with the mistress sick and all—well, I can't do everything. Not with the girls crawling around the kitchen like thieves, and the baby needing a change, and dinner on the fire."

He picks up the toppled chair and then his cap and then his criminal daughter. He seats her roughly in the chair without a word. She is too frightened to cry. Late afternoon September light comes through the wrinkled panes of the tall window. The fire crackles, pots and pans dangle like victims, the beams cast shadows against the gray-white walls and ceiling. He mumbles what might be a grudging apology and goes out.

ii

Christopher Marlowe sits among the ruins of the Abbey of St. Augustine outside the walls of Canterbury. He is waiting for Friar Martyn, who, they say, has discovered a secret passage to hell among the crumbled stones of the once magnificent monastery.

Clutching the shoes that he has not yet delivered to Sir Roger Manwood, Kit calls out the name of the old monk. "Friar Martyn. Friar Martyn. It's me, Kit Marlowe." He waits. He listens. The Roman arches of glassless windows rise above him in the half-demolished wall. Broken pieces of statuary mingle with the heavy blocks of stone. He sees a corpse's eye, remnants of an effigy, and shudders in the September breeze as white-gray clouds briefly cover the sun. He has come out with only a shirt and breeches, and his stockings have fallen around his ankles. He looks this way and that, and, seeing no one, he says aloud, "Hobberdidance, Flibberti-gibbet, Modo, Mahu." From behind a heap of crumbled brick and mortar a humped figure appears in monk's robes, his hood up, so that he seems to be a faceless demon rising from the dead. Friar Martyn flings back his hood and laughs, his gray hair flying, his toothless mouth open wide.

"Ah, it's you, my friend," he says. "Bringing gifts to the wise men." He chuckles. "But be careful what you conjure with those potent words. Be careful of Modo and Mahu. There may be a new comet in the sky. Sun, Moon, Mars, Mercury, Jupiter, Venus, Saturn, Trine, Sextile, Dragon's Head, Dragon's Tail, I charge you all to guard this house. The Queen comes tomorrow. Give her an almanac. Let her consult her stars. These are times for purging and bloodletting. Stay away from the water, Kit. Christ in crystal. Mary in the moon."

"You promised to tell me about Mother Hudson," says Kit.

"Screech owls and ostriches shall walk in her houses, apes and satyrs shall dance in her beautiful buildings," says the monk. "Come sit by me, my son."

Kit sits beside him on a wide stone, a piece of the Catholic structure smashed to ruins by King Henry the Eighth.

"First the gift," says Friar Martyn, reaching for the shoes.

"No, no," says Kit, drawing back. "These are not for you. I've got to deliver them to Sir Roger Manwood in Hackington."

The monk tears the shoes from Kit's hands and examines them. They are made of polished leather and silk and cork, with a delicate heel and silver buckle. "Ah, such finery for such a fine gentleman. Not for the likes of such low creatures as us, eh, Kit?" He tosses them back. "A year of bread and a month of wine to decorate a man's feet. The world's an ugly place."

"I'll bring you some food tomorrow," says Kit, "and maybe some wine. But I have to be careful."

"Good. Good," says the monk. "In the meantime I will fast and pray, fast and pray." He laughs. "Or eat rocks."

"And now can you tell me about Mother Hudson?" says Kit.

"Of course, of course, my boy. After all, I was there. I saw it all, every bit of it, the billowing flames, the hand of death. There are forces in this universe—forces that we cannot even imagine, cannot even guess at. Invisible forces. Forces that descend out of the darkness of space and rise from the bowels of the hot earth." He looks this way and that for eavesdroppers and spies. His face comes very close to Kit's. His breath is vile. "I have it on good authority," he says. "Good authority. And that is not all. I know the secret connections—how to make visible the invisible. How to lay open the future."

"But Mother Hudson," says Kit. "What about Mother Hudson?"

"Ah yes," he says, his blazing eyes scanning the ruins. "No less than fifteen murders could be traced to her door. Yes, fifteen. She killed the Mistress Warden's third child and threw the municipal clerk's assistant from an upper window in his house. She brought the pox on William Verson and killed poor Mary Drew in childbirth. She was found singing in the graveyard and howling at the full moon. No, no, there never was any doubt about it. She was the devil's own creature. 'Tis magic, magic makes this black world go round. Dogs snapped at her. Children spat on her; unborn babes kicked with terror when she passed. And when she was taken and brought to trial they found in her possession a thumb, a toe, a nose, and an eye, all used in her black art. But she was never burned, never tortured—for as they led her to the place of judgment a whirlwind surrounded them. The sky cracked open and a bolt of lightning set fire to the woods. She disappeared in a cloud of flames that I saw for myself was the devil's hand. For in another moment the sky was clear and the trees that seemed to be on fire were not so much as scorched."

Pale with astonishment, Kit rises and steps away from the mad monk. "Is it true?" he says. "Is that the way it happened?"

Friar Martyn explodes his wheezing laugh. "Lies, my boy," he shouts. "All lies. The truth is all lies. Do not be deceived by it. Lines and circles and symbols. Give me magic every time."

Kit backs away. "I have to go. It's late. I have these to deliver." He holds out the shoes.

"Yes, go, little one," he says, "but not without first swearing me an oath."

"An oath?" echoes Kit.

"Yes, in the old biblical way," says the monk, smiling with a wet mouth. "Come, I'll show you." He grabs Kit roughly by the hand. "You see, you place it here—thusly." He shoves Kit's hand between his withered legs. "And swear, by Christ and his Virgin Mother, that you will never repeat a word of this meeting to any living soul. Now swear!"

Kit feels the limp flesh of his groin. He cringes but cannot escape. "I s-s-swear," he says. "I swear!" And then he is free and flying over the fallen stones and through the town to the West Gate.

iii

The following day the people of Canterbury put on their finest, their feathers and furs, to greet the Queen, her courtiers and train, a cortege of perhaps two hundred people.

The excitement has been building all day. The open market closed early, sold out of everything from shallots to sheep's eyes.

There will be enormous dinners of fifteen courses at the elegant houses, notably at the Archbishop's palace, but there will also be celebrations in the more ordinary households. After all, it is not every day that one can actually lay his eyes on the divinely appointed Queen of the realm.

Local officials and gentlemen and merchants have spent small fortunes on their costumes: knitted hose, bombasted breeches, elaborate ruffs, decorated doublets, cloaks with standing collars and tippets of velvet. They and their wives vie with each other, hoping for the unlikely miracle of a special gesture or even a glance from her Royal Majesty, a sign of recognition on which they might feast for the rest of their lives.

The arrival of royalty has cured Katherine Marlowe of her ailments, at least temporarily, and she manages to walk the half mile across town from St. George Street to the West Gate with her husband and half a dozen neighbors. Her farthingale cannot conceal her condition. If anything, it only exaggerates it.

She chats with Mistress Livingston, who wears a beaver hat over hair which is tinted a fashionable red. "The Guild is presenting a leather-bound chest, studded with silver."

Mistress Livingston makes henlike noises of approval and proudly describes the silver chalice fashioned by her husband and his fellow craftsmen.

John Marlowe makes do with an old outfit—black and conservative in the Spanish style, with lace at the collar and cuffs. He is unaccustomed to these rituals and a bit short-tempered. "I don't see why we have to go all the way to the other side of town," says John, "when the whole procession will be passing through to the Cathedral and then, afterwards, out again to the King's lodging at St. Augustine."

"But we'd miss the welcoming ceremony at the West Gate," says Katherine.

John glances across the street and sees Will Hartley in blazing green and his feather of a wife in pink and pearls. He sees also his friend Plesington the baker, the municipal clerk, Constable John Hart, and several Huguenot weavers.

Coaches and wagons and horses are forbidden beyond a certain point, and the crowds fill the streets. The wide skirts of the ladies brush against one another, and the children tear away in general rebellion.

The welcoming party waits. Dr. Matthew Parker, Archbishop of Canterbury, is in conversation with Sir Roger Manwood. The bishops of Lincoln and Rochester stand rigid and silent, like effigies of themselves, their bodies already entombed and their souls fled to heaven. The nervous Grammarian rehearses his oration, his lips moving visibly. The mayor bustles about, and the aldermen make pompous jokes. They are flanked by a small army of clerks and miscellaneous gentlemen.

Archbishop Parker is almost seventy years old now. His round, firm face is a record of years of discipline and benign ambition. "Something must be done about the roads in Sussex and Kent," he says.

Sir Roger agrees. He has the kindly and somewhat dissipated look of a man with a secret vice. "And did Her Majesty, by any chance, stop at Mr. Guildford's house in Benenden?" he says.

"Yes, briefly," says Parker. "And then we were a week at Croydon. A somewhat exhausting week. And thence to Orpington, where Sir Percival Hart presented a most magnificent water entertainment. And then to Knole, Sissinghurst, Boughton Malherbe, Hothfield, and Westenhanger."

Martial music from the dual turrets of the West Gate announces the arrival of the royal procession. The crowd presses forward with gasps and shrieks of excitement. "It is about to begin," says his Suffragan to Archbishop Parker, whose expression does not change.

Kit Marlowe, an escaped prisoner from his own room, crouches and runs through the deserted alleyways and streets of St. George parish. He knows he must not be seen at the celebration, having been punished in this way for "willful disobedience." He turns a corner and sees the tower of St. George the Martyr. It is a stone's throw from the Cathedral of Christ Church and has a commanding view of the main road.

He plunges into the musty interior, and his footsteps echo in the vaulted nave. He knows the church well, attends it regularly, and was, in fact, baptized in it. He goes through a heavy door and down a narrow corridor with a low ceiling, almost a tunnel. Then up stone steps to a higher level, and still a higher level, until he is in the belfry, among the heavy bells. Then he goes up a ladder and through a trap door and emerges into sunlight on the square rampart.

He hears trumpets and bells and then stretches of silence. He knows what is happening, though he can't quite see. Edmund Carey, his schoolmaster, has described it all. After the Grammarian has made his oration, the Queen gets off her horse. They kneel and say the Psalm *Deus misereatur* in English, and certain other collects. Then the Queen is borne in a magnificent canopy by four knights to the Cathedral, while the choir, the Dean, and the prevendaries line the way for her. After she hears evensong the procession moves from the great church to St. George Gate.

It is an endless wait until the crowds reach the Cathedral, and he sees the Queen go in as the choir sings. And it is another eternity until she emerges and draws closer to his fortress. But now he sees them all clearly: the noblemen, the bishops, the knights, the ladies, and the Queen herself, borne aloft on the shoulders of four beautiful men, their swords gallantly draped, their high ruffs giving them an arrogant air. Thin rods of gold support the chair and the bejeweled canopy. The Queen herself is in a cloud of white, studded with emeralds. She glows as though she is the center of light, and he is dazzled.

Then they are directly below him, a strange sea of bobbing heads, truncated and a bit absurd. His excitement turns to laughter and borders on hysteria. He has an urge to spit on them—or worse. But he is assaulted suddenly by the tolling of bells directly under him. He holds his ears and closes his eyes until it stops. And when it does and he looks again, the eye of the royal hurricane has passed through the gate, and he sees in the surging crowd his own parents and Mary May. He retreats in a panic, knowing that he has but a few minutes to get back into his room.

iv

It is almost Christmas, a clear and windy afternoon that has been preceded by three days of December rain. John Marlowe, in good spirits, has declared a half holiday and sent his apprentices away. After lunch he is planning to take his family to a play at the Guild Hall.

In the five years since Queen Elizabeth's visit, John has grown thicker and more prosperous. They live now in St. Andrew's parish in the heart of town. Katherine has, at last, given him a second son, who is alive and well at the age of two and a half. He is Thomas Marlowe.

John goes from the shop into the large kitchen, where Mary May is preparing lunch. She is bent over the fire as he passes her, and he gives her a playful pinch. She straightens up with a little shriek and shakes her head disapprovingly. "Don't you let the mistress catch you doing that," she says.

He hums his way out and finds, in the next room, what he calls his covey of females. "Handy, dandy, prockly pandy," sings Margaret to her younger sisters, "which hand will you have?" Margaret is thirteen, and, since she does not go to school, she has assumed some of the household responsibilities. She holds out her hands to Dorothy, who is now five.

It is Saturday noon, and the city is alive with bells. Joan, who is nine, sings out:

"Jack boy, ho boy news,
    The cat is in the well:
Let us ring now for her knell,
    Ding-dong, ding-dong bell."

"Why can't we go to the play, too?" says seven-year-old Anne.

"Because you're too young, my dear," says Katherine. Anne pouts and stamps and asks again, "But why can't we go?"

John picks up little Thomas and holds him high in the air. "How about you, Tom?" he says. "Do you want to go to the Guild Hall too and see the old dragon roar?"

"I think you should wear your Venice breeches and a heavy doublet," says Katherine to her husband, "and a cloak to boot. It's turned quite cold."

"I'll wear what I please, madam," he says.

"And what will that be?" she says.

"Why, my Venice breeches and a heavy doublet, of course," he says.

The play proves to be a lot of shouting and stamping in gaudy costumes, flashing swords, clanking armor, invisible music-makers and flying dragons. With a few choice words the actors transport themselves miraculously over the geography of Never-Never land: Denmark, Norway, the Court of Alexander the Great, the Forest of Marvels, and the Isle of Strange Marshes. Christopher is rigid with concentration, his mind coiling itself about each ridiculous piece of fantasy and invention. For him it is all more real than the real world, but doubly absurd.

"What's happening now?" says Katherine in a loud whisper to her husband. "Who is that funny-looking man?"

John turns to his son. "Kit, who is that fellow there?"

"That's Subtle Shift the Vice," says Kit. "He promises to serve Clyomon, but he can't be trusted."

John passes back the information to his inquisitive wife, who nods as though satisfied. But in another moment she passes along another question: "Who has to kill the Flying Serpent, and in what country are they now?"

"Clamydes has been sent by his Lady, Juliana the Princess of Denmark, to kill the dragon. Her brother is Prince Clyomon, but Clamydes doesn't know this. Now they have come to the court of Alexander the Great to have a trial at arms, because Clyomon has pushed Clamydes aside when his father was about to knight him—thus stealing his knighthood."

Katherine is leaning across her husband and listening to Kit's explanation. "Oh," she says.

When they finally emerge from the Guild Hall into the waning light of the winter afternoon, it is like emerging from a dream. So deeply involved was Kit in those imaginary lands that the stones and steeples and shuttered windows of Canterbury seem ghostly and insubstantial.

They come to a curb, and suddenly Kit's mother takes his arm. "Help your mother across," says John from behind him. Kit pauses to look down into the miniature river. "Come on, come on," says John. "Cross over!" And Kit feels the weight of his mother on his arm as she tries to take a long step.

v

John Gresshop, headmaster of the King's School, sits at his desk in a cluttered office and goes through a set of Latin themes with the calm indifference and efficiency of a man who has been at his post a long time and can be surprised by nothing, even occasional flashes of talent, or abysmal displays of ignorance. He has seen his boys come and go, ranging in age from nine to fifteen when they enter, and some of them almost men when they leave—often for one of the universities.

He looks up at the sound of a tapping on his door. "Come in," he says, and the door opens. Standing there he sees his lower master, Robert Rose, with the new boy, Christopher Marlowe. Rose is a lean young man in black with a scholarly brow, a bit too nervous for Gresshop's taste.

"Well," says Gresshop for the thousandth time, "how does it feel to be a member of our little family?"

"I am very pleased to be here, sir," says Christopher.

"Good, good!" says Gresshop and motions Robert Rose out. When they are alone, he says, "I asked Master Rose to bring you here so that we could have a little chat. I like to see to it that the new boys are comfortable and that they understand our way of doing things."

"Yes, sir," says Christopher, not quite sure what to do with his hands.

"It is too bad that John Emtley had to leave us so suddenly, but his misfortune is your good fortune, which is so often the way in this world." He clears his throat. "Now, as I understand it, you are here on the usual scholarship. I suppose you know the terms. One pound, eight and four per year, with allowances for commons and a new gown each Christmas, for a total of four pounds, which comes to one pound per quarter. You made a very favorable impression on the selection committee and you come to us highly recommended by Sir Roger Manwood. I hope that you will not prove a disappointment to us. Everything indicates that you are, indeed, 'apt for learning.' I understand you also have a fine voice and that you dabble in verse."

Christopher blushes and glances down at his feet.

"Master Rose has undoubtedly explained your schedule to you. You are coming into the fourth form, which means a fairly advanced level of Latin, poetic tales, familiar letters of learned men, and other literature of that sort. In the fifth there will be oratory, classical rules of literary composition, and Greek. By the sixth you should be able to handle Erasmus and to vary speech in every mood in Latin. You will read Horace and Cicero and other Romans and Greeks. There will be competitions in declamations and participation in plays, as well, of course, as the choir, throughout your stay. My personal examinations will take place weekly, and you will advance at the usual times if your work is adequate. Lessons conclude at five, but there is an additional supervised study period between six and seven, which you will be expected to attend. You will take your meals with us and spend your evenings at home." His voice has flattened into routine, and Christopher is only half-listening. "Is all that clear, my boy? Do you have any questions?"

"No, sir," says Kit.

"Well, then," says Gresshop, "welcome to King's and good luck." Christopher is dismissed and goes out.

vi

The boys linger in the garden before choir practice, angelic in red and white, shifting from foot to foot under the elms and evergreens, urinating in the labyrinth of privet. In a few minutes the counterpoint of their sweet unaccompanied voices will rise heavenward in a moving motet, polyphonic praise for the Creator and Protector of poor mankind. In the meantime a little scatology lifts their spirits, and they giggle among the geraniums and along the sacred paths.

Thomas Russell, fine-featured as a knife, amuses his younger followers from the podium of his family heritage. He has just finished a story about chamberpots and chambermaids when his attention is drawn to Robert Groves, a slight lad with intelligent eyes, who comes around the hedge, sucking his finger. "Oh, look at that," says Lord Russell. "The poor fellow has pricked himself in the bush." His audience howls, pointing at Robert and echoing his line. "Come here, dear boy, let's have a look," says Russell.

"It's only a scratch," says Robert.

"If it itches, scratch it," says one of the boys.

"But not in God's garden," says another.

"Hush up," says Thomas Russell. "Robert can scratch it all he wants. Nothing will come of it." More laughter. Robert looks confused.

"A sheet of music flew into the bushes, and I was reaching in to fetch it."

"So you stuck your hand in the bush," says Russell with mock sympathy.

"And got pricked," says his friend William Playfer.

"Yes," says Robert. "Exactly. And I don't see what's so funny about that."

"Why, nothing at all," says Russell. "Your little digit must be tender."

"I'll wager his bum's tender, too," says ugly Richard Lecknor.

"Tender, indeed," says Russell. "To buy and sell with. And what little gifts have you bought lately with your tender bum?"

Robert pulls away. The laughter subsides. And in the theatrical split-second of silence, one of the boys farts. "Well done, well done," shouts Russell, imitating the choir master. "You're in fine voice today."

The boys shove each other playfully. Kit joins them, but he is too late for the joke. "What's His Lordship up to now?" he asks Robert Groves.

"Oh, his usual foulness," says Robert. "I scratched myself in the bush, and he's been making fun of me."

Kit smiles and puts his arm around the boy. "Time to go in," he says, seeing the choir master emerge.

vii

A wagon moves slowly toward Canterbury along the Dover Road in the late afternoon. It contains a few sacks of flour and a large pig, which is tied to the uprights. It also contains Kit Marlowe and his now inescapable friend Robert Groves. They have been to Dover to visit Kit's grandfather, William Arthur, and to see the cliffs and the sea.

The metal rims of the wheels grind against the gravel, and the wagon echoes the rhythm of the horses, two thick-footed, fly-bitten plow horses. Kit and Robert lie on their backs and stare into the drama of the billowing sky. "There's a lion," says Robert. "See?" He points eagerly. "See his head, his mane, his mouth."

"I see the holy city of Jerusalem," says Kit.

"And now he's fading," says Robert. "His face has gone all flat. He's turning into a fish."

"I see a Spanish galleon and the billowing waves," says Kit.

"No, not a fish," says Robert. "A dragon. See his forked tongue and the lash of his tail?"

And then they are silent, and the wheels crunch and the wagon squeaks as the fields spread out on both sides. A flight of crows disappears into the distant woods. A group of cows pose motionless under a broad tree. There is a farmhouse and then another. The pig grunts and struggles suddenly to free himself. His snout is hairy and damp, and there is fear in his small eyes.

"Quiet, you beast," says Kit, "before we eat you."

Robert laughs. "There are certain religions of the East that claim that when a person dies he comes back to life as an animal or a bird

or an insect. This pig might have been a very important man once."
Robert's face is soft and animated. He seems always about to laugh
or cry and he has the habit of licking the corners of his mouth.

"Or he may have been a very unimportant person," says Kit,
"who came back to life as an important pig."

Robert laughs again and raises himself up on his elbow so that his
face comes closer to Kit's. The driver's back is to them. His
shoulders are broad and round, and he moves with the limpness of a
man who might very well be asleep at the reins.

The two boys continue to stare at the reincarnated pig, Kit still
lying against a flour sack, his hands behind his head. Robert's face
gradually grows more serious. "Kit," he says, his voice subdued.

Christopher does not acknowledge him, but his smile relaxes and
his eyes wander back toward the sky, where he sees maps and
mountains and towers.

"Kit, you're not angry with me, are you?" says Robert.

"Angry?" says Kit. "Why should I be angry?"

"I mean because of last night," he says.

Christopher says nothing.

"I only meant to show you," says Robert.

"Show me what?" says Kit.

"How I feel," he says. "It's hard to explain, but I hope you
aren't angry. I don't want you to be angry with me."

Kit sits up impatiently. "Oh, Robbie, for God's sake, don't be so
dramatic. I didn't mind." He shoves him playfully.

"But did you enjoy it?" says Robert.

There's ridicule and affection in Christopher's laugh. "No," he
says, "I hated every minute of it. Of course I enjoyed it, you little
idiot. Who wouldn't?"

"I'll do it for you again, if you want," says Robert.

"When?" says Kit.

"Anytime you say," says Robert.

"Now, for instance?"

Robert looks at the back of the farmer and then at the pig, as if
he too were capable of moral judgment. "If you want me to."

Christopher grabs him by the shirt front and pulls him very close to himself, so that their faces almost touch. "Well, I don't want you to," he says in a rough whisper.

He holds him for another moment and then shoves him away as the driver coughs. The horses slow from a trot to a walk and then stop. The driver turns and shouts something at them through his old sunken mouth and points up the road. They get off the wagon and start to walk. The farmer turns into a narrow lane and disappears behind a row of poplars.

"It can't be more than three miles or so from here," says Robert. "We were lucky to get a ride part of the way at least."

They walk along the side of the road, Kit striding quickly and frowning as his little friend breaks now and again into a run, babbling apologetically, cajoling, struggling to make jokes, repeating gossip already chewed over.

Christopher stops listening. He is thinking of his grandfather, who is not well, and of the white cliffs, and the rough excitement of Dover, the teeming port, the ships at anchor, the sailors speaking an English he has never heard. The sails of *The Flying Dragon* billow in his mind. He soars halfway around the globe, cavorts with zebras and two-headed savages with bones in their noses.

And then Robert's voice intrudes again. "You're not going to Tom Russell's for Whitsuntide, are you?"

Christopher stops short and flashes his anger. "And what's it to you if I do?"

Robert shrugs. "Nothing. I just thought—"

"You just thought what?"

"I just thought I would ask, that's all," says Robert.

They walk on again, and after a while Kit says, "Well, the answer is, I don't know."

"Mind you, I'm not jealous or anything like that," says Robert. "But—"

"But what?"

"Well, all I meant to say is—well, you might be out of place there. The Russells are very important people, and—"

Once again Kit stops. He looks with a cruel smile at his trembling friend. "And I'm a very unimportant person. Is that what you were going to say?"

"No, that's not what I meant at all," says Robert.

Kit stares at him for a moment. "Well, you're right," he says. "For once you're right. The Russells *are* very important people. And that's precisely why I *am* going with Tom for Easter. And if you think I can't hold my own among the gentry, you're wrong."

They walk on in silence. A horse gallops by, raising dust. The sun expands into a fat orange blaze behind snow-covered Himalayas and golden cities in the sky, and sinks visibly toward the horizon. And before long the silhouette of Canterbury comes into sight, and Robert says cautiously, "We're almost home."

viii

The Russell estate is on the banks of the Lesser Stour. The manor house has the thick stone walls of an earlier era and half-timbered recent renovations and additions. There are swans in the lake, and lily pads, and oak trees and beech trees and woods and fields. Inside there are arras hangings and linen-roll paneling and a main hall that can easily accommodate thirty people for a fifteen-course meal.

It is mid-afternoon, and the holiday guests have dispersed to their several amusements. Henry Russell, having taken a physic, sits on his "Apostolic Seat," as he calls it, behind a little screen in his bedchamber. He is a somewhat apoplectic, red-faced type. He has taken advantage of the lull in the Whitsuntide celebrations to perform his "meditations"—his third favorite pleasure after hawking and cock-fighting. Self-accompanied by gaseous eruptions, he rehearses his gorgeous life: his hounds, his house, his running geldings, his guests, his son, and his new tennis court.

His wife, Elizabeth, has been resting in the adjoining bedroom. She comes in talking (as she departed talking an hour earlier), and then shrieks and gasps and covers her face with the garment she wants her husband to approve of before wearing it to supper. "Henry," she says in a muffled voice, "you are absolutely incredible."

"All right, all right," he shouts from behind the beautifully decorated screen, "open the window."

"What!" she says. "And destroy all the vegetation for half a mile around? No, thank you. Perfume yourself, darling, perfume yourself. A little of Mr. Carey's remedy." She has found a fan and is using it with all her might. "Do hurry, Henry," she says. "I want you to look at my new dress. I'll not be outdone by that awful Jane Flood with that outrageous bosom of hers. Did you see her at dinner? Did you see what she was wearing?"

Henry grunts and chuckles from his semiprivacy. "How could I help but notice? I was afraid they'd be mistaken for melons and be eaten by one of the guests."

"Henry, don't be naughty," she says, standing in front of a mirror in her underthings and holding up in front of her the elaborate dress with its wheel farthingale, the very latest thing from France. She is a thin, flat-chested woman, from whom her son Thomas has inherited his leanness and fine features. "It was your idea to invite them. And not a very brilliant idea at that, what with all the gossip about her, and her poor husband forced to sit at the same table with a pair of her lovers."

"I thought it would be amusing," says Henry.

"Well, nobody is amused," she says.

"I am," he says.

"Least of all that nice Vincent Randall," she says. "He's in the garden, brooding like a lovesick adolescent. I saw him from my window."

"He's not lovesick at all," says Henry. "He suffers from acute indigestion. We had a long talk about it. He suspects his liver but is afraid of leeching."

"Nonsense," she says. "It is common knowledge that Jane Flood and Vincent Randall were lovers, and that she has tossed him over for Robert Copell. Can't you tell by the smug look on the man's face? And he the rector of Throwley. A fine rector! Collects his tithes and disappears for six months at a time. I don't like him. I don't like him one bit. He has an evil look about him—an absolutely evil look. Oh, Henry, do hurry, I'm afraid this dress will never do and I'll have to wear the green satin, which is terribly outdated."

His reply is a gutsy eruption that rattles the windows and sends his wife out of the room in angry suffocation.

While Alexander Flood, the cuckold, is out in the field hawking with Edmund Bull, Robert Copell, rector of Throwley Park, has an assignation with Jane Flood, a handsome and insatiable lady in her mid-twenties. They are rowing on the lake, scattering swans and ducks as they make like mad Vikings for a small and deserted island. "Faster, Robert, faster," she says, "they'll be back from the hawking before us." And Robert, who is not accustomed to physical labor, tries to increase his stroke but succeeds only in skimming the surface and falling backward off his seat. Jane Flood, her bosom loaded with compassion (and passion), rushes to comfort him. She throws herself on him. "Oh, Robert," she pants. "You haven't hurt yourself, have you? You poor darling." She kisses him from stem to stern, and he is unable to rise. That is, he rises but cannot regain his seat. "Never mind about the island," she says in a hoarse whisper.

The enormous kitchen of the Russell mansion is an inferno of roaring fires and boiling caldrons. The cooks shout orders through the meat-scented smoke to the greasy Joans who stir the pots and wash the pans. There will be boiled beef, roast veal, mutton in pottage, chickens, rabbits, pigeons, and pigeon pie. There will be kid, and moorcocks, calves' feet, and soused pig. There will be jellies and fruits, tarts and marzipan, suckets, codiniacs, marmalades and gingerbread.

In an indoor court of stone and wood, George Hawkes plays tennis with Reginald Bolton. Neither one is very good at the game, and they move about awkwardly, trying to get the ball across a tasseled rope with their short-handled racquets. They are dressed more for dancing than for tennis, with their padded breeches, their ruffs, and even their decorative daggers. Fortunately, no one is watching.

"A ridiculous game," says Reginald, swishing at the ball but catching only air. He is thin, with very large joints and a bony face. "The French must be out of their minds."

"Oh, they are, they are," says George Hawkes. He puts another ball in play but overpowers it into the gallery. They begin again and manage a dim approximation of human grace and motion. After a few more minutes of this, they pause and refresh themselves with wine.

"Tell me, George," says Reginald, "why do you suppose Henry Russell invited young Walsingham to this gathering? He must have a reason, a practical reason."

"I haven't the slightest idea," says George Hawkes. "Unless he's planning to match him up with his daughter Alice. She must be close to eighteen years old by now, and very pretty—very pretty, indeed."

"Not a chance," says Reginald. "When a Walsingham marries, it is usually political. And besides, they say young Thomas is not especially inclined toward women—if you get my meaning."

"Nonsense," says George. "Everybody is inclined toward women. Only some men are shyer than others."

"No, no," says Reginald, "you don't understand. They say he likes boys."

George Hawkes looks puzzled. "Well, what's wrong with that? Boys are all right. Everybody likes boys. Good sturdy boys. Got a boy of my own. Good fellow. What's that got to do with it?"

"Never mind," says Reginald, rolling his eyes skyward and finishing his wine. "Shall we try again?"

"No, thank you," says George. "I'll save myself for the hunt tomorrow. I don't feel quite natural unless I've got a horse under me, and you can't very well play tennis on horseback, can you?" He chokes out a hearty laugh, and Reginald responds with a wincing smile.

In the Blue Room, as the Russells call it, the ladies are playing cards and gossiping. And what better subject for gossip than the Queen herself?

"She had her opportunities, God knows, with Robert Dudley," says Frances Hawkes, a plain and practical woman of thirty-five. "Probably the only man she really cared for, anyway."

"She can't afford to care for any man, not in the usual way," says Marian Bolton. "She is, after all, the Queen, which makes the whole thing different, and besides—"

"I do not believe for a moment that the Earl of Leicester can be trusted," says Katherine Reynardes, squinting suspicious eyes.

"She might very well be too old."

"Nonsense," says Bess Porter. "Women have been known to have children when they are almost sixty."

"She's forty-seven now."

"It's my contention," says Marian Bolton in a loud whisper, "that she simply cannot."

"Cannot what?"

"Well, my dear, I'm sure you know what I'm talking about. She simply cannot. A physical defect of some sort. It's been rumored for years. An obstruction."

"No, no," says Katherine Reynardes, the vixen, "it's all politics. All politics. She cannot afford to have a husband. She doesn't want a husband."

"Every woman wants a husband," says Bess Porter, who never had one and is now seventy years old.

"But what if she had died in childbirth? What of that, with Mary Stuart still alive?"

"Ladies, ladies, play your cards."

A small child of six appears, and Katherine Reynardes blinks rapidly, as though she has a mote in her eye. There are other children in the house. They are a conspiracy of mice—ordered to stay out of the way, stealing sweets from the kitchen, dashing from hiding place to hiding place in secret games, giggling under the stairs, spying on the adults.

Thomas Russell, of course, is not a child. At fifteen he is

considered a young man. In the fall he will be going to the University. He and his school friend freely tour the house and grounds, Thomas pointing to this or that with inherited pride.

"That," says Thomas Russell to Christopher, "is my grandfather Richard Russell." He is pointing to a portrait over a fireplace. The man depicted in the painting is smiling as though he is in pain. He is severely buttoned into his clothes and wears a shameless codpiece that implies miracles of virility. "He was, I understand, illiterate, but a genius at lechery. I've overheard my father boasting about his exploits. I think it is fair to say that he is something of a local legend."

"I suppose he's wenching among the worms, now," says Kit.

"Oh, yes, dead, quite dead," says Tom.

They go through a door and find themselves suddenly in the Blue Room. They try to back out without being noticed, but Aunt Bess calls them in and insists on introducing them.

"Ah," says Katherine Reynardes, "so this is the handsome heir apparent we've heard so much about. Your father is very proud of you."

Thomas makes polite gestures. Aunt Bess falters in her introduction because she cannot remember Christopher's name. Thomas explains to the ladies that this is Christopher Marlowe, his good friend from the King's School. "Oh, yes," says Frances Hawkes. "I seem to know that name, but I can't quite place it at the moment. Did your family, by any chance, have an estate near Faversham?"

"No, madam," says Christopher. "My father has a shop in Canterbury. He's a cobbler."

"Oh," she says, "I'm sorry."

"So am I," says Kit.

She brings her lace handkerchief to her mouth to cover her embarrassment, and Aunt Bess reprimands Thomas with a glance. "Well," she says, "I hope you young men are enjoying yourselves." They all suddenly become intensely interested in their card game, which they have lost track of ages ago.

Tom and Kit wander out to the garden. "Did I say the wrong

thing?" says Kit. "I could have lied for your sake, but I don't really care."

"Neither do I," says Tom. "On the other hand, it seems to me that with a little effort you might have been born into a better family."

"Perhaps your father would like to adopt me," says Kit.

"Not likely," says Tom. "But why don't you marry my sister Alice? She's only two or three years older than you, and very pretty."

"Do you think she'd consider a fifteen-year-old pauper?" says Kit.

"I don't suppose she would," says Tom. "And besides, I suspect Father is trying to marry her to Thomas Walsingham."

They are in a small maze of hedges, and a voice comes from the other side of the row. "Is that so?"

Tom and Kit are startled and embarrassed. In another moment a young man turns the corner and comes face to face with them. It is Thomas Walsingham himself. Though he is only, at best, a couple of years older than the boys he confronts, he seems more mature by far. Perhaps it is the elegance of his clothes or his poise. He is handsome. He is graceful. And he is also the heir, after his brother Edmund, to a large fortune.

"You must be careful what you say when you are walking in a maze," says Walsingham. He looks from one to the other of the boys, his eyes clear and quick.

"I'm sorry," says Tom Russell, "just repeating a little gossip. Surely it's nothing new to you."

"As a matter of fact, it is," says Walsingham. "And you can tell your ambitious father that I am far too young to marry. Besides, I've got other things in mind." His gaze stays with Christopher. "Tom, you're an awful host. You haven't introduced us."

"My name is Christopher Marlowe," says Kit. "Tom and I are at the King's School together."

"Isn't that interesting," says Walsingham. "A fine school, a very fine school."

"We were just walking down to the lake," says Tom.

"Do you mind if I walk with you?" says Walsingham.

"Not at all," says Tom.

At the lake they are approached by hopeful and hungry swans. "Well," says Tom Russell, "if you didn't come down here to marry my sister, then why did you come?"

"I came to listen to the scintillating conversation of George Hawkes and Edmund Bull," says Walsingham. "And to contemplate the magnificent bosom of the notorious Jane Flood. With a body like that, she can't possibly drown."

"Seriously, Thomas," says young Russell, "why did you come? I'm sure you have an ulterior reason for being here."

"If you must know," says Tom, "my family have all gathered at Scadbury for the holidays, and, frankly, I was bored. I thought you and I might find a way to get into a little trouble."

"Oh, Kit and I are very good at that sort of thing," says Russell. "We've already arranged an *adventure* for this evening. Don't ask any questions; just be ready about eleven."

That night, after an immensity of food and an immensity of small talk, after tarts and marzipan and wine, after singing and music and Morris dancing in the courtyard, the guests begin to grunt and sigh and yawn and wander off toward their beds.

At last the candles are out and the house is dark. Christopher waits in his room for the other conspirators against the country-plump daughters of Farmer Staley. He has never even kissed a girl, let alone made love to one. And the only naked female body he has ever seen has been his sister's—surreptitious glimpses that filled him more with wonder than with lust.

He sits down and thinks of women. He tries to imagine the act itself. The woman in his mind is an enormous landscape of flesh—all hills and valleys. And he is a small boy, an explorer in as yet undiscovered continents. He forces himself into the appropriate posture but can go no further in his imagination. Fear grips his heart. He has a sense of falling and suffocation. Her red mouth gapes. Her black pubic chasm threatens to absorb him.

He is startled from this nightmare by a tapping at his door. It is

Tom, his finger across his lips, his eyes wide. He beckons, and Kit follows. In the garden they meet Walsingham, who has a skin of wine. They all drink and laugh in whispers, huddling together.

And then they are off, under a good moon, down a narrow path, through some woods and across a field. In the distance they see the silhouette of a small house, one upper window dimly lighted. Thirty yards from their objective they crouch in the shadows and review their strategy. "The girls are in the lighted room," says Tom. "When we toss a pebble against the window, they will sneak out to join us."

Walsingham tips back the wineskin and passes it. "Have you fellows ever had a girl before?" he says.

"Of course," says Tom.

"Liar," says Walsingham. "And you, Kit?"

"No," says Kit. "That makes *you* the expert."

Walsingham smiles ambiguously.

They move closer, and Tom tosses up a few fine pebbles. They make a louder noise than he had hoped they would. The trio retreat at the sound, stumbling over one another. Walsingham catches Kit around the waist and holds him for a moment, as if to steady him or perhaps to steady himself. They wait, hearing only their own breathing and the night sounds of crickets and toads. "Perhaps they're asleep," whispers Tom, hopefully. "Perhaps we ought to leave."

Kit is not accustomed to wine, and it begins to make him bold. "No," he says. "We've come this far, and there's no turning back. If they don't come down, we'll go up and get them."

But the frontal assault is not necessary. In another minute they hear footsteps. A dark form moves toward them. Tom goes forward and whispers. The form comes closer and proves, indeed, to be a girl—a young girl no more than sixteen. "Where is your sister?" says Tom. He knows the entire family. They are, in fact, tenants of his father.

"She wouldn't come," says the girl. "She was too frightened."

"But she won't tell, will she?" says Tom.

"No, no, of course not," says the girl.

Tom takes her by the hand, and they go across the field and into the woods. When they are safely away from the house they all laugh quietly and nervously. "This is Ann," says Tom to his friends.

She giggles, having had her share of wine at the festivities earlier. "And who are you?" she says to Kit and Walsingham.

"Never mind," says Walsingham, handing her the wineskin. "Come, we'll drink a toast to Diana." He looks toward the moon.

"We saw you at the dancing," says Tom. "You were lovely."

"Did I do all right?" she says, wiping her mouth with the back of her hand.

"You did fine," he says.

"I really shouldn't have come out. If my father ever finds out—oh, I hate to think of what he might do. One more swallow and I'll be on my way. I came down mainly to tell you that my sister can't come."

"All right, then," says Tom, "but first give us a kiss good night."

"What, all of you?"

"Why not?" says Walsingham.

She shrugs and kisses them—first Tom, then Walsingham, then Kit. But as her lips meet his, he grabs her impulsively and pulls her toward him. He has no idea what he is about to do. His head is muddled. His blood is warm. She struggles to get away, but he is very rough with her. He tumbles her down on the ground and tears at her gown. "Stop it! Stop it!" she says, but she is afraid to scream.

Tom tries to interfere, but he feels Walsingham's hand on his arm. "No, leave them alone." And they stand there trembling in the night as Christopher assaults the girl.

Moonlight falls on her naked breast. "Go to her, Kit," says Walsingham in a hot whisper. And he and Tom form a fascinated audience.

ix

Christopher walks through the cloisters of the Cathedral and through the Dark Entry. It is the fall of the following year,

Michaelmas term, 1580. A heavy November sky hangs over the world. The air is damp. The chapel is cold in the pre-dawn. Many people in Canterbury are suffering from a severe cough. Some have died. Old women exchange remedies. There are prayers for those who suffer.

Robert Rose conducts the morning service. He is himself afflicted. His eyes are shadowed and his voice is low. "Let us consider the warmth of His universal love in these cold days. Let us rise above the frailty and pain which have been our heritage from the first fatal disobedience. Let us renew our faith in a just God—the only Judge. In our smallness and ignorance we cannot hope to understand how the everyday events of our lives fit into His divine plan. Do not resist Him. Do not be proud. Do not commit over and over again the sin of our first father and mother. And pray with me: 'Lighten our darkness, we beseech Thee, O Lord; and by Thy great mercy defend us from all the perils and dangers of this night; for the love of Thy only Son, our Saviour, Jesus Christ.'"

Later, as Kit is ascending the steps of the Norman staircase, he is overtaken by Robert Rose, who invites him to his room for a cup of hot wine.

When they are seated comfortably before the fire, Robert says, "Christopher, I have some interesting news for you. You've been recommended for one of the Archbishop Parker scholarships to Cambridge University." He waits with a smile of satisfaction for Kit's response.

"Good," says Kit, without much enthusiasm. "I rather thought I would be."

"Oh," says Robert. "You're not exactly overwhelmed, then, are you?"

"I'm very pleased, but not surprised," says Kit. "I mean, who else is more qualified?"

"It's quite an honor, you know," says Robert. "Old Parker was very fond of Corpus Christi. He gave them a fine collection of manuscripts. And then these several awards, the first of which must go to a Canterbury boy who is a graduate of King's. Three pounds six and eight per annum. Not bad, eh?"

"But there are conditions, I hear," says Kit.

"Well, yes, of course," says Robert. "There are always conditions. You are expected to continue in residence for six years as a divinity student, after which the assumption is that you will take holy orders."

"That's a bit awkward, isn't it?" says Kit.

"I don't understand," says Robert.

"Well, naturally, I want to go to the University, but I'm afraid my interests lie elsewhere."

Robert tries to laugh away Kit's concern. "Now, now," he says, "six years is a long time. You can think about all that later on."

"And if I don't take holy orders?" says Kit. "What then?"

Robert shrugs. "If you don't, you don't. The choice will be yours. But who's to say now that you don't *intend* to?"

He smiles significantly, and slowly Kit responds with a smile. He puts an affectionate arm around Kit and draws him close, but then, almost immediately, he clears his throat and withdraws into his involuntary privacy. "We will, of course, miss you here at King's," he says, staring into his wine. "The annual agony of the schoolmaster—parting with his star pupils."

"I'm sorry," says Kit.

"No, no, don't be sorry. Go! Go with joy and high expectations. But do let us hear from you from time to time, will you?"

II

CAMBRIDGE

i

IN the simple black robe and skull cap of the undergraduate, Christopher Marlowe walks with Thomas Lewgar and Christopher Pashley on the campus of Corpus Christi College, Cambridge University. Thomas Lewgar is one of his two roommates. Christopher Pashley has preceded him as a Canterbury scholar. He will be leaving shortly as a Master of Arts.

"It's not an easy life, mind you," says Pashley. "Up before five, morning services, breakfast at six, lectures and studies until noon. Then dinner, if you can call it that—a penny's worth of beef divided four ways, with luck, and maybe a pottage of the broth with salt and oatmeal. Unless, of course, you've got a little money of your own. Well, then, it's quite different. Quite different. But you'll have your barber free, and your laundry. Nothing to worry about on that score." Pashley is a kind of middle-aged youth, heading, like a cannon ball dropped from St. Paul's, for holy orders—an orderly and holy life in the Church, perhaps in a country parish where he can raise bees.

They walk around the Old Court. A gust of December wind billows their black gowns. The light is failing in the gray afternoon sky. Thomas Lewgar is a head shorter than the other two, looking like a child or a dwarf next to them. The buildings that surround the Old Court are grim, more than two hundred years old, reflecting a certain antique austerity.

"You'll find the old storeroom bearable," says Pashley.

"Storeroom?" says Thomas Lewgar.

"Well, it's not a storeroom any longer, of course," says Pashley, "but the name lingers. You know how it is with names. Before Archbishop Parker endowed these scholarships, the space was used as a storeroom. I think you'll manage all right there. A bit cramped and certainly cold in the winter, but you'll get used to it. Run up and down for a few minutes before leaping into bed at night. It helps!"

A scattering of scholars is blown across the court. Latin and laughter envelop them. Two young men pass them on the path. They are dressed in gaudy doublets and capes. One is leading a greyhound. Marlowe stops and stares after them. Before he can ask the obvious question, Pashley says, "The rules, of course, are not absolute. Nothing is absolute here. Officially, one may speak only in Latin or Hebrew on campus. And officially, one must wear a gown of a sad color. One may not leave the grounds unaccompanied. One must not wear long hair or visit the taverns or other places of pleasure in the town. But times are changing. Times are always changing. And, of course, if one has money, it does make a difference. But I would not, if I were you, try to compete with the upper classes. We are only pensioners, not fellow commoners. And count your blessings that you did not arrive as a sizar to be booted about by gentlemen. My advice to you both is to conduct yourselves in a quiet and conservative manner and to stay out of trouble."

"Is there much trouble?" says Marlowe.

"Enough," says Pashley. "More than enough, in fact."

Thomas Lewgar, who is not quite fifteen, blinks his eyes very rapidly and waits for an explanation.

"To begin with," says Pashley, "there's The Eagle in Bene't Street, opposite the entrance to the College, where some of the local wags roist it out, drinking and carousing when they should be at their books. And strutting like peacocks in their finery and brawling like baboons. Full of words and noise. Flashing their swords and fancy daggers. And that's not the only tavern between Trumpington Street and Bridge Street. Is it any wonder that the local citizens are up in arms against us? We wake them up with bawdy songs in the middle of the night, make water in their doorways, molest their daughters, and generally act like drunken children. When I say *we,* of course, I do not include myself, though all our reputations are tainted because of the unruly few."

Kit smiles at the prematurely middle-aged puritan. "Do go on," he says. "What other sort of trouble ought we to be on our guard against?"

Pashley clears his throat and casts a suspicious frown at this new undergraduate. "Well," he says, "the usual things—gambling, drinking, bear-baiting, cock-fighting, not to mention baser sorts of lewdness, if you know what I mean."

"What does he mean?" whispers Thomas Lewgar to Christopher, almost trotting to keep up as they leave the quad and go past St. Bene't's Church.

"I haven't the foggiest idea," says Marlowe, a hint of Walsingham in his tone.

"What's that?" says Pashley, who has just overheard them.

"Nothing," says Kit. "Where are we going now?"

"Oh, well, I thought we might just wander over to the King's College Chapel. Wonderful church. Beautiful piece of architecture. I'm sure you'll agree."

Lead on, little priest, says Marlowe in his mind, and they cross Trumpington Street in front of a noisy horse-drawn wagon.

"And, of course," says Pashley, speaking into the wind, "there are all these new books. All these dangerous ideas. Stay away from them. Remember that even the devil can quote scriptures. Stay with your prescribed reading. Do not be seduced by heretical wits and wags."

"What books?" says Kit.

Pashley stares straight ahead like a horse with blinders. "Oh, books! Books!" he says, waving them out of existence with his long preacher's arm.

"I have heard they read Machiavelli here," says Kit.

Pashley coughs and clears his throat. "Oh yes, that and worse. Certain Turkish discourses. Leroy's Exposition on Aristotle's Politics. French and Italian stuff. Radical in the extreme. And utterly useless except to feed the unwholesome curiosity of certain restless minds. You will soon discover that learning is a double-edged sword. It can be used to strengthen your fundamental faith or to destroy your brains. There have been cases of madness, you know, brought on by this nonsense and heretical rot. Ah, but here we are. Forget all that and feast your eyes on this magnificent structure."

They are standing before the King's College Chapel, their eyes moving slowly upward, over the vastness of the central window, over embroidered masonry. The sky beyond the spires is a drama of dark and darker clouds that billow and sweep and rise, announcing bad weather.

"Is it going to rain?" says Thomas Lewgar.

"I think it is the most perfect church I have ever seen," says Pashley, and the rain drops that streak down his face are like tears.

"Perhaps we should go back," says Thomas Lewgar.

"Nonsense," says Pashley. "Only a little shower. Won't hurt you. See, the sky's lighter there. It will all pass over in a moment or two. Clare Hall," he shouts, above a roll of thunder, and sweeps them along to Trinity Hall and then across to Trinity College Chapel, whose protection they seek for two or three minutes until the rain subsides. Then on into St. John's they go and across Bridge Street to Jesus College. Then back across Bridge to Market Hill, Slaughter Street, and Pembroke Hall. And once more up Trumpington to Bene't Street, where suddenly they find themselves standing in front of The Eagle Tavern.

"Now that you know where it is, stay away from it," says Pashley, urging them toward the rear entrance to Corpus Christi. But a wild figure in a flying black cloak emerges from the dark interior of The Eagle and hails them.

Pashley takes his boys firmly by the arms and leads them away. "Pretend you can't hear him," he whispers.

"But who is it?" says Marlowe.

"It's Kett," says Pashley, "Francis Kett, a very dangerous man." They escape through the gate, past the graveyard and into the chapel. There Pashley leaves them with noisy apologies, and there they linger until the rain lets up again.

ii

In the lecture hall at Corpus Christi, old Professor William Lyne tries to explain Aristotle's way of arriving at the truth. He stands at an ornate podium and addresses his audience of distracted scholars. His voice is a monotone that conspires with the cruel balminess of spring to drive his students to fantasies and revolution. In their minds they are romping in green fields and lying with beautiful companions beside waterfalls and lakes. Or else they are exploding the university into extinction, including the antique lecturer who now pours his questionable wisdom into their unwashed ears.

Professor Lyne's ideas are orthodox. For almost fifty adult years he has carried in his mind the beautiful vision of a contained universe, with the Earth as the center, with the contending elements of water, fire, earth, and air; a perfect sphere, a divine envelope of stars in the firmament, contained within the crystalline layer and then within the *primum mobile,* about which one can say nothing, except that it is God's will that it should be thus. Oh sweet harmony! A universe that is orderly, purposeful, and intelligible. Eternal, immutable heavens, free of flux and decay. What a comfort forever and ever and ever. What a consolation to take to one's grave.

With his wide, watery eyes, William Lyne stares beyond his restless students and studies an ornate molding close to the ceiling. It is a symptom of concentration. And also a way of escaping the small sounds of adolescent boredom. He leans heavily on the podium, as though his robes and beard and black cap are weighing him down. "There are two distinct sources from which we can reconstruct Aristotle's methodology," he says. "*The Organon,* which we might call his *theoretical* method, and the large group of works sometimes called his scientific treatises, or his *practical* method. Unless we can see the two methods as compatible and not contradictory, we cannot be justified in talking about the one, indisputable Aristotelian approach. No, Aristotle does not contradict himself, as we shall see."

In the audience Christopher Marlowe is flanked by John Burman and Edward Bennett. In front of him is the playful Charles Walford, who is scribbling with exaggerated enthusiasm, his illegal longish hair escaping from his skull cap and twisting into blond curls. After a while he folds a sheet of paper—once, twice, three times—turns suddenly to flash a red mouth and comedian's eyes, and to deposit, with a swift motion, the square white wad in Kit's lap.

"For Aristotle," says Professor Lyne, "there are several distinct varieties of knowledge: intuitive knowledge, demonstrable knowledge, and knowledge of the fact. The problem in the *Posterior Analytics* is how to achieve demonstrable or scientific knowledge . . ."

Christopher cautiously unfolds the sheet of paper passed to him by Walford. There he finds a piece of verse accompanied by a crude drawing of the venerable professor hoisting up his robe to reveal an exaggerated rump and impossible genitalia.

> He studies the world with prisms
> And talks in silly gisms.
> And when he's in the mood
> And in the nude
> The sweetest sound he hears
> Is the music of his spheres,
> *A posteriori* in the hay,
> Preaching of *primum mobile.*

iii

When Tom Walsingham comes to Cambridge he usually stays at the Gregory Hostel near Trinity College. On this occasion he has arranged for a small dinner party in his rooms. Four other guests are already there by the time Kit arrives. Tom sweeps him into the room and introduces him to Gabriel Harvey, Tom Watson, Robert Cecil, and Robert Greene. "Mr. Marlowe is not only a Matthew Parker scholar," he says, "but a poet."

"How interesting," says Harvey with an affected yawn. He is an elegant man of about thirty, but not handsome. His carefully arranged hair is abundant, but it is already beginning to retreat somewhat from his forehead. He has a sharp nose and thin mouth. And he has a lizardlike habit of wetting his lips. He is dressed in expensive velvet and silk. His bright yellow hose, cross-gartered, draws attention to his shapely legs.

Tom Watson, on the other hand, is open and friendly. Kit can feel in the firm but gentle grip of his hand the man's humanity. He has just returned from a long love affair with France and Italy. "I write poetry, too," he says to Kit.

"Everybody writes poetry," says Gabriel Harvey.

"Don't listen to Gabriel," says Watson. "He has a very possessive attitude toward poetry."

"Yes," says Robert Greene, his fleshy, bearded face flushed with wine. "He and Edmund Spenser have been granted the hexameter monopoly. You have to be licensed now to pound out a verse. Poetic license, one might call it."

"Don't you listen to him, young man," says Harvey. "He is green with envy." Roberto winces at the pun. Harvey's whole air is condescending. He is a fellow at Trinity and speaks always as though he is in sole possession of the truth.

Robert Cecil, an undergraduate at St. John's, is barely a year older than Kit. He is a diminutive man with a malformed back, almost a hunchback, though otherwise quite normal. He is the son of the famous William Cecil, Lord Burghley, Chancellor of the University and the Queen's chief counselor.

"I hear there's a play in preparation at Trinity," says Robert, "that makes some unflattering references to you, Gabriel."

"In English or Latin?" says Harvey.

"Latin," says Robert.

"You mean, it makes fun of me!"

"Yes, indeed. A great deal of fun."

"I wonder why? Whom have I offended?"

"My dear Mr. Harvey, whom have you not offended?" says Greene.

Dinner is brought in, and the conversation becomes fragmented. There are comments on the food. Wine is passed. Several people talk at once. It is not a situation that Gabriel Harvey can tolerate for too long. Conversation makes him uneasy. He must turn it as quickly as possible into a monologue, because, after all, no one else in the world ever really has anything interesting to say, except perhaps Edmund Spenser, his dear, dear friend.

He is still picking his teeth with a silver toothpick when he begins his pompous explanation. "The trouble, you see, is that in *Three Proper, and Wittie, Familiar Letters* I accuse the university of giving preferential treatment to certain wealthy students . . ." He goes on for three-quarters of an hour, reviewing his entire relationship with Edmund Spenser, his poetic theories, his connections at court, his feud with the Earl of Oxford and with sundry other persons, and, of course, his great disputation before the Queen at Audley End. He punctuates his impeccable sentences with wine. After a while, everyone is so hypnotized by his performance that no one is able to speak. Hope fades, and the other guests subside into their own thoughts, praying that this egomaniac may finally exhaust himself.

Then, suddenly, he stops talking. They are all taken by surprise, as though one of the eternal spheres stopped moving in its appointed direction. When they remember how to speak again, they desperately try to change the subject. "I understand," says Robert Greene to Walsingham, "that your cousin, Sir Francis, is sending spies all over Europe and that he is trying to provoke a war with Spain. I think it's a marvelous idea."

"Sir Francis is not trying to provoke a war with anyone," says Walsingham. "But if the war is inevitable, as many of us believe, perhaps we ought to get it over with before the Spanish forces in the Lowlands get any larger. They've got about forty thousand troops there already."

"Tell us about the spies," says Robert Greene.

"It's probably the world's worst-kept secret," says Tom Watson, "that hundreds of English seminarians are being trained at Rheims and Rome and shipped back into England to convert the countryside and preach rebellion and treason. Their activities have to be carefully watched. As long as Mary Stuart lives, the English Catholics abroad will be tempted to assassinate Elizabeth and bring that lusty whore to the throne."

"I still think the answer is diplomacy, not war," says Robert Cecil.

"What kind of diplomacy is possible with a fanatic like Philip the Second?" says Watson. "He sees himself as divinely appointed to restore European unity and the domination of the Catholic Church. No, my friends, there will be a war. Take my word for it. I have been abroad for several years and I can smell it in the air."

"Oh, the war be damned," says Gabriel Harvey. "Let's talk about something really important. Let's talk about literature. I hear, Tom, that you've done a Latin version of *Antigone*."

"Never mind *Antigone*," says Robert Greene. "Let's talk about me, the world's swiftest writer of English prose. Pamphleteer, playwright, poet, polemicist, preacher, and propangandist for the good life."

"And boozer *extraordinaire*," says Gabriel Harvey.

"Nothing in moderation is my motto," says Greene.

"Except modesty, of course," says Harvey.

"Be careful what you say, Hobbinoll; I shall satirize you all to pieces in my next play."

"Why don't you give up this literary hustling," says Harvey, "and do something respectable for a living?"

"Such as?"

"You could be a butcher, for instance."

"Ah, but I am a butcher."

"What do you butcher, besides the English language?" says Harvey.

"Inflated reputations," says Greene.

"You mean you prick them," says Robert Cecil.

"Yes," says Greene, "with my trusty *dispenser!*"

When all the others have gone and Kit and Walsingham are alone, they sit by the fire and laugh at both men. "They are incredibly amusing when you can get them into the same room," says Walsingham.

"Mr. Greene has something to recommend him, but Mr. Harvey is a pompous peacock," says Kit.

"He is also a man of considerable accomplishments and certain connections who will, no doubt, rise in the world," says Walsingham.

"Rise in the world!" echoes Kit. "Rise in the world, indeed. Only Jesus Christ can do that."

"What should I have said? Rise in bed?"

"A lot more likely," says Kit. "Haven't you ever risen in bed?"

"Oh, frequently," says Walsingham. "A situation that must not get out of hand."

"Ah, but there is no political advantage in it, is there?" says Kit.

"No, but there's a political lesson in it," says Walsingham.

"And what might that be?"

"A sudden rise, if too vigorously handled, will lead to a crisis and instant decline."

Kit applauds, and Walsingham bows from the neck. "You should go to London," says Kit, "and be a playwright. You could write dirty comedies for shopkeepers and questionable ladies."

"No, thank you," says Walsingham. "I'd rather go to Rome and spy on the Pope for Sir Francis."

There is a long pause. They stare into the fire. At last Kit says, in a very quiet voice, "Do you really think you will go?"

"Eventually, perhaps, but not tonight." Another pause. The candles burn low.

"I would like to be a spy," says Kit. "I would like, in fact, to go to war."

"You might have to kill people," says Walsingham. "Think of that. Plunging a sword into human flesh! The guts of a thousand disemboweled warriors spoiling the flowers."

In the fire of his imagination Kit sees a battle. "I swoop among Spaniards or Turks or Blackamoors," he says, "armed with a magic sword drawn from a stone, and wearing a vest of gold. I am surrounded. I am alone. I am the King of Samarkand. I am Richard Coeur de Lion." He grabs the fire poker and dances around, stabbing at pillows and chairs. "I am King Arthur at Mount Badon. I will defend the bridge. They shall not pass. God is on our side. Kill or be killed. For honor, for country. Ah, there, and there, and there." He collapses onto the rug, clutching his heart as though he is wounded.

Walsingham comes to him. He stands over him and looks down. Kit's face is wet with perspiration, and he has torn his shirt in his dream war. Walsingham puts his foot on the fallen man's chest and allows some red wine to trickle onto his face. "This is your blood, now," says Walsingham. "You've been wounded, maybe killed, at the Siege of Cambridge."

Kit looks up at the figure who bestrides him like a little Colossus. "Yes," he says. "I have been killed at the Battle of Corpus Christi, but I have come back from the dead to seek revenge and to complete the requirements for the Bachelor of Arts degree. Archbishop Parker is watching me from heaven. I am a divinity student."

"You're a heathen," says Walsingham. Kit grabs him by the legs and topples him down. The wineglass flies away and breaks against the stone fireplace. They wrestle on the rug. Walsingham finds his young friend surprisingly strong. Kit gains the advantage and pins Walsingham's shoulders down. Their bodies strain. Their legs tangle. Kit's face is close to Walsingham's. "Surrender!" he says. Walsingham shakes his head and heaves his body. Kit's shadow of a mustache and his dark eyes give him a sinister look. "Then I will have to kill you," he says.

"Heathen!" cries Walsingham again.

A small lightning flashes in Kit's eyes. But almost immediately he smiles, relaxes his grip and gets up. "All right," he says, "you win. I'm a heathen."

iv

Kit and Robert Cecil have been to see *Pedantius*, the satirical attack on Gabriel Harvey. They laugh all the way back to Robert's room at St. John's and sip sweet liqueur when they arrive.

When the conversation turns to Tom Walsingham, Robert says, "Please don't repeat anything that Tom tells you about his government service. He's inclined to speak too lightly of his cousin's work. It is really quite a serious business."

"I understand," says Kit. "I certainly won't discuss the matter at all—with anyone."

"Good," he says, and laughs. Because of his condition, he looks at times, not like a little boy, but like a little old man. "You have a good and useful friend in Tom. My advice to you is not to do anything to spoil the opportunity. You see, I am just as bad as my father—giving such serious advice, and to someone only a year or two younger than myself. If I'm not careful, I'm going to grow up to be a very boring old man."

v

It is the first of December, and the air has turned colder. An east wind has come up, and great swollen coffins of clouds sweep across the spire-infested sky of London. Fires burn in the huddled herds of houses and the damp mansions of the largest city in Europe. The rain of the past few days has settled the dust into mud in the unpaved lanes and washed away some of the stench of human waste. But the noise of trade is undiminished in the markets and shops. And the wharves along the Thames digest the commerce from far and near, as a thousand boats, small and large, make a colorful traffic on the watery highway.

Kit is on his way to Canterbury to visit his family on one of Mr.

Hobson's hired horses. He has come as far as London, where he plans to stop over. So jammed are the streets that it is a major struggle to go by cart or horse or foot from St. Paul's to London Bridge. Swarms of men, women, and children jostle one another roughly. And there is a riot of clothing, from the rags of the lowest beggars to the finery of the finest gentlemen and the bizarre costumes of visiting foreigners. Peddlers hawk their wares at every corner. Hammers smash against anvils. Tubs are hooped. Porters stagger under their burdens. Merchants hug their bags of money. And cutpurses and prostitutes ply their trades.

A quarter of a million people move about in the organized chaos, in search of wealth or power or merely a crust of bread. And the symphony of survival is very, very loud, though human life is the cheapest commodity in the marketplace.

Behind the thick walls of his Westminster house Thomas Walsingham does not hear the distant hum and throb of ordinary life. Nor does he have any desire to. It is not that he is unsympathetic to their plight; it's just that they are essentially boring, with their dirty feet and their greedy eyes. He prefers to have nothing to do with them. Besides, they are not to be trusted. They are too poor to have any real sense of honor.

He is with Tom Watson, who paces back and forth. Watson stops by a large window and looks down into the river. "When I came back to England," he says, "I thought perhaps I had left all this behind."

"Yes," says Walsingham, "but we can't really blame Sir Francis, can we?"

"Nevertheless," says Watson, "these barbaric intrusions on one's sensibilities are very disturbing." He turns away from the window. "I mean, how in God's name is one supposed to dedicate himself to the writing of poetry and other such civilized pursuits when people go on killing one another over such ridiculous theological disputes? What difference does it make what one says the wafer of bread is? Who cares how the individual approaches his God? We all crawl to him in the end anyway, don't we? So much desperate hocus-pocus." He pauses. *"Hoc est corpus."*

"Ah, but weren't you saying just a few months ago that the danger is very real?" Walsingham faces his friend in the middle of the large room. "Weren't you lecturing us at Cambridge about the army of priests who were being infiltrated into England by the Jesuits? About how they are here to win souls, to convert and persuade, and to assist in the overthrow of the government?"

"Of course the danger is real," says Watson. "I don't deny that it is. That's what makes it all so depressing. I'm losing my faith in humanity."

"Your faith in humanity!" says Walsingham, laughing. "An odd place to have ever put your faith. The mob is a many-headed monster that knows no reason except appetite. Why do you think they're hanging Campion up at Tyburn today? It's for the mob. A public spectacle—to please them. To terrify them. They know no other language but fear and food. They are like dogs. To train them you either whip them or toss them a bone. Faith in humanity, indeed!"

"Where, then, my young and noble friend, would you put *your* faith?"

"The orthodox answer to that," says Walsingham, "is that I put my faith in God, sir." He stiffens to imitate certain rather puritanical members of his family.

"Yes, indeed, my Lord," says Watson with a mocking bow. "I did not mean to suggest for a moment that you would place anything before your God. But I mean on this earth, man. On this earth!"

"On this earth?" says Walsingham, as though he has been forced to think about the question for the first time. "I really don't know. I mean, when you consider the sad state of affairs on this earth, what is there to believe in?"

"Well, let me give you a little catalogue, if you can forgive a little pedantry. To begin with, there is Nature. You know, the rose, the wind, the wine-dark sea. And, of course, there is pleasure, that great Roman preoccupation—after politics. And poor humanity, of course. Poor humanity. Our brothers and sisters in God's special creation. And power! *There's* something to put your faith in. The domination by brute force or wealth or political advantage of your fellow men—those very same diminutive creatures who this very minute are out there at Tyburn enjoying the disemboweling of a vastly superior, if somewhat misled, human being. That man on the gallows is worth a thousand of those fat merchants and ragged apprentices who have been making a holiday of his death today."

Walsingham goes to the fireplace and stares at the flames. After a moment or so he says, "These are confusing times in which we live. I don't suppose one can trust anyone or anything." He pauses. "But to answer your question, now that you've forced it upon me, I suppose what I believe in, more than anything else—after an Almighty Intelligence, of course—is my *self.*"

Watson also comes to the fireplace. "Your *self?*" he says.

"Yes," says Walsingham. "I don't quite know what I mean by that, but at least it is right here." He pounds his narrow chest.

"Yes," says Watson, "I suppose I know what you mean. There is a kind of universe in us, isn't there? And one hardly knows what to make of it. It is easy enough to say that we are part of a larger design; and yet, at times, I feel so utterly separate. From everything! I mean, I feel contained within this fragile skin, within the globe of my private soul. I am tempted at times to think that, beyond these tiny limits, we shall never know anything for sure."

Walsingham breaks out of his frowning seriousness. "Oh, Mr. Watson. Heresy! They'll have you up before the Privy Council for that. A few minutes on the rack should bend your logic in the right direction."

"Ah, the rack, the manacles, the *peine forte et dure,*" says Watson. "The ultimate rhetorician is Richard Topcliffe."

"He's a horrible man, but very effective, my cousin tells me," says Walsingham.

"How a man like Sir Francis can tolerate that kind of vulgarity, I don't know," says Watson. "I know he is a man of conviction. But I also know that he is a sensitive man, an intelligent man. What walks we had in Paris. What poetic readings in the long foreign nights.

But I suppose you're right: he finds Topcliffe effective—a weapon in his mad war against Popery." He pauses. "Still, I thought he might have found a better solution to this Campion business."

"But do you think he had any choice in the matter?" says Walsingham. "What else could he have done?"

"He could have held him in prison," he says. "He could have avoided this—this martyrdom."

"The martyrdom was apparently what Campion wanted."

"Precisely the reason to avoid it," says Watson. "Yes, I know he wanted it, longed for it. It was part of his twisted nature, his exhibitionism. They say he laughed all the way to Tyburn as they dragged him through the mud. I wonder if he is laughing still? I couldn't stay for his final performance. Perhaps even now he is haranguing the crowd, amusing them with his bravery. Or are they howling at the ludicrous way in which his head rolls around the platform and his limbs twitch as the executioner jerks him by the throat into the air?"

"Stop it, Tom," says Walsingham. "It's too disgusting to think about."

"I'm sorry," says Watson. "I am very upset about Edmund Campion. I knew him and admired him. Which is not to say that I have all that much sympathy with the Catholic cause. Still, one must admire any man who has as much pure conviction as he had, as much certainty of what he is doing."

"I think, possibly, he is quite happy where he is at the moment," says Walsingham. "And I frankly don't much care."

"He could have gotten away with it, you know," says Watson. "With a little common sense, he could have survived. He was well hidden. He did not have to be caught. He could have gone on ministering in Lancashire, Northamptonshire, and Berkshire, or wherever he felt he was needed. But no, he had to come to the graduation ceremonies at St. Mary's and distribute his little *Decem Rationes*—four hundred copies. Whatever made him imagine that he could get away with *that?*"

"I don't believe for a moment that he imagined he would get away with it," says Walsingham. "I'm convinced that he wanted to be caught, wanted to be tortured, and wanted to be martyred. It is a form of insanity."

"I suppose so," says Watson wearily. "I suppose so. But I will never quite understand what drives a man into such tragic circumstances."

Their conversation is interrupted. A servant comes in and says to Walsingham that there is a young man named Marlowe to see him and that he is in a rather disheveled condition. "I will be glad to turn him away, sir, if you choose not to see him."

"Please, William, show the man in. And bring us all some sherry."

It is a while before Christopher is able to speak. His face is bruised. His hat is gone and his riding cape is torn. The drying stains on the front of his jerkin and his knee-length breeches are a mingling of mud and blood. He sits by the fire, flanked by Watson and Walsingham. They comfort him and offer him brandy. At last he begins:

"I came into London on the Kingsland Road. It had been a slow trip. Lots of rain. Had to go home to Canterbury. Mother sent a letter, all about my sister's difficulties." He drinks, Walsingham refills his glass. "I stayed over at an inn. Edgewater. Didn't want to kill the horse. And fell in with an old sailor. There's where I first heard about it. Campion, I mean." He takes a deep breath, as though he has been running uphill.

"I don't know London. I've only been here once before. I kept asking the way—not to Tyburn, but to here, to Westminster. I moved through narrow streets, through mud, through crowds so thick I had to abandon the horse at last. God knows where he is. All those streets and lanes a vast muddle in my mind: St. Agnes le Clare, Old Street, Aldersgate, Saffron Little, Dorset, Bell Yard, and suddenly the river. I was in a crowded tavern, trying to get something to eat, but everyone was drinking. A rough crowd. Rufflers and whipjacks. One-eyed veterans and a drunken boatman bellowing at the top of his voice, 'The rose is red, the leaves are green; God save Elizabeth, our noble Queen.' And then I was out in the streets again, drowning in the desperate cries of peddlers and beggars. Smoke swirled down upon us from the heavy sky. Steam rose from the sweating horses. Drivers cursed. Wheels groaned. Once again I asked my way. Threadneedle, St. Paul's, Hog Lane, Holborn, Oxford . . .

"Suddenly, I was at Tyburn. Ladies and gentlemen all in a row in the wooden galleries, chatting, waving lace handkerchiefs, settling in for the drama as though they were at the theatre. And on the stage, the gallows, the caldron, smoke curling up to join the smoky sky. The cast of characters—executioners and victims. I was pressed against a bear of a man who kept drinking from a bottle and coughing and spitting. He was vast and hairy, and stank as though he had been dead a week. He had no teeth and kept shouting something that I did not understand. He wrapped his paw around me and laughed with poisonous breath right into my face. He offered me his bottle, and I dared not refuse. He was explaining something with fat lips and bugged-out eyes, but I could not understand a single word of his strange dialect. I put the bottle to my lips and drank. I winced and shook my head. He hugged me to him and laughed at my agony. 'Usquebaugh,' he roared. He grabbed the bottle and put it to his toothless mouth. 'Ahhhh!' he said, letting out a ghost of steam. I expected him to fall down dead or to go up in flames, but he only seemed to grow stronger.

"I was dizzy. The crush of the crowd and the strong drink took my breath away. I felt myself gasping for air. And yet I was fascinated by this beast beside me, fascinated by the heat of his body, his hugeness, his stench, the fire that failed to consume him.

"A hush fell over the crowd. I strained to see. Heads bobbed before me. My eyes would not focus. I struggled forward and then caught the sharp sight, in the eye of the silence, of the hanged man. Was it Campion or one of the others? I could not tell. But then someone was speaking, his words blowing away into the smoky heavens. I caught only fragments. The crowd applauded. Someone shouted Campion's name, and suddenly there he was, his head grotesquely twisted to one side by the rope. 'Cut his heart out!' they chanted. The ladies in the stands covered their faces but peeked bravely through the lace. They would not miss the twitching of the strangling body for anything. How they leaned forward. How they shivered. A gasping excitement ran through the crowd, as though they were the collective victim, as though they were caught up in a grim orgasm, raped by death into a final affirmation of life. And when the still-alive priest was cut down, a great sigh went out of them—not of relief, but of satisfaction. And he was flung roughly on a block by his muscular butchers, and there he was disemboweled. He did not stop moving until the executioner's hand was rammed into his cut-open stomach, in search of that symbolic center of the man—his heart. And then the quartering of the corpse! Oh, sweet barbarism!

"I broke away from my beast and pressed closer. Suddenly I caught sight of a shadowy figure under the platform. He was the man who feeds the fire to keep the caldron boiling—an ordinary man, no doubt, unconcerned about the politics of his job, unable to read or write. What in the world could have been running through his mind as he rammed more wood into the fire? Perhaps he was thinking of his fee or what he might have for supper. In the shadows his face seemed black and his eyes very white. It was more terrible even than the hanging itself . . ."

Kit's face is buried in his hands. He is sobbing and trembling. "What shall we do?" says Walsingham, his hand on Kit's shoulder.

"We'll get him to bed," says Watson. "He'll be all right in the morning." And they lift him gently from his chair by the fire and support him across the room to the door, where they are met by William, who picks him up as though he is a large child and carries him off to a bedroom.

vi

Winter subsides into spring. The deadly routine of chapel, lectures, meals, and bed is rarely disturbed. Everyone seems to have turned serious over the winter. They are reading Machiavelli and Ramus like mad and discussing, from hearsay, the ideas of Giordano Bruno. The language is heavy, the concepts frightening.

Thomas Walsingham has gone off to the continent on a mission for Sir Francis. All very confidential. Tom Watson is in London being very famous for his newly published *Passionate Century of Love*, a collection of a hundred love poems derived from the French and Italian poets with whom he is so familiar, but written in English—a new departure for him.

Robert Thexton has completed his studies and has been replaced in the "storehouse" by Thomas Munday. Kit finds him talkative and boring and seeks refuge in books and long walks.

In April, Kit hears that his sister Joan is going to marry John Marlowe's apprentice, John Moore. He is invited to come home for the wedding but refuses. Joan is twelve and a half years old.

The only bright part of the spring and summer is the arrival at St. John's of Thomas Nashe. It doesn't take him long to fall in with Robert Greene and his crowd and to fall out with Gabriel Harvey and his brothers. Before long he is in serious trouble, and there is talk of his being expelled.

The invitation that comes from Scadbury rescues Kit from his books, his dreary roommates and his malaise. He accepts greedily.

At Scadbury the days are clear and dry and very warm. Kit and Tom Walsingham spend their time walking and reading and hunting. Occasionally there are a few guests from nearby estates. Once Tom Russell comes by, but he cannot stay for long. Everything is leisurely for a change, and Kit luxuriates in the dreamy gorgeousness of his surroundings. Cambridge slips out of his mind. He even considers not going back at all. "That would be a mistake," says Tom. "I mean, for me it was all right, but for you it's different. You need your degrees. Besides, I think the discipline is good for you."

They linger on a stone bridge that crosses a moat. It is August. Summer has come to a fat and luscious ripeness. They sit on the low stone wall and look into the water. Kit lets fall a small stone. It breaks the surface of the water with a swallowing sound and sends its circles out. "I suppose I should be grateful," he says, "that my daily work is so precisely laid out for me. Otherwise I'm not sure what I would do. Go to London, perhaps, or Paris."

Walsingham smiles. "To be swallowed up by literary vultures. Oh, they would love you in London."

He drops another stone into the moat. "I don't suppose I really want to leave Cambridge, anyway. I'm learning a great deal and meeting some excellent people. Except that sometimes everything is boring—and everybody. And I just want to leave for a while."

"Well, Kit," says Walsingham, "if you really have an itch to travel, I could probably fix up something for you with Sir Francis. Something simple. Confidential courier, or something like that. You have no idea how few people can be trusted in this business."

"What makes you think you can trust me?" says Kit.

"Are you suggesting that I can't?"

Kit hesitates before answering. He seems to be amused by some thought that's running through his mind.

"Well?" says Walsingham.

"If you couldn't trust me," says Kit, "do you think for a moment I would tell you?"

Walsingham laughs and pokes his friend playfully. "Oh, Kit, you'll make a marvelous spy. It's really quite exciting. And, of course, terribly important."

"If I agree to do it," says Kit, "will you tell me all about your trip to Rheims?"

"I'm afraid I can't tell you *all* about it," he says. "But I'll tell you what I can."

They walk on, and Walsingham describes the English universities at Rome and Rheims. "It's quite an impressive group, you know. Very scholarly, very dedicated. There's no better place to learn Greek and Latin. And those Jesuits, you know, have an unbelievable capacity for hard work. Not quite my style. And the building that houses the college in Rheims is a bit dreary, I must say. But Rome—ah, Rome! What a fine city. It's enough to turn one into a Catholic."

"But what about the work?" says Kit.

"Oh, yes, the *work*, as you call it," says Tom. "You see, we have men at both colleges. I can't even mention their names. They provide us with all sorts of information."

"What sort of information?" says Kit.

"Mostly about what the Catholics are up to," says Tom. "They have a kind of network by which they communicate with one another. All of Europe from Rome to Spain to England is covered. They must coordinate their activities. They must confer. It is our job to penetrate this network, intercept their messages, decode them, and at times feed into the network false information to mislead them. If there is to be a Spanish attack on England, it will no doubt be coordinated with an attempt to assassinate the Queen and with a general Catholic uprising at home, which will free Mary Stuart and try to bring her to the throne. There are people running all over the place wearing false whiskers, writing with invisible ink, and carrying vital documents in the hollow heels of their boots. It's really quite fantastic."

Kit looks interested but puzzled. "But how can you tell whether or not the information you gather is accurate?"

"You can't," says Tom. "But that's all part of the game."

"And did you go with your own identity or in disguise?" says Kit.

"Oh, in disguise, of course. I was an ordinary wine merchant. I had all the necessary papers to prove it. I was brought across the Channel by small boat at night and given the names of my contacts. Everything went quite smoothly. I was even courted by an important French wine producer, who imagined I might make a large purchase. His wine was quite excellent and had I really been in the wine business I would, indeed, have made a deal with him. A charming man. He even had a smattering of English, which is more than one can say for most Frenchmen."

They have come halfway around the lake. They sit on the bank, remove their shoes and hose, and dangle their feet in the cool water.

"Do you really take all of this seriously?" says Kit.

"I most certainly do," says Tom. "So much so that I am considering a permanent position with Sir Francis. He has offered me the supervision of Kent in his organization. It would be very convenient, of course, and not terribly dangerous. I would have half a dozen agents or so. We would keep an eye on things and report back to him. It's not as exciting as going abroad, but then one can take just so many chances in this life without losing it."

"Do you really think that you can get me an assignment?" says Kit.

"I'm reasonably sure that I can," says Tom. "I mean, Sir Francis has asked me to look out for promising young men. And I told him that it would be a great pleasure to look out for promising young men." He is smiling and kicking up the water.

Kit pretends to be angry and shoves him off the bank. He goes into the lake with a splash and a howl, only to find that the water is barely knee-deep. They burst into boyish laughter in the stillness of the August sun and are mocked by a flight of crows, who rise from a field of ripening corn.

vii

At the home of Sir Francis Walsingham in London, several men are in the midst of a very serious conversation. They are Lord Burghley, his son Robert Cecil, Thomas Walsingham, Thomas Phelippes, and Sir Francis himself. After a rather Spartan dinner, they have retired to the privacy of the study, where they have before them on a large desk certain confidential documents and maps.

"Knowledge is never too dear," says Sir Francis. He is a man in his fifties who has always looked fifty. His face is firm and his eyes steady. He has the habit of self-discipline, and his real religion is hard work. His clothes are black and simple, his collar a small white ruff. He is bearded, as are all the others, except Thomas Walsingham. "It is not the cost that matters; it is the accuracy, gentlemen. The accuracy." He is talking to the younger men in the room, not to Lord Burghley, from whom he learned the art of secret surveillance. He paces back and forth beside his desk. "Very few men are totally reliable these days. Too many swear their allegiance to gold. Nevertheless, we need information, and we will have it. England's survival depends on it."

He stares down at a map on his desk. The others come closer and gather around. He points to the Lowlands. "If the Spanish plan an invasion of England, they will want to move their troops from here in ships."

"Impossible," says Lord Burghley. "The water's too shallow."

"They may use shallow-draft barges," says Sir Francis, "and keep their galleons in deep water."

"Parma would be a fool to try to move his troops out before taking a deep-water port," says Lord Burghley, running his finger along the Channel coast. "The Dutch Sea Beggars with their fast sloops would cut them to pieces. They would never reach the galleons."

"Nevertheless," says Sir Francis, "the Spanish in the Lowlands represent a serious threat to us. Therefore, we must have as much information about them as possible. We must infiltrate Parma's army and, if possible, his staff. We must intercept whatever messages pass between Parma and King Philip."

Lord Burghley looks a bit impatient. "Francis, I really think you tend to exaggerate," he says. His tone is donnish, and he seems to be lecturing the somewhat younger man. "We have had no indication that an armada is being formed. As for information, you are quite right. We need as much as possible—abroad and at home. But here in England is where the real danger is. We must expand our surveillance, especially in the north and in London. No Spanish invasion of England can succeed unless there is an uprising here to support it. And we must see to it that there is no uprising. If we are to increase our espionage staff, first consideration must be given to domestic problems. We must, at all cost, protect the Queen's person. She is herself rather reckless, as you know. She appears too often in public. She is fond of a progress into the country. She likes festivities and plays. How she can abide those roaring masquerades, I'll never know. There are countless occasions on which some madman could reach her. One thrust of a sword, one pellet of poison from such a deluded martyr would be more dangerous to England than fifty thousand Spanish troops on our beaches. I would personally like to see our surveillance at home doubled. Tripled! I would like a catalogue of all the important families in each county. I would like the movements recorded of every person with the potential for conspiracy. I would like to monitor all messages that cross the Channel."

"I don't see how that's possible," says his son Robert.

"It's not possible," says Lord Burghley, "but we can do it."

There are eighteen men in Her Majesty's Privy Council, but the burden of the work is borne mainly by Lord Burghley, Walsingham, and Leicester. Some say that Lord Burghley is the real power behind the throne. On the other hand, there is a rather formidable power *on* the throne, and no one, not even Lord Burghley, is about to force Elizabeth Tudor to do anything against her will. But she trusts him above all the others, even Leicester, with whom she has been romantically involved. She admires Burghley for his talents and loves him as a personal friend and servant. In fact, his long-standing intimacy with the Queen has, for years, disturbed Leicester, who has been urging war, while Burghley advances more cautious policies, preferring to achieve his ends more subtly and more inexpensively. Leicester and Walsingham are the vigorous anti-Catholics on the Council. They would like to plunge England into a war on the continent.

"If the Spanish succeed in the Lowlands, we are next," says Sir Francis.

"War is expensive," says Burghley. "And men get killed."

"But how can it be prevented?" says Tom Walsingham.

"How has it been prevented thus far?" says Lord Burghley. "By diplomacy, my dear fellow. Diplomacy."

"If you mean the marriage game," says Sir Francis, "I'm afraid our time is running out. Her Majesty can't go on playing that game forever. She's fifty years old."

"There are other considerations," says Burghley.

"If Mary Stuart were out of the way, the situation would be much simpler," says Sir Francis.

"On this point I think we all agree," says Burghley. "All of us, except Her Majesty, of course. And one must appreciate her reasons. They are not altogether emotional, you know. To bring to trial another queen, divinely appointed, is a very dangerous precedent to establish. It might one day be used against *her*. The very concept of monarchy requires that a king not be judged by his subjects."

"Mary Stuart is not the Queen of England," says Walsingham.

"Yes, but she is the Queen of Scotland," says Burghley.

"You forget that she has been driven out of her own country and been called a whore in the streets of Edinburgh."

"Nevertheless, she is by birth the legal and rightful queen," says Burghley.

Walsingham turns away from the desk and strides across the room and then back again. "William, you know as well as I do that this is all a lot of nonsense. Her Majesty is only afraid of antagonizing the Catholics by doing away with Mary."

"No, no, no. You don't seem to grasp this very subtle point. Nor do you fully understand the relationship between these two women. And you must never forget that the Pope has declared our Elizabeth a bastard and a heretic, and designated Mary Stuart the rightful queen. One can put aside such actions, but they still affect one's thinking."

"You don't mean to suggest that the Queen has doubts about herself?"

"Doubts?" Burghley savors the word. "No, not doubts. It's very complicated and very difficult to explain. Mary and Elizabeth are enemies, but they have a good deal in common. They are both queens. And in this sense sisters. Cousins, in fact. They share common blood from Henry the Seventh. And they share some secret knowledge that only a king or a queen can have. Such people are different. They are set apart."

Walsingham makes a fist and pounds on the desk, disturbing the maps. "Subtleties be damned!" he says. "Mary Stuart has to die."

"Why don't you dispatch her privately?" says Burghley with a sly smile.

"You know why as well as I do," says Walsingham. "First of all, I don't believe in murder. It is against my religion and my conscience."

"And, secondly, should you get caught at it, it would mean your head."

"She must be brought to trial," says Sir Francis. "Throckmorton has confessed everything. His plan to raise the Catholic gentry, to rescue Mary, to assassinate the Queen. He will go to the gallows. Mendoza, the Spanish Ambassador, for his part in this ridiculous conspiracy, will be asked to leave the country. It is the perfect occasion for getting rid of that Jezebel."

Burghley shakes his head. "You will never get Her Majesty's permission for such a trial."

Walsingham throws up his hands and lets them fall against his sides in a gesture of sheer exasperation. "It makes our job so much more difficult."

"Ah, that brings us back to the more practical issue," says Burghley. "Your cousin and my son seem to have had some success in recruiting couriers and agents for our service."

"Yes," says Robert Cecil. "As a matter of fact, I have the names of four people I would like to recommend, and Thomas has three others."

"Good," says Walsingham. He sits down. Robert hands him a sheet of paper. One of the names on it is Christopher Marlowe.

viii

At the Cambridge Scribblers' Club, organized by Robert Greene, Kit reads one of his translations of Ovid:

Corinnae concubitus

"In summer's heat, and mid-time of the day,
    To rest my limbs upon a bed I lay;
    One window shut, the other open stood,
    Which gave such light as twinkles in a wood,

Like twilight glimpse at setting of the sun,
Or night being past, and yet not day begun.
Such light to shame fast maidens must be shown
Where they may sport, and seem to be unknown.
Then came Corinna in her long loose gown,
Her white neck hid with tresses hanging down,
Resembling fair Semiramis going to bed,
Or lais of a thousand wooers sped.
I snatch'd her gown; being thin, the harm was small;
Yet striv'd she to be covered therewithal;
And striving thus as one that would be cast,
Betrayed herself, and yielded at the last.
Stark naked as she stood before mine eye,
Not one wen in her body could I spy.
What arms and shoulders did I touch and see,
How apt her breasts were to be press'd by me!
How smooth a belly under her waist saw I!
How large a leg, and what a lusty thigh!
To leave the rest, all lik'd me passing well;
I cling'd her naked body, down she fell;
Judge you the rest: being tir'd she bade me kiss;
Jove send me more such afternoons as this."

"So that's what you do in the middle of the night at Corpus Christi," says Greene.

"I love that 'lusty thigh,' " says Thomas Nashe.

"Why do you do it line by line?" says Evance. "It forces you into certain awkward constructions. Perhaps you should give yourself more freedom."

"I take liberties in the phrasing," says Kit.

They argue about the nature of Corinna's gown. " 'Nec multum rara nocebat,' " quotes Greene. "All he means, damn it, is that the gown is already virtually invisible and cannot hide her charms, so what's the difference if he tears it off. Surely that's what you mean, Kit."

"That's exactly what I mean," says Kit. "But I had to jam it all into one line and find a rhyme for it."

"It's not altogether clear," says Richard Harvey, one of Gabriel's two brothers. "And I'm not sure I approve of rhyming 'small' with 'therewithal.'"

"Nothing wrong with that," says Greene.

"I've seen worse," says Nashe.

"You've written worse," says Harvey.

Greene reads the first act of his new play. It is awful, and everyone tells him so.

Nashe offers up a satirical poem in which a lady eats her lovers. He is so violently attacked that he tears the poem to pieces and scatters it about the room. "Temper, temper," says Greene. "The Muse rarely visits an angry man."

When Kit gets back to his room he finds a perfectly ordinary message from Tom Walsingham. But it is written in French, which is the private indication that Kit's assignment abroad has been approved.

ix

In his rented house in Bishopsgate Street, between Norton Folgate and the old wall, Thomas Watson works on a new play. He sits at a handsomely carved desk, shipped back from Padua, where he was a student of Roman Law. His shirt is undone, his sleeves rolled, and his hair disheveled from a habit he has of running his hand through it and then over his face. Beside the window a caged bird sings, and along the sill potted plants lean toward the light. He pauses frequently and stares blankly out the window, where he sees neither the houses across the way nor the busy traffic of the street below. What he sees is a stage floating in the air. A stage on which is unfolding a scene from a comedy called *Don Alberto's Revenge*.

With the help of some important friends, his natural charm, and his enormous talent, Tom Watson has settled into an active literary life in London, having decided, after all, not to pursue law as a career. For money he tutors the son of the wealthy William Cornwallis and writes entertaining dramas full of sophisticated puns and social allusions. For satisfaction of a higher sort he writes poetry, both in Latin and in English, and spends a good deal of time with musicians and composers, for music is his other passion.

On the airy stage of his mind the characters come and go in *Don Alberto's Revenge*. They pose, they speak, they dance their way through satirical agonies—verbal jugglers, rhetorical gymnasts, in love with language and clothing and themselves. He is lost in composition. His pen moves rapidly across the sheet of paper, a tiny meticulous script, rushing to keep up with his galloping imagination.

A knocking at his front door confuses and disturbs him. It seems a part of his play at first—the way a morning noise sometimes intrudes itself into one's dreams. He stops in the middle of a line. He waits. And then it comes again. "God's blood and damnation!" he mutters and puts his pen down.

Kit apologizes for his sudden appearance. He hesitates in the doorway. "I seem to have arrived a day too soon. I mean, for Tom Walsingham."

Watson brushes aside his explanation, orders him into the living room and puts a glass of wine in his hand. "Of course you've arrived too soon. Tom's going to a dinner party tonight for the famous Nolano."

"For whom?"

"Giordano Bruno," says Watson. "At the home of Sir Fulke Greville. In fact, I'm going too and should be getting ready."

"You mean Bruno himself is in London?" says Kit.

"You are an admirer of his, I suppose."

"We talk about him a great deal at the University," says Kit.

"He is very difficult, I understand," says Watson.

"I would love to meet him in person," says Kit.

"I wish I could invite you, but it's not my party," says Watson. But, almost at the same instant, he leaps up as though inspired. "Come," he says. "We'll hunt up Tom and see if he can fix it up for you." He rushes off to dress, dragging Kit behind him by the hand.

X

Dr. Giordano Bruno of Nola, notorious professor of philosophy, sits at the head of one of the two tables in the elaborate dining room of Fulke Greville's house. The great man looks annoyed, and *is*, in fact, annoyed, because it had been his understanding that the gathering would be small and very selective, so that there could be a sensible discussion. Two or three guests at a light supper would have been ideal. After all, how can one talk about the immensity of the universe when his belly is distended with mutton and his mind dulled by wine?

"You English are all exhibitionists," says Bruno. The remark is received with polite laughter by those around him, but Bruno's face remains grim, and they can see that he is quite serious. "You dress like peacocks and eat like vultures."

"Not half so bad as dressing like a vulture and eating like a peacock," says Tom Watson. His remark extracts from Bruno a very reluctant smile and a nod. He is a handsome man, clean-shaven, with a strong face and a low forehead. His eyes are deep shadows under a ridge of bone, which gives him the appearance of being perpetually lost in thought. His nose is large and elegant and suits the forcefulness of his chin and his whole face. He is all confidence and dominance, and his voice is musical and deep. He talks very slowly, moving among several languages. He speaks English with a heavy accent and is more comfortable in Latin or French, but frequently, especially when excited, slips into Italian.

He is only thirty-six years old, and yet his work is known all over Europe. In some circles he is considered a very dangerous man. He has gone beyond Copernicus. His cosmology is either the vision of a genius or the work of the devil. He has fled from several churches, beginning as a Dominican friar in Naples, where he was suspected of heresy, and winding up in prison in Geneva as a bad Calvinist for having attacked Professor Antoine de la Faye. He preaches intellectual freedom and a concept of the immortality of the soul that few people can agree with without risking ecclesiastical difficulties. He is a philosopher, a scientist, and a poet, clearly one of the leaders of the "new age."

Marlowe instantly recognizes in him all those qualities that he admires: daring and courage and swiftness of mind. He sits quietly and listens from the lesser of the two tables. Both Tom Watson and Tom Walsingham are at the main table, along with such dignitaries as Walter Ralegh and Philip Sidney. Present also are two prominent Italian emigrés, John Florio and Albericus Gentilis.

"Where, may I ask, is our friend Thomas Harriot?" says Bruno.

"I am afraid he was unable to come," says Ralegh. "A slight indisposition."

"Too bad," says Bruno. "A mathematical wonder, he is, and we have had so little time to talk."

"There will be other occasions," says Ralegh. His pointed beard tends to exaggerate his long face. He wears an ermine-trimmed vest over his embroidered doublet, and a pearl dangles from his left ear.

A small army of servants moves in and out of the room and about the tables. It is not a modest supper at all; it is a small feast, and even Fulke Greville realizes that perhaps he has overdone it.

At Kit's table is Michel de Castelnau, the Marquis de la Mauvissière, the French Ambassador in London, who took in Bruno when he came to him with letters of recommendation from Henry the Third. Though he is himself a Catholic, he has often come to the defense of beleaguered Protestants. He has a gracious and fatherly air about him.

Also at Kit's table is Gabriel Harvey, whose greeting is abrupt, as though he does not want to be associated, in the minds of the others, with a mere undergraduate. The only other person of any note at the table is Edward Dyer, who is something of a dilettante as a writer, but a charming fellow with a good sense of poetry.

During dinner several discussions take place at once. Those who are not directly involved lean this way or that to eavesdrop.

Edward Dyer and Gabriel Harvey are talking about Montaigne. "His mother is a Spanish Jew, you know," says Dyer. "Antoinette de Louppes. The family is Catholic, of course, having converted ages ago. But you know they keep their cultural identity, so they are quite literally Catholic Jews!"

"I understand you're much taken with this Montaigne," says Harvey. Kit listens in on the conversation, but he is distracted by hunger, not having eaten all day. With his hands he dismembers a pigeon while he eyes the roast beef, the venison, and the several varieties of fish.

Closer by, and in competition with Harvey and Dyer, there is a serious discussion of the St. Bartholomew's Day massacre. Mauvissière is trying to explain how such a thing could have happened, how, out of frustration and rage, over two thousand Huguenots could have been slaughtered by rampaging Catholics. "You must understand that the atmosphere was most hysterical," he says, "and that there was much disagreement. I don't believe that anyone could have foreseen such an extensive . . ." He searches for a word. A tall, hawkish man sitting next to Kit provides him with one. "Slaughter!" he says, causing Mauvissière to wince and purse his French lips.

In his borrowed clothes Kit looks almost as though he really belongs in this company. He wears a small white ruff and a black doublet with red slashes. He laughs quietly into his wineglass at Mauvissière's expression. "But it is too ridiculous to go on about," says the Ambassador. "It is an unfortunate piece of history. We can only hope that it will never happen again." Someone farther down mentions the name of Catherine de Medici, but he is generally ignored.

Philip Sidney chats in Italian with John Florio. Giordano Bruno reaches for a strawberry. Someone explains to him where and how they are grown. Sir Francis watches silently, his dark face a study in puritanical restraint. His plate is clean but for one lonesome bone, and his wine is untouched.

"Harriot has figured it all out algebraically," says Ralegh. "I'm not sure I can follow his calculations, but I trust his genius."

" *'Chaque homme porte la forme entière de la condition humaine!'* " says Edward Dyer. "It is an entirely new way of looking at things.

Study yourself and you will know the world. It is all in us. My mind to me is a kingdom. This is what Montaigne teaches us."

"Is it true that you've been translating him into English?" says Gabriel Harvey.

"It is the Pyrrhonism," says Mauvissière. "The Scepticism." He has leapt out of the St. Bartholomew conversation into the safer atmosphere of metaphysics. "But he will die in the arms of the Church, believe me. In the end, you see, it is a great comfort."

"But is there any truth in it?" says Marlowe, surprised at his own audacity. The table goes dead for an instant, and the sudden silence at one of the tables draws glances from the other. Kit's neighbor is staring at him as though he is an uncatalogued species of worm.

"Ah, the truth, the truth," says Edward Dyer. "How elusive! How immense!" And then he tells a long anecdote about his visit with Montaigne in Bordeaux.

But the conversation cannot find a focal point. It slips this way and that. The eating goes on, and the drinking. Someone coughs. Someone laughs. There are references to the courtship of the fifty-year-old Queen and the Duke d'Alençon. Mauvissière, who has been handling the negotiations in this long, terribly drawn-out maneuvering, refuses to say anything about it, except that he believes it will succeed. Ralegh and Francis Walsingham tilt their heads at this remark and look to the other table. But already the dominant noise from that quarter is about whether or not one can trust the evidence of his senses. The abundance of wine at the table has made everyone bolder and more relaxed. "There are those, in fact," says Kit, "who believe that there is no such thing as the truth."

"But that is ridiculous," says his neighbor. "Whatever is, *is!* How can it be otherwise, even if we perceive it otherwise? I mean, we can be deceived or misled. God knows, men have been proven wrong from time to time—but wrong in relation to what? Surely, there is a collection of truths that make themselves known to us—in glimpses, in visions."

"And this is not to say that there is a contradiction with the doctrines of the Church," says Mauvissière. He hesitates and clears his throat, realizing that there is more than one Church involved at the table. "Whichever church," he says, drawing several sympathetic chuckles. "What I mean to say is that the Church is the guardian of the revealed truth. This does not mean that any individual within the Church knows everything—or anything, for that matter, except this important fact. The rest becomes a matter of faith. Obedience, supplication, humility, acceptance. So we are caught, in a way, between the irrepressible urge to explore our world and the demand that we accept the revelation. Hence, the feeling that science may very well be, in itself, a heresy."

"If learning is a heresy and a sin," says Marlowe, "would you advise me, sir, to leave the University?" Several people are listening now, and there is amusement.

"There are certainly those who would advise you to do so," says Mauvissière. "Ironically, the universities, which were founded by the Church and are dominated by the Church, are the very places today where the Church is being undermined. This is most certainly true of Cambridge. My own opinion? Well, that is an entirely different matter. I was never able to take vows of silence. I love to talk, as you all may have noticed."

Giordano Bruno is smiling at his friend's little speech, and then, suddenly, he begins to pound the table, as though for attention. "It is a confrontation!" he says in a loud and resonant voice that cuts off five conversations at once. "It is a very great confrontation. The free quest for knowledge and the absolute acceptance of the dogma. Our struggle to reconcile these two things is the dance of an idiot. And the suppression of certain ideas is more political than theological. How much difference can it make, really, if you English are Protestant or Catholic? We are all Christians. And in a thousand years from now perhaps even that won't matter. Ah, but the politics. That is very important. The Vatican is very powerful. The Unity is their wish. And the wish of King Philip. It is the unity of the old world, of the enslaved mind. The crawling on one's knees up the rough stones of the Church. The total submission. It is too old. It is ridiculous! You think a Hail Mary can destroy an algebra? Nonsense. Look around you. Use your eyes. Use your minds. You sail around the globe. It is round—no? And it turns on itself, once around every day. We are discovering movement. Everything moves. The sun, the stars, the moon, and all the infinite spheres of this immense universe. We are just beginning to see this. We are just coming out of the cave. All things heavy and light move upward or downward, and the wave swirls through the water, and all is infused with a mysterious vigor. How can we go on believing in miracles when our calculations already confirm what our senses have told us? No wonder King Philip is frightened. For him and the Pope the sky is, indeed, falling. Consider the Huguenots, the Unitarians, the Puritans, the Calvinists, the Mohammedans, the Epicureans, the *esprits forts* and *libertins,* the free-thinkers, and the atheists. Among the infinity of religions, what man does not believe that he possesses the truth? And what is his impulse? To immediately kill all the rest. *Vox populi est vox Dei.* Off with their heads. Nonsense! Utter nonsense! And it is not only in the Church, in the religion, that we find this foolishness; it is also in the universities. I must tell you a little story of my visit to your Oxford University." He pauses and mutters, *"Vedova de le buone lettere,"* and John Florio cannot suppress his laughter. "I spoke there on the immortality of the soul and the fivefold sphere. You know, the system of Copernicus. Nothing too new for those who are mature. Nothing too frightening for those who are not already frightened to begin with. But do you know what they did? They hooted me. They called me *pig.* They whistled. They made the vulgar noise. Perhaps it is the only kind of logic they know. And foremost among them the rector himself of Lincoln College." He throws up his hands. "Such a constellation of pedantic and obstinate ignorance, presumption and incivility. Fantastic! *Incroyable!"* He pauses again. "Forgive me," he says, but his tone is hardly humble. "It is the blood. It is the Neapolitan." His eyes blaze. His fist comes down on the table, rattling the silver and crystal. "You must understand," he says. "If you do not understand, no one will. It is for the love of true wisdom and contemplation that I torment and crucify myself."

Kit Marlowe, struck by the lightning of his language and conviction, is seared to the very soul. And when Bruno stops speaking and lowers his head as though he is exhausted, Kit starts an applause that the others quickly join, happy to escape the awkward silence and tension that has followed in the wake of the philosopher's blast.

xi

Somewhere between Fulke Greville's house and Bishopsgate Street, three young men walk arm-in-arm down the middle of an unpaved lane, avoiding puddles by a three-headed maneuver that is not always successful. When one of the three is dragged through muddy water, he curses good-naturedly as the other two laugh. They have had their share of wine, but they are not drunk. They are Tom Watson, Kit Marlowe, and Tom Walsingham.

"But won't Sir Francis be expecting you at his place in Seething Lane?" says Watson, as though completing a thought started half an hour earlier and interrupted by puddles, brawling cats, and observations about the dinner party.

"No," says Walsingham. "I told him this evening that I would not spend the night there after all, and that Kit and I would come around in the morning."

"Then you're expected at your own house," says Watson.

"No," says Walsingham. "My man Albert thinks I am spending the night with Francis."

"Then you aren't expected anywhere," says Kit.

Watson and Walsingham laugh. A puddle looms. They pull and drag, and the man in the middle catches it, which means Kit, who lets out a yelp and tries to leap clear over it, only to fall in the middle with a splash. Their arms are unlinked and Kit brushes away water and mud. "God's bloody arse, you've ruined my clothes."

"Not *your* clothes, Mr. Nimble-Foot," says Watson. "*My* clothes."

"I thought you looked a bit more respectable than usual," says Walsingham, putting his arm around Kit's shoulders.

"Oh, I'm getting more and more respectable every day," says Kit. "I have excellent tutors. Watson here, for instance! Versifier *par excellence,* world traveler, fancier of French wines and Italian sonnets, master of Latin literature, translator, friend of that literary puritan Sir Francis Walsingham and other people in high places, such as the bell ringer at St. Gabriel's and the man they hanged at Tyburn this afternoon."

"A very high position, indeed!" says Walsingham.

"But, above all," says Kit, "he is a maker of poems, a shaper, a creator, a laborer in the vineyard of language. He will make you a poem of whatever kind you want—whatever shape or size or length or subject. Is it love you fancy? Or death? Or heroism? Or terror in the night? He will make you a square poem about it, a round one, an elliptical one. If you prefer that it be anagrammatical, he can arrange that too. A very remarkable man. Especially adept at the sonnet, which he can deliver in a variety of languages, from Portuguese to Arabic. He also knows his philosophers, from Aristotle to Zeno and back to St. Augustine. And, besides, he doesn't mind lending an acquaintance a pair of breeches on occasion. A fine fellow, all in all."

Watson staggers with laughter and almost falls down. "He sounds quite magnificent," says Walsingham.

"Oh, he is, indeed," says Watson. "And not bad-looking either."

"Except for a rather arrogant nose," says Kit.

At Watson's house they have a fruit brandy before going to bed. They kick off their shoes and strip to their shirts. "Thank you for the borrowed rags," says Kit to Watson, handing him the handsome doublet.

"Don't mention it," says Watson. "Just drop it anywhere."

"And the ruff and the chain and the jerkin and the silken hose," says Kit slowly as he removes each item and lets it fall to the floor.

"How poetic!" says Watson. "The ruff and the chain and the silken hose!"

Walsingham unlaces his shirt and sprawls himself in a wooden armchair padded by cushions. "The trouble with dinner parties," he says, "is all that sitting around on hard chairs. Gets you right in the hindquarters, doesn't it?"

"I don't have that problem," says Watson, "being a little sturdier than most."

"So I've noticed," says Walsingham suggestively.

"Well, it won't do you any good, my dear," says Watson. "What's more, I'm exhausted, talked out, and drunk. I'm going to bed."

"A marvelous idea," says Walsingham, leaping to his feet.

"Where shall we all sleep?" says Watson.

"I don't know," says Walsingham. "What are the choices?"

"Not many, I'm afraid," he says. "It's a very small house. Just two bedrooms upstairs."

"Well, then, one of them must be yours," says Walsingham. "In that case, Kit and I will take the other."

Watson glances at Kit, who offers him nothing more than an inscrutable smile. There is a slightly awkward moment.

"I mean, if it's all right with you," says Walsingham.

"Well, of course," says Watson. "Of course it's all right with me. Why shouldn't it be?"

On the landing they say good night in a cobweb of shadows. Kit is carrying his brandy in one hand and a candle in the other. Walsingham steadies himself between the railing and the wall. "Sleep as long as you want to in the morning," says Watson. "If you hear any noise downstairs it will be Mistress Potter. She talks to the cat and to herself. Perfectly harmless old crone."

Their bedroom is small, with two dormers in the slanted ceiling and two small windows. Walsingham lets himself fall on the double bed and stretches out. "Well, here we are," he says. "All the luxuries of home."

"Privacy itself is a luxury," says Kit, "after life in the storeroom at Corpus Christi. I can't tell you how stifling and boring it is to live with a pair of serious, unimaginative divinity students." He puts the candle in a holder on a table between the dormers and then lights another on the mantel over a narrow fireplace.

"Ah, but there are other people at the University—more interesting people. I don't suppose you are always quite as bored as you claim you are."

Kit begins to undress and then hesitates. "No, not always."

Walsingham sits up and slips off his shirt to reveal a white and hairless chest. He is well formed, but perhaps a bit too lean. The bones of his shoulders protrude, and he has a thin neck that is a bit feminine. He rubs his breast and studies Kit. "Tell me, Christopher," he says, "how do you amuse yourself there?"

"Do you mean intellectually?" says Kit.

"No, you idiot, I mean amorously."

"You promised not to ask," says Kit.

"That's right, I did. But, as you can see, I'm asking anyway."

"I might ask the same of you," says Kit. "But I know it won't do me any good."

"I understand you spend a lot of time with a young man named Tom Nashe. Who is he?"

"A very bright boy," says Kit.

"But who is he?" says Walsingham.

"What do you mean, *who* is he? He's nobody. At least, in your terms. I mean, he comes from a perfectly ordinary family—Herefordshire, I think. His father is a minister. You needn't bother yourself too much about him. Besides, I thought jealousy was not your style."

"Don't misunderstand me, Kit," he says. "I'm not jealous—just curious."

"You and the cat that got killed," says Kit.

"Now you're angry," says Walsingham.

"No," he says, and then pauses. "I think I know what's bothering you."

"Do you?"

"Yes. You imagine that I am bartering affection for influence."

"And are you?"

Kit hesitates. "How much difference would it make to you if I said *yes?*"

"More than you imagine."

"Well, the answer is *no,*" says Kit.

Walsingham looks at him intensely and then allows himself to smile. "I prefer to believe you, even if you lie," he says.

"Very clever," says Kit, and cups his hand around the candle to blow it out.

xii

The secret conference at Barn Elms, Sir Francis Walsingham's estate near Richmond, begins, for one of the participants, in Marshalsea Prison half an hour before dawn.

The man who rises at this early hour is Robert Poley, a prisoner. He has a rug on his floor, a desk, a bed, and a collection of wine bottles. Behind a curtain hang his clothes. There is a washstand and a pitcher of water. For a prisoner, his circumstances are fairly luxurious—and all arranged for, in advance, by Sir Francis.

In addition to these physical accommodations, Robert Poley is allowed visitors, especially one Joan Yeomans, generally acknowledged to be his mistress, though she is married and still living with her husband.

Poley is a sturdy man of thirty-two with a dissipated boyish quality. Most people describe him as "affable" or "congenial," though they often pause in their description, puzzled by some reservation they cannot name. He has been to Cambridge, or at least he says he has—Clare, to be exact. In an ordinary conversation it is impossible to tell whether or not he is lying. In fact, this quality informs all his activities. Is he a scholar or a rogue? Is he kind or cruel? He has the chameleon's ability to adapt himself instantly to his surroundings and circumstances. Among Catholics, he is a Catholic. Among Protestants, he is a Protestant. He moves instinctively toward ambiguous language.

In Marshalsea he has what they call "liberty of the house," and is free to come and go as he pleases within the prison. This is an essential arrangement for a government agent. And there is no better place for an agent to collect information than in prison.

At Barn Elms, Sir Francis, the Queen's "Moor," is already at his desk by mid-morning, having risen early to make the trip from his house in Seething Lane. With him are several other men: his

secretaries, Lawrence Tomson and Francis Milles; his chief
assistant and code expert, Thomas Phelippes; Thomas Rogers, alias
Nicholas Berden, one of his key operators; Maliverny Catlyn,
whose current assignment is Cambridge, where he uses the alias
Benjamin Roberts; and Robert Barnard and Walter Williams. They
are expecting any moment the arrival of Thomas Walsingham and
one of his new recruits—a certain Christopher Marlowe.

Sir Francis sits at the head of a long table. He has the strained
look of a man who is overworked or unwell. In fact, a rumor has
circulated for some time that he is suffering from an ailment that is
not sufficiently respectable to name, and that this ailment has
severely affected his urinary system. But he never discusses these
matters with anyone.

"Gentlemen," he says, "let us begin." He glances slowly around
the table at each of the faces and then nods to Thomas Rogers, who
is sitting, once removed, on his left.

Rogers knows as much as anyone in England about the activities
of Catholic priests. They, in fact, imagine that he is an agent of
theirs. Their faith in him has been confirmed by his ability to secure
the release of certain suspects through influence in high places. He
has shrewd eyes and a neat small beard. His hair is black and his
face is hard, with sharp lines in his cheeks, as though he might have
some teeth missing. He has a nervous way of releasing a sudden
tight smile that gives him a sinister look. From time to time Sir
Francis has been warned that it is perfectly possible that Rogers is,
indeed, a double agent, but he is unpersuaded.

Rogers is reporting on the activities of a Catholic agent whom he
merely refers to as Richard, as though everyone is already familiar
with him. He is Dr. William Allen's man. And Dr. Allen is the
founder of the English College at Douay (now in Rheims). "I was
very interested," says Rogers, "in the means by which these
seminaries are brought into England. Richard says that Dr. Allen
gives every priest for his journey six or seven pounds in money and
a new suit of clothes; and that the priests usually come over in
French boats, coming to Newcastle for coals. They land either at
Newcastle or nearby. They choose this place because Robert

Higherlife, the Queen's officer at Newcastle, is a papist at heart, and his wife also. The priests with their books enter securely and are given further directions by Higherlife, as well as the names of certain sympathizers who form a kind of secret organization to assist these priests and to feed them and hide them. One such person here in London is known as William Bray. Not only does he provide protection for these seminary priests, but he is also probably the chief conveyor of papal books into England. I fell into his confidence quite by accident at The Bell in Aldergate Street. I learned from him that a new means of communication has been established between the Catholics and Mary Stuart, in spite of her close imprisonment."

Walsingham interrupts Rogers and questions him more closely on this point. "It seems to me most unlikely," he says, "though, as you know, we are preparing such an avenue of communication— one, however, that is filtered through our hands. Is it possible that the reference is to this connection?"

"No, I don't think so," says Rogers. "Nor do I entirely trust Bray's remarks. He was a bit far gone in liquor and was inclined to indulge in a little self-importance, if you know what I mean, sir."

Walsingham rubs his face and beard meditatively. "It is extremely important that there be no other line of contact with Mary Stuart but our own."

There is a brief silence in which nothing is heard but the swift scratching of Lawrence Tomson's pen as he records in a tiny script the vital matters of the conference. Walsingham waits until Tomson stops and looks up. Then he begins again.

When Rogers has completed his report, Walsingham turns to Robert Barnard, a slight blond man with dry red lips. He reports with excessive conciseness that the Earl of Westmoreland has been to Rome, where he received 500 crowns from the Pope, and that he is now returned to Flanders. That since St. Bartholomew's Day last some twenty-four Jesuits and seminary priests have entered England. That one of the members of the association to aid these priests is a Mr. Gardiner. He and his wife have a house not far from Uxbridge, though sometimes they stay in London or at Hogsden and rarely continue in one place. They have a priest who is called Mr. Gimlet. He goes on in this manner, his voice a monotone. Tomson the secretary makes a scratching duet out of his performance. Walsingham seems pleased, though not surprised at anything he has to say.

Walter Williams is about to report on his disagreeable sojourn in a Rye prison when the conference is interrupted by the appearance of Robert Poley, who is shown into the room by the man posted outside the door. Sir Francis indicates an empty chair next to Rogers, and Poley sits down without a word. His face is still moist with perspiration and has collected a streak of dust across the forehead.

There are no introductions, and Williams is asked to proceed. His looks and speech betray his lower-class origins. He is large-boned and broad-shouldered. There is only a shadow where a beard might be, and his eyes are dark under thick untrimmed brows. He has the advantage of once having worked for Thomas Copley, an English Catholic refugee in Paris. By what device he was persuaded to join Walsingham's invisible little army no one is quite sure.

"I want to thank Your Honor," he says, "for releasing me at last from that hell-hole in Rye. Not that I wasn't glad to do my duty as I understand it, but, begging your pardon, sir, it is a place more fit for dogs than for men. For a long time I slept on the bare ground and in my clothes and lived among thieves and rovers. I did, of course, seek out this Pasquinus Romanus, that notorious papist, and did, indeed, get thick with him. I confessed to him what seemed to be the innermost secrets of my heart, including the fact that I was a secret Catholic, born and bred, and tossed in prison on the suspicion of aiding the seminaries. Perhaps he believed me, perhaps he did not. In any case, he was not forthcoming for a long time. But little by little I got from him a few facts, and his promise that he would write a letter of introduction for me to certain highly placed friends in Paris, so that I might proceed there at some future time to be taken into the confidence of other refugees."

Walsingham interrupts him. "And do you think, Williams," he

says, "that on the basis of this flimsy promise we should send you as our agent to the continent?"

"If I am to follow up this contact," says Williams, "it is the logical next step, your Honor. Besides, it's a much more comfortable assignment than being tossed into another prison. I think I've had my share of lice and rats and rotten food."

"Did it ever occur to you," says Walsingham, "that this Pasquinus Romanus might very well be shipping you into the hands of the enemy and that you might not only wind up in a Paris prison but in the hands of a skillful tormenter who might try to wrench from you some information about us?"

Williams hesitates and looks around at his stone-faced colleagues. "It was not my impression that Romanus was lying."

"Did he show you the letter?" says Walsingham.

"No," says Williams.

There is another dramatic pause. Walsingham holds out his hand to Phelippes, who is seated to his right. Phelippes produces a sheet of paper. "Do you want to know what he said in that letter?"

Williams nods. "Of course, sir, but—"

"Well, then, listen," says Walsingham. "And listen very carefully." He reads: " 'Having the opportunity of knowing Mr. Williams, gentleman, who had been for a long time my fellow prisoner, arrested on suspicion, I could not but, at his special request, write this much about him, which is that his devotion toward the good ale is very substantial, for every morning he had much conversation with the clerk of the town touching the same. He is a great faster, but he prays little, unless it be somewhat before dinner that God may give him a good appetite to the same, which being down, his delight is to be among his white bears with whom he has by practice gotten great experience, using to wash them often with claret wine and sugar. He contents himself with this exercise only until supper, at which time he has very little meat, keeping an order in his diet for the quinsy in his throat; and for that cause, sack only suffices him, by which means his disease is reduced to his legs so that he can hardly stand.

" 'Besides this he suffers from severe headaches and can hardly

see. He has a good conscience, though, and prays only for those
things he takes. When he needs money he pawns his clothes. Ah,
but he is honest, for I have heard it reported of him that he never
touched a maid but from the knee upward. But I am too tedious in
writing all this to Your Reverence, whose wisdom is such that you
can, by these few remarks, conjecture and judge of the rest. I
beseech you, therefore, for my sake, to further him in his affairs,
which as I can learn is nought else but to seek remedy for these
diseases.' "

"God's body, he was on to me all the time," says Williams. "And
must have known that this letter would be intercepted by you. He is
trying to destroy my reputation."

"Your *reputation!*" shouts Walsingham, tossing the letter in the
direction of Phelippes, who rescues it in mid-air. "What reputation?
You squander the money allotted to you on drink and then
complain about the awful conditions in prison. They are only as
awful as you choose to make them. Now what are we supposed to
think about all this?"

"Only that the man is lying," says Williams weakly. "Why else
would he write such a satirical letter?"

"Perhaps because it's true," says Walsingham.

"I assure you, Your Honor," says Williams, "that I carried out
my assignment to the letter, making a brother of this prisoner and
trying to learn of his continental contacts and whatever else he
might divulge."

"Perhaps he was doing the same to you, you fool," says
Walsingham. "And in this drunken state of yours, how much did
you divulge?"

"Please, Your Honor—" says Williams.

"Not now, Williams," says Walsingham coldly. "We have
serious matters to discuss here. You may leave now. Go back to
London and stay there until we send for you again. Do you
understand?"

Williams gets up from the table, his broad face pale, his lips
twitching at the corner. As he reaches for the door, it opens in front
of him, and he nearly collides with the two men who are being let

in. He sweeps past them without a word. There is some confusion. Heads turn from the conference table to see what is happening. Thomas Walsingham comes into the room followed by Christopher Marlowe. They are all impaled by the awkwardness of the moment.

"Dear Cousin Francis," says Thomas, "how dreadfully sorry I am that we are so late. I cannot begin to explain what happened en route."

"We are not interested in your explanations," says Walsingham. "If you will have a seat, perhaps we can continue."

Christopher and Tom sit down and receive no greetings, except a smile from Robert Poley.

"It is my sad duty," says Sir Francis, "to report the death of our young courier Richard Corey, who was found murdered in a tavern outside of Rheims, his throat cut, apparently in his sleep. The significance of this event escapes us for the moment. It is quite possible that it was a personal matter. On the other hand, we must consider the possibility that he was discovered or betrayed. We expect a further report within a fortnight. Among other things, he was carrying confidential communications from our man at Rheims, whom we call simply Roland."

He pauses and turns to Marlowe. "Providing that your qualifications meet with our approval, you will have the unenviable task of repeating Corey's mission. You will go to Rheims as an ordinary student with Catholic leanings and establish contact with Roland. He will place in your hands certain important documents and reports, which you will return to us with all good speed and secrecy. After this general conference is adjourned, you will confer privately with Phelippes here about the details of your mission. However, before we go that far, I will ask those of you at this table who have any questions to put to Mr. Marlowe to do so now. And I will ask Maliverny Catlyn to comment on his recent stay at Cambridge."

Christopher follows Sir Francis's gaze to discover who this Maliverny Catlyn is; and there, amidst the other faces, he discovers one that is familiar—not as Catlyn but as Robert Benjamin of Trinity. He is a young man with red hair, thin lips that spread to reveal small teeth, and quick hands that produce, as if from nowhere, a notebook with a black leather cover. Among his colleagues at the table he is known as a man who is well educated and something of a religious zealot. At Cambridge he is known as a rather shy divinity student, a candidate for the M.A. degree, with a fondness for Greek.

"I have very little to report about Marlowe," says Catlyn, turning the pages of his notebook. "Undergraduate. Corpus Christi, candidate this term for the B.A. degree, Archbishop Parker scholar from Cambridge, son of a cobbler named John Marlowe. Superior intelligence, average performance, excellent in Latin, gifted in the making of verses, and given to argumentation, especially on matters of religion. He is inclined to associate with the more literary people at the University, and it is generally agreed that he will not be a serious candidate for holy orders when his scholarship is expired. Beyond this there is nothing to report, except that he has the proper recommendations and seems suited for an assignment as courier to the continent, especially in the light of his knowledge of several languages."

"Thank you," says Sir Francis. "Gentlemen, are there any questions you would like to address to this young man?"

Thomas Rogers leans forward to indicate that he would like to speak. "Marlowe," he says, "may I ask why you have sought out this—this less than respectable profession?"

"In the first place," says Kit, "I do not plan to make it a profession. Secondly, I was sought out by Thomas Walsingham and did not volunteer. When I was made aware of the possibility of both serving my country and making some money, I was naturally interested."

"You are in need of money, then?" says Rogers.

"Yes," says Kit, "though not desperately."

"And we can assume that your loyalty to your country is absolute?" says Sir Francis.

Kit hesitates. "Insofar as anything in this world is absolute," he says, evoking a glance from Tom Walsingham. "That is," he adds hastily, "I consider myself a loyal subject of Her Majesty and would, under certain circumstances, surrender my life on her behalf."

"You have heard, of course, of the papal bull denouncing the Queen as a bastard," says Sir Francis.

"Yes," says Kit.

"And?"

"The Pope is a man as any other man," says Kit. "And, to me, he speaks with no authority whatsoever."

"You recognize, then, the supremacy of Her Majesty in matters of religion?"

"Yes, sir," he says.

There are no further questions, and the business is concluded. "We have reports remaining," says Sir Francis, "from Derbyshire and Stratfordshire, from Yorkshire and Durham, but I am sure these will be too tedious for your young ears, Christopher. You may amuse yourself in the garden, where I trust Phelippes will find you in due course."

In the garden of Barn Elms, Kit collects himself among the granite scrolls, the water nymphs, the roses, and the conversations of the busy birds. He had not imagined that his adventure would be like this, and, for a moment, he considers the possibility of running away.

He dips his hand into the cool water and brings it to his face. The coolness tightens his skin and clears his eyes. Birds flirt with the spray that issues from the phallic spout.

"Fascinating, aren't they," says a voice very close to his left cheek, so close he can feel a hint of warm breath. He turns with a start into the triangular face of Thomas Phelippes. "Fountains, I mean."

"I didn't hear you approach," says Kit. "The noise of the water."

"I didn't mean to frighten you," says Phelippes, sitting on the stone rim of the fountain. There is a curious smile on his face that almost contradicts what he says. His eyes are very wide, and his narrow chin is brought to a more acute point by his carefully trimmed black beard. There is a touch of gray in his tightly curled hair, but he is not old. He is, in fact, quite young, though in an ageless way. As Kit stares at him, he imagines that he is the sort of man who will always look young. He has the cautious grace of a magician or a surgeon. Kit moves away a step or two but follows his example and sits on the rim of the fountain, just outside the reach of the falling water. The man has neither said nor done anything unusual, and yet Kit is more than mildly afraid of him.

"We are supposed to discuss the next step in your induction into the service," says Phelippes. "But I can see that your mind was a thousand miles away. Whatever could you have been thinking about? Don't tell me. Let me guess. It's my business, after all, to decipher things. Nothing magical, of course; merely a matter of observation. It's a habit you will have to learn if you are to succeed in this business. Now let me see. You are young. You are handsome. Is it possible you were thinking of a woman—a special woman?" He considers his own suggestion and rejects it. "No. No, not very likely on an occasion such as this. No, what you were thinking probably is that you would like to change your mind, that you would like to go through that gate, out of this garden, across the lawn to the stables where your horse is, and gallop as fast as that horse would take you all the way back to Cambridge. Is that right?"

Marlowe cannot believe what the man is saying. At first he frowns, afraid that this precise, intelligent fellow has indeed read his mind; and then he smiles, amused at the accuracy of his guess. But he will not give him the satisfaction. "Nothing of the sort," he says. "I was wondering how passable my French would be."

"Ah, very good! Very good!" says Phelippes. "Nevertheless, it's a difficult decision—I mean, this business of putting yourself in danger. And you *are* quite young. If you do have second thoughts about the matter, please feel free to voice them now. There will be no embarrassment, no price to pay. You will be absolutely free to go."

"I assure you, sir," says Kit, "I have every intention of going through with this assignment. And I am not all that young anymore. Twenty on my last birthday in February."

"Ah, all of twenty," says Phelippes. "A fifth of a century. A fiftieth of a millennium. Think of that!"

"I don't understand the point of your calculations. I thought you were going to provide me with instructions for my going abroad."

"In due time, Christopher," he says. "In due time. But, you see, it is as much a part of my duty to be absolutely sure that the people we select are suited for the role they are hired to play."

"I thought that was already determined inside," says Kit.

"Oh, it was. It was. But the habit of observation is almost a vice. One keeps coming back to the beginning. Repetition is important. It is deadly to be too impulsive. You're not, by any chance, an impulsive type, are you?"

"I've never given the matter much thought," says Kit. "I don't think so."

"Ruled by your head instead of your heart?" says Phelippes.

"I've always enjoyed logic," says Kit.

"And common sense?" says his instructor.

Kit begins to understand the game. "I have very little respect for anything common," he says.

Phelippes laughs out loud and leans forward to pat him on the shoulder. "All right, then, let's get on with the practical details. I trust you have a good memory. You should be careful to write down as little as possible, lest you be intercepted somewhere along the way. First of all, you are to return to Cambridge immediately. There you will stay until you receive your degree, which, if I am not mistaken, will be on Palm Sunday. Between now and then you are to make a point of voicing certain opinions that will not endear you to your Protestant friends. This portion of the scheme I will leave entirely up to you, but be careful not to go too far. You don't want to jeopardize your position entirely at Corpus Christi. You merely want to sow some seeds of doubt, so that, should there be a Catholic agent at the University, your attitudes might come to his attention. Do you understand?"

"Perfectly," says Kit.

"The Wednesday following your commencement you will go to the tavern known locally as The Gate in Ludgate Street. There you will inquire after Nicholas Berden, who you will discover is actually Thomas Rogers. Be careful never to call him anything but Berden. It is the name by which he is known in Catholic circles. He will provide you with the necessary documents. Your story will be that he is an old friend of yours and that because you have expressed a desire to visit the English College at Rheims, and because you are disenchanted with the ways of your Church and government, he has made your trip possible. His Catholic friends understand that he has ways of doing this for sympathizers to their cause as well as for actual seminaries and Jesuits. However, you will not go to Rheims as a convert. Not having been a practicing Catholic, you might find this too risky. You will merely go—well, very much as you are: an intelligent Cambridge student in whose mind there are troublesome doubts and Catholic leanings. You will be given the names of certain people and letters of introduction. If all goes well, you will be received as a potential student and a potential convert. You need not go that far, of course. And your visit will prove to be a short one, and, I hope, a profitable one. Not only will you be expected to bring back reports from Roland, but you will be expected to make whatever other observations are possible. Is all that clear?"

Christopher nods. Phelippes stands up, a little detached and bored, as though he has just made love and is eager to be on his way.

"Am I to use my own name?" says Kit.

"I don't see why not," says Phelippes. "It's a perfectly good name, and it keeps you closer to the truth, doesn't it?" He flashes one more empty smile, nods, and walks away, leaving Kit alone by the fountain.

xiii

Back at Corpus Christi, Kit sets about his twofold task of completing the requirements for the B.A. degree and damaging his reputation with the establishment. However, what is counterfeit coin for the forces of orthodoxy proves coin of the realm among the rebels, and he is soon something of a notorious celebrity on campus.

In The Eagle Tavern he makes fun of the *responsios* and *opponencies* before an appreciative audience of John Penry, Richard and John Harvey, Richard Proud, and Simon Aldrich. He is prepared to defend, he says, the proposition that man is by nature a sodomite. Laughter and wine encourage additional suggestions for these rhetorical exercises which are required for graduation. From Richard Harvey comes the somewhat too serious proposition that all logic is dialectical, to which Kit responds by saying, "Petrus shall Ramus full of persuasion, and Norgate shall deny us thrice e'er the cock crow twice."

"That the nature of things is a Hereclitean fire," says Penry. "Try that in your public schools against your vacuous opponents and watch them scream 'foul.' "

"That fair is foul and foul is fair where parallel lines meet," says Simon Aldrich, whose father would surely suffer a stroke if he knew what his son was up to at that moment.

"That choice can exist without free will," says Kit.

"That the good life is impossible without good wine," says Penry.

"That Aristotle was the illegitimate son of Plato," says John Harvey.

"That man created God in his own image," says Kit.

"Now, now, you go too far," says Simon Aldrich.

"It is only disputation," says Kit. "I may be proven wrong."

"That disputation is an instrument of the devil," says Richard Proud.

"Ah, very good! Very good!" says Kit. "We are all victims of language. And logic, and rhetoric, and dialectic, and all things square, round, and verbal. Beware the lecherous word. Beware the sound of your own voice. Beware the forked tongue of the devil and Beelzebub's magic syllogism. We are all fools. After the Tower of Babel we have never really understood one another."

"That faith is an act of heroism against an army of heresies," says Richard Harvey.

"That suicide is a religious act of self-humiliation," says Kit, "and should be rewarded by instant resurrection."

No laughter follows this remark, and Richard Proud says in his pimply way, "I once knew a boy who committed suicide. He drowned himself in the Serpentine with a large rock around his neck."

There is an awkward silence that Kit breaks by knocking his glass against the table and singing out, "That the Queen knows better than the Pope what's good for Tommy Tweedle's immortal soul."

In spite of his somewhat tarnished reputation, Kit is granted his B.A. The Palm Sunday ceremony delights and depresses him all at once. He is touched by Norgate's speech and by the singing, in which he takes part. And he feels suddenly as he did when he was fifteen years old, that a large part of his life has managed to slip away without his quite noticing it, and that one day he will be "surprised by death."

xiv

Within ten days Kit is on his way to Rheims. He is on the outskirts of Abbeville and hopes to reach Amiens that evening. Following his instructions, he exchanges horses at the stable of a M. Corot and presses on. He moves along the unpaved road within sight of the river at a steady canter. He leaves behind the clustered houses and chimneys of Abbeville, and once again the level land stretches out behind hedges and rows of trees. There are meadows reaching to a patch of woods on a slight rise. There is an oxcart in front of him, now beside him, now behind him. There is a herd of swine, and pigeons circling, and the long ridge of billowing clouds in the new air.

The sun is very warm. Kit removes his cape, then his traveling coat, and drapes them across the horse's rear, over the canvas bag in which he carries his clothes and other necessities, and a smaller leather bag that contains papers for Roland. These papers are skillfully coded to seem innocent and personal. If he is apprehended and questioned, he is to say that they are letters from friends and relatives and that he is delivering them as a favor to Roland's father.

He is a few miles past Abbeville when he hears someone calling out to him. He turns to see a frantic monk galloping on a mule with no saddle. His impulse is to spur his horse and run. He does so, but the surprised horse rears and nearly tosses him. He reins him in and steadies him. And then it is too late to escape. The monk rides up, shouting, "Wait, wait." He is wearing a long brown frock and sandals. His pate is shaven. He has lost his cap. His untrimmed hair falls about his ears and over his eyes. There is dust in his face. He comes up beside Kit and, unable to catch his breath, says only, "Please, please." Then he adds in a moment, "You are the English for Rheims, no?"

"What do you want?" says Kit.

"Do not be afraid," says the monk. "I am your friend." And again he asks, "You are the English for Rheims?"

Kit is afraid to answer. "You have made a mistake," he says. But then he adds, "How do you know who I am?"

The monk slides off the mule and ties it to a tree. "Come down for a moment," he says. "I must have some words with you. You are Monsieur Marlowe, no?"

Kit is too taken aback to do anything but dismount. He joins the monk beside the tree, whose broad branches shade them from the sun. The monk is a short man with stubby arms and protruding eyes. His belly has an unascetic roundness to it and bulges past his sunken chest. His small quick hands seem to be creating words out of the air around him. "I explain. You must give me a moment to explain. My English is not grand. It is very small."

Kit takes a skin of wine from his canvas bag and offers it to the monk, who is now sitting on the ground and leaning against the tree. The monk thanks him profusely and takes a long drink.

"You see," he says, "we have papers for Monsieur Parsons. He has come from Rouen to Rheims for only a short time. And Father Michel is with the fever and cannot go even to Amiens. We have word that there is an English for Rheims from the University in Cambridge. We have watched all day and it is you. We are sure it is you—Monsieur Marlowe."

"Incredible!" says Kit. "How can you know such a thing?"

"Ah, but we do," says the monk. "We have been told before that you would come, by friends of Monsieur Berden. It is the same way always as for the other students who come. You go to the inn, Au Mouton d'Or, no? You see, we know everything. No, no, not everything. But we are told that you are to trust and that perhaps you will be a priest. Is that not so?"

"No, that is not so," says Kit. "It is true that I have come from Cambridge and that I will visit the English College, but it is not true that I will become a priest. About that, I cannot say now. It requires a great deal of thought. I am sure you understand."

"Oh, but of course, monsieur," he says. He puts a fatherly hand on Kit's shoulder and tilts his head to one side. He is perhaps twice Kit's age and does, in fact, seem to understand. "These are very grave decisions. Very grave. To give up the world. A very grand commitment. You will pray for guidance and your prayers will be answered. And I will pray for you, too." He makes the sign of the cross.

Kit studies the monk and considers the possibility that this is a trap of some kind, perhaps even concocted by Walsingham to test him. "What are these papers?" he says.

"Who knows," says the monk. "It is not for us to know. They are for the English Jesuit, Robert Parsons, a man of much importance and power. He gets many letters, many papers in his business. We must only deliver them. And we must deliver them privately through friends. You are a friend, I am sure."

"Yes, yes," says Kit, cutting him short. "Well, all right, then, let me have them and tell me who to turn them over to."

"Ah, good," he says and struggles to his feet. From inside his robe he produces a small packet. "Here. For John Ballard at the seminary. He is another English priest. He meets with Robert Parsons, who comes for a grand meeting. He explains the rest to you."

Kit takes the packet and smiles. "But are you sure you can trust me? Suppose I am a spy for the enemy."

The monk shrugs. "I do not believe. I have the good words for you. And I can see in your eyes that you are honest. It is a very large favor for all of us. You will do it? No?"

"Yes, I will do it. I will give these letters to John Ballard. But that is all I will do. Nothing more. Do you understand? I am only a student. I am only going for a visit. I do not want to get involved in your politics."

"It will be no trouble," says the monk. "No trouble at all. And you will be well paid. You will see." He backs toward his mule and unties him. "And now, I must be back to Abbeville. Good fortune and God be with you."

And in another moment Kit is standing under the broad tree looking up the road as the monk retreats at a gallop, raising dust behind him. He is puzzled and amused. He puts the packet away in his canvas bag and mounts his horse. He shakes his head and mutters aloud, "Incredible!"

xv

The director of the Jesuit mission in England, Robert Parsons, comes to the Rue de Venise in Rheims for an urgent conference at the college with Gilbert Gifford, John Ballard, Christopher Hodgson, and Dr. William Gifford. They sit at a long table in a plain white room and discuss the assassination of Queen Elizabeth.

Parsons is an intense man with an angular face and penetrating blue eyes. He is thirty-eight years old, at the height of his ability, and dedicated to bringing England home to the Catholic Church. He has lived on the continent as an exile for ten years, having given up his fellowship at Baliol and embraced the "true" Church as a convert.

"You will pardon me for saying this," says Parsons to Gilbert Gifford, "but your brother George is an ass. An incompetent Braggadochio. A bungler. A fool. And though in my own heart I cannot condone murder, I find stupidity even more revolting."

"You did not actually ask him to kill the Queen," says Gilbert in his lethargic way.

Parsons gets up from the table and paces across the room. He is wearing a simple white gown and a skull cap. "Though the Pope has made it clear that the man who kills Queen Elizabeth will be absolved from all guilt, and will, in fact, be a hero in the eyes of the Church, I cannot, in all good conscience, order anyone to commit an act of murder."

"Still," says Gilbert Gifford, "you wouldn't mind if some fanatic were to bury a dagger in her royal neck."

Parsons stops pacing. He stares at Gilbert, who calmly stares back, a trace of a smile on his somewhat dissipated face. "I would consider it an act of God," he says.

Dr. William Gifford clears his throat loudly to interrupt the exchange. "If we may put aside this unfortunate episode and turn to a piece of new business," he says, "I would like to introduce a young man who has been waiting outside for quite a while. His name is John Savage. His family is Catholic, and he was forced to flee from England a few years ago. He came here to the College, but stayed less than a year and took no holy orders. He returned to England briefly and then came back here for a second time. Still restless, he went off to the Lowlands to volunteer his services to the Duke of Parma. There, he felt, he might help the Spanish to develop their invasion plans for England. What he discovered was that the military life, especially under Alessandro Farnese, was less than glamorous, and that the war against the rebels in the Lowlands might very well go on forever. Disenchanted, he returned to us for a third time. Now he has come forward determined to sacrifice his life, if necessary, to strike the blow that will free England from its Protestant tyranny."

Parsons sits down. "It all sounds so simple. So romantic. And so familiar. What these young men need is *brains,* not bravado. But bring him in. Bring him in."

John Savage strides in, his movements rather rehearsed. He takes an unusually long stride, perhaps to give the effect of decisiveness. He is tall, handsome, clean-shaven, and dressed expensively in the Spanish style. His doublet of pinkish white silk seems lavish in these plain surroundings. And over his left shoulder, carefully draped, is a fur-collared cape.

Parsons stands briefly and says, "Welcome, Mr. Savage. It is a pleasure to meet you."

"The pleasure, sir, is all mine," he says.

"Please sit down," says Parsons. "Make yourself comfortable. This is a very informal meeting."

"Thank you," says Savage, arranging himself at the table with the others.

"I hope you don't mind if we ask you a few questions," says Parsons.

"Not at all," says Savage. He puts his hands on the table and then removes them to his lap. He seems uneasy.

"Well," says Parsons, "I guess the best way to begin is simply to get to the heart of the matter. I understand from Dr. Gifford, Gilbert, and Father Hodgson that you have taken an oath of some sort—that you have sworn to do away with the Queen of England."

"Yes, sir," says Savage. "I have sworn it before witnesses."

"These witnesses?" he says, indicating the men at the table.

"Yes, sir, before these three men within these last several days here in Rheims."

"And may I ask you, John, what brought you to this desperate course of action? I say *desperate* because it means almost certainly that you will give up your life in the attempt, even if you fail."

"I understand that," says Savage.

"Still, you are determined to try?"

"Yes."

"Can you tell me why?"

Savage looks puzzled. "The answer should be obvious," he says. "It is what we all want, isn't it?"

"But why *you*? Why should you be the one to do this? Do you—do you feel that you have somehow been singled out for this task? I mean, divinely singled out?"

"I do not know, sir, what my destiny is," says Savage. "I would like my life to be useful, to be meaningful in some way."

"You mean you would like to feel important," says Parsons.

"I feel I have certain talents, sir."

"And what exactly is your principal talent, Mr. Savage? Surely not persistence. I mean, you seem to move about from this to that."

He coughs nervously. "I find it rather embarrassing to talk about myself in this way."

"I did not mean to be facetious," says Parsons, "I am trying to understand your motives. Do you, for instance, hope to gain anything specific for yourself by this heroic act—aside from the glory of being, in the minds of some people, a hero? In the hearts of many others you will be a terrible villain."

"I realize that," says Savage. "No, I am not looking for material rewards. I understand that George Gifford was promised eight hundred crowns by the Duke of Guise if he would do the job. I might need certain expenses, of course, but nothing for myself."

"And afterward?" says Parsons.

"Afterward?"

"Yes. Would you expect something from the new government? An appointment of some sort? Surely, you would expect something for your trouble."

"Assuming that I succeed and that I am still alive," says Savage, "I see no reason why I should not be offered a position."

"Master of the horse, perhaps," says Parsons. Gilbert Gifford lets escape a subdued chuckle. "You find that amusing?" says Parsons.

"No, no," says Gilbert in his relaxed way, waving the whole matter aside.

"Well, then, may I ask your opinion in this matter?" says Parsons.

"First of all," says Gilbert Gifford, "I think you are wasting your time examining John's motives. What difference does it make? Perhaps John is fired by religious fanaticism. Perhaps he would like to hurl himself into the pages of history. Perhaps he is a gambler for high stakes. As long as the job gets done. Isn't that what matters?"

Parsons looks at Gilbert with a smile. "I feel thoroughly chastised," he says unconvincingly. Then he turns to John Savage.

"I did not mean to probe. If I embarrassed you, please forgive me. What specifically do you have in mind? Do you have a plan?"

"The Queen, as you know, moves about frequently. She goes from Whitehall to Greenwich, Richmond, Oatlands, or Nonesuch or Hampton Court. Not to mention her summer progresses into the country."

"I understand that her travels have been curtailed because of the tenseness of the times," says Parsons. "I have heard that she may not go into the country at all this summer."

"Well, that remains to be seen," says Savage. "I doubt that Elizabeth herself knows at this point. She might go on an impulse."

"Burghley and Walsingham will scold her," says Dr. Gifford.

"I personally think there is a fair chance that she will at least go to Theobalds or Kenilworth," says Savage.

"And if she does?" says Parsons.

"Well, there may be an opportunity en route, if she goes far afield."

"She goes with an entourage of two hundred and a large military force," says Parsons.

"I have considered also the possibility of securing a position with the officer of the hunt at one of these estates. I am an excellent horseman, if I do say so myself. And the Queen is fond of hunting and a royal picnic. Under these circumstances, who knows what might present itself?"

"Is there any way that you might become a member of the entourage?" says Gifford.

"I don't know. I could talk to Anthony Babington or some other friends—"

"You must be very careful what you say to your friends," says Parsons. "When you are involved in a business such as this, you must assume you have no friends." He leans back, rubs his forehead and eyes, and studies the young adventurer. "Tell me, Mr. Savage, why did you come to us and what do you expect from us?"

"I am only one person," he says. "Though I am determined to do the deed, I feel I need assistance. What's more, immediately following this assassination certain other things should happen.

Mary Stuart should be freed instantly and proclaimed Queen of England. Catholic forces should rise and be organized. Perhaps there should be a move from the north. But I am not well versed in all this. These operations are for other people—you, the Pagets, Morgan, Arundel. I only offer myself as the hand that holds the dagger. Should you devise a total plan into which that dagger can fit, I am your man."

"I think it would do no harm to take up the matter with a few other people," says Gilbert Gifford.

Parsons stands up to bring an end to the discussion. "Mr. Savage," he says, "I want to thank you for your frankness and for your enthusiasm. As Gilbert says, we will want to give the matter some thought and perhaps discuss it with some other people."

After Savage leaves the room, Gifford turns to Parsons and says, "Well, what do you think, Robert?"

"My first impression is not favorable," says Parsons. "And yet, who knows? He might be the very one to do the job. He's a little mad, but he may be able to throw away his life and keep his wits about him at the same time. May God forgive him if he should succeed." He walks out of the room.

Gilbert Gifford also goes out. He goes down a corridor, down a narrow staircase and out through a side entrance into the Rue de Venise. The street is busy. There are many carts and wagons and men on horseback. The market has closed. People are returning home. Bells are ringing. The Cathedral looms above the town.

He turns into a side street, from which emerge a group of woolen workers. They part as they move around him, talking their rapid French. He finds room on the narrow sidewalk just in time as a large cart bears down on him, its driver crying out to the crowd and to the horses with their shaggy hair and wide feet.

Gifford turns into a shop under a sign that indicates that books are bought and sold here. He is greeted by a man with a large nose and thick glasses that are held in place by loops that go completely around his ears. "Ah," says the shopkeeper, "Monsieur Gifford. What a pleasure to see you."

"Henri," says Gifford, "I have an important message to send."

"I understand," says the shopkeeper. He takes a book from under the counter behind which he stands. He opens it to reveal a shallow place carved out of several pages. "These books will be delivered personally into the hands of Sir Francis Walsingham."

Gifford goes around the counter and into a back room that is so jammed with books he can hardly move. At a small desk in the light of a shaded candle he writes the following: "The seed has been sown. I have persuaded William, and William has persuaded Savage. He imagines that he will make history, as, indeed, he will, though not the sort he expects. If the High Priest agrees, a plan will be set in motion. We must find a way to link it with the Queen Bee. I await further news from you."

xvi

Meanwhile, in London, in a private chamber in Whitehall, Queen Elizabeth sucks on a black tooth from which the pain is gradually subsiding. She sits in a high-backed, highly carved chair and listens to her "Moor," Sir Francis Walsingham.

"Under the circumstances," he says, "I think it is imperative that Mary Stuart be moved at once to more secure quarters. I have, at last, the full report of the Creighton business. It is much more serious than we imagined it would be."

"Creighton? Creighton?" she says. "Who is Creighton?" She rests her cheek in her hand and looks as though she has been betrayed by some invisible force. She is wearing a black gown, mourning, perhaps, for the dying tooth. Her ruff is small and mounts to her chin and cheeks. It is lined with gold, as is the small velvet hat she wears. A necklace of pearls in decorative gold settings crosses her chest and ends in a circular pendant and a final tear-drop pearl.

"Creighton, Your Majesty, is the Jesuit priest who was involved with Francis Throckmorton in his despicable plot to remove you from your throne and separate you from your life."

"Why wasn't he apprehended and brought to trial with the rest?" she says.

"He was in France," says Walsingham. "Inaccessible. However, I learned from an agent of mine not long ago that he was trying to get to Scotland. I had his ship intercepted by the Admiral of Zeeland, a very competent man, and had Creighton taken prisoner. Just before he was seized he took from his doublet a document of some sort and tore it to pieces. Hoping to scatter it in the wind, he tossed it away but in the wrong direction, the fool, and it all flew back on deck, where most of it was recovered. It proved to be an extremely important discourse, written in Italian. I have a copy of it here. It sets forth very explicitly the entire plot against you and the plan to liberate Mary Stuart. In addition—something Throckmorton never revealed to us—it sets forth in detail invasion plans much more elaborate than we guessed. Not only did the Duke of Guise and his confederates intend to invade us from the north, but they also intended a full-scale invasion of Scotland. Such a twofold assault might have proved disastrous to us. My guess now is that Throckmorton himself did not know about the second invasion."

She sighs, as though in pain or despair, rubbing her somewhat swollen jaw with a very white, long-fingered hand, decorated by two jeweled rings. The arches of her thin eyebrows collapse into a frown. Her thin mouth tightens. Suddenly she looks all of her fifty-one years of age, and perhaps more. Everything about her betrays her tension. Her entire body seems to contract into a concentrated effort at control, exaggerating the prominence of her nose and the height of her forehead as it rises to the small border of carefully contained red hair. At last she says, "Sir Francis, must you always bring me such awful news? Can't you put an end to these ridiculous conspiracies?"

"I'm sorry," he says, "but I think Your Majesty knows as well as I do that these plots against your life and your throne will continue as long as Mary Stuart is alive."

Her hand falls away from her ailing jaw and, as a fist, pounds against the arm of her chair. "Mary Stuart, damn her," she shouts. "Christ in heaven, why can't the wretched whore be stricken dead by some natural cause? She is forty-two years old. Surely, God in his wisdom can find some disease with which to ship her into eternity, so that we can live out our lives in peace and concentrate on our more immediate pain. What sin do you suppose I have committed, Walsingham, to be thus cursed with rotten teeth and an ungrateful cousin? I have saved her life time and time again. What more can she want?"

"She is a very ambitious woman," says Walsingham.

"She is a lecherous strumpet," says Elizabeth. "But, God help me, she is also a queen, whatever her faults."

"She is a criminal and must be brought to justice," he says.

"Oh, justice! Justice! What in hell is justice, anyway? Your solutions, Walsingham, are expedient, not just."

"My deepest concern is for my country," he says.

"You needn't remind me again of your marvelous integrity and patriotism. If I didn't trust you and need you, you wouldn't be here. What would you have me do?"

"Shrewsbury is eager to be quit of his duty as Mary's keeper," he says. "Put her in the hands of someone more severe and move her to a place where her confinement can be more absolute."

"And what exactly do you suggest?" she says.

"I suggest you put her in the hands of Amias Paulet and remove her to Chartley Castle," he says.

"Amias Paulet! That humorless puritan!"

"A very effective and scrupulous man."

"Your man," she says.

"No, not my man," he says, "but on this matter we stand in agreement. He will be sure to see that no communications pass between Mary and her allies—here or abroad."

With a grinding motion of her teeth, she seems to be considering the suggestion. "I have been thinking about Sir Ralph Sadler," she says.

"He is not nearly as good," says Walsingham, "but I have no objection, as long as you remove her from Sheffield Castle. She has had too much freedom there. It is a situation that is hard to control. Move her, at least, to Wingfield. We will manage better there."

"I will think about it, I promise you," she says.

"And you will let me know tomorrow what your decision is?"

"I will let you know, sir, when I am good and ready!" she shouts. "Now leave me alone while I meditate on the brevity of life and the stinking corruption in my mouth."

xvii

Having completed his solitary journey, his conquest of France, Christopher Marlowe marches in triumph through Rheims, re-creating in his mind the victory and tragedy of Joan of Arc. His ragged post horse is a prancing stallion. His ordinary doublet is silver armor. *"Maintenant il faut aller à Reims."*

Houses thicken and cluster, church spires pierce the low gray clouds, the Cathedral rises like a city within the city. Was this how it was for her a hundred and fifty years earlier? he wonders, wrapping the story of the miraculous maid of Orleans in spontaneous poetry, savoring the names of the places that were her personal stations of the cross: Orleans, Patay, the bridge at Meung-sur-Loire, the castle of Beaugency, Montepilloy. He sees her in her male clothing, leaping from the top of a tower of the Castle of Beaurevoir. He sees her standing before her judges, the Bishop of Beauvois and Jean Le Maistre. He sees her at the altar with Charles the Seventh. And he sees her burned at the stake in the Place du Vieux-Marché. *"C'est moi,"* he says aloud. *"C'est moi!"*

And then, suddenly, he is none of these things. He is a stranger in a strange city known to him only in his dreams. He is thirsty and tired. His horse snorts like an ordinary horse and tugs him toward a public trough. Bells mingle with the rattle and yelping of the increasing crowd. A coach lumbers through the street and shouts him out of the way. He dismounts and lets his horse drink. On the ground he feels stiff and heavy and a little dizzy. He splashes water in his face and sits to rest on the edge of the trough.

From a leather pouch strung across his shoulder he takes a piece of paper on which are written the directions to the Rue de Venise and the Seminary.

Some hours later he sits in an attic room of a small inn called La

Tour. His instructions demand that he stay there until he is contacted by Roland.

Nothing happens until after midnight. By then he has dozed in his chair. The knocking at his door wakes him, and his heart leaps. He stands. The book falls. He reaches for his dagger but does not draw it. "Who's there?" he says.

It is Roland, at last. Kit unlatches the door and looks out before letting him in. "You have a word for me?" he says.

"The word is 'unicorn,'" says Roland.

Kit opens the door wider to let him in. Their greeting is abrupt. There are beads of perspiration on Roland's forehead. He does not remove his cape. "I have only a few minutes," he says, "and much to tell you."

"But I will be here for some days," says Kit. "I don't understand. Are you in difficulties?"

"Yes, I think so," says Roland, "but I cannot be sure. I think I was followed here. If someone else comes to your door tonight, do not answer." He produces a packet and hands it to Kit. "These," he says, "are various letters for Walsingham. See to it that they do not fall into anyone's hands. If you are taken, try to destroy them."

Kit motions for him to sit, but he refuses. He accepts the packet and then, noticing his fallen book, stoops to pick it up. "I was asleep—" he starts to explain, but Roland is not listening.

"In addition you must tell Walsingham," says Roland, "that Parsons is here in Rheims and that he has been in conference with the Giffords, Ballard, and Savage. Tell him, furthermore, that letters from Mary have reached Paris and that our attempt at interception has failed. You can say that it is my opinion that one of Parson's men in Paris is a traitor."

Kit nods, committing all this to memory.

"I am sorry about the hastiness of this visit," says Roland. "Perhaps we will have a chance to talk at greater length; perhaps we won't. We should not be seen together at the Seminary. If we do meet, you will pretend, of course, not to know me. And now, I must go." At the door he turns and says, "I assume you have a letter of introduction to Dr. Allen."

"Yes, I do," says Kit. And at this very moment he remembers the messages for Robert Parsons given to him by the monk in Abbeville. He is about to mention them, but then decides not to. He allows Roland to leave.

He puts away the packet and then throws himself on his bed. It is all done, then, he thinks. How simple! He stretches his legs with a sense of accomplishment. The rest is different. It is something that is entirely up to him. He welcomes the chance to use his own initiative, though he has not decided yet what exactly he will do. He will present himself in the morning to Dr. Allen and then to Ballard. With luck, he imagines he can see the famous Robert Parsons.

xviii

His interview with Parsons does not come for another three days. At the College he has been treated as a visiting student and a potential convert. He has attended lectures. He has been shown the city. With an older student, William Baldwin, he has even attended mass at the Cathedral—an impressive ceremony, full of embroidery and incense and relics of the dead saint. *"Et unam sanctam ecclesiam catholicam,"* explains Baldwin at one point, but Kit is not listening. He is drawn into the ritual. "As long as you shall do these things, you shall do them in memory of me." The small bell rings at the altar, the candles flicker in the airless room as though moved by ghosts, the light is tinted through decorated glass, and there is a conspiracy of mystery and spectacle aimed at his vulnerable heart. He leaves the Cathedral shaken by doubts and filled with contempt. It is all so childish. It is all so grand!

His invitation to meet with Father Parsons is an imperative. It leaves him no choice. A young priest informs him at his room at the inn that he must come immediately and ask no questions. He has already delivered his unopened packet to Ballard and assumes that Parsons has heard by now.

He is received in a small study at the Seminary. It is very early in the morning. Parsons sits behind a table in a simple black gown.

His face is composed, his blue eyes clear from a day of fasting and prayer. Kit is brought in by the young priest, who immediately departs. He is alone with the Jesuit leader, and the room is suddenly like a small prison.

There are no introductions. Parsons says nothing for a long time. His intensity fills the room, paralyzing Kit out of even the most normal congeniality. He waits, feeling himself in the presence of a man to whom he will not be able to lie.

Parsons leans forward against the bare table, his hands clenched, his elbows supporting him. "Your name is Christopher Marlowe," he says.

"Yes," says Kit. "I am from—"

"You are from Cambridge," says Parsons.

"Yes."

"You are a student."

"I have just recently taken my Bachelor of Arts degree at Corpus Christi."

"And you write poetry, I understand," says Parsons.

"Yes, I write poetry."

"Well, that's neither here nor there, is it? If I may come directly to the point, I think, young man, that you are an agent for Sir Francis Walsingham. Am I right or wrong?"

"I don't know what gives you that idea," says Kit.

"Am I right or wrong?" shouts Parsons.

There is a long pause, after which Kit says, "You are both right and wrong, sir."

"I would prefer a simpler answer," says Parsons.

Kit finds himself breaking into a smile. "May I sit down?" he says.

"By all means," says Parsons, indicating a chair beside his table. As Marlowe takes the chair, Parsons comes back to the table and also sits.

"Well, now, where shall I begin?" says Kit. "Obviously there is no point in lying to you. Yes, I am a courier for Walsingham. No, I am not a spy. Yes, I am a courier for you. No, I am not a Catholic."

"Well, then, what are you?" says Parsons.

"Shall I be honest?"

"I think you had better be."

"I will begin at the beginning, then," says Kit. "I am a student at Cambridge. Through some friends I was given an opportunity to come to France, provided I delivered certain letters to certain people. I have done so, though I shall not tell you, under any circumstances, to whom. In addition, I was given the opportunity to deliver certain letters to you. I have done that also. To me it is a matter, in either case, of total indifference. I wanted only to come to France and to Rheims."

"You are, then, an opportunist," says Parsons. "Is that right?"

"No," says Kit. "Not in your sense."

"Then what do you want in Rheims?" he says.

"A chance to study," says Kit. "A chance to see things from another point of view. Like many of my friends, I am very troubled by what is happening in England, especially in the English Church. I am on a scholarship at Cambridge and I am expected to take holy orders. But how can I? The Church is all politics, all very secular. It is really quite disgraceful."

"You are saying these things to please me," says Parsons.

"No," says Kit, "I believe them—and worse. Things I dare not mention to anyone."

Parsons smiles. "You are a young man and a poet. You probably imagine that you have lost your faith."

"How did you know?" says Kit.

"We all lose our faith at least once before we are thirty," says Parsons. "It's nothing to worry about. If you are pure of heart, it will come back."

"And if I am not pure of heart?" says Kit.

Parsons stands up. "Come, my son," he says, "let's take a walk in the garden."

They talk for about an hour about religious matters. Parsons is refreshingly blunt, and Kit is surprised to discover that he can, indeed, be honest with him, though much of what he has to say would hardly be tolerated in his own country—even at Cambridge.

When they are back in his study, Parsons says, "I have no reason now to doubt that what you tell me is true. I hope you will stay in Rheims for a while and that you will study with us."

"I would like to stay," says Kit, "but I must be back before long or lose my standing at Cambridge. And I am not ready yet to abandon my scholarship and my Master's degree."

"If you decide to come here to study, we will make some arrangement for you."

"You trust me, then?" says Kit with a smile.

"Why shouldn't I?" says Parsons. "You were quite honest about your mission here. And you delivered my letters intact. Why didn't you open them?"

"Because I don't care what's in them," says Kit.

"What do you think Walsingham will say about that?"

"Sir Francis will never know, unless I tell him," says Kit.

"And do you plan to tell him?" says Parsons.

"No," says Kit. "Why should I?"

The priest shrugs. "I don't know. Out of loyalty, perhaps."

"Loyalty to what?"

"To your country," says Parsons. "Don't you feel a certain loyalty to your country?"

"Do you?" says Kit.

"England is also my country, though I have been away for a long time," he says. "Yes, I feel a great loyalty to it, and I often miss it."

"It is beautiful, isn't it?" says Kit.

"Yes, very beautiful in places," says Parsons. "I am from Somerset. Have you ever been there?"

"No," says Kit.

"I think often of those hills and those fertile valleys," he says. "We had orchards and cows. And when I was a boy, my father took me to see the Roman ruins. It was very exciting. I have not been there for years and years."

"But you have been in England," says Kit.

"Yes, in another part, with Campion. You know, of course, about that."

"Everyone knows about that," says Kit. "I was there—at his execution."

Parsons looks at him as though he must see him in a different light now. "You saw it all, then?"

"Yes, the whole thing," says Kit. "It was terrible—and wonderful. He was very brave."

"I sometimes think I should have been there with him," says Parsons. "But, had I been there, I wouldn't be here now talking with you, would I?" His smile is sad and meditative. "Do you think that the government of Elizabeth is a harsh government?"

"All governments are harsh," says Kit.

"Did you know that a hundred thousand people a year are fined for failure to attend church in England?"

"No," says Kit, "I did not know that, but I am not surprised. The English are not very pious."

"No, no, it's not that," says Parsons. "It's because most of the English are Catholic. They prefer their own rites, their own priests. There are hundreds and hundreds of priests still in England. More than anyone imagines. The government is a Protestant tyranny that has created its own church to strengthen its political hold on the country. Sooner or later you will find yourself at odds with the very people for whom you are now working. They cannot tolerate the kind of freedom you want."

"I am already at odds with them," says Kit, "but would I be better off here or in Italy or Switzerland?"

"Yes," he says, "you would be better off here. You would not be so closely watched. There is greater intellectual freedom and tolerance."

"Is that why Giordano Bruno has had to flee from city to city all over Europe?"

"Ah, Bruno," says Parsons. "We cannot talk about Bruno. He is a special case. A rare case."

When, at last, their conversation comes to an end, Kit has agreed to consider enrolling at the College. He has also agreed, for a certain compensation, to make himself available as an informant, if and when the opportunity occurs. "We will know where to reach you," says Parsons. "Until then, God be with you."

xix

On All Saints' Eve, Kit returns to his room at Corpus Christi to find someone sitting at his desk. He is startled. In the dim light he does not at first recognize the broad-shouldered blond man. "Ah, there you are," says the intruder.

As soon as the man speaks, Kit remembers who it is. "Is it Mr. Poley," he says, "of Marshalsea?"

"*Formerly* of Marshalsea," he says, smiling boyishly and coldly and making no move to rise. He is wrapped in his black cape and seems, except for that boyish face, an appropriately sinister figure for All Saints' Eve. "Been out these five months now."

"A hard price to pay, it seems to me, for—"

"For serving my country?" says Poley. "Nothing is more important than that, is it? But let's not talk about me. Let's talk about you."

Kit sits down on his bed, and the two men look at each other for a moment. "What exactly did you come for?" he says.

"Let me get right to the point," says Poley. "We have another assignment for you."

"What sort of an assignment?" says Kit.

"A mission not unlike your first one," says Poley. "You see, now that certain Catholics on the continent seem to trust you, we would like you to serve as a courier for them."

"I don't understand," says Kit.

"It's really quite simple," says Poley. "We have reason to believe that a major conspiracy against our Queen and country is now being hatched on the continent. A vital ingredient in their plans is the conviction that a Catholic uprising is possible here in England. Nicholas Berden, who, of course, they believe is one of them, is already gathering relevant information. He needs assistance in getting his material into the proper hands abroad. The information he sends them will, of course, be prepared by us. And, what's more, it will show that Catholic strength here is much greater than it actually is, and that an organized uprising can be guaranteed. This will encourage them to make certain bold moves. And when they do—well, you can imagine the rest. There's no telling what we may catch in our net."

"But why would you want to encourage a conspiracy of this sort?" says Kit. "I mean, suppose it works? Suppose some madman manages to kill the Queen?"

"I don't think it's very likely," says Poley. "We are too thoroughly in control of the situation. You see, it's not the little fish we want. We want to flush out the big ones—and, well, one in particular. But I don't think we should go into that right now. Some of these things must remain confidential."

"I understand," says Kit.

"So what do you say, Christopher?"

"What if I refuse?" says Kit.

Poley smiles and leans forward, emerging from his batlike cloak, the orange slashes of his jerkin catching the light and seeming for a moment like wounds or perhaps the feathers of a rare bird. "I don't think, Christopher, that you are in a position to refuse."

"What do you mean?"

"You see, there's been some serious question about your last trip," he says. "About whether or not you went over to the other side. I mean, there *could be* some misunderstanding about this, should I want to make an issue of it with Sir Francis. Now do you follow me?"

"You would do that?" says Kit.

"You would be surprised what I would do."

"But if you force me to go, what makes you think I won't betray you?" says Kit.

"First of all, we will know if we are betrayed," says Poley. "Second of all, I consider myself a good judge of character, and you do not strike me as the sort of person who is ready to chuck everything for something as trivial as this—your education, your country, your friends, your family. You don't want to give up all that, do you?"

"You may be overrating the value I place on these things," Kit says.

"I don't think so," says Poley. "Besides, what we ask of you is really quite simple—except for the minor risk that you might lose your life." He lets escape a whisper of a laugh and shrugs his shoulders. "Speaking of which, did I tell you that poor Walter Williams is dead? He was found at an inn in Ipswich. Apparently died of natural causes. That is, he died, quite naturally, after somebody let all the blood out of his body. It seems he went over to the other side after Sir Francis withheld his fees, and he was on his way to France. A thoroughly disreputable fellow." He sighs. "Ah, but that's neither here nor there. Come now, Christopher, give me your decision."

"When would I have to leave?" says Kit.

"Oh, not until sometime after Christmas," says Poley. "We wouldn't want to interfere with your holidays."

"Very generous of you," says Kit.

They look up at the sound of someone at the door. "Good," says Poley in a hasty whisper. "I will be in touch with you."

XX

In Poley's house in Bishopsgate, which he calls "The Garden," he entertains Anthony Babington.

"What marvelous good fortune," says Babington, "to have fallen into such an advantageous position. It's really quite amazing that you, of all people, should be living in Sir Francis Walsingham's house—you, a Catholic born and bred, courier for Mary Stuart, former religious prisoner. I can't quite believe it. How in the world did you manage it?"

"It wasn't easy," says Robert Poley. They are in that part of the house from which it draws its name: a small but lovely garden with miniature paths and grape arbors. Babington sits on a low stone bench and stretches out his long legs. He is tall, handsome, wide-eyed, and young, about twenty-five. He has the physical appearance and poise of an aristocrat. He is a Derbyshire squire and a Catholic. His family is part of a whole society of Midlands Catholics.

"Well, do tell me, will you?" says Babington. "I'm dying of curiosity."

Poley has the ability to digest people while he seems to be pleasantly relaxed. He is lying now on a small patch of grass, propped up on his left elbow. He is virtually at Babington's feet, a position, in his mind, of considerable advantage at the moment. "It was a very complicated process, a very curious set of circumstances," he says. "I will have to back up a bit and fill you in. You see, several years ago I had some incidental employment with Sir Francis Walsingham. Unfortunately, I was forced to spend part of my employment in prison as a recusant. This merely served to improve my reputation with my friends. I struck up a connection with Charles and Christopher Blunt. For Christopher I did a number of useful things, the most difficult of which was to deliver letters to Thomas Morgan, who happened to be in the Bastille in Paris at the time. My reward for this rather daring exploit was a letter of recommendation from Morgan to Mary Stuart, suggesting that I might be of some help to their cause. I then persuaded Christopher to use his influence with Leicester to get me an appointment in Sidney's household—which means Walsingham's household. He was convinced that I would spy on Walsingham, and Sir Francis was convinced that I would be made privy to Catholic schemes, being so crucially placed. So, you see, it has worked out quite well."

"Remarkable. Absolutely remarkable, Robin," says Babington.

"But it is you who have the really important news," says Poley. "Tell me, dear friend, what is happening?"

Babington looks around before speaking. "Are you sure we are secure in this garden?"

"Oh, absolutely."

"Well, then," he says, "everything seems to be coming along quite well, except that communications are so slow and so difficult—especially with Mary herself. I have yet to have any direct contact in that direction. Sir Amias Paulet has her in a cage."

"Not entirely," says Poley with a smile. "She has been reached, and very recently. But more about that in a moment. Do go on."

"There are three aspects to the whole thing," says Babington, "not all of which are within my control. There must be assistance from abroad. There must be a rising at home, and there must be a force to free Mary and depose Elizabeth. Savage is still sworn to do the deed, but he and Ballard have just recently arrived in London, and we have, as yet, developed no specific plan. However, I will personally undertake the task of liberating Queen Mary. I have a following with which to do this."

"Such as?" says Poley.

"I think I can raise a hundred men," says Babington, "with the help of such close friends as Chidiock, Tichborne, Dunn, Charnock, Travers, Bellamy, and Jones. Salisbury is with us, and Gate. They have all promised to deliver a group. And I have the funds to back it up."

"What sort of funds?" says Poley.

"Well, I have personally about a thousand a year," he says.

Poley's expression indicates that he is impressed. "As much as that?" he says.

"And more, if I need it—I mean, through friends. There are some very wealthy families involved. They have kept out of it thus far, and I hesitate to mention their names."

Poley has risen to a sitting position on the grass, cross-legged and attentive. "I understand," he says.

"At any rate, I have just had an interview with Ballard. He is all enthusiasm about the possibilities abroad. He brings word from Parsons and Dr. Allen and Lord Paget, all of whom are convinced that Philip will move in at least thirty thousand men. The Guises can be counted on also."

"But how can you be sure of all this?" says Poley. "What are the details?"

"I also have it from Thomas Morgan directly," Anthony says. "He has been in constant touch with Mendoza, who is now in Paris also. It is through Mendoza that we have these guarantees from Philip. He says only let them know the date of the uprising and help will appear. They may have ships in the Channel already, for all I know. Or perhaps the troops will come from Parma in the

Netherlands. The details will have to be worked out. Nevertheless, isn't it terribly exciting?" He stands up and starts to pace with his long stride. Poley also rises, but more slowly. He watches the younger man, and once more urges him to go on. He moves with the slow sureness of a predator who knows he has his prey.

"Morgan says he will write to Mary, if he can reach her, to recommend me and to ask her to contact me. Certain letters also will be coming to me from Scotland from another source. These I am to deliver to her. And this, too, will reassure her of my reliability. God, how I long to see her, to look directly upon her face. You know, Robin, when I was a child I was a page to Shrewsbury, who was then her jailer. I used to see her from a distance from time to time, and I had such wild notions of one day rescuing her. I mean, there she was, the Queen, imprisoned in the castle. And I could see myself like a knight out of the old days, sword in hand, banners flying, sweeping up to the walls, laying down the challenge, and then hacking to pieces whoever stood in my way. It was a boyhood dream, but it's actually like that in a way, isn't it? I mean, here we are, about to do just that."

"Oh, Anthony," says Poley, "you are very brave." His earnestness verges on the satirical, but Babington doesn't catch it.

"But, of course, I can't do anything without Her Majesty's approval," he says. "I must somehow lay the whole plan before her. You said earlier there might be a way to do this."

"Yes, I think there is," says Poley, "in spite of Sir Amias's security measures at Chartley. It's quite ingenious and extremely confidential."

"Of course, if you think you shouldn't confide—" he begins.

"Oh, nonsense," says Poley. "I just want you to understand that there are very few of us who know about this arrangement. I am one; Gilbert Gifford is another. This is how it works. Chartley Hall is supplied by a brewer who makes regular trips between there and Burton. Gilbert has managed to enlist his help, for a sizable fee. In the bunghole of his casks there is a corked tube. Into this tube Mary's secretary, Claude Nau, can put a leather packet of messages. He must, of course, hand them secretly to the brewer. Sometimes he does this through the laundress, sometimes personally. The brewer cannot risk carrying these letters on his person, because he is regularly searched as he comes and goes. But where in a cask of beer is one liable to hide anything? Tap out the bung and you'll be washed away. So the letters go, via the brewer, to Burton, where they are given to Gifford, who then takes them up to London. He usually delivers them to the French Embassy—to Guillaume de l'Aubespone, in fact, the new Ambassador."

"And it has actually worked?" says Babington.

"It has worked for the first time just recently," says Poley. "Gilbert was finally able to persuade the Ambassador to allow him to attempt the delivery of about a year's worth of letters that had piled up there for Mary. They were wary, of course, but Morgan reassured them that Gilbert was reliable. The letters went through and the responses came back. Hence, we know that the system works. If you want to reach Mary Stuart, I suggest you write your letter, give it to me, and I will get it to Gilbert, who, in turn, will get it to Mary through the brewer. Her reply should come back to you by the same route."

Babington agrees, and the trap is baited. The letters will, indeed, be delivered through the brewer of Burton, but not until Gifford has had them deciphered and copied for Sir Francis. And the same is true of whatever passes from Chartley Hall to the outside world. As soon as Mary gives her approval in writing to the Babington scheme, the ax will fall.

xxi

It is not until the summer of 1586 that the long-delayed reunion at Scadbury takes place. Tom Watson has married Ann Swift, and Kit has been to the continent again. He has done his job without fully appreciating the grand scheme of which his trip is a small part. In fact, the whole adventure was disappointingly uneventful. And now, with the plague in London, the time seems ripe for a holiday.

Kit is the first to arrive, and Tom sweeps him instantly away for a long walk before Edmund Walsingham, the new Lord of the

Manor, can trap him into one of his plodding conversations. "Ever since Father died, Edmund has come out of his shyness," says Tom. "He walks up and down counting his inheritance and making long lists of the inventory of lands and houses and furnishings. He has also taken up Father's habit of drinking himself to sleep every night. What a clod he is!"

"And how do *you* get off to sleep at night?" says Kit.

"I read myself into oblivion with your boring translations," he says.

Tom takes Kit by the arm and leads him along a path into the woods. They move from the warm sunlight into the cool shade of giant oaks and beeches. "It's like going into a cathedral," says Kit.

They go, single file, deeper into the woods. They hear the dead debris of nature under their feet—the stiff leaves and brittle branches. Rare spots of sunlight filter through the heavy foliage of the trees, and the breeze makes a rustling sound high above them and lazily moves a half-dead limb so that it creaks eerily. At last they come to a small clearing where some rocks form a natural place to sit. "This is my very own place. A very private place," he says. "No one ever comes here except me—and Ingram, of course."

"Ingram?" says Kit.

"Yes, Ingram Frizer," says Tom. "He helps me keep the path open. He's been with us almost a year now. Edmund brought him up from London to help manage things. He's very good with the men, having been a farmer himself."

"And what else is he good at?" says Kit.

"For God's sake, Christopher," says Tom. "He's a servant, that's all. Sometimes you are impossible."

"I'm sorry," says Kit. "I caught a certain tone in your voice. I can almost always tell when you are concealing something. You turn a little more formal, a little stiff."

"It's not that at all," he says. "It's just that it's been a long time, and—well, you seem different. You've changed."

"For the better, I hope," says Kit.

"You seem less innocent."

"I have never been innocent," says Kit.

"Perhaps you're right," says Tom. "I've seen the devil dancing in your eyes."

"There is no such thing as the devil," says Kit.

"Oh, nonsense," says Tom. "You speak such nonsense at times."

They sit in the secluded clearing and argue themselves amorously into their old familiarity. The tension between them disappears, and an audience of birds applauds them with a song.

Suddenly, Tom catches Kit by the arm and says, "Listen!"

They hold their breaths and listen. There is the crunch of footsteps moving toward them. They are frozen into a parody of Greek statuary. The sound is upon them. The curtain of the grove parts, and out of the foliage steps a dark-haired man, his country clothes tight about his muscular body, a leather band about his wrist. He is obviously more than a servant but less than a gentleman. His dark mustache tends to droop at the corners, giving him a sinister look, and he does not try to hide the scar on his cheek with a beard.

"Ingram!" says Tom. "What are you doing here?"

Ingram Frizer shows no sign of being disturbed by the idyllic scene, except a certain tightening of his impassive face that gives it a slightly Oriental look. "I came to tell you that Mr. Watson is here, sir. What shall I do with him?" The corner of his mouth twitches toward his scar, and he seems to be suppressing a smile.

"Tell him we've gone for a walk and will return instantly. Tell him to make himself comfortable. See to whatever he needs."

Frizer lingers for a moment, his eyes more on Marlowe than on Walsingham. Then he turns away and plunges into the forest.

"Does he always follow you around that way?" says Kit.

"He's very attentive," says Tom.

"Well, whatever he is, I don't much like him," says Kit.

"Then neither do I," says Tom with a cajoling smile. "Come on, let's get back to the house and see what Tom and his bride are up to."

xxii

At midnight the dogs begin to bark at the sound of a horse galloping across the drawbridge and up to the house. Everyone is asleep, except Kit. He goes to the window and looks down into the courtyard. A shadowy figure has drawn his horse to a scuffling halt. He descends, the night breeze wrapping his cloak about him and swirling dust into the moonlit air. A yellow glow blossoms in an upper window. Edmund Walsingham flings open a window and bellows, "What in hell is going on down there?" His own light has blinded him, and his brain is muddled from too much drink.

There is a silence. The stranger does not answer. Once more Edmund calls out. Kit sees a second figure emerge from the shadows. Then he hears the voice of Tom Walsingham. "It's all right, Edmund," he says. "It's a friend of mine. Go back to bed."

Spluttering and cursing, Edmund slams shut his window and douses his light.

Kit also puts out his light and makes himself less visible at the window. The two men below are talking quietly together, but the stranger's gestures are animated. Tom indicates a place where he might tie his horse and then leads him by the arm into the house.

Kit puts on his breeches and goes, barefooted, into the hallway. He makes his way downstairs, stepping softly past Edmund's chamber. He goes past the Great Hall and the Great Brown Parlor, through a passage to another parlor, past several rooms along another passage, and eventually approaches a small chamber just past the Andrew Room. There he hears muffled voices and sees a line of dim light along the bottom of the door. He listens but cannot distinguish what the men are saying. It occurs to him that he might just knock at the door and announce that he too was awakened by the arrival of a stranger in the night. Instead, he rushes down the corridor and finds his way outside. He circles hedges and finds his way to the window of the room in which the men are talking. There, lurking in the dampness of the night, his feet cool, his face flushed, he watches from the security of his darkness, and, since the window is open, he hears them as clearly as though he were in the room with them.

The stranger has removed his cloak and hat. He sits stiffly on a severe chair and leans forward to talk, one booted foot advancing past the other, as if he is already in motion or prepared to run. The characteristics of the man gradually assemble themselves in Kit's mind, and, suddenly, he knows who the intruder is—it is Gilbert Gifford, whom he first met in Rheims, and who, to this moment, he assumes is a Catholic agent. What then can he be doing here at Scadbury talking to the cousin of Sir Francis Walsingham? Kit has an impulse to fling himself through the window and in the midst of the flying glass announce treachery and betrayal. But who is betraying whom?

"The sky is about to fall in London," says Gifford.

Walsingham, in his wide-sleeved brown robe corded about the waist, looks like an exotic monk. He paces the floor in front of his visitor, stopping frequently to absorb what the man is saying or to ask a question. "Is he going to move so soon?" he says.

"Any day now," says Gifford, "he will swoop down on Babington and his whole group. Plans are already laid. He wants to take them all: Ballard, Tichborne, Savage, Salisbury, Dunn, Jones, Charnock, Travers, Gate, Bellamy—the whole lot. And, of course, Mary Stuart and as many of her cohorts as he can accuse of some complicity. There will be widespread peripheral arrests, I understand. Even Robert Poley will be taken into custody."

"But why Robert? I don't understand," says Tom.

"Sir Francis says it's for appearance's sake," says Gifford. "He says he wants the Catholics to go on thinking that Poley is one of them. Personally, I don't think Sir Francis trusts him any longer, and he wants him in prison where he can lay hands on him."

"Does Robert know this?"

"Yes, we discussed it. I decided to flee to the continent until things quiet down. But he decided to stay and take his chances. At this point Sir Francis doesn't trust anyone, and I don't want to be around when there's a lot of hysterical hanging going on. I'm getting out while I've got the chance—even if it means never coming back again."

"But of course you can come back," says Tom. "You're an agent of Her Majesty's government."

Gifford laughs. "You have no idea what's going on right now. There is a kind of madness in London. There is a smell of blood in the air. Sir Francis has the old bitch cornered, and he is going in for the kill. It is the culmination of years of planning and maneuvering. Now he has the evidence. He has it in writing—from the Queen of Scots herself. Elizabeth will never know that the documents are somewhat altered or that Mary Stuart's secretaries were bribed. He's got twenty witnesses against her, and her signature and seal. That fool Babington will spill out everything as soon as he's accused. He's that type. Besides, it doesn't matter; he's lost anyway. They're all lost."

"But how can you safely go to the continent now that you've had a hand in all this?" says Tom. "They'll kill you if they find out."

"As far as they know, I have been working for *them*," he says.

"Perhaps you ought to risk a short stay in prison instead," says Tom.

"I have an aversion to prisons," says Gifford. "Poley doesn't seem to mind. He spends half his time in them."

"What are your plans, then?" says Tom.

"I'll have a few hours' sleep here, if you don't mind. Then I'll be off before dawn. I have an arrangement outside of Dover for a quick passage. On the other side I am among friends, so to speak. By tomorrow or the next day, Sir Francis will begin sealing off every port from Plymouth to Hull. You will have to be Jesus Christ himself to get a license to leave the country—and then you might have to walk across the Channel."

It is only as Kit listens to this account that he realizes what part he has played in it all. Like Poley and Gifford, he has been part of a plan to mislead the Catholics into a false move. He has assumed all along that the conspiracy was real, but now it occurs to him that there might never have been a plot if it were not "arranged" by Sir Francis. He is both thrilled and appalled. How ruthless! How clever! And then, suddenly, he wonders about his own vulnerability. Will he, too, be tossed into prison until the authorities decide which side he is really on? Should he, like Gifford, flee to the continent to avoid that possibility? He has a moment of panic in which he sees himself galloping desperately through the night toward the coast. But then he calms himself with the more rational argument that he has been only one of many couriers and agents involved in this grand scheme.

As Gifford and Walsingham show signs of putting an end to their conference, Kit quickly retreats into the garden and back into the house.

In his room he spends a restless night and cannot fall asleep until just before dawn, only to be awakened by the sound of a horse stirring in the courtyard and then galloping away. He hears the sound of its feet in the crushed stone and then that awful drumming on the wooden bridge.

xxiii

It is Saturday. Thomas Hobson's university carrier is due to arrive any moment. Sunlight brightens the colors of everything along the Cambridge streets that lead to Hobson's stables. Scores of students make their way in that direction, hoping for further news about the great conspiracy to kill the Queen. Everyone who comes up from London is pumped for information. Letters are shared or read aloud in packed rooms or noisy courtyard crowds.

News has reached them already about the arrests and the trials. They expect any day a description of the executions and news of the fate of Queen Mary herself. By twos and threes they move along the street, Kit Marlowe amongst them, Charles Walford by his side.

The carrier is late. The crowd at Hobson's stable grows larger. The sun fattens into an orange ball as it descends in the late afternoon sky. "There will be a massacre in the streets," says someone. "You mark my words." He is not a student. "It'll be a vengeance for St. Bartholomew's Day."

"And a good thing, too," says another man. He is dressed as a baker, and his hands are ghostly white with flour. "A little bloodletting will cure the body politic."

"Violence only leads to more violence," says a student. He wears the cap and hood of a Bachelor of Arts.

"Then how are we to defend ourselves?" says the baker. "How are we to prove that we mean business? There must be executions."

"Oh, there will be executions, all right," says another. "But let's hope there won't be mobs in the streets and unjust murders."

"There may yet be an invasion. There are rumors of Spanish ships off the coast of Cornwall."

Kit and Charles stand to one side of the main discussion. They lean against a half-timbered wall near the entrance to the stable. The odor of manure is strong. It dries to hay on the ground. Overhead a breeze moves the sign with Hobson's name on it. Mr. Hobson himself comes out and looks down the street for some sign of his carrier. Then he goes back in, muttering to himself. Someone shouts after him, "If you'd feed your animals decently, they'd be a little more eager to come home, Hobson."

"They could have died of old age between here and London," says another man. Hobson waves a thick hand at them without looking back and goes into the cool darkness of the stable.

By the time the wagon is seen in the distance, lumbering and squeaking into town, the crowd at Hobson's has increased by half. The carrier is so late that some of the impatient waiters are now more curious about its fate than the fate of England.

As it approaches the stable, one can see that it is heavily loaded with cargo. What one cannot see, until the very last moment, is that there are also two passengers: one an old man, the other Robert Cecil, now a member of Parliament from Westminster at the age of twenty-three.

The carrier comes to a halt and is immediately surrounded by townspeople and students. Kit and Walford hang back and see Robert Cecil climb down from the wagon. He is greeted by several friends.

"Did you know he was coming up?" says Walford.

"No," says Kit, "but while he's here I've got to talk with him."

They move into the crowd, which is now firing questions at everyone on the wagon, especially the driver, who, from his high seat, seems about to make a papal announcement. He holds up his hands and shouts: "If you will give me a chance to speak, I will tell you the news from London. But I ain't going to say it over and over a hundred times. My throat's as dry as sand, and I'd like some supper."

The crowd grows quiet, and the driver, a potential actor, has his moment. "The news from London is that fourteen conspirators against the life of Her Majesty, Queen Elizabeth, have been executed in St. Giles Field near Holborn. I have seen with my own eyes these terrible deaths. The first seven, amongst them the priest Ballard and the leader of the plot, Anthony Babington, were executed in the most painful way possible. They were hanged, cut down while still conscious, and forced to witness the carving out of their private parts. And then, still alive and aware, they were drawn—so skillfully that their guts were on the ground at their feet before they fell into darkness. They were most carefully attended to, in order to achieve the highest degree of bloody torment. Their genitals were rammed into their mouths. Their bodies were quartered and the limbs and torsos plunged into boiling caldrons. Their heads were raised on poles and carried to London Bridge. The second seven victims were treated more kindly, at the request of certain highly placed persons.

"There were celebrations in the streets both before and after the executions. As the prisoners were paraded to St. Giles Field, people lined the streets to hoot and holler and sing, out of vengeance and relief. They threw stones and rotten fruit, they cursed and gave out indecent gestures. Afterward there was much drinking into the night and much talk of killing Catholics. There are rumors of some murders but nothing confirmed, and yesterday the city seemed quiet enough. There has been no general uprising and no invasion. And Mary Stuart is in the Tower, awaiting her trial."

At this piece of news, the crowd lets out a cheer.

"They say there will be a trial in regular and official fashion. And that the Parliament will be asked to ratify the judgment."

Thomas Hobson comes out and breaks his way through the crowd that surrounds the carrier. "Here, here, here, here," he says, "make way, make way. We've got a wagon to unload and goods and letters to deliver. Now make way, make way, so's we can get about our business. And you, Henry Norris, get down from your pulpit and give us a hand. Never mind all that talk. There's people in the government can take care of all that."

"Sorry, folks," says Henry Norris, "me lord and master has spoken, as you have heard, so off with you now and let me be."

xxiv

In the Cambridge house of Lord Burghley, Kit Marlowe and Robert Cecil take a light supper in a small room with an enormous fireplace. In this season the fire is out and the unused cavity is a huge black mouth. Kit has not seen Robert in some time, and he is amused at the shape of his maturity. He has moved inevitably in the direction of his father, assuming some of his characteristic gestures along with some of his responsibilities. And here he is, sitting in his father's chair in this comfortable room in his father's house, talking, in his twenty-three-year-old way, about great affairs of state.

"Oh, they've got her now," he says, "unless the Queen intercedes. Her moods are hard to gauge."

"How much do you know about the so-called Babington Plot?" says Kit.

"Not as much as Walsingham, of course, but not much less."

"Do you think it was a real conspiracy?" says Kit.

"What do you mean?" says Robert.

"I mean that the whole thing may have been an invention of Sir Francis Walsingham's, that's what I mean."

"You're not serious," says Robert. "Of course, we know by now how he arranged to trap Mary and her cohorts, but surely they were serious. I mean, damn it, they're all dead, hanged for treason."

"I still think Sir Francis created the whole scheme," says Kit. "I think he infiltrated the Catholic ranks to the extent where his own agents could invent this plot. After all, who persuaded Savage to attempt an assassination? It was mainly the Giffords—Gilbert and William. And they were working for Walsingham. And God knows what Robert Poley has been up to, aside from spurring on that idiot Babington."

"I doubt that even God always knows what Robert Poley is up to," says Cecil. "But perhaps you are right. Perhaps Ballard and Babington were merely being used."

"I am personally sure of it," says Kit. "They and their friends are a bunch of incompetents who could never have managed alone— that is, without the fatal aid of people like Robert Poley and Gilbert Gifford. What pathetically easy victims for the old hawk."

"It's a serious accusation," says Robert.

"I can carry it one step further," says Kit. "I happen to know that the crucial letter written by Mary Stuart to Anthony Babington was altered by Walsingham. I happen to know also that both her secretaries were bribed."

"In other words," says Robert, "you're accusing Sir Francis of a kind of legal murder."

"Under the circumstances," says Kit, "I think *murder* is not too harsh a word."

Robert frowns and lowers his voice. "I hope you realize that you are saying very dangerous things, Christopher. And I hope to God that you have the good sense never to utter them in public. I myself would not condemn Sir Francis for his tactics, but the Queen might feel differently about it. She may yet spare Mary's life, believe it or not. It is a difficult situation for her. Who knows how she would react to such a rumor about Sir Francis."

"Well, don't worry, Robert," he says. "I am not about to stick my neck out for anyone anymore. I've had my fill of it. It's a dirty business."

"I think that's a wise attitude, Kit," says Robert, "and a safe one. Stick to your poetry. No one can ever hang you for a false rhyme."

"No, but I may yet be roasted here at Cambridge for a false impression."

"So I've heard," says Robert.

"What exactly have you heard?" says Kit.

"A number of things," he says. "You're much talked about, you know. That, at least, should please you."

"It doesn't please me at all," says Kit. "I want my Master's degree, and I want to stay out of trouble."

Robert laughs. "For a man who wants to stay out of trouble, my friend, you carry on an outrageous flirtation with it."

"What have you heard?"

"I hardly know where to begin," says Robert. "That you are a free thinker. That you are merely *using* your Parker scholarship. That you have no intention at all of taking holy orders. That you associate with known Catholics. That you have. been to Rheims."

"How in the world did *that* get out?" says Kit. He stands up and paces in the small room.

"How does anything get out?" he says. "Sometimes by accident. Sometimes by calculation."

Kit stops suddenly and leans toward the small young man in the large chair. "Are you suggesting that Sir Francis wanted that news circulated here?"

"It's possible," says Robert. "It would be consistent with all the rest."

"Do you think I may be denied my degree?" he says.

"It's quite possible," says Robert.

"And if I am, do you think Sir Francis will set the matter straight for me?"

"I wouldn't count on it," says Robert. "It might be more convenient for him to have you tossed out of Cambridge—and even into prison. But we mustn't cross that bridge before we come to it."

"No wonder Gilbert Gifford fled to the continent," says Kit.

"Gilbert Gifford is a thoroughly bad fellow," says Robert. "No one trusts him, least of all Sir Francis."

Kit empties his glass and slumps back in his chair.

"Now, now, don't despair," says Robert. "Should you get into difficulties with Norgate, we will lend you a hand. If an appeal of any sort should be necessary, make it through Copcot and my father, not through Walsingham. In fact, make it through me and I shall have it taken up in the Privy Council. They can bring some pressure to bear in the right places. Norgate is down on you; there's no question about that. And what's more, Norgate is in difficulties because of his generally liberal attitude and laxness at Corpus Christi. He may use you as an example—proof that he can crack down occasionally. Do you understand?"

"All too well," says Kit. "But I'll be damned if I'll be anybody's scapegoat. If anyone tries to get me, I warn you, Robert, I'll tell everything I know—about everybody. And that includes Sir Francis."

"Does it include Tom Walsingham?" says Robert.

"If necessary, yes," says Kit. He pauses. Then adds: "But I don't see what that has to do with it."

"Not much, really." He is almost smiling as he raises his glass to his lips.

xxv

On a cold February evening in 1587, William Short of Corpus Christi College, Cambridge, returns, on one of Mr. Hobson's hired horses, from Fotheringhay, where he has gone to visit his ailing father. Mr. James Short has done service for Amias Paulet at the castle in Fotheringhay, where Mary, Queen of Scots is imprisoned, having been found guilty some months earlier of a capital offense. Mr. Short, a local yeoman, had been expected to appear at the execution of the Scottish Queen, which, though private, was to be witnessed by several hundred people, most of them from the immediate vicinity. Eager to go but unable to rise from his bed, he had sent his son in his place.

After some supper and some hot wine to soothe his winter-afflicted chest, William Short sits before the fireplace in the hall and goes over the details of the execution before a small hushed crowd of crouched, kneeling, reclining black-robed students. His mono-tone is punctuated with a cough. He looks, not at his audience, but mainly into the fire, recalling, perhaps, the huge fire that burned in the main hall at Fotheringhay Castle to drive out the double chill of winter and death.

Kit is among the listeners, his imagination translating into reality every ordinary phrase that the ineloquent William Short uses. "Nobody in the village knew what to expect. After all, how many months had it been since Babington and his crowd went to the gallows at St. Giles Field? And there were rumors in the neighborhood, according to my mother, that Mary might be spared, because of political considerations. They said that Elizabeth wanted the full consent of James the Sixth, and that the Anglo-Scottish alliance was more important to her than the death of Mary. Old Abraham, who works for my father, said James was looking out for himself and didn't give a damn about his old lady, hardly having known her personally. I suppose he was as right as anybody, since the death warrant was signed and, as far as I know, nothing has happened to destroy the alliance. Abraham says James will be the heir to the English throne. There was a rumor afloat, in fact, that he had made a proposal of marriage to Elizabeth—imagine that! And he some thirty-odd years younger. He was probably advised to get some assurance of succession before granting his approval for the execution. For public consumption he ranted and protested and fulminated. After all, his mother was still the Queen of Scotland, and though she had been called a whore in the streets of Edinburgh, there weren't many who wanted to see her killed by the English.

"At any rate, when I arrived in Fotheringhay, there was such a large garrison there that one might have imagined we were at war. I understand that there were seventy foot-soldiers and fifty bowmen. I suppose that they imagined, because of the remoteness of the place, that a force of Mary's supporters might try to free her at the last minute. But after what happened to Babington and his followers, I didn't think it was likely that anyone would rush physically to her aid.

"My father said that Mary had already been separated from all her servants, though they continued on at the castle. Only her physician, Bourgoing, was allowed to see her. Still, at this point, there was no definite news of the death warrant. But we all expected it momentarily. What a cloud hung over the whole place! People

CAMBRIDGE

121

met in the market and spoke in whispers to one another. They commented on the comings and goings of everyone at the castle. There were superstitious predictions based on numbers, or stars, or peculiarities in the weather. My mother was convinced that they were going to kill her secretly and call it a natural death. My father, his voice sounding like a rusty hinge, argued to the contrary.

"Shortly after I arrived, we heard a rumor to the effect that Mary had been deprived of her priest, her steward, her rod, and her dais, because she was no longer a queen but a condemned woman. Most of the villagers took this as a sure sign that the end was near. King Richard the Second, they pointed out, had been treated the same way.

"Then came an even surer sign. On Sunday, the twenty-ninth of January, there was a mysterious fire in the sky that three times lighted up the Queen's room but was not seen elsewhere in the castle. Mary's guards were nearly blinded by it. The heavens, they say, show forth the deaths of the great and divinely anointed. At church we were asked to pray for the soul of the Scottish Queen, so that she might be delivered from the fatal grip of her popish faith.

"But still nothing was definite, and there was a great suspense everywhere. Would Her Majesty, after all, have a change of heart? She was, as we all knew, notoriously indecisive at times. And then there was the whole legal question of whether or not an ordinary court could convict an anointed queen. This was the big debate in the taverns throughout Northamptonshire, and, I suppose, throughout all of England and Scotland, and perhaps all of Europe as well. There were many in our parish who thought not, and who felt that as long as Mary was locked away and allowed to live out her life in religious meditation that that would be sufficient and safer punishment for her ambitions.

"On the fifth of February all speculations came to a stony halt. Robert Beale, clerk of the Privy Council, arrived in Fotheringhay. He is also, as you know, brother-in-law to Sir Francis Walsingham. He could have come for one reason only. Two days later Shrewsbury and Kent and some others arrived. And then, grimmest rumor of all, we heard that a certain Mr. Bull was brought secretly to Fotheringhay by Walsingham's man Digby, and that he was disguised as a serving-man and his ax hidden in a trunk."

Kit listens to all this on the rim of the leaning crowd in the main hall of Bene't College. He has a vision of Mr. Bull: a thick, dark, muscular man with broad features and enormous hands. He has an image also of the sharpened ax, lying in the coffin of a trunk. A chill goes through him. He feels his heart beating rapidly behind his ribs.

"There was no longer any need for secrecy. Those who took part in the preparations in the hall told us what was happening. There was a platform being erected there, about twelve feet by twelve feet, and two feet high. And arrangements for perhaps as many as three hundred spectators. We heard later that Mary was not told the news until the evening of February seventh, which gave her but one night to prepare herself. The execution was scheduled for eight o'clock in the morning on the eighth. And, since Mary's room was directly above the great hall, she must have heard the hammering, which went on all through the night."

Kit's imagination flies to Fotheringhay, to that bedroom above the hall. He hears the hammering. He sees the Queen at her prayers. He sees himself locked into this small room the night before his own execution. In his mind he falls to his knees, then rises, then screams, then threatens heaven with a clenched fist, then weeps. He cannot imagine his own actual death, but the very thought of it fills him with terror, and he almost runs from the room before William Short has finished his recital. What a personal thing one's own body is, he thinks.

"She came into the hushed hall, accompanied by her oldest and dearest servants: Melville, Bourgoing, Gervais and old Didier, Jane Kennedy, and Elizabeth Curle. All one could hear was the crackling of the huge fire and an occasional cough. She seemed to me very tall, and her step was firm, even arrogant. It was very dramatic. Very frightening. Oddly enough, I think the audience was more frightened than she was—she who was about to die. She was in black satin and embroidered black velvet, except for a long white veil that hung down her back, so that she looked like a strange combination of bride and widow. Her hair seemed very red under a white headdress. Red and white and black. Those were her colors. While all around her, pale faces, wrapped to the chin in woolens, stared at her, an audience of drab gray and brown by comparison. Their colors were somber for the occasion. But under Mary's black exterior was a crimson velvet petticoat.

"She clutched a crucifix and a prayerbook and, I think, some beads. She was led up the three steps to the stage, though she did not need assistance. And she stood for a moment, surveying the place where her final act would be played—a small kingdom, draped in black, a little stool where she might sit to disrobe, the block and the ax. Shrewsbury and Kent were with her on the platform. Paulet and Drury, her other custodian in her last days, were just off the stage but very close. And all around was a circle of soldiers to separate her from the audience, the commoners and the official witnesses. Because of the suddenness of the decision to carry out the sentence, there were not many dignitaries. A few local people: Lord Talbot, Sir Edward Montagu, and a few others. Walsingham's strategy, apparently, was to have sufficient ceremony but as little publicity as possible, in order to avoid the feeling of martyrdom and rouse sympathy in the hearts of the people.

"As she stood there, her face fixed in an almost pleasant expression, the commission was read to her, the authorization for her execution. It was like the prologue of a play. And then it was all to be carried out. Next came Dr. Fletcher, dean of Peterborough, who tried to preach to her, presumably to save her from damnation. He was very pompous and she was very adamant. I half-expected the crowd to cheer when she said, 'Mr. Dean, I am settled in the ancient Catholic Roman religion and mind to spend my blood in defense of it.' But Dr. Fletcher went on with his prayers, convinced that it was his duty, I suppose. He kneeled and prayed aloud. And against him Mary too prayed, but in her own way, in Latin. She was seated on her little stool, but then she too went to her knees. It was a very moving contest, and many tears were shed by the onlookers—including, I must confess, myself.

"And when at last Dr. Fletcher stopped praying, Mary prayed on, but aloud and in English, stopping from time to time to kiss her crucifix and cross herself. She prayed for the English Church, for her son, for Elizabeth. Kent tried to stop her, but she went on, ending at last with these passionate words, as near as I can recall them: 'Even as Thy arms, O Jesus, were spread here upon the cross, so receive me into Thy arms of mercy and forgive me all my sins.'

"The executioner, eager to get on with his business, quickly asked her forgiveness for what he was about to do and was gladly granted it. 'I forgive you with all my heart,' she said, 'for now I hope you shall make an end of all my troubles.' Then she was helped off with her outer garments and revealed the red bodice and petticoat, to which were added red sleeves, so that she stood there all in blazing red in that drab hall.

"It is apparently customary for the executioners to take the victim's ornaments for themselves. Part of their compensation, I suppose. And as they did this there was some struggle about a golden rosary that Mary wore about her neck. It was resolved somehow. Perhaps Mary promised them money instead. I don't really know, but she managed to keep it. And all through this she kept her pleasant air and composure, though her servants were now dissolved in tears.

"It was Jane Kennedy who came forth to cover Mary's eyes with a white cloth. It was embroidered in gold, and, they say, had been chosen by Mary herself the night before. Jane Kennedy kissed the cloth and wrapped it gently round and round her eyes and over her head.

"Unafraid still, the Queen knelt on the cushion before the black-draped block and, by feeling her way, arranged her head there. Then, as though she were prepared to fly to the next world, she spread her arms and legs and cried out: *'In manus tuas, Domine, confide spiritum meum.'* Over and over she said this until the ax fell. The first blow did not strike home, and her lips still moved. It was the second that almost severed her head, but still they had to carve through as with a knife before the job was done. A ghastly business. Several ladies were sick. Even some men were unable to watch these last barbaric moments. Finally the executioner held up her head and cried, 'God save the Queen.' And, would you believe it, the lips of the severed head still seemed to be moving. And then a terrible thing happened. The red hair that the executioner held came loose from the head, which fell onto the platform with the most awful sound in creation. And we could see that her real hair was quite gray and very short."

Though the room is cold, in spite of the fire, Kit's face is damp with perspiration. William Short's account has made him sick with terror. He feels in his heart the thud of that head on the stage. He imagines that the head can still think and that the eyes move. Perhaps they catch a glimpse of the body from which the head has been cut. He thinks of his own head cut from his own body, and he is suddenly dizzy. What a horror that last moment of consciousness must be! And those lips still trying to speak but without breath to form words. O God, O God! His own lips form the words. He cannot swallow. He feels the blood rushing from his face. His hands are ice. His heart thumps, and he is afraid that he will faint. But the noise of the dispersing, gasping, inquisitive students distracts him. Charles Walford is suddenly standing beside him. "Are you all right, Kit?" he says. Kit takes him firmly by the arm and steadies himself. They go out into the icy night, where Kit, looking up at the clear sky, breathes great drafts of air, until he has driven the nightmare out of his mind.

xxvi

In the private study of Dr. Thomas Norgate, two men confer. One is Dr. Norgate, Master of Corpus Christi College; the other is John Copcot, Vice-Chancellor of the University, an appointee of Lord Burghley and his chief representative at Cambridge when the Chancellor is away.

The April glow comes through the latticed windows and draws color out of every grain of wood and loop of rug. It reveals in the jowled face of Dr. Norgate, as he sits at his desk, a spidery network of capillaries, expanded by brandy.

John Copcot is another sort of man: spare and calm and neatly

bearded and moderate in all things. Rumor has it that he would like
to succeed Dr. Norgate as Master of Corpus Christi College.
Rumor has it also that with the help of Lord Burghley he may bring
about this administrative change before Dr. Norgate himself is
ready to retire or prepared to die.

They are discussing Christopher Marlowe's *supplicat* for the
M.A. degree. "I am recommending to the fellows of the College
that we deny his application," says Norgate.

"But, my dear Norgate," says the Vice-Chancellor, "aside from
your personal distaste for this young man, do you really have
sufficient grounds for such a drastic course of action? You must,
above all, consider the consequences for the College and for the
University. It is not the sort of publicity that we want, you know. I
mean, it's difficult enough to maintain the impression around here
that all is well. All is not well. You know it, and I know it, and Lord
Burghley knows it. But will it do any good to create an open
disturbance of this sort?"

"It has recently been suggested, Mr. Copcot," says Dr. Norgate,
"that I have been lax with the students, that I have been inefficient
with the finances, and that I have allowed the College to fall into a
kind of chaos. I don't know what the source of these criticisms
is—perhaps you do—but I will not leave myself open to them any
longer. This Christopher Marlowe has broken the rules and has
conducted himself in a totally reprehensible manner."

"Nevertheless," says Copcot, "I understand that his academic
record is excellent and that he is highly regarded by the more
artistic and intellectual elements at the University."

Norgate leans heavily forward on his desk, putting aside a large
book with slow deliberation as he says, "Did you know that during
his several long unauthorized absences from the University Mr.
Marlowe has been to the Catholic College at Rheims?"

Copcot raises his eyebrows and tightens his mouth. "And did you
know," continues Norgate, "that he has no intention of taking holy
orders, even though he has held an Archbishop Parker scholarship
for six years? He has made no effort to get a title. He has been in
touch with no vicars. And, in fact, he shows every indication of

leaving here and going directly to Rheims, where, for all we know, he may become a Catholic priest."

Copcot is somewhat subdued by these arguments. "You can't make that assumption," he says.

"Furthermore," says Norgate, "interviews with students closely associated with him indicate that he supports some strange doctrines. One young man, I understand, is known to have said that Marlowe converted him to atheism."

"That's a serious charge, for which proof will be necessary," says Copcot.

"I offer it up as part of a pattern," says Norgate. "It is my contention that Marlowe may be a secret convert to Catholicism, and even that he may be in the service of the Catholics while here in England. Why else would he spend such long periods of time abroad, and why would he be so secretive about his movements?"

Copcot stands up and paces back and forth. "You sound like Sir Francis Walsingham all of a sudden. Wherever you look you see Catholic spies." He stops in front of Norgate's desk. "Look at it this way," he says. "Here is a young man of exceptional intelligence and imagination. And here we are in complicated times. You must give him a certain amount of leeway to explore himself and his world. Granted, it is our duty to keep the young from going astray. Nevertheless, Thomas, you know how it is with the young, don't you?"

"All too well, apparently," says Norgate. "I have been very tolerant, very easy about the usual vices: the deviltry, the inevitable sexuality, the endless fracturing of little rules. But this business is different. Marlowe is no ordinary person. I think he has deceived us, and I think he is dangerous. These are not the pranks of an undergraduate. He is twenty-three years old and must be held responsible for what he does."

"You are determined, then, to withhold his M.A.?" says Copcot.

"Yes," says Norgate.

Copcot throws up his hands. "Well, then, there's not much I can do about it, is there? I mean, you *are* the Master of Corpus Christi and you have certain prerogatives."

"That's right, Mr. Copcot," he says. "I am the Master of Corpus Christi."

xxvii

As soon as Kit is notified that he will not be granted his M.A. at this commencement, he writes an urgent letter to Robert Cecil. The very same carrier who delivers his letter to London has brought him news from Tom Nashe that Robert Greene has made an arrangement, through friends, for a production of Kit's play, *Dido, Queen of Carthage*. It will be done in Norwich, where Robert Greene was born. The excitement about this pleasant surprise eclipses Kit's suspense about his scholarly career. He even persuades himself for a while that, if he is to have a career in the theatre, it really won't matter so much about the M.A.

It takes Nashe and Greene three days to travel from London to Cambridge, because Roberto has periodic attacks of dryness that he swears must be the first symptoms of a rare disease, curable only by large quantities of dry sack and Rhenish wine. "Besides," he argues, "I may one day want to write a short history of country inns and taverns, and there is nothing so valuable as firsthand experience." He is overdressed in somebody's ill-fitting secondhand clothing, once-expensive garments purchased from a thief in Cheapside out of the fee for his latest pastoral romance. His red beard is brushed to a devilish point, his untrimmed hair falls almost to his shoulders.

Each time they mount up again, it is with greater difficulty. Once Nashe boosts his friend into his saddle only to have him slide off the other side and go howling to the ground. "You're an impossible man, Robert Greene," he says. "I don't see how your wife tolerates you."

"I didn't marry my wife to be tolerated," says Greene, struggling to rise, with a helping hand from Tom. "Besides, I've left the wench and her bawling babe and gone to live with Em Ball in Holywell. I don't believe I'm fit for family life." Nashe is brushing the dust from his fur-lined cape. Greene stoops to pick up his highly feathered hat and almost falls on his face. Nashe steadies him. He puts his hat on backwards and shouts, "No, no, my dear friend, we were not made for dull domesticity. We are the courtiers of the Muse." He draws his sword and points it toward heaven. "We are the soldiers of the spirit. The guardians of the human imagination." He begins to sag again, and, once again, Tom sees that it will be necessary to spend the night on the road and hope for better traveling conditions in the morning.

The trip from Cambridge to Norwich is much swifter. Kit is nervous and can talk about nothing but his play. He shouts over the sound of hoofbeats and into the rush of wind. He forces the pace. He will not stop often to eat or drink. Greene curses him as a man "possessed by the demon of ambition" and suggests that he remember how all is dust and returns to dust. "Great success shall be as ashes in your mouth."

"If you wouldn't talk so much, you wouldn't get so thirsty," says Kit, and gallops off to see what lies over the next rise.

They arrive in very good time. Instantly Roberto is seized with an attack of nostalgia. "Oh, Norwich, Norwich," he sighs, "city of my boyhood. How many little dreams I left behind here. Oh, Guild Hall and marketplace. Oh, sweet mother gone to heaven, under the old churchyard dirt. Amuse me, boys, before I weep."

"We've traveled hard," says Nashe. "I think we've earned a little beer; don't you, my friends?"

"Yes, indeed," says Greene, "lest the fluids of the body be too dangerously depleted. Ah, but then, you must come with me on a little tour of my marvelous city. Neither of you has been here before, and I must show it all to you."

After a brief stop at The White Dolphin, they are ushered through the avenues and alleys of Norwich. They pass through the marketplace in the center of town, where only a few stalls remain open. "That," says Roberto, "is the flint Guild Hall." He is pointing to a handsome structure. "And that is the church of St. Peter Mancroft." The traffic is thinning as the day wanes. The square is littered with manure and feathers and straw. A group of ragged boys play war with rotten fruit. One of them runs accidentally into the scholar-actor-poet-pamphleteer. Roberto grabs him roughly by the arm and exhibits him to Tom and Kit, as though he were a stuffed toy. "You see this pathetic creature, this gaunt-eyed, starving little rat. Well, there I am at the age of nine or so. Dirty, hungry, and uncivilized. And here I am now at the age of thirty—"

"Yes," says Nashe. "Dirty, hungry, and uncivilized."

The frightened boy escapes, and Greene curses after him. "Damn him," he says. "I wanted to give him a coin. It might have altered the entire course of his little life."

Greene takes his friends by the arms and sweeps them around a corner and into a narrow street. "Ah, here we are: the sunless alley in which I first experienced the world as a puking child. I recognize the stench. After all these years it is a horrible perfume. It draws me on and repels me all at once, like those ghastly, painted, Cheapside whores. See how cozily the buildings all lean together." He points to a tall, narrow house. "An uncle of mine lived here years ago. A very disreputable fellow." He lowers his voice to a hoarse whisper. "Murdered, he was—right there." He stops dramatically and points to a spot in the middle of the lane. "A pimp and conycatcher on my mother's side. The Greenes were more respectable. Honest laborers, they were. But my father is very old now and makes a profession of staring out of his bedroom window and playing landlord to some foreign young men who work in the woolen trade. Let's hope he's got a vacant room to put us up in."

"I'd prefer an inn, myself," says Kit.

"So would I," says Nashe.

"Nonsense," says Greene. "When we are in Norwich, my house is your house."

The interview with Robert Greene's father is brief and painful. They find him sitting at his window. From that distance he cannot recognize his own son. He shouts down that there are no available rooms, and then, mishearing the reply, he spits at them and ducks inside to find a full chamberpot. But in a few moments all is rectified. There is a recognition scene in the small living room on the ground floor. Mr. Greene is a small, toothless man, too hard of hearing to converse with. He neither kisses his son nor shakes his hand. He looks at him suspiciously, as though he might be a stranger disguised as his son for some nefarious reason. They all sit there awkwardly for a while. Roberto explains about the play and about his work and about London. All the time Samuel Greene nods and forces a smile, but eventually it is obvious that he either cannot hear what is being said or else he simply does not understand. Finally he clears his throat and says, "Well, son, I see that everything is all right, but you needn't have come this far just to say hello. I'd offer you and your friends a room, but we've got a full house right now. Why don't you all go out to the Wensum Inn? More your style, anyway. All you fine gentlemen."

There is nothing more to say. They all leave and walk back up the narrow street in silence. The hour is struck by a medley of bells from the many churches in the city. It is not until they are approaching the Cathedral Church of the Holy Trinity that Roberto forces himself to smile and says, "So much for family reunions."

Darkness closes in on the city. Dull lights appear where windows were, dull earthly stars, weary yellow eyes. The streets are almost empty. A bony dog pads by, his tongue lolling from the side of his mouth.

"We've seen everything but the theatre," says Kit.

"Oh, there's no theatre," says Greene. "Not like The Theatre in Shoreditch, or The Curtain. They play their plays in the nave of the old church of St. John the Baptist, the Dominican church, closed down when the country was bled of popery half a century ago. It makes a wonderful playhouse, as you will see in the morning. We'll go around early and meet William Hunnis and his lecherous little boys. But now it's time for kidney pie and Burgundy and perhaps a little tart for dessert. I'm for a room and a meal at The White Dolphin if we have the price of them among us."

The performance at St. John's Hall takes place in the late afternoon of the following day, about four o'clock. A large platform protrudes into the nave, and the play is given virtually in the round.

Kit is fascinated, but not altogether pleased. He had not expected

that some of the boys would be so small or that their voices would
be so feminine. He had imagined his play in terms of Olympian
gods and earthshaking heroes. It is all a kind of miniature world
that they create. They are like puppets, like toys, with their
musical, precise voices. No one can fault their pronunciation. They
are trained to the language as puppies are trained to sit and beg for
a bone. They can parrot the master's tone. They can gesture and
strut and faint and fall. But it is no more convincing than a brigade
of wooden soldiers falling in battle. They do not bleed; they merely
go *thud*.

Kit studies the audience. He wants them to like his play, to
respond to every bit of humor and every ounce of tragedy; but they
seem only mildly interested. They have come, and only half-filled
the wooden benches, to be amused before settling down to the
serious business of dinner. "Haven't we seen this before?" he
overhears a portly lady say to her portly husband, puffing
extravagant feathers away from her extravagant face. The husband,
who has been startled out of a delicious doze, says, "No, no, no, my
dear," as though he has been accused of infidelity.

A thin boy, padded out to be a bosomy Dido, and appropriately
taller than his Aeneas, sopranos away Kit's marvelous lines:

> I'll frame me wings of wax, like Icarus,
> And, o'er his ships, will soar into the sun,
> That they may melt, and I fall in his arms;
> Or else I'll make a prayer unto the waves,
> That I may swim to him, like Triton's niece.
> O Anna, fetch Arion's harp,
> That I may tice a dolphin to the shore,
> And ride upon his back unto my love!
> Look, sister, look! Lovely Aeneas' ships!
> See, see, the billows heave him up to heaven,
> And now down falls the keels into the deep!
> O sister, sister, take away the rocks!
> They'll break his ships. O Proteus, Neptune, Jove,
> Save, save Aeneas, Dido's liefest love!

Now is he come on shore, safe without hurt:
But see, Achates will him put to sea,
And all the sailors merry-make for joy;
But he, remembering me, shrinks back again.
See, where he comes! Welcome, welcome, my love!

But these are all fantasies, and Aeneas does not come. The play rushes to its inevitable conclusion. "Go, Anna, bid my servants bring me fire," says Dido. She burns all relics of Aeneas and then throws herself into the flames. The fire in this production is left to the imagination, and the whole scene is unconvincing. In Kit's feverish mind he envisions an outdoor production with a huge bonfire onto which are heaped furniture, weapons, clothing, and then onto which leaps the howling Dido. A real fire, a real woman, and a real suicide.

Polite applause and shuffling feet wake him from his reverie. The play is over. A babble of voices makes its commentary. An occasional yawn indicates that the interest was perhaps less than universal. "Not bad. Not bad at all," says Greene, taking Kit by the arm. "I mean, for a bunch of yelping boys."

Back at The White Dolphin, Roberto collapses across the bed and falls into a drunken snore. Tom takes off his boots and rolls him over. Then he and Kit sit for a long time and talk about the play.

"It needs work," says Tom. "I wouldn't mind having a go at it. That is, if you trust me."

"Of course I trust you," says Kit. "But somehow the prospect of a long series of revisions strikes me as boring. It's the initial act of creation that excites me. It's like making love. After it's over, you don't want to sit around and fuss about it. You want to go home and do something else."

"You mustn't be disappointed," says Tom. "Your play is good. It is full of excellent poetry. And quite erotic!"

"Then what does it lack?" says Kit.

"I don't know," says Tom. "A certain discipline, perhaps. A

certain flexibility in the structure. You just can't have your characters standing there on the stage shouting marvelous poetry at the audience."

"Perhaps I stuck too literally to the original," says Kit.

"It might help to work with more original material next time," says Tom. "It would give you a greater sense of freedom."

"I thought you said I needed discipline."

"I meant in your language," says Tom. "You tend to fall in love with your own booming voice. And yet—that's precisely what I admire in the play. It's something of a dilemma. Your greatest weakness and your greatest strength are almost one and the same."

Kit smiles. "That which nourishes me, destroys me!"

"I hope not," says Tom. "And yet I suppose we are all that way—little fires consuming ourselves."

"All that can matter, then," says Kit, "is the brightness with which we burn. Not how long!"

"Yes, but one must be careful not to die too young," says Tom. "There is something to be said for ripeness."

"All I can say for ripeness is that it is followed almost instantly by decay. Witness the rose!"

"Oh, the rose be damned," says Tom, "and all the rest of your grim philosophy. Let's talk about something practical, something immediate."

"All right," says Kit. "Pour us some wine and I will tell you all about Tamburlaine, the subject of my new play, a fascinating fellow . . ."

xxviii

It is less than a week before commencement. Cambridge has gone soft in the embrace of summer. The days are long; the discipline is lax. Though it is forbidden, students have been sneaking off to swim in the river. Many have abandoned their black gowns in favor of more comfortable clothes. At Corpus Christi, Master Norgate keeps to his quarters and seems to be ignoring the mass breakage of rules. There are rumors that he may resign.

Kit has abandoned all hope of receiving his M.A. degree. He is in the storeroom, packing away his books and clothes and small accumulation of other belongings. Tom Lewgar comes in. At first they say nothing to each other. They have not spoken in almost a month, except for a few cold civilities. Tom has not abandoned his hood and gown, nor has he gone bathing, nor has he stopped reading, though he plans to graduate in a few days. He has found a place as a curate in a respectable parish in Kent. His life is arranged. Out of his monstrous respectability, as Kit sees it, he will pluck a wife and three small children, and they will all sit, evening after evening after evening, at an oval table in the small dining room of the parsonage, and there, sipping their soup and smiling at one another, they will fade into history, a small group of tilted tombstones in an old graveyard, the letters on the stones gradually worn away by the weather, so that years later visitors who come by will have to squint and guess at the real names and dates of all these unreal people.

Kit holds in his hand the finished manuscript of *Tamburlaine the Great*. From the trunk he removes some books and a pair of shoes and tries to find a level and secure place for it.

"Look, Christopher," says Tom Lewgar. "I'm awfully sorry about everything. I mean, about your degree and all. We've had our difficulties, God knows, but I hate to see it all end this way." He shifts from foot to foot, and his small hands move awkwardly.

"For the love of Jesus, what are you trying to say, Tom Lewgar?"

"Just that I'm sorry that our time here has not been better. And that, well, from my point of view, anyway, things have not been all bad. We've had some good times—haven't we?"

"I suppose we have," says Kit, "though offhand I can't remember any."

"I don't blame you for being bitter, Kit," he says. "I mean, I think it's terribly unfair denying you your degree and all."

"To hell with it," says Kit.

"You'll be putting your stuff on the carrier for London tomorrow, I suppose."

"Yes," says Kit. "The sooner I get out of here, the better."

Lewgar blinks his eyes very rapidly. "My father's coming up from Canterbury for commencement," he says.

"How nice," says Kit, a stiletto in his tone that he cannot hide.

Fortunately, this awkward conversation is interrupted by a knock at the door. It is Charles Walford, who shoves the door open and breathlessly shouts, "Kit, you're wanted urgently at Dr. Norgate's office."

"What for?" says Kit.

"I don't know," says Walford, "but I was told to get you there instantly—a matter of the utmost importance."

All that occurs to Kit as he walks across the courtyard is that he is about to be informed of some terrible calamity. Perhaps his family has been wiped out by the plague. Perhaps his father is dead.

He finds the Master's study open, and he pauses in the doorway. "Come in, come in," says Dr. Norgate, who does not rise from behind his cluttered desk. "And close the door behind you. Come and sit down." He indicates a chair with a leather seat.

Though it is summer, Norgate is still dressed for winter, with a fur-lined robe over his ordinary academic gown and a black velvet hat. His face is worn, and he seems to Kit to have aged a good deal since he last talked with him. In his hand he holds a piece of paper, but he cannot hold it steady because of a pronounced tremor. He clears his throat. "It seems, Mr. Marlowe," he says, "that we have done you an injustice. I received this morning this letter from Her Majesty's Privy Council. Since it is self-explanatory, I would like you to read it." He hands him the letter and then leans back heavily in his chair to watch Kit's reaction.

Kit reads the following to himself: "Whereas it was reported that Christopher Marlowe was determined to have gone beyond the seas to Rheims and there to remain, Their Lordships thought good to certify that he had no such intent, but that in all his actions he had behaved himself orderly and discreetly, whereby he had done Her Majesty good service, and deserved to be rewarded for his faithful dealing: Their Lordships' request was that the rumor thereof should be allayed by all possible means, and that he should be furthered in the degree he was to take this next Commencement: Because it was not Her Majesty's pleasure that anyone employed as he had been in matters touching the benefit of his Country should be defamed by those that are ignorant in the affairs he went about." The letter is signed by Whitgift, the Lord Archbishop; Sir Christopher Hatton, the Lord Chancellor; Lord Burghley, the Lord Treasurer; Lord Hunsdon, the Lord Chamberlain; and Sir James Crofts, the Comptroller.

Kit reads it through twice and then hands it back to Dr. Norgate, who is frowning and smiling at the same time. "How were we to know, Christopher," he says, "that you were engaged in such important matters?"

"I was not free to explain myself," says Kit, "even at the risk of losing my degree."

"I find that extremely noble and commendable, Christopher," says Dr. Norgate. "And I will, of course, recommend instantly that your degree be granted. Since it is the wish of the Privy Council, you may rest assured that it is as good as done."

Kit thanks him and gets up to leave. Dr. Norgate also gets up and follows him to the door. There he takes him by the arm and draws him close. "I don't suppose you can say what your business on the continent was," he says.

"I am sworn to secrecy," says Kit, "but I can assure you that the whole matter has been brought to a successful conclusion."

Norgate's eyebrows arch and his eyes widen. "The Babington Plot!" he says.

Kit smiles noncommittally and goes out, leaving the Master of Corpus Christi somewhat in awe.

He strides across the courtyard and then out of the grounds of the College and into the bell-drenched air and startling sunshine of the streets of Cambridge. London beware, he says to himself. Your time has come!

III

LONDON

i

ANN SWIFT, now Mrs. Thomas Watson, is a tall, handsome woman. Her blond hair is simply parted in the center and plaited close to her head under a white cap. Her dress, too, is simple; it hugs her shoulders, reveals the shape of her delicate arms and the thinness of her waist.

It is August. The aggressive sunshine of high summer filters through curtains, slashes across the wide boards of the living room and dances against the wall of the small kitchen.

The widow Potter has come and gone, having accomplished her morning chores. Ann Swift is working on a piece of embroidery. She is seated in a straight wooden chair in front of the living-room window. She hums to herself. The cat, back-arched and amorous, rubs against her leg. So lost is she in the serenity and precious solitude of this noon hour of a summer day that she does not hear the footsteps that descend from upstairs. It is not until Kit is actually standing in front of her that she looks up, startled for the blink of an eye before she greets him with her full-lipped smile. He is a dissonant note in the music of her moment. He stands there, disheveled, unwashed, his shirt open, his black hair down to his shoulders, his eyes shadowed with sleep and exhaustion.

"You're a bit of a horror to look at this morning," she says.

"It wasn't my fault," he says, collapsing into a chair opposite her and holding his head.

"Of course it wasn't your fault," she says. "It was the devil made you do it."

"Well, if you must know, it was more Tom's fault than mine." Her hands stop. She looks up. "Tom's fault!" she says. "Why, Tom and I were in bed a bit before dark. And, what's more, we heard you go out, trying to tiptoe down those squeaky stairs like a thief."

"I wasn't tiptoeing," he protests. "I was trying to be considerate. I heard the two of you laughing and sighing in there. Disgusting domestic rituals."

She blushes but faces up to him. "And what sort of rituals were you up to last night?" she says.

"It so happens that I worked very hard yesterday—all day," he says. "By nightfall I had finished the translation of Tom's *Rape of Helen*. I was so wrought up I had to show it to *somebody*. I didn't think it was appropriate to bang on your door and thrust the damn thing between your naked bodies. Now I'm sorry I didn't. Instead, I took it around to The White Bear near Holywell Lane, where I was sure I would find some familiar faces."

"I can imagine by your own face which faces you found," she says.

"You don't have to be able to read stars to know that Roberto was there," he says. "And so was Tom Nashe and half a dozen others. Pretty far gone already by the time I arrived."

"And what did you do," she says, "read them Tom's poem?"

"I had to read it to *someone*," he says again.

"You might have waited until the morning and showed it to Tom first," she says. "After all, it *is* his poem, you know."

"It may be his in Latin," says Kit, "but it's mine in English. And my version is infinitely better."

"Oh, Christopher," she says impatiently, "what nonsense you talk sometimes!" She lays aside her embroidery and stands up. "Let me get you something to eat."

He gets up unsteadily and follows her into the kitchen. "If you doubt me, ask those who were there last night," he says.

She cuts a piece of bread from a round loaf and dips warm broth from an iron pot. "I don't give a fig for what they think—always posing and boozing and showing off their university ways."

"Be careful what you say, madame. I too came down from one of those exalted institutions."

"Came down is right," she says. "You squander yourself, Kit. You squander your talents."

"Don't worry, my dear," he says. "I'll have a play on the boards within a month. My *Tamburlaine* this very moment is in influential hands."

"Who in his right mind in a Christian society is going to put on a play about a madman who goes around murdering men, women, and children and daring God out of heaven? It makes no sense. He doesn't even die in the end. He just goes on and on and on, spraying the audience with noise."

"I didn't know you had read it," he says.

"Tom let me have a look at it," she says.

"And does Tom feel the same way?" says Kit.

"Ask Tom," she says.

"Where is he?"

"He's gone around to St. Paul's Churchyard to talk with Dick Smith the stationer about something or other," she says. "Now be still and eat your breakfast, you naughty boy."

ii

In a dramatic mild grayness and intermittent rain, Kit follows the familiar route down Bishopsgate Street to Threadneedle, Poultry, Cheapside. He cuts down Bread Street to Watling and then over to St. Paul's Churchyard. The Churchyard is lined with bookshops: The Holy Ghost, The Green Dragon, and The Candle. Books are proliferating like flies in summer, he thinks as he browses. Perhaps they have a way of copulating. *The Chronicles of England, Ireland, and Scotland*, massive and masculine, couple grotesquely with *The Three Ladies of London*, a little play by Robert Wilson. Kit smiles to himself and takes down a translation of the *Ten Tragedies of Seneca* by Thomas Marsh. He considers it, asks the price of the

bald-headed dealer, and then decides not to buy it after all. He goes
on to another shop.

It is early. The crowd in the Churchyard is comparatively thin.
Inside the Cathedral it is sermon time, though it's business as usual
in the aisles. At The Candle he finds himself buying a copy of John
Lyly's *Campaspe* before he knows why. Perhaps he imagines that
this way lies success.

It begins to rain in earnest, and he retreats to the enormous
ugliness of the Cathedral. He does not like the place: that great
expansive, yawning cavity, empty of spirit, empty of feeling,
stamping ground for whores and lawyers and peddlers of liquor and
illicit literature. He goes down the south alley of the nave, drawing
closer and closer to the small gathering that listens attentively to the
visiting Dr. Peale, an ineffectual speaker from Salisbury, come to
talk, presumably, about the true meaning of salvation, but lured by
patriotic fervor and the nature of the times into a meandering
diatribe against the Catholic conspiracy and the preparations of the
Spanish fleet. "We pray, along with our Queen," says the minister,
"that God will erect a wall around our island, that he will protect us
from these barbaric intruders into our garden of prosperity and
right-mindedness."

Kit stops short of the seated audience, prepared to retreat should
his impatience drive him away. *Prosperity* resounds in his mind.
Behind him he hears the hum of that prosperity. It's all commerce,
after all. He has a vision of the twin snakes of spiritual poverty and
secular power entwined and at the very same moment recalls the
Catholic mass at Rheims. It's magic that makes it work: pageantry
and magic. If one is to deal with miracles, he thinks, one has to be
seduced by images and incense, by music and ritual. Logic leads
nowhere—except maybe here. He looks back over his shoulder at
the milling crowd in the aisles and at the rear. Small groups of men
gather in whispered conversations. Goods are exchanged. Exhibitionists strut in leather and feathers, hoping to be noticed, hoping to
be invited somewhere, anywhere, as long as it is in the direction of
profit.

It is a weekday service and soon draws to a close. After all, Dr.

Peale is not terribly important and it's a business day. The small group shuffles away and mingles with those who infest the Cathedral for less elevating purposes than sermons on salvation. Salvation for them is a silver-lined chunk of the visible world. Kit moves along with them. He can see through the open doors in the distance that the rain has stopped.

As he moves down the aisle he senses someone close behind him. Before he can turn around, he feels a hand on his shoulder and a voice saying quietly, "Mr. Marlowe?"

He turns calmly, concealing his apprehension. He comes face to face with a gaunt and beardless man not much older than himself, a man who might be handsome behind the shadows of intensity that tighten his jaw and widen his eyes. His clothes are a bit shabby, but they are the clothes of a gentleman, castoffs perhaps from a more prosperous friend. "My name is John Hunt," he says. "May I have a word with you?"

"A word about what?" says Kit. They step to one side, out of the path of the emerging crowd and into the dampness of an unlighted corner.

"I'm not sure this is a very good place," he says.

"If it's a matter of business," says Kit, "it seems to me the perfect place."

"May I be so presumptuous as to offer you a glass of wine at The Mitre?" says the stranger. "It's not very far and much more private."

"I know where The Mitre is," says Kit, "but I don't know who *you* are."

He lowers his voice. "I am a friend of Nicholas Berden. Is that a sufficient introduction?"

Kit studies him for a moment. "I notice the rain has let up. Perhaps we can get there before it begins again."

iii

"Robin the Bobbin,
the big bellied Ben,
He ate more meat

than threescore men.
He ate the Church,
   he ate the steeple,
He ate the Priests
   and all the people.
And yet he complained
   his belly wasn't full."

John Duke's recitation is followed by laughter and applause at
The Unicorn, John Alleyn's tavern. He and his friends have thrown
two large tables together to accommodate their party. They are
actors and writers, several women, and a few men of questionable
character from the narrow streets: Richard Tarleton, the great
comic of Her Queen's Men; Robert Greene; Tom Nashe; Robert
Armin, a young protégé of Tarleton's; Black Dick and John Duke
of Lord Strange's Men; Will Monox, reputed cutthroat; and three
charming and lusty ladies: Em Ball, Roberto's mistress; Kate
Tarleton, the comic's playful wife; and Joan Duke, wife of John and
close friend of Kate and Em.

Tom Watson and Kit and the actor John Bentley sit at another
table and enjoy the noisy celebrations. It is someone's birthday, but
they cannot figure out whose.

Roberto, in his red beard and goose-turd green cloak, rises,
goblet in hand, overfull and dribbling, to top John Duke's
performance:

"The rose is red, the grass is green,
Serve Queen Bess, our noble Queen!
   Kitty the spinner
   Will sit down to dinner,
And eat the leg of a frog.
   'All good people
   Look over the steeple,
And see the cat play with the dog."

He is whistled and booed back to his bench, where he takes a giant swallow of wine. The fiddler, the lutist, and the two singing boys in the background are drowned out by the din of the crowded tavern. It is a warm and friendly evening on the far edge of summer, and everyone seems to be there. The tables are full. The waitresses shout orders to the cooks and the drawers of ale and sack, and the drawers curse and spit.

One of the ladies rises from the table where Greene seems to preside. It is Kate Tarleton, who recites her ditty through bubbles of giggles that threaten to bounce her bosom clear out of her dress.

> "My little old man and I fell out,
> I'll tell you what it was all about;
> I had money and he had none,
> And that's the way the trouble begun."

Richard Tarleton whacks his wife on her bottom, through her abundant skirt. He laughs, his squinting eyes disappearing, his flattened nose broadening. His clothes have all the inelegance of a strolling player or a vagabond, though he is the most celebrated comic actor of his time. He is, in fact, dressed off stage much as he is often dressed on stage, in russet and buttoned cap, from which a fringe of curling hair escapes. His mustache is elaborate and somewhat shaggy, but his poor chin has never been able to produce much of a beard, a fact to which Kate Tarleton, when in her cups, attributes her somewhat loose nature, complaining that she has an unnatural desire for men with great, bushy beards. Her husband is also rather short, though what he lacks in stature he makes up in flexibility, being able to do fantastic things with his legs.

Kate tumbles backward, not into her seat, but into the lap of Black Dick, who has earned his nickname not as a player of minor parts (rogues, gravediggers, and servants) but as a lewd man with incredibly quick hands. When Kate bounces with a shriek from his lap, it is not out of embarrassment. She has been catapulted back toward her husband by the deftness and accuracy of the smiling man's fingers.

From the leather moneybag slung at his side Tarleton takes a coin. He flips it onto the table in front of his wife and says, "I hear there's a virgin in Holywell Street who can pick up pennies without using her hands." They all collapse in laughter, and Kate leaps for the coin before her husband can recover it.

The other tables at The Unicorn that evening are less boisterous. With Tarleton and Greene to amuse them, they need nothing more than food, drink, and private conversation. One such conversation takes place at a small table between Edward Alleyn and James Burbage. Alleyn, though still in his early twenties, is a veteran tragic actor of great reputation. His companion, James Burbage, considerably older, is the man who built the first public theatre in London, called simply The Theatre and located outside the jurisdiction of The City in the Liberty of Shoreditch. He is a sturdy man of considerable commercial imagination and torridness of temper. He and Ned Alleyn are talking about Henslow's new Rose Theatre on the other side of the river. They speculate about the possibility that Bankside in Southwark will become, after all, the center of theatrical activities.

At another table we find Matthew Roydon, George Chapman, George Peele, and Thomas Lodge—all writers, all fairly young, all well known to the rest of the crowd.

Somewhat secluded and deep in conversation are Edward Blount and the most talked about man in England, Sir Walter Ralegh, holder of the monopoly of wine licenses and the export of broadcloth, Warden of the stannaries in Cornwall, Lieutenant of Cornwall, Captain of the Queen's Guard, member of the commission for the defense against Spain, and, some say, suitor for the Queen's hand.

Kit catches sight of Ralegh and nudges Tom. "Yes, I know," says Tom. "The great man himself. I wonder what he's got to talk over with young Blount."

"They say Ned Blount is going to open a book stall soon in the Churchyard," says Bentley. "Working with Ponsonby and publishing Sidney and Spenser has earned him something of a reputation. He should do well on his own."

"Do you suppose Ralegh's going to back him?" says Tom.

"It's possible," says Bentley. "He's always looking for ways to publicize his point of view. He would turn England into another Spain, with colonies and explorations all over the known world. And, at the same time, he would drive the Spaniards from the high seas. He dreams of El Dorado."

"In more ways than one," says Tom. "Ah, El Dorado is in your eyes, and would I were in your golden arms!"

"There's a good chance for you, Kit," says Bentley, with a quick glance at Tom Watson. "You could write a play for Sir Walter. He'd pay you well. He might even write it for you. A play full of Indians and sun-gods and waterfalls of pearls and diamonds. *Roanoke Revisited, Heliogobulus, The Kingdom Beyond the Sea.*"

"No, thank you," says Kit. "I'll write my own plays, my own way."

Bentley affects an effeminate gesture. "My, my, such independence from one so young."

Tarleton and his friends are clearing a table, tossing plates and cups on the floor, cursing at waiters and waitresses to pick them up and to bring more wine and ale. "How can a man perform cold sober like this?" shouts Greene, supervising the operation, with his cup moving, as though of its own will, between his hand and his mouth. From time to time he turns to look in Marlowe's direction.

Tom Nashe arranges benches. The three bosomy ladies form a chorus of shrieking laughter. Tarleton is taken by the arms and lifted onto the improvised stage by Black Dick and John Duke. There he does a jig that evokes a round of applause. Even Ralegh and Blount turn to see what is happening. A waitress falls with a trayful of uneaten dinners, and the applause increases, as though she is part of the show.

Will Monox and Tom Nashe try to help Robert Greene up onto the cleared table, but he fights them off. "Unhand me, you slaughterers of the Queen's English," he shouts. "The Tower of Pisa may lean, but it shall not fall." He brushes them aside, tosses away his goblet, and, with an enormous effort, hauls his hefty form first onto a bench and then onto the table where Tarleton is still performing. He stamps his foot for silence and calls for a trumpet.

The musicians oblige. "Ladies and gentlemen," he bawls. "I have an announcement to make. For your special entertainment and to celebrate the natal day of the king of comedy, we have for your mirth and intoxication a new play to perform." He leans over to Nashe and nearly falls from the table top. Little Tarleton rescues him with elaborate gestures. Nashe hands him up a manuscript, somewhat abused, the pages crudely stacked and out of order. One drifts from Greene's hand and floats to the floor. "Never mind," he says. "It will never be missed. And the actor who might have played the part has probably starved to death by now." He stamps again. "We must have your absolute attention. I have here in my hand a new play, written by an anonymous playwright, newly arrived from a great center of learning."

"Black Lucy's Goose-Egg Farm," shouts Black Dick, splitting the temporary silence and forcing even Greene to laugh.

He coughs, recovers, and goes on. "It is the touching story of a poor Scythian shepherd who by hard work, perseverance, and enormous slaughter rises from obscurity to conquer half the world."

Kit Marlowe leaps to his feet, knocking over his chair, but before he can say anything, Tom Watson grabs him firmly by the arm and says, "Sit down, you fool, you'll start a riot."

"But that's my play," says Kit, his voice a hoarse whisper. "That's my *Tamburlaine*. I gave it to them to read."

Tom forces Kit down, and Bentley picks up his chair. "Let them have their fun," he says. "No one will know the difference."

"Treacherous son of an infected whore," mutters Kit.

"You've got to learn to take this kind of thing," says Tom. "Consider it your initiation. They will think all the better of you if you take it as a joke."

Kit takes a long drink and nods grimly. "All right," he says. "All right!"

"You will understand before long," says Greene, "why the author prefers to remain anonymous, though he may, for all we know, be right here in this very room."

The crowd buzzes and looks about. Silence cannot be maintained for very long in this busy, smoky, informal place. Greene has to shout to be heard.

"I may have my wits about me," he says, indicating Tarleton, who breaks into a quick dance step and then bows, "but I cannot for the life of me give you an accurate summary of the action. But I remember especially the slaughtered virgins of Damascus hoisted on the walls of that conquered city. And I remember the Emperor of the Turks, imprisoned in a cage like a grotesque nightingale, to be shown off and tormented. Marvelous stuff. Absolutely marvelous. Truly the stuff of great tragedy. But let us begin." He shuffles through the pages. "Surely there must be a beginning in all this. A beginning, a middle, an end. Or perhaps it doesn't matter. Just keep on beginning to the very end, a wise man once told me. There's a free piece of philosophy for you, which you can easily change into expensive philosophy when the boy passes among you with my cap.

"Ah, here, at last, is the beginning. I shall read the prologue. My giant of a friend here shall play the part of Tamburlaine." He looks up in Tarleton's direction, finds nothing, and then looks down and pretends to be startled by the flat-nosed comedian.

"From jigging veins of rhyming mother-wits,
And such conceits as clownage keeps in pay,
We'll lead you to the stately tent of war,
Where you shall hear the Scythian Tamburlaine
Threatening the world with high astounding terms,
And scourging kingdoms with his conquering sword.
View but this picture in this tragic glass,
And then applaud his fortunes as you please."

He turns with bowing, staggering, and hiccupping to introduce Tarleton, who steps forward on tiptoe, stretching himself to his most potential height, which is perhaps shoulder-high to Greene. "I'll find you a speech before the night is through, oh terror of Asia," says Roberto, "but you, as central figure of this romance, may play only one role, while I must play a thousand insignificant parts. And you know what sort of memory I have. Like another part of me, it leaks!"

The audience joins the fun. Someone shouts, "We can't tell the play from the commentary."

"The play is the commentary; the commentary is the play," says Greene.

"And both," says another voice, "are very *common*, indeed, and *airy*."

"When all the air goes out of you, sir," says Greene, "there will be very little left to contend with."

"Which *end*," says the same man, "is the *cunt end?*"

"The bearded end, through which some men can speak poetry with their tongues," answers Greene.

From another part of the taproom someone shouts, "Stand him on his head. We want to hear what his other *end* has to say."

"Quiet, you illiterate sons of ungrammatical whores. A little respect, please, for the educated gentlemen and the immaculate ladies amongst us. The Captain of her Queen's horse is not familiar with such language. It doth offend his ears."

Ralegh smiles from his table in the alcove.

"They say the Queen can curse in twenty languages."

"But, alas," says Greene, "the Queen's horse can only sneeze and laugh."

"A hoarse laugh is better than no laugh at all," says Tarleton, "when you earn your living by your wits."

"Play the play!" comes a menacing shout from a bruiser of a man in the rear.

Others join him and begin a rhythmical clapping that demands action. Greene finds a passage that suits him and cannonades the audience. "This speaker is called Menaphon," he says. "A Persian, I believe, though who can tell one Mohammedan from another, or the Mongols from the Moors, or the Moors from the Spaniards, or the Spaniards from the Jews? With a name like Menaphon he should be Greek."

He clears his throat, plants his feet firmly, throws out his arm in the direction of Tarleton and reads:

> "Of stature tall, and straightly fashioned
> Like his desire, lift upward and divine."

He is interrupted by roars of laughter. Tarleton flexes his muscles
and poses as the terror of Asia.

> "So large of limbs, his joints so strongly knit,
> Such breadth of shoulders as might mainly bear
> Old Atlas' burden. 'Twixt his manly pitch,
> A pearl more worth than all the world is plac'd,
> Wherein by curious sovereignty of art
> Are fix'd his piercing instruments of sight,
> Whose fiery circles bear encompassed
> A heaven of heavenly bodies in their spheres,
> That guides his steps, and actions to the throne
> Where honour sits invested royally."

Ned Alleyn and James Burbage watch with as much amusement
as anyone in the crowd, but, as Greene continues, Alleyn's smile
turns to a frown, and he tilts his head as though he is trying to listen
more closely to the butchered lines. "Who wrote this play?" he says
to Burbage.

"I have no idea," says Burbage, "but if Greene and Nashe can
turn it into a comedy I'll pay them handsomely for it."

"I have a feeling it's no comedy," says Alleyn.

"Well, it's a comedy tonight," he says, "and people will pay as
much to laugh as to weep."

Tarleton mugs and mimics, trying to act in pantomime the lines
that Greene speaks. Someone hands him a chamberpot, which he
puts on his head over his cap as a helmet.

> "Pale of complexion, wrought in him with passion,
> Thirsting with sovereignty and love of arms,
> His lofty brows in folds do figure death,
> And in their smoothness amity and life.
> About them hangs a knot of amber hair,
> Wrapped in curls as fierce Achilles' was,
> On which the breath of heaven delights to play,
> Making it dance with wanton majesty.
> His arms and fingers long and sinewy . . ."

Tarleton shows off his stubby hands. Some lines are lost in the noise.

"Betokening valour and excess of strength.
In every part proportion'd like the man
Should make the world subdu'd to Tamburlaine."

Tarleton tugs at Roberto's turd-green cloak, like a little boy trying to attract his attention. "Is it not time for Tamburlaine to speak?" he says.

"Be still, you moral monster you, while I complete my scene," says Greene. "Only a true writer knows how difficult it is to break a scene. One might more easily break the wind."

One of his cohorts obliges with a simulated fart that stops the performance for a full minute while the audience laughs and coughs and stamps its feet.

Greene flips through the manuscript. "Enough of that nonsense. Let's give our hero a speech to speak. Here!" He thrusts a page at Tarleton, who holds it away from his face as though he is farsighted. He draws himself up, adjusts his chamberpot of a helmet and speaks with an effeminate lisp:

"I that am term'd the Scourge and Wrath of God,
The only fear and terror of the world,
Will first subdue the Turk, and then enlarge
Those Christian captives which you keep as slaves . . ."

He is repeatedly interrupted but goes on, his comic timing perfect.

"These are the cruel pirates of Argier,
That damned train, the scum of Africa,
Inhabited with straggling runagates,
That make quick havoc of the Christian blood.
But, as I live, that town shall curse the time
That Tamburlaine set foot in Africa."

A fat and aging waitress is coaxed onto the table beside Tarleton. Greene retreats to find himself a drink and to rest. It is Tom Nashe now who hands Tarleton his lines from the confused manuscript.

Tarleton circles the small mountain of a female that has been thrust at him, as though he is looking for a foothold to scale her. And then he whistles, and then he jigs, and then he reads whatever it is that Nashe has placed in his hands:

> "Zenocrate, lovelier than the love of Jove,
> Brighter than is the silver Rhodope,
> Fairer than whitest snow on Scythian hills,
> Thy person is more worth to Tamburlaine
> Than the possession of the Persian crown,
> Which gracious stars have promis'd at my birth."

Tarleton makes amorous and lewd gestures toward the smiling wench. She, still clutching the coin they have placed in her hand, does not seem to understand what is going on, but she laughs because everyone else is laughing, and she thinks of the bolt of cloth at the mercers that the coin in her sweating palm will buy.

> "With milk-white harts upon an ivory sled
> Thou shalt be drawn amidst the frozen pools,
> And scale the icy mountains' lofty tops,
> Which with thy beauty will be soon resolv'd.
> My martial prizes, with five hundred men,
> Won on the fifty-headed Volga's waves,
> Shall we all offer to Zenocrate,
> And then myself to fair Zenocrate."

With these lines Tarleton throws himself at the feet of the startled waitress and makes elaborate kissing noises. But when he rises, his head is under her giant skirts, and he has done something that makes her scream and lose her balance. She staggers. She falls. Fortunately for her, unfortunately for them, she falls amidst a group of Tarleton's friends, as the crowd gasps and laughs all at once.

Kit notices that Robert Greene has withdrawn to another table, where, face down, he snores away his wine. The new master of the revels is Tom Nashe, who announces that because of a plague of drunkenness the theatre will be closed.

Before he can draw the entertainment to a close, however, he is interrupted by someone who shouts at him in a strong voice and rushes toward his table. "Just a minute! Just a minute, gentlemen!" It is Ned Alleyn, the actor. He mounts the stage and, though he speaks to Nashe, he also seems to be addressing the audience, which has fallen silent. "I ask you kind actors and performers who have so amused us this evening to give me a moment or two of your time. You have had your fun at the expense of some writer whose name I don't even know. But I do know that there is beauty and brilliance in the lines that you read with such destructive delight. I beg you, in all fairness to that anonymous poet, to me, and to yourselves, to allow me to read just one speech as it was written to be read. You may choose it, since you know the play and I do not. All I ask is your silence and attention."

His announcement is greeted with wild applause and shouts of approval. "Give us Ned Alleyn! Let him read!"

Tom Nashe readily agrees and, thumbing rapidly through the manuscript, finds for Alleyn one of the passages he himself most admires in Kit's play.

Alleyn takes the sheet of paper, glances at it and then fixes the audience with his eyes. In the dramatic pause before he speaks, they settle into their seats and hush each other into silence. Even before he begins he has gripped them by his presence. Most of them have seen him on the stage and have been moved to elation and tears.

When all is settled and the tension in the room is almost beyond endurance, Ned Alleyn begins:

> "Now clear the triple region of the air,
> And let the Majesty of Heaven behold
> Their scourge and terror tread on emperors.
> Smile, stars that reign'd at my nativity,
> And dim the brightness of their neighbour lamps;

Disdain to borrow light of Cynthia!
For I, the chiefest lamp of all the earth,
First rising in the east with mild aspect,
But fixed now in the meridian line,
Will send up fire to your turning spheres,
And cause the sun to borrow light of you.
My sword struck fire from his coat of steel
Even in Bithynia, when I took this Turk;
As when a fiery exhalation,
Wrapt in the bowels of a freezing cloud,
Fight for passage, makes the welkin crack,
And casts a flash of lightning to the earth.
But ere I march to wealthy Persia,
Or leave Damascus and th' Egyptian fields,
As was the fame of Clymene's brain-sick son
That almost brent the axle-tree of heaven,
So shall our swords, our lances, and our shot
Fill all the air with fiery meteors.
Then, when the sky shall wax as red as blood,
It shall be said I made it red myself,
To make me think of naught but blood and war."

He stops. The audience is so stunned by his performance and so
awed by the unfamiliar power of these lines that it is fully thirty
seconds before the applause begins—slowly at first, seeming to
come from the rear in the direction of Ralegh's table, and then
building to a shattering uproar that lasts for what seems to Marlowe
a thousand years.

Alleyn smiles and takes several bows, then leaps athletically from
the table to be embraced by writers and players alike, by tradesmen
and gamblers, by gentlemen and hired assassins.

At his now isolated table, Robert Greene raises his head at the
noise, looks around bleary-eyed and then lets his head fall once
more into his folded arms.

Alleyn rejoins Burbage, who hugs him and kisses him on both
cheeks. "If we can find the author of this *Tamburlaine*," Burbage

says, "we'll have it at The Theatre, with all the pomp of Persia, before the month is out."

Kit does not have to overhear the remark to know that his career in London has begun.

iv

A few weeks pass in which everything happens. His play is in rehearsal at The Theatre. Tom Walsingham comes up to London for a prolonged visit. And Tom and Ann Watson go off to the country to visit friends. They are actually driven off by Kit, who has overflowed his small room and works furiously on Part II of *Tamburlaine* all over the house.

Tom and Ann have argued over whether or not they should ask Kit to find lodgings of his own. Tom has at last agreed to speak with him about it, and Kit has promised that he will move out just as soon as he has "captured" the first draft of his play. "It would be a disastrous distraction to stop now," he says. Faced with this kind of frenzy and disorder, Ann and Tom decide that the best thing to do is to get out of the way for a while. Besides, Ann has a childless uncle in Essex from whom she hopes to inherit a bit of money or property. It seems a good occasion to be kind to him.

The day after the Watsons leave, old Mary Potter comes down with a fever and cannot come to work. The house falls into ruins and chaos. There are books and papers and empty bottles everywhere. In a drunken attempt to visualize the action of his play, Kit has rearranged all the furniture into an exotic symbolic geography that he personally conquers. He doesn't wash. He sleeps in his clothes. He drinks more than he eats. But he writes. And what he writes reveals the fever pitch and near madness of his mood:

> Give me a map; then let me see how much
> Is left for me to conquer all the world.
> That these, my boys, may finish all my wants.
> Here I began to march towards Persia,

Along Armenia and the Caspian Sea,
And thence unto Bithynia, where I took
The Turk and his great empress prisoners.
Then march'd I into Egypt and Arabia;
And here, not far from Alexandria,
Whereas the Terene and the Red Sea meet,
Being distant less than full a hundred leagues,
I meant to cut a channel to them both,
That men might quickly sail to India.
From thence to Nubia near Borno-Lake,
And so along the Aethiopian sea,
Cutting the tropic line of Capricorn,
I conquer'd all as far as Zanzibar.
Then by the northern part of Africa,
I came at last to Graecia, and from thence
To Asia, where I stay against my will;
Which is from Scythia, where I first began,
Backwards and forwards near five thousand leagues.
Look here, my boys; see, what a world of ground
Lies westward from the midst of Cancer's line
Unto the rising of this earthly globe,
Whereas the sun, declining from our sight,
Begins the day with our Antipodes!
And shall I die, and this unconquered?
Lo, here, my sons, are all the golden mines,
Inestimable drugs and precious stones,
More worth than Asia and the world beside;
And from th'Antarctic Pole eastward behold
As much more land, which never was descried,
Wherein are rocks of pearl that shine as bright
As all the lamps that beautify the sky!
And shall I die, and this unconquered?

He has just finished this passage when a knocking at the door
hauls him out of his drama and back to the reality of Bishopsgate
and London. The last time he was conscious of his surroundings
there was daylight in the windows of the living room. Now there is

darkness, and he has no idea what time it is or who his visitor might be.

The insistent knock comes again, and he goes to the door. In the dim light he cannot see clearly the face of the man who is standing there. "Who is it?" he says.

"May I come in?" says a familiar voice, a voice that he remembers well, though he has heard it only twice before. "I didn't mean to frighten you."

It is Thomas Phelippes, chief aide to Sir Francis Walsingham. He removes his hat and looks around the room. "I hope I'm not disturbing you," he says, a small smile on his thin face, his wide eyes taking in the chaos.

"The old lady is sick," says Kit, as if that will explain everything.

"May I?" says Phelippes, picking up an overturned chair.

"I'm sorry for all this confusion," says Kit. "I was working. Tom and Ann have gone off somewhere."

"Yes, I know," says Phelippes. He sits down, noiselessly, catlike, beside the table and removes his gloves slowly, finger by finger.

Kit is too nervous to sit down. He paces back and forth, picks up some papers and books and then puts them down again. "What is it you want?" he says. And then adds, before Phelippes can answer, "Can I offer you something?" He looks around and finds a wine bottle, but it is empty.

"No, no, don't bother, Christopher," says Phelippes. He pronounces Kit's name with a frightening precision.

Kit turns his attention from the empty bottle to his visitor. "Well, now," he says. "To what do I owe this—"

Phelippes interrupts him with a laugh. He shakes his head. "Relax, dear boy," he says. "I am not here on official business. I wanted a word with you—merely out of curiosity, that's all."

"About what?" says Kit.

"Why don't you find a place to sit down," says Phelippes. "I find it rather uncomfortable looking up at you like this."

Kit removes some books from a chair and sits down at the other side of the table. "I'm sorry about the wine," he mutters. "More for my sake than for yours." He rubs his mouth with the back of his hand.

"I've been hearing all sorts of things about you lately," says Phelippes.

"Good things or bad things?" says Kit.

"Neither good nor bad," he says. "Just—mm—things."

"About my play, you mean?" says Kit.

"Yes, of course, there's that, isn't there?" he says. "I must congratulate you. It should be an enormous success. I found it very interesting. We will have to talk about it one day."

"You've read it?" says Kit.

"Yes, as a matter of fact," he says.

"But how—I mean, where did you get it?" says Kit.

With his gloves he waves away the whole conversation. "Well, never mind about all that," he says. "I wanted to ask you about something else. It has come to my attention, quite by accident, that you have been in some discussion with a priest named John Hunt or John Edmunds. Is that right, Christopher?"

"Yes," he says. "That's right. What about it?"

"You can't blame me for being curious, can you? I mean, the man is deeply involved in sedition and treasonous activities, for which he could easily lose his head."

"I thought this was not an official visit."

"It's not," says Phelippes. "I was not sent by Sir Francis or anyone else. As I say, it is idle curiosity that brings me here. And, given the circumstances, I think you owe me a bit of enlightenment on the subject, don't you?"

"Since you seem to know everything else, you probably already know exactly what our conversation was all about."

"I can probably guess, but I would prefer that you told me."

"It's very simple," says Kit. "He approached me at St. Paul's one day and asked me if I would work as a courier for him and his friends in the north. They wanted some information gathered and brought to the continent."

"To Parsons?" says Phelippes.

"Yes," says Kit. "And perhaps others. I don't know much about it. I told him I wasn't interested. And, as you can see, I am very much involved right now."

"So you told him *no,* flat out?"

"That's right," says Kit.

"In that case," says Phelippes, "why was it necessary to see him again the following day at The Mitre?"

Kit gets up and stalks across the room angrily. "Good lord, man," he says, "what have you been doing, following me around? Must I look under my bed before I go to sleep at night? Do I have no privacy left at all?"

"Now, now, Christopher, calm down," Phelippes says in a quiet voice. "These are very difficult times. I'm sure you understand. Relax. I'm not accusing you of anything."

"Aren't you?"

"Not at all. But I am curious to know why you met this John Hunt the following day. If you were in my position, wouldn't that strike you as rather peculiar, since, as you say, you turned the man down flatly?"

"I am not you, sir," says Kit. "I don't know what strikes you as peculiar. Personally, I find it very strange indeed that you should know so much about me."

"Actually, I wish we knew a bit more."

"My life, sir, is an open book," says Kit, waving his hand around the room at the books and the pages of his new play, which are scattered everywhere.

"Well, then," says Phelippes, "put my mind at ease and tell me why you met with John Hunt a second time."

"I met with him a second time because I needed time to think."

"To think about what?"

"To consider the various possibilities."

"Such as?" says Phelippes, leaning slightly toward Marlowe.

"I was considering taking the information to Sir Francis," says Kit.

"And why didn't you?"

"Because I decided that I was through with all that. I decided that I did not want to get involved again. Had I gone to Sir Francis, he would have insisted that I pursue the matter, and it would have been difficult for me to refuse."

"But you did refuse John Hunt?"

"Absolutely! Why would I want to work for them, when I don't even want to work for you?"

"I don't know," says Phelippes. "Some people do, you know. They have their reasons: political, religious—*monetary!*"

"I don't need money," says Kit, "and I am not interested in politics. I'm a writer."

"There was a time when writers restricted themselves to Olympian gods and sighing lovers," says Phelippes. "But many a pen has been turned to politics and religion. Be careful what you write. You can be hanged for an unpleasant rhyme, you know. As Mr. Marprelate will soon discover—that is, as soon as we discover who he is."

"Thank you, sir, for your kind advice," says Kit sardonically. "If I am visited by the Muse, I shall tell her to restrict her offerings to benign nonsense."

"Well put," says Phelippes with a smile. He rises, takes his gloves from the table and prepares to leave. "I'm sorry if I have offended you, Christopher. I meant no harm." He seems genuinely apologetic.

"That's all right," says Kit, eager for him to leave.

He pauses at the door. "And, oh, yes, all good fortune with your play. I hope to be there when it opens at The Theatre."

Kit closes the door behind his visitor and paces twice across the room and back again before kicking over the chair in which Phelippes was sitting.

v

"Well, what do you think, Anthony?" says Stephen Gosson. "Shall we go around to The Theatre this afternoon to see this new play?"

"I don't think either one of us would be very welcome at The

Theatre," says Anthony Munday. "Since you gave up writing plays you've been very hard on your former associates and friends. They will never forgive you for your *School of Abuse.*"

"But you still go from time to time, don't you? And you have been at least as critical as I have been—in your own way. I hear they fairly hate you."

"Oh, but that's somewhat different," says Munday. "You see, I'm a journalist of sorts, still a writer."

"And a priest-hunter, a pursuivant. A pamphleteer," says Gosson. "I took my stand against the theatre out of principle. They feel that you have been merely an opportunist. I took holy orders. I *had* to make a choice. I mean, I take my calling quite seriously."

"Then why even consider going to The Theatre this afternoon?"

Gosson, a man in his early thirties, clears his throat, tucks in his receding chin, only to expose a second chin, and says, "Well, now, I can hardly preach an intelligent sermon against the evils of our public theatres without keeping current with them, can I? And I am often in the country and rarely in London these days, as you know."

They are sitting in The Spire, a tavern near St. Paul's. Neither of them goes anymore to The Mermaid or even The Mitre for fear of running into certain theatrical types whom they have accused of corruption, immorality, hedonism, heresy, and sedition. Both men are about ten years older than Christopher Marlowe. They have known each other for a long time, but they have gone their separate ways: Gosson into the Church, Munday into the ranks of professional scribblers and into government service. Both have had connections with the very institution that they now denigrate; both have written plays. Worse yet, Stephen Gosson was even a player. "But all that is behind me now," he constantly protests. "And a man should not be condemned for the foolish things he did in his youth. After all, one matures, one learns, one profits from experience."

Ambition reveals itself in Anthony Munday's hungry eyes. It was he who went abroad with Thomas Nowell to write an exposé about the English Catholics in exile. It was he who bore witness against

Luke Kirbie and Campion and Bristow. And on the scaffold where Campion was executed, it was he who read aloud the justification for the execution.

"I haven't been to the theatre in ages," says Stephen Gosson, sniffing his sherry and then holding it up to the light to examine it for sediment. "I confess I am curious to see how things have changed. Besides, they say this Marlowe is a cut above the others. A good scholar. Corpus Christi and all that!"

Anthony Munday spreads his beard away from his large red lips and feeds himself some shreds of beef. "He's no better or worse than the others," he says.

"Well," says Gosson, "I suppose there's always Blackfriars. Or a visit to Reverend Starke. I suppose I should drop around. But he's so awfully boring, if you know what I mean."

"All too well," says Munday, pushing his plate away, drawing his goblet closer and failing to contain an enormous burp.

"And you? Do you never go to the theatre anymore?"

"Of course I do. From time to time. I prefer the inns—The Bell, The Cross-Keys, The Bull, The Bel Savage. I generally stay away from The Theatre. Mr. Burbage doesn't like me, and Mr. Burbage has a very hot head. I don't trust him to keep his temper."

"Well," says Gosson, "that's too bad. I mean, it's something to take into account, isn't it? And yet, I would like to see this *Tamburlaine* before I leave London. It might be worth a few hard stares. We could go amongst the groundlings, I suppose, and never be noticed."

"Good lord, Stephen, you're not serious? I'm not about to stand for two hours among the stinkards and have my purse stolen to boot."

"Perhaps, then, high up in the *porticus* we would be inconspicuous," says Gosson, tugging at the skin of his naked second chin.

"Perhaps," says Munday, consulting his wine for advice.

The Theatre is alive with activity some hours before the performance of *Tamburlaine*. The galleries are being swept down, cushions are being set out. In the tiring house James Burbage marches up and down, cursing the spectators from the day before who have made a ruin and garbage heap of his theatre. There had been a program of juggling and tumbling and gymnastics that had attracted a very common class of people, who managed to consume more than a common amount of wine and ale. There had been a fist fight that threatened to break out into a riot. A lady had fainted. A partition in the galleries had been broken, along with several benches. "God's blood, these whoresons expect too much for their penny!" he shouts. "If they want to fight so badly they should be mustered into the army and shipped to the Netherlands, where, with luck, they'll have their scabby heads blown off by Spanish muskets. Curse them and the diseased women of the streets who brought them into the world. I should shut the place down. I should sell out and move to the country. This is no life for a man my age."

All around him the players bustle, trying on costumes, complaining, laughing when oranges are plunged into their clothes to make them ladies. "The virgins of Damascus," shouts an effeminate voice. The book-holder complains that certain lines are illegible, so hastily were the copies made. Ned Alleyn prompts the prompter from his infallible memory. The tireman arrives with Tamburlaine's costume, which proves to be too tight in the crotch. "I'll split my britches," complains Alleyn. "Under all those Turkish robes, who in God's heaven will know the difference?" says Burbage, a vein bulging at his forehead, his face red with exasperation. The tireman reports that the crown is missing. "How am I supposed to conquer the world without a crown?" says Alleyn. "Use Henry the Fifth," says Burbage. "What's the difference? A crown is a crown." Edward Dutton overhears him and says, "I'm using that one. This play is full of kings."

Burbage turns away in disgust, only to face a complaint from the musicians that they have not been given enough room for their drums. "Then use the pit under the stage," he shouts.

The stagekeeper, the grooms and attendants fuss with curtains and move about pieces of furniture, testing their weight, arranging them so that they can be conveniently shoved onto the stage. Some visitors have arrived to chat with the actors and add to the confusion. They cannot be asked to leave since they are good customers. "Is the Lord's Room ready?" calls out Burbage to one of the grooms, who doubles as a collector at the main entrance. He shouts back that it's Tom Daley's turn to do the Lord's, and Burbage shoves his way through the crowded quarters with murder in his eye.

When Kit arrives at the theatre, he is tempted to go directly to the tiring room to make sure that they have gotten it all right, but he does not. He does not even go up to the gallery, where he has promised to meet Ann and Tom Watson. He goes, instead, into the crowd of groundlings, under the open roof. He wants to see his play from there, anonymously, without the distraction of being with friends.

He is bumped and shoved as the large crowd maneuvers for a good vantage point. Hawkers peddle fruit and candy and cakes. The lesser folk scan the Lord's Room, which is just above the tiring room to the rear of the stage, for dignitaries. "There's Sir William," somebody says. They argue about whether or not it is Sir William. Someone near Kit coughs and spits. He is a large man. Two women clutch each other for protection but eye the men who eye them. The house is full. Kit sees Tom Walsingham, who is with Ann and Tom Watson. He also sees Thomas Phelippes, who sits alone in the second tier of the gallery. Roberto is there with Tom Nashe. He is delighted. It is a cool day, but the heat of so many bodies, packed so closely together about the protruding stage, soon warms things up. He is bumped from behind and turns to stare into the ugly face of an unshaven man with tangled blond hair and a smile full of broken teeth. He turns back to the stage. There are trumpets and drums. The noise of the crowd first rises, then falls, almost to a silence but not quite. It is about to begin.

And then it does begin. An actor comes forward to speak the prologue. Players enter from the right in marvelous costumes suggesting the exotic and wealthy cultures of the East. The crowd applauds. Drums join them. Kit can tell already that he has caught them and that his play will be a success. The Persians confer. They

talk about Tamburlaine, whose force is gathering, and who means
to menace all of Asia.

Kit knows his play by heart. He notes some missing lines. They
are little amputations inside of him, but he sweeps along with his
own action, feeling that the movement is swift and good, noticing
that the crowd is understanding what he is talking about. He has
aimed for clarity—the simple, loud, clear music of powerful
language. The musicians are almost superfluous, he thinks. Who
needs them? Tamburlaine pounds his own drum. When at last he
appears, the audience is ready to receive him. They applaud. They
cheer. Is it for Tamburlaine, or for Ned Alleyn, or for the
marvelous costume?

High-sounding words. Threats. Booming pronouncements. Here
is a hero to satisfy every heart. Ruthless, handsome, strong, blond,
tall. Who has not dreamed of being just that man, that man who
would be a king, because to be a king is half to be a god? No!
Because "a god is not so glorious as a king."

> I think the pleasure they enjoy in heaven,
> Cannot compare with kingly joys in earth;
> To wear a crown enchas'd with pearl and gold,
> Whose virtues carry with it life and death;
> To ask and have, command and be obey'd;
> When looks breed love, with looks to gain the prize,
> Such power attractive shines in princes' eyes.

It is not until the play is over and he is outside the main gate that
Kit notices that his purse is gone. There is nothing there but a cut
piece of leather from which it had hung. His curse dissolves into a
laugh. What does it matter? he says to himself, and shouts across
the emerging crowd to Tom and Ann and Walsingham.

vi

November is a large gray hand that descends upon England,
pressing the damp sky closer, shortening the days, strangling the

last stubborn bits of greenery. A few late roses die before they bloom, hardening into corpses before they fall.

In new clothes and silk-lined shoes, Kit boards a boat at the end of Old Swan Street and travels up the Thames to a convenient landing near the Strand, where Ralegh's Durham House is located. He has heard much of Ralegh and his circle and imagines that he is about to attend a dinner party of the foremost intellectuals in England. Instead, he finds that he is the only visitor and that the large house is dark but for a few dim lights in several windows. He is greeted by an elderly servant who leads him into a book-lined study, where Sir Walter sits, not in his courtly, bejeweled garments, but in a simple black doublet and a fur-lined robe. His shirt is unlaced. On his desk there are many books, all open, as though he has been hunting for something—more the scholar than the courtier.

He rises and offers his hand to 'Kit. "So good of you to come. I had hoped to meet with you sooner, but there seems to be no end to the work in these trying times. I'm sure you understand. Come, sit down here. Peter will bring in some wine. A little brandywine, perhaps, to take away the chill, or do you prefer the *eau de vie*?"

"It doesn't matter," says Kit.

"I wanted to talk with you about your play," says Ralegh. "And other things. They say you are a very bright young man."

"A bright young man?" says Kit, his eyebrows raised. "It seems to me I first heard that expression when I was about ten years old."

"I'm sorry," says Ralegh, amused. "I didn't mean it quite that way."

Peter appears with the "water of life" and sets the tray down on a corner of the massive desk. "I hope you don't mind my informality," says Ralegh. "I did not intend this as a social occasion. God knows, I've got enough of those. No, I wanted merely to talk with you, to exchange a few ideas. You see, I was quite deeply moved by your *Tamburlaine*—both parts. Though Part II struck me as a hasty job."

"They wanted it in a hurry," says Kit.

"I understand," says Ralegh. He raises his glass to Kit, who sits

beside the desk, his cloak draped over the back of the chair. "Here's
to your gift and your grasp," he says, "which is still greater than
your reach. But you must be careful."

"Careful of what?" says Kit.

"I see in your play a fascination with the exotic and the
unorthodox. Your hero, for instance. Not only is he not a Christian;
he is a man incapable of any religion, except the religion of his own
wonderful self. He is the man who would be God. Even the man
who would destroy God, if he could. The Anti-Christ, if you will.
He is an atheist in the profoundest sense of the word. And yet he is
very appealing. Though he dies, he is never punished. He is never
defeated. All his battles on earth are victories. The whole thing is a
terrible heresy."

"I did not have heresy in mind," says Kit.

"Now, now, don't feel accused. When you are in my house you
are among friends. People who understand the free spirit."

"I've heard rumors about these friends of yours," says Kit.
"Who exactly are they?"

"Well, there's Tom Harriot, of course. A fine mathematician.
And Arthur Gorges, my cousin's son and a very good poet. There's
Robert Hughes, the geographer, and Robert's patron, William
Sanderson, who is married to my niece. There's Walter Warner,
the third most brilliant man I have ever met after Hughes and
Harriot. And Richard Hakluyt. And Robert Sidney, who is married
to my cousin Barbara Gamage. Let me see. George Chapman,
Michael Drayton, Matthew Roydon, Laurence Keynes, Sir George
Carey, Ferdinando Stanley. Oh, yes, Nicholas Hill with his atoms,
and Nathaniel Torporley, another mathematician."

"And what is it that you all talk about?" says Kit. "Witchcraft?
Atheism? Sedition?"

"You are less amusing than you imagine, my friend. We talk
freely—that's all. Away from official scrutiny. We run before the
wind of new knowledge, and it is very exhilarating. Forget the
vicious rumors." He refills his glass and then takes out a pipe and a
bowl of tobacco. "Will you join me?" he says, offering another pipe
to Kit.

"Yes, thank you," says Kit.

"I find it very soothing, don't you?" says Ralegh. "Very conducive to meditation. It is particularly pleasant when one is writing poetry. The Muse's very own weed. I predict that eventually every writer in the world will be using tobacco. It will become as essential as his pen."

Ralegh lights a taper from the candle on his desk, and the two men play the bellows to their pipes until there is a dense cloud of smoke between them that ascends lazily toward the beamed and decorated ceiling.

Two hours later, Kit comes away from Durham House, his head whirling with new ideas. They have talked about everything from the war with Spain to the existence of the human soul. He has come away also with an invitation to attend those gatherings that have already been labeled as Sir Walter's School of Night. It is another triumph, another stride away from being merely the cobbler's son. He struts. He sings. His footsteps echo in the empty streets.

vii

Twelfth Night, and a gentle snow is falling on London. It falls on the tile and thatch of the huddled rooftops, on the stiff ruts of the frozen mud and the glistening cobblestones. It is a dusting of white hair on Tower Hill and Moor Fields and the Artillery Grounds, where unattended, impotent cannon stand dutifully in a row. It falls on Whitehall, where the Queen's Men prepare an entertainment for the Queen; and on Newgate Prison, where there will be no celebrations. And on The Curtain, The Rose, and The White Bear, where the revels thicken as the afternoon fades into evening. It is, after all, the eve of the Twelfth Day, the Epiphany. Let the bells ring and the wine flow to preface the giving of the gifts, the baptism of Christ, the end of the journey of the Wise Men from the East.

Elizabeth the Queen talks quietly with the ladies of her chamber as she prepares herself for the festivities of this significant eve. She is concerned, above all, with her hair—a red wig now, over the

desolation that once was the free-flowing fire of her youth. Her face
is powdered. Her cheeks are rouged. She sits before a mirror,
watching her public self created once more. She is oddly and coldly
objective, her thin eyebrows raised, her mouth fixed by curiosity, as
though she, the real woman (the girl), were standing to one side and
watching her busy ladies create The Queen—another creature
entirely. This fretting and fussing over each fold and frill is not
mere feminine vanity; it is more a political act. Her appearance is
very important—more important, in fact, than her pathetic reality.

Almost a thousand miles away, King Philip of Spain kneels at
prayer in his private chapel in the seclusion of his vast Escorial
Palace. He wants no company, no conversation, no talk of war on
this eve of the miracle of the manifestation of God in the child
Jesus. He has fled the fiestas that accompany the Epiphany. While
his nation prepares for the Feast of the Kings, he fasts and prays,
rising occasionally from his stiff knees to peer through a narrow
window at a skyful of stars, and then returning to his cushioned
altar, eyes closed, to imagine that single star that dominated the
heavens and lured the Magi toward Bethlehem, where the spirit was
made flesh and the union with God was made possible. He struggles
to fix his mind exclusively on this central fact of his being and the
central fact of all earthly and heavenly existence. Before this birth
he sees only the chaos of a confused and misguided world; and
beyond the denial of it he sees the raging fires of eternal damnation.
He comes back again and again to the familiar prayers in the book
he holds in his hand, but his eyes wander to the crucifix, to the
tormented body of Christ, to the child in the arms of Mary,
depicted in stone and gold, reflected in multicolored glass. His mind
wanders, too, in spite of his efforts at concentration, to the
hammering and yelping and squeaking of wheels in the ports of
Spain and Portugal, where the preparations go on for his crusade
against the bastard queen of the Protestant heretics—she who
would place herself above the Pope, above the Church itself, against
the judgment of God and His Son and His Son's disciples and the
whole heritage and hierarchy of Christianity from the beginning

down to this very moment, in this chapel, behind these vast walls, under the silent dome of His obvious design and irrefutable harmony.

In London the snow continues to fall. Not only does it fall on the immense structures of church and state, commerce and personal wealth; it falls also on cold ruins, cottages, and tenements. Some of these are in Shoreditch, in Norton Folgate and Bishopsgate. Though Kit Marlowe has lived up to his promise to move out, he returns often to visit Tom and Ann Watson.

"This is the first real snow we've had in years," says Ann.

"The corpse of the Holy Ghost," says Kit from inside the cave of himself.

Tom Watson, who is sitting nearby, going through a manuscript on the table, looks up. "What was that?" he says.

"The corpse of the Holy Ghost," says Kit. He has a glass in his hand, which he raises heavenward, as though toasting some deity or fallen angel. "When I was a child I asked an old monk what the snow was, and that's what he told me—the corpse of the Holy Ghost, who permeated the world and, when he died, crystallized and showered himself down on us all, in white disappearing ashes that rose again invisibly and formed once more the universal spirit of the world. He was a madman. They burned him in Canterbury when I was a boy."

Tom puts aside his manuscript and stands up. "It's getting late," he says. "We've got to decide about this party—this masquerade. Have you figured out who you are going to be?"

"I haven't even figured out who I am," says Kit. "How can I know who I shall be?"

"Be a king," says Ann.

"And you?" says Kit. "Shall you be the Virgin Mary?"

"If she can be the Virgin Mary," says Tom, "then I can be the Baby Jesus. There is a limit, even to miracles."

"Well, then," says Kit, "we'll all go as donkeys and goats. Who can deny that there were animals in that manger?"

"How does one disguise himself as a goat?" asks Ann.

"Why, with a pair of horns and a tail," says Kit. "Isn't that right, Tom?"

"I think you jest with me, Christopher," says Ann, her hands on her slender hips.

"Yes, my love," says Kit. "I confess I would plant horns on this fellow here—this husband of yours—and turn him into an ass and a cuckold, were he not practically my brother."

They are all laughing. "I never saw an ass with horns," says Tom.

Kit takes Ann by the arm and forces her into his lap. "Brother Tom," he says, "lend me a kiss from your fair Helen. I have a great need for kissing tonight."

"There are kisses and there are kisses," says Tom. "What are your intentions, sir?"

"Adoration, my lord," says Kit. "On this, the eve of the circumcision of Christ, I come as a king and a magician out of the East to adore this miracle of a woman with kisses as pure as Persian gold and as warm as Babylonian fire."

"*Venite, venite, quid tardatis,*" says Tom, standing over his friends, his hands outstretched like a pagan priest.

"Sweet Ann, sweet Mary, sweet Helen," says Kit. "Come, make me immortal with a kiss." He kisses her passionately, his hand cupping her breast. She struggles but not seriously. Tom laughs and draws his sword.

"Put up your sword," says Kit, "I meant no harm. But find me a woman like your Ann and I swear that I will marry her and retire from this reckless bachelor's life. I can't tell you how jealous I am of your good fortune." He is between them. He kisses them both. Then Tom leaps up suddenly and says, "What disguises shall we wear for Tom Walsingham's party tonight?"

"We should have thought of this a long time ago," says Ann, adjusting her hair and then her bodice. "I could have made us all something a bit original. I suppose now we will all have to go as shepherds and kings."

"But everybody there will be a shepherd or a king," says Kit.

"I hear Sir Walter plans to play Herod for the evening," says Tom.

"If I had a lily and a trumpet," says Kit, "I could go as the Archangel Gabriel, bugling up the beginning and the end of things. A nice role for a poet."

"I'd like to go as Cleopatra," says Ann.

"She had nothing to do with it," says Tom.

"You could go as one of the ladies of Samaria," says Kit. "I understand he knew them well."

"In what way?" says Ann.

"Oh, in the usual way," says Kit, "being a man of the flesh."

"You vile, awful, naughty man, you!" says Ann. "Tom, tell him to behave himself."

Tom leaps up. "Ah, I have it!" he says. "I shall go as Joseph. A simple solution. We'll go around to The Theatre and borrow some costumes from Burbage's tiring house. I know the fellow who keeps the key—Peter Short of Cock Lane."

"If you go as Joseph," says Kit, "I'll go as the soldier named Panthera, who they say was the real and earthly father of Jesus."

"Where in the world did you get that blasphemous thought?" says Tom.

"From a very reliable and alcoholic astrologer at The White Bear," says Kit, "who shall remain nameless."

"Christopher," says Tom, "you must behave yourself tonight. Tom Walsingham will never forgive you if you embarrass him. Remember, it is a social event of considerable importance to him. Sir Francis will be there, and Ralegh, of course, and Robert Cecil, and the Sheltons, including Audrey."

"Audrey?" says Kit, suddenly serious. "Who is Audrey?"

"Audrey Shelton," says Tom. "Daughter of Sir Ralph Shelton, High Sheriff of Norfolk. A very wealthy family, indeed. The Norfolk and Suffolk Sheltons. Surely you've heard of them. They've owned enough land since before the Conquest to make a separate nation of their own."

"I've heard of the Sheltons, of course," says Kit. "But I haven't heard of Audrey. You mention her as though there is something special about her I should know."

"Only that there is a rumor that a match is being attempted between her and Tom Walsingham," says Watson.

Kit frowns, then laughs. "Not likely," he says. "Tom's not ready to marry."

"There is an old saying about younger sons," says Tom. "They should marry wealthy and far from home. You forget that Edmund Walsingham inherited his father's estates. Tom's greatest asset is his good name. It would be a logical match."

Kit tosses off the rest of his wine and dismisses the whole subject with a slightly bitter laugh. "It seems everybody's getting married these days except me and the Queen. Perhaps we should get together and shock the world. I've always been drawn to older women."

Ann, who has been standing by patiently, says, "Well, what are we going to do? It's getting late."

"We're going up to Cock Lane," says Tom, "to find Peter Short and the key to the tiring house. There we will find costumes enough for all of us. Christopher will be a king, after all—one of the three kings from the East who followed the star of Bethlehem."

"I'd rather follow my nose to The Unicorn," says Kit, "than a star to a stable."

"We'll find you a paper crown with some glass diamonds," says Tom, "and some of those Persian robes from your *Tamburlaine*."

"All right, all right," says Kit, rising reluctantly. "But I want you to know that they were not kings. They were magicians and followers of Zoroaster. A whole caste of priests. Babylonian jugglers. Astrological manipulators. I'll be damned if I know what they were doing in Bethlehem. Probably carrying on a little trade, what with all that gold, frankincense and myrrh. They could hardly have come all that way in the worst time of the year to lay these things at the feet of a miscellaneous and probably illegitimate child."

"For God's sake, Kit, save your wit and theology for Durham House and the taverns," says Tom, "and let's be on our way."

Ann has already put on a coat, and Tom is lacing his shirt. "If you insist," says Kit. "But if I must be one of the so-called kings, I want to be the black one. Which one was he? Gaspar? I shall be Gaspar. We shall find at The Theatre the black dust they use to turn us white men into Moors."

They go out into the dying light, and, in the white dust of the still-falling snow, they walk arm-in-arm up Bishopsgate and Norton Folgate to Cock Lane, singing:

> "Love me little, love me long,
>   Is the burden of my song.
> Love that is too hot and strong
>   Burneth soon to waste:
> Still, I would not have thee cold,
> Not too backward, nor too bold;
> Love that lasteth till 'tis old
>   Fadeth not in haste.
>   Love me little, love me long,
>   Is the burden of my song . . ."

At The Leopard's Head in Shoreditch, the fires roar and the tapmen sing out their echoes of orders from the unruly mob of players and the still more unruly stagehands and theatre laborers who have gathered here to celebrate the Twelfth Night of Christmas in their singularly irreligious way. Richard Jones, the actor, leads a group of huddled, swaying men in a round of bawdy songs. His wife's parents own and run the tavern. It has none of the comparative respectability of The Mermaid. It is said of The Leopard's Head that it is a good place to be introduced to the disease that will one day kill you, by which is meant that it is frequented by a shabby clutch of whores.

"We'll have one drink here and then we'll be on our way," says the black king in the pseudo-Persian robes and crown of Tamburlaine.

"It's no fit place for a lady," says Tom Watson, the false-bearded Semitic cuckold, as Kit calls him. The slow-witted father of the cannibalized god-man. Joseph, whose tender-hearted wife, Mary, took a roll in the celestial hay with the Holy Ghost. "I don't mind," says Ann. "But one only, Kit. On your word." Her adornments are exotically modest, some costumer's idea of what biblical ladies must have worn. Her robes are somewhat livened by a "gold" chain about her waist and a pendant about her neck. She wears also a headband of imitation gold that suggests a fallen halo. From it her loosened blond hair flows angelically. She could be, they decided in the tiring house, the infamous lady from Samaria they had envisioned earlier, or, if necessary, the Virgin Mary herself. It was a decision they could make later on, they agreed, and they might prefer the ambiguity for the sheer fun of it.

The three ghosts of the unreal past go into The Leopard's Head, Kit leading the way. They cannot help but attract attention. Kit throws out his arms, as if to embrace them all, and shouts, "We've come ten thousand miles on the humps of camels in search of our little Saviour, and we're dying of thirst. Here's gold from Byzantium for a draft of your rotten ale." He flings a coin toward the pig-faced tapman and tumbles two drunken actors to the floor to make room for himself and his friends. His flamboyance is met with cheers and jeers. Both he and Tom are known by most of the crowd.

Richard Jones breaks off his song and comes to greet them. Others gather around to joke good-naturedly. "Well, if it ain't King Marlowe and the Whore of Babylon," says Jones. "But who's the funny-looking Turk in the sticky whiskers?"

Among those who laugh in the small circle is Robert Pallant, a clean-faced, effeminate young man, used on the stage to play the parts of fair ladies. "Come, come, my pretty one," says Kit, taking Pallant by the waist and forcing him down beside him on the bench. "We'll put some color back in those pale cheeks of yours and make you cherry-ripe to play the Lord Mayor's daughter."

Glasses arrive and toasts are drunk all around, mostly in the form of congratulations for plays well written or acted or in the form of mock insults, which are really compliments. Tom stands and announces to Kit and Ann and all their friends that they are expected at a gala celebration at the house of an important member of the aristocracy.

"Hobnobbin' with the snobbery, eh?" says John Duke.

"Take us along, mate," says Robert Goffe, "and we'll make a real party of it. None of that sippin' and singin' in whispers and lace, and 'How do you do, Your Honorable Lordship, sir?' "

"Oh, these are real gentlemen, they are," says Jones. "Too good for the likes of us. Let 'em go. Let 'em go to their fancy ball. They'll be back when times turn hard—and they always do, sooner or later."

Kit stands up, his arm still around Pallant, who rises with him, apparently enjoying the attention. "You dare speak thus to the terror of the world, who has leveled all the lands from Scythia to Zanzibar and captured prisoners and slaves by the thousands to man his warlike galleys. I shall have you all put to the sword—as soon as it is convenient. In the meantime, I shall hold this lad as a hostage. He may be redeemed, in time, for a thousand crowns or a small barrel of dry sack."

To applause and laughter they sweep out of The Leopard's Head with young Robert Pallant, indeed a prisoner in the strong right arm of Kit the King. "Come on," says Tom. "It's getting late. Send the boy back and let's be on our way."

Ann is laughing uncontrollably and is moved to kiss the young captive. "Such an adorable boy," she says. "Must we throw him back to the dogs and swine?"

"We can't very well take him with us," says Tom.

"Wait! Wait!" says Kit. "I am being visited by a vision." He pauses melodramatically. "I can see it now. This lad, who is, in the real life of the stage, a virgin girl, shall be our Mary. We'll make one more quick trip to the tiring house of The Theatre, which is but two minutes away, and disguise her with Arabian veils as a mystery guest who chooses to conceal her real identity. How it will titillate all those boring people."

"You'll never get away with it," says Tom. Then he thinks for a moment, smiles, and agrees that it would be great fun.

Ann claps her hands with delight. The boy says, "I don't understand," but they sweep him away before offering him any further explanation.

It is not until they are at the door of Walsingham's house, which is ablaze with celebrations, that he finally comprehends what his role is to be. "Don't forget," says Kit, "you are a visitor from the west country, where your father is an enormously wealthy and influential man. But be evasive and flirtatious and coy and when asked your name, answer always and simply that it is Mary."

And then they are all inside in a riot of costumes, glittering with jewelry, real and artificial. "The theatre of the world," says Kit to Tom, searching the gathering for his host and friend Tom Walsingham.

Tom comes across the room, masquerading as something Roman. Their meeting is cordial, but not affectionate. He takes Watson briefly by the hand and gives Ann a small kiss. "And this charming girl?" he says, indicating Pallant dressed as Mary.

"My name is Mary," says Pallant.

Walsingham waits, looking at his friends as though for an explanation. "It's a game, Tom," says Kit. "She said she would come to your masquerade as long as she did not have to reveal her identity. But it is a fact, to which I will swear, that her true Christian name is, indeed, Mary. Her family name is the mystery." He leans closer to Tom and whispers so that only he can hear. "But I assure you it is a name somewhat better than well known."

Walsingham looks pleasantly puzzled. "I rather like games," he says, "but I don't quite see the point."

"And who are you supposed to be?" says Watson. "No, no, let us guess. Isn't that the fun of a masquerade?"

Ann, who has not quite recovered from her giggles, says, "Ask him if he's got anything on under his sheet."

"You are not likely to be Julius Caesar," says Watson. "That would be irrelevant to the occasion."

"Oh, relevance has nothing to do with it," says Tom. "There are several King Arthurs here, one Charlemagne, a Salomé, a Tristan, and a man with a large black beard who wants to be a Russian of some sort. Not to mention those too unimaginative to wear anything but their ordinary clothes."

"I see Robert Cecil has come as Richard the Third," says Kit.

"Don't be nasty, Christopher," says Tom. "He's come as himself, and with apologies, having just gotten back to London a few hours ago."

"I have it," says Watson. "You are Cicero."

"Good lord, no," says Tom. "Why would I want to be someone as boring as all that?"

"Petronius perhaps," says Kit, "or Ovid?"

"Isn't he clever?" says Tom to the others. "It's the trimming on my robe that gives it away, isn't it? I mean, the border of tiny hearts."

"Ah, *Amores,* of course," says Watson. "How subtle!"

Walsingham offers Pallant his arm. "Come, my mysterious Mary," he says. "I will introduce you to some of the other guests. Perhaps they will be able to discover your secret."

Pallant smiles and takes Tom's arm. The others follow, Kit walking with exaggerated formality as they wander among the kings and queens, among wise men, heroes, and disciples of Christ.

"George Chapman has made a small entertainment for us, which I am sure you will all enjoy," says Walsingham. "And then there will be music and food and general merriment on into the night. It is our one big effort of the season."

William Fleetwood, "Leicester's mad recorder," turns suddenly away from one group only to intrude himself, quite by accident, into Tom Walsingham's group. He looks like a startled monkey with his black mask. He coughs, grumbles, apologizes, tries to escape, but is caught by the arm by Tom, who introduces him to the Watsons and the mysterious Mary. Having thrown them together, he turns away with Kit. Fleetwood is a man in his fifties, a conscientious and rather severe judge, a bit mad on the subject of vagrants, priests and papists. Like Watson he is a man of wit, and it is not long before he and the poet manage a civilized discussion.

Unfortunately, it is almost wrecked by Mary's flirtatious smile. In the little holes of Fleetwood's black mask one can see his small eyes darting from Tom Watson to the sexy Virgin Mary. He does not suspect that the bulges that are her bosom are, in reality, a pair of enormous and delicious Spanish oranges.

Among the guests is Lord Burghley, accompanied by his fifteen-year-old ward, the third Earl of Southampton, a lad of exquisite platinum-blond beauty. Robert Cecil is there, not as Richard the Third, after all, in spite of the physical resemblance. Also with Lord Burghley is his nephew Francis Bacon, a man in his late twenties, generally acknowledged to be brilliant if a bit unorthodox. He and his cousin Robert do not always see eye to eye.

Sir Francis Walsingham is there, of course, in black, as usual, refusing to play games. He is engaged in quiet conversation with his brother-in-law Robert Beale, whose only concession to costuming is a rather ridiculous turban with a glass ruby in it. With Sir Francis came also the old poet Thomas Churchyard, now almost seventy and close to poverty, in spite of all his military services to this country, his courtly pageants and his most recent book, *The Worthiness of Wales*. Still another member of Sir Francis's contingent is Thomas Phelippes.

Of the poets present, three arrived together: Gabriel Harvey, Edward Dyer, and Robert Sidney. They have thrown themselves into the spirit of the occasion and have come as Arthurian knights, presumably prepared to defend the faith with razor-sharp pens against those lesser poets, those tavern wits, who would violate all the classical rules and play to the rabble merely to keep alive—a vulgar ambition, indeed.

With Walter Ralegh came Ferdinand Stanley (Lord Strange) and Thomas Harriot, recently back from the Roanoke settlement in Virginia and full of facts and anecdotes.

Circulating freely in this illustrious Elizabethan circle are some Thornboroughs, some Sheltons, including the beautiful Audrey, and poor John Lyly, who has come specifically to persuade everyone that he should be the next Master of the Revels after

Tilney. He has come as a court jester, but his complicated syntax strangles his wit, and he proves to be rather boring.

Tom Walsingham takes Kit aside and says, "Now tell me, Christopher, who is this Mary of yours? You are up to something bad. I can see the devil in your eye. What is she to you?"

"To me?" says Kit, all innocence. "Why, she's nothing to me at all—except, of course, the Virgin Mary. Rather a marvelous-looking creature, don't you think?"

"I don't mind a little joke, Kit," says Tom, "but please don't embarrass me. I invited you here to meet some very important people and to help you gain a little respectability and prestige. Now don't ruin it."

"I promise, Tom, on my word of honor," he says. "I will behave myself in a gentlemanly and kingly fashion. After all, I am an Eastern potentate, as you can see, humped all the way from Persia by a camel in my regal rags. Come, introduce me to someone—anyone. I will charm him all to pieces. How about that sweet boy with the golden hair? Who is he?"

"He happens to be none other than Henry Wriothesley," says Tom, "third Earl of Southampton."

"He may be an earl, but he's a pretty boy," says Kit.

"Well, you stay away from that pretty boy," says Tom. "Lord Burghley is his guardian, and he guards him well."

"Perhaps I should dedicate a poem to him," says Kit. "Does he like poetry?"

With brass horns the musicians announce the formal entertainment prepared for this occasion by George Chapman. Tom's conversation with Kit is interrupted.

A group of musicians and dancers come in through the main door and perform in the center of the room, almost amidst the guests. They are costumed as nymphs, satyrs, and sileni, their simple veils and robes decorated with miscellaneous jewelry, their faces covered with elaborate masks.

"We must have a better look at this," says Tom. "After all, I *am* the host. Come."

They move politely through the crowd of guests until they are at the edge of the circle. There they find George Chapman, creator of the entertainment, a congenial smile on his face. "Ah, Thomas," he says. "I was looking for you. I do hope you enjoy this. It's been great fun putting it together."

Chapman and Kit greet each other politely. They are only slight acquaintances. "You may have to explain to your host what's going on," says Kit. "He's not well versed in this sort of erudition."

"Oh, there's nothing very erudite about it," says Chapman. "The dancing nymphs and satyrs are being led in by Hermes. They are singing to the audience and inviting them, a bit symbolically, to take part in thir revels. There was a time when the guests would have joined in, but it's no longer done that way, as you know."

The guests show their appreciation noisily and seem almost inclined to join in the revels of these mythological characters. A group of torchbearers enter and are followed by a gorgeously attired woman on a litter born by attendants in improbable and slightly Oriental costumes. "Diana," explains Chapman to his host.

"Inevitably," says Kit, but Chapman seems not to hear him. He is absorbed in his own creation and preoccuppied with impressing Walsingham. "You see, there's to be a song contest between the mountain gods Cithaeron and Helicon, each of whom represents a distinctly different school of art. Diana herself will be the judge."

"What a marvelous idea," says Tom.

"But hardly original," says Kit.

"Only the idea is borrowed," says Chapman. "It belongs to Corinna, the poetess of Tanagra in the fifth century before Christ. Hence the title—*Corinna*. That's credit enough, don't you think?" he says to Kit.

"If Diana doesn't mind, I certainly don't," says Kit.

"Are you suggesting, by any chance, certain contemporary parallels?" Tom asks.

"Ah, I leave that to the imagination," says Chapman.

Cithaeron and Helicon appear. Since they are gods, their attire is extravagant. Cithaeron wears a fur-lined, bejeweled blood-red robe, and his false blond hair falls to his shoulders. A radiation of golden rods decorates his head, suggesting the rays of the sun. Helicon is all in white silk, with a velvet cap studded with pearls. The dancing ends, and Diana recites the rules of the competition in rather disappointing and stiff couplets.

"I've never seen a real god before," says Kit. "Is that what they look like?"

"Mr. Marlowe," says Chapman, "it is a spectacle, not a piece of theology."

"Never mind him, George," says Tom. "He's been carrying on with old Bacchus."

They are all amused and turn their attention to the stage gods, who are now reciting in turn like mad. Not all of it is awful poetry, but instantly Kit understands that Chapman has pitted one modern school against another, and he knows which one is destined to lose. From time to time they break into song and are accompanied by their respective supporters of nymphs and satyrs.

"I think it's absolutely wonderful," says Tom Walsingham and keeps turning to Chapman to nod his approval. "Well done! Well done!" The guests agree and punctuate the performance with applause.

At last the judgment is made. All eyes are on Diana. That she is the queen of these revels no one can deny. That she is also intended to be the current Queen of England is equally obvious, and everyone is quite delighted, even Kit, who ordinarily has nothing but contempt for this kind of display.

When it is over, the participants join the guests. They are not players in the ordinary sense. They are amateurs and socially appropriate to the occasion. All during the performance there were whispered attempts at identification. The two celebrations amalgamate into one, and soon it is impossible to tell the original guests from the visitors out of ancient Greece and out of the imagination of George Chapman. He is very pleased with himself. He and Tom and Kit become dispersed, distracted by introductions and shifting conversations.

More food and drink are brought in. The music continues. Some of the guests break into impromptu dances. Female laughter rings in the room over the deeper sounds of satisfaction made by the men. There are some chairs and tables on the perimeter of the room, but most people prefer to stand and move about freely. There are some quiet conversations. Perhaps even some business is being transacted. Certainly there is much political talk and much discussion of the significance of Chapman's song competition. Did he have in mind those hexameters of Mr. Harvey? some wonder. Others are so ignorant of poetry they cannot tell a hexameter from an Irish jig.

Kit falls into a conversation with Thomas Harriot, who is talking about the Indians of the Roanoke settlement in Virginia. So fascinating is he that he soon attracts a rather large circle—too large, in fact, for Kit, who slips away to refill his glass.

He finds himself alone, unable to connect, as though he is a foreigner and cannot speak the language. The hall is hot. He is momentarily muddled. Sweat from his throbbing forehead and temples makes little trails in the black powder on his face. He feels suddenly ridiculous and oddly afraid. The grotesque masks and the blazing costumes swirl about him in a nightmarish dance. Lacquered papier-mâché faces. Frozen smiles. Ghastly shrill laughter. Genghis Khan bobbing like a puppet. Lucretia Borgia, bleeding at the mouth, laughing through blue eyes. And Leda afloat on a sea of tremulous silk. A wave of desperation swells in him, rises, folds over itself and breaks against his chest. He takes a deep breath and tugs at his tight collar. His eyes search for the door. He forgets for a moment where it is. He talks to himself. He calms himself. He repeats his own name over and over. It's all very simple, he says. Turn to the nearest person. Smile. Say something—anything! The sea of faces parts for an instant, and there, miles and miles away, across the room, stands the tall and enchanting Lady of Samaria, Ann Watson. She is staring at him, waving at him, moving toward him. And then the sea closes again and swallows her up. When she appears again she is standing beside him, holding his hand and whispering to him, "Kit, darling, are you all right?"

"I'm not sure," he says. "Such a confusion of characters." He forces a laugh. "I had a feeling that the house was going to collapse on us. I mean, I wish it would. And kill us all."

"Is it as bad as all that?" she says. "I thought you were having a good time."

"Oh, I am, I am," he says. "But I couldn't remember for a moment why I was here."

"Why, to see and be seen," she says, taking him by the arm. "Come, we'll talk to poor Thomas Churchyard. See how they've abandoned him in his old age."

The antique poet is standing alone with a glass of wine in his hand. His wasted body is a skeleton in the musty outfit of an artillery officer, relics of his youthful adventures in Her Majesty's service. Ann goes up to him boldly and says, "Mr. Churchyard, how good to see you again. Do you remember me? Tom Watson's wife?"

"Oh, of course, of course," he says. And then, suddenly, they are joined by Robert Cecil, who has with him Audrey Shelton. There are some introductions as Kit considers the interesting contrast between Robert's ugliness and Audrey's beauty. Audrey, by some strange coincidence, has chosen to come as Dido, Queen of Carthage. Her costume is an expensive creation, more appropriate to courtly occasions than to this lesser celebration. Her conversation is almost wholly devoted to the old poet, but her even more charming eyes are surreptitiously devoted to the young man about whom she has heard so much from Tom Walsingham.

"I am fond of reading," she says, "especially when we are in one of our country places. You know how it is in the country, I'm sure. Not really very much to do, and so many boring people. The men are always out hunting or examining properties or building things. And in the evening they drink entirely too much. And then before ten they are all exhausted and drag themselves off to bed, their heads swimming with pigs and porticos and port."

She is barely twenty, but she has the poise and wit of an older woman. Her skin is very white, her hair very black, her bosom full and generously displayed. Her height and form are extremely feminine, and the high sweetness of her voice is matched by the softness of her whole aspect. Only in her large eyes might one detect something beyond the ordinary woman—an intelligence, a smiling shrewdness, and another quality, an unnamable but distinctly unfeminine quality. Kit is fascinated and welcomes his exclusion from the conversation. Finally Robert Cecil puts an orthodox end to the brief encounter and leads his lady away.

Kit's attention drifts across the room to the beautiful Earl of Southampton, who now, surrounded by only two or three people, seems, for the first time, approachable.

Christopher Marlowe, black potentate of the East and magician of Babylon, discoverer of the Christ Child and author of *Tamburlaine*, moves without excuses through imitations of mythology toward the golden boy, from whom now fall away two more parasitical pharaohs, leaving only one unconvincing Robin Hood— actually Francis Bacon, the bright and ambitious cousin of Robert Cecil. They are alone in quiet conversation when Kit, who knows neither one of them, moves in with a predatory smile. He is about to introduce himself when Southampton breaks off his conversation with Francis and says, "Don't tell me, let me guess. I like games."

Francis Bacon eyes his competition for the attentions of this very influential young man. "Something Moorish, no doubt," he says.

"No, no," says Southampton. "More likely Nubian. One of those sooty kings out of remote history. I should know more about these things, but they are cramming me so full of Aristotle at St. John's that I don't really know anything."

"Let me help you, then," says Kit. "My friends and I, navigating by the stars, across a sea of sand, arrived here this very day, bearing gifts for a special child who they say will leave his mark upon the world. Is that a sufficient hint?"

"Too much of a hint, I am afraid," says Francis.

"You're too clever for me, Francis," says Southampton. "He should be a king, but he's so black."

"Perhaps he came down the chimney with his incense," says Francis. "Or was it myrrh?"

"Actually," says Kit, "I came by way of Canterbury and was quite white until I arrived in London."

The game has gone far enough as far as Francis Bacon is concerned. He turns like an impatient schoolmaster to the young earl and says, "Dear Henry, what *do* they teach you at St. John's? Surely you know that one of the three kings who arrived in Bethlehem was black. And this young man, whoever he is, is that black king. Gaspar, is it? Or Balthasar?"

"Take your pick," says Kit. "They were probably all fairly dark. Besides, it hardly matters. It's only a masquerade. The room is so full of Magi tonight it practically trembles with miracles. But there is still but one star in this room worth following, sir, and you are that star. May I beg the honor of your acquaintance?"

Southampton laughs boyishly. "Well put, whoever you are. But let us have introductions. I am Henry Wriothesley. This is Francis Bacon. And you?"

"I am Christopher Marlowe," he says.

"But of course," says Southampton. "I should have known. You have quite a reputation at Cambridge. Corpus Christi, wasn't it?"

"Yes," says Kit, "Corpus Christi. Six years of labor in the mines of the mind."

"And now a scribbler for the public theatres," says Francis.

Kit cannot conceal the anger that flashes from his dark eyes. "And how am I to take that remark, sir?" he says.

"Take it, Christopher, with my apologies. I have seen your *Tamburlaine* and should not classify you with the—what shall I say? The gang of starving entertainers who for a few shillings or pounds will grind out any absurdity to titillate the vulgar mob. They make a mockery of genuine poetry. If art were a religion, their motley efforts would be sins against the Holy Ghost."

"But, Mr. Bacon," says Kit, "art *is* a religion."

Southampton, his blue eyes full of bright innocence, his face as smooth as a child's, turns to Francis and says, "Is that a proper thing to say? I mean, has he spoken a heresy of some kind to call art a religion?"

"It is certainly not the state religion," says Kit.

"The understatement of the evening," says Francis.

"Tell us about your costume," says Kit.

"It was John Florio's idea," says Southampton. "I mean, I come as an Italian courtier. He has me reading Castiglione. You know, *Libro del cortegiano.* I know one is not supposed to admire the Italians too much these days—because of their religion and all that. But, frankly, I find them fascinating. So civilized. So intelligent. I adore Florio. He is the most brilliant man I have ever met."

"And you?" says Kit to Bacon. "Who are you supposed to be?"

"Why, Robin Hood," says Bacon, "as you can plainly see by my costume."

"Was he the gentleman who robbed from the poor and gave to the rich?" says Kit. "Or was it the other way around?"

They are interrupted by Lord Burghley and Tom Walsingham. The conversation turns stiff and formal. Lord Burghley is almost three score and ten. Age has shortened and squared him a bit, but it has not dulled his mind. His eyebrows arch over his blue eyes in an expression of eternal observation and understanding. Nothing escapes him. Is it any wonder, then, that, with half a shoulder turned to Marlowe, he addresses himself almost exclusively to Francis Bacon and Southampton. "Tell us, Francis," he says, "about this entertainment you're giving for Her Majesty next month at Greenwich. I hear it's going to be quite magnificent. Something about King Arthur."

"It's called *The Misfortunes of Arthur,*" says Francis. "It will be presented to Her Majesty by the gentlemen of Gray's Inn. I mustn't take too much credit for it. Thomas Hughes really wrote it. I am helping to devise the dumb-shows, along with Christopher Yelverton and John Lancaster."

"Is it a play, then?" says Tom Walsingham.

"Not really," says Francis. "It's closer to pageantry. A series of scenes and devices in the life of Arthur."

"Sounds a bit old-fashioned," says Kit, speaking almost over the shoulder of Lord Burghley, who does not give ground to allow him further into the conversation—a true guardian of his handsome young ward. Burghley, too, has heard of Marlowe's reputation at Cambridge.

When they are alone, Walsingham says to Kit, "You should know better than to intrude yourself where you are not wanted. People of that sort are very wary of strangers—and flattery."

"People of what sort?" says Kit, looking beyond Tom with the raised eyebrows of a bored aristocrat.

"You know damn well what I mean," says Tom.

"You mean people of *your* sort," says Kit. "Besides, I was only carrying on a civilized conversation with young Henry what's-his-name and that lawyer nephew of the Lord Treasurer."

"They are not families to tamper with."

"It's not the family I'd like to tamper with."

"Sometimes, Christopher, you try my patience."

"In all fairness," says Kit, "I should allow you to try mine, but fortunately I have none. I'm not very good at sitting still."

"If you're so restless," says Tom, "then go and find yourself some street boy. Have yourself a drunken fling and sleep it off. But don't play the fool in my house."

"I can think of no better place to play the fool, considering how courtly your atmosphere is tonight. And isn't that why I am here, after all? Tom Walsingham's little poet. His monkey-on-a-stick. If I am a good fellow, you will toss me a piece of fruit. And if I am naughty, you will take back my velvet breeches, not to mention your patronage."

"Whatever I have given you, Christopher, I cannot take back."

"And what exactly have you given me?"

"My friendship," says Tom. "My affection."

"And—?" says Kit.

"And my influence," says Tom.

"I half-expected you to say your love," says Kit.

"I think, in the long run, that you will find my influence more useful than my love."

A few minutes later, Kit locates his vagrant Virgin Mary and leads her quietly out of the house. "Where are we going?" asks Robert Pallant in his female voice.

"Back to The Leopard's Head," says Kit, "to drink ourselves to death among some real people. I'm sick of all these masks."

viii

Barn Elms, July 22, 1588. Small lights burn near midnight in the study of Sir Francis Walsingham. The gusty wind out of the southwest plays in the summer plumage of the invisible trees, tugs at the shutters, and moans in the chimneys like a locked-out ghost.

The household has gone to bed, except for Sir Francis himself, his aide, Thomas Phelippes, and his secretary, Laurence Tomson. Sleep is an elusive mistress for the Secretary of State in these critical days. He no longer even tries to court her, though he is drawn with exhaustion and the constant discomfort of his old malady. Fortunately, after a period of seclusion and treatment, he is somewhat improved, but he has sensed for some time now that the weeds of death have driven their roots deep into the substance of his body. The candlelight shadows sketch in his face the outlines of a skeleton beneath his pale and diminishing flesh.

Were it not for a greater danger than mere mortality, his thoughts might sink into personal preoccupations. It is not his own life or death that keeps him up into the dark hours, but the life or death of his nation—of England. The situation with Spain has come to a head. They are, indeed, at war, and in his hands, more than in the hands of the army or the navy or even the Queen herself, rests the responsibility of determining the right course of action and of organizing the country's defenses. Because he is the intermediary between the Queen and the Privy Council, everything passes through his hands: all reports from the fleet, all reports from the land forces, such as they are, in the various camps and deployments, all information from agents and ambassadors abroad and at home, and all requisitions for funds, for victuals, for munitions and supplies.

"We are ill-prepared for this conflict," he says for the hundredth time. He is seated at a large table, a gaunt figure in puritan black, trimmed and formal, containing in the tightness of his expression not only his personal pain but all these thousand facts and figures, these digested reports and messages, the peculiar moods and vacillations of his Queen, the maneuvers of Burghley and Leicester and other influential figures, and lists in his mind of work still to be done.

"You must try to get some rest," says his secretary, Laurence Tomson. He is himself very weary. His lids droop. His hand, still clutching a pen, is cramped. There is a long silence. Thomas Phelippes sits calmly to the right of Sir Francis, unmarked by the long hours of working and waiting, apparently unmoved by the unfolding drama, his phenomenal mind ready to receive, to collate, to disgorge treasuries and dung heaps of data. He is indispensable.

Sir Francis looks toward the draped windows and the sound of rustling leaves in the night beyond. "I don't suppose there's been a shift in the wind," he says.

"South-southwest," says Phelippes, with the certainty of a man who knows what he's talking about.

"That means the fleet is still pinned in at Plymouth," says Sir Francis. "How long has it been now?"

"They arrived back on the twelfth of this month," says Phelippes. "And this is the twenty-second. Ten days now since they had to give up the offensive against the Spanish coast."

"If the Spaniards have put to sea again," says Sir Francis, "we will have no choice but to take up purely defensive positions."

"They would be fools not to be at sea at this very moment," says Phelippes. "And with the wind at their backs it is a wonder that they are not at this very moment on our coasts."

"Perhaps they have been delayed, after all," offers Tomson. "For repairs and supplies, I mean. At Corunna."

They have been over and over the problem a hundred times, but still Sir Francis, shifting maps and papers on his table, says, "Let us review the situation once more before we give it up for the night. Let's go back to May twentieth. We have reliable reports that it was on that day that the Spanish fleet set sail. Sometime earlier we had what is supposed to be a copy of Santa Cruz's own detailed report on his ships, his stores, and his forces. This is Anthony

Standen's report. Tom, is there any chance that we have been misled as to the size of this fleet?"

"I have no reason to doubt the accuracy of this information," says Phelippes, "though it is always possible that something has gone wrong. Pompeo Pellegrini has been one of our most reliable agents. As Anthony Standen, he left England some twenty years ago. For some time he has been in the service of the Grand Duke of Tuscany, where he is highly regarded. He himself placed the agent in the household of the Marquis of Santa Cruz, the Grand Admiral of the Spanish Fleet and predecessor to Sidonia in this venture."

"You do not think, then, that we were fed an erroneous report?" says Sir Francis. "It seems somewhat incredible to me that so huge a force as that described in Standen's report should prove to be so elusive. They left Lisbon, presumably on the twentieth of May. They probably put into Corunna for some refitting. But then some fragments of the armada were sighted off the Scilly Islands, at the very mouth of the Channel. What were they doing there? Was it the main force? Or were they stray ships, driven off course by bad weather?"

"Our best reports indicate that the entire fleet was to rendezvous off the Scilly Islands," says Phelippes. "But now it seems that those plans were wrecked by the weather. Seymour was stationed in the Channel. And when Howard finally put out from Plymouth to intercept these ships, he couldn't locate them. They no doubt were forced back to Corunna with the rest of the scattered fleet. Drake scoured the French coast with ten ships, but still no Spaniards."

"Isn't it possible," says Sir Francis, "that only a portion of their fleet put into Corunna and that the rest of them regrouped elsewhere and are perhaps at this very moment sailing north?"

"If they are," says Phelippes, "we will know about it before very long. And since time is on our side, I don't think they will delay much longer. They cannot afford to sustain such a force for very long. While we, on the other hand—"

Sir Francis tosses aside a map and shouts, "While we pinch pennies and listen to Lord Burghley and The Queen grumbling about taxes and expenses! It was not until the Spanish had actually put to sea that we were allowed to mobilize the fleet and raise troops. And at the slightest hint of peace or even delay we will be stripped again of what little we have. How in God's name are we supposed to fight a war of survival when the woman who rules us is counting her coins and crying poverty?"

He slumps into his chair with a heavy sigh and covers his eyes for a moment with his hand, as though to regain his poise and control. "I'm sorry," he says. "We must, of course, do the best with what we have. But let us pray to God Almighty that we can prevent the enemy from setting foot on English soil. Whatever troops they have will cut to ribbons those unarmed, untrained, ragged mobs we call our army. And if, by some chance, the Duke of Parma is able to move his forces across the Channel, we will indeed be in grave trouble. We must keep them at sea. There we can manage them. There, if our dear sovereign allows us sufficient food and ships, we will be more than a match for them with their lumbering floating fortresses. We can outrun them. We can outfire them a quarter of a mile. We can cut them off from Parma or drive them north through the Channel." He pauses. Silence descends for a long moment. The candles flicker. The unpredictable wind haunts the night. "But if only—if only we had been allowed months ago to carry the fight to them. What a difference it would have made!"

He leans over a map, his slender finger making configurations in the seas between Spain and England, as though he is hunting for the enemy's ships. "With all our sources of information," he says, "why can't we be more sure of their movements?"

"We have people in Corunna, but it takes time," says Phelippes. "Besides, everything has happened so quickly in the past few weeks that we can be certain of nothing unless we see it with our own eyes. No doubt a new rendezvous point has been selected—perhaps only a matter of days ago. And my guess is that it is not far from the original place. They will prefer the first landfall."

"You don't think they will try to put ashore some men in Cornwall?" says Sir Francis.

"There is no indication at all that they are prepared to do anything but provide an armed escort for Parma's troops in the

Low Countries. They have been, thus far, enormously unimaginative. I don't see why they should suddenly be visited with any
special inspirations. Besides, with Ralegh in the West Country it is
not likely that they will want to squander their meager forces there.
No, they need Parma. Without him, their whole cause is lost."

Sir Francis sighs again. His thin lips twitch into a sad smile.
"Isn't it ironic, gentlemen," he says, "that the thing we have most
to dread at this point is that Her Majesty will negotiate a
last-minute peace settlement? Even now we are at the conference
table with Parma."

"There's little fear of that," says Phelippes. "They are too far
committed. They have been fanatically committed for years. They
never intended to arrange a peace. They have been stalling for
time. They have won the diplomatic war."

"Through no fault of ours," says Sir Francis. "Had Drake been
allowed to follow up his raids at Cadiz and along the coast, we
would have destroyed them in their own waters. But here we are
now with our backs to the wall because our Queen was deluded into
believing that she could bring about a settlement. Incredible! A
settlement with Philip! Even while the presses in Antwerp were
running off a roaring hellish papal bull denouncing Her Majesty
again as a bastard and usurper of the Catholic throne. Even while
those cumbersome forces were gathering in Lisbon and the Pope
was donating a million ducats to the cause. God forgive me for
saying it, but sometimes I think Her Majesty has lost her reason
and that her inability to part with money is a disease."

"Unfortunately," says Phelippes, "there are many who agree
with her."

"They have been spoiled by too many years of peace," says Sir
Francis. "They have grown fat and complacent. They imagine that
because we are an island we are invincible. But let us face it: we
have no army. We are a nation of farmers and weavers and
shopkeepers. And whatever navy we now have we owe to the
pressures and persuasions of Howard and Hawkins and Drake." He
pounds the table. "She has crippled and castrated all the good men

on whom we most depend—Leicester and Ralegh and Drake. She's a stubborn, acquisitive, indecisive old woman."

"You cannot blame her, sir, for being a woman," says Phelippes. His calm, intelligent smile is not lost on Sir Francis. They tacitly agree that what they need at a time such as this is a man on the throne, a strong man, but they can say no more.

"It is very late," says Tomson. "Past midnight now. The Privy Council meets at Richmond in the morning."

"Yes, yes, I know," says Sir Francis. "We have had enough of this for one night. Our brains are beginning to thicken with fatigue. Go to bed. Go! I need a little time alone and then, I promise you, I too will rest. This unfortunate body of mine drags me down. I would give all I own to trade it for a healthy frame so that I could bear the weight of that new suit of armor of mine and join the forces in the field."

"You are worth ten thousand troops, sir, right here at this table," says Phelippes. "Besides what you have given personally already: fifty lances, ten petronels, two hundred foot-soldiers. More than anyone in England except for Hatton and Essex. And you can ill afford it."

"You put it too mildly, dear Tom," says Sir Francis. "The truth is that I have nothing left—nothing! Only this corpse I carry around to contain my brains. Now go. Please! Give me a moment's peace that I may gather myself for sleep."

They go out, leaving Walsingham alone at his cluttered table amidst half-consumed candles, some of which have already died. He listens once more to the wind. He does not have to go to the window to know that it is still unchanged.

His hands are folded limply in his lap. He tries to pray but cannot. His mind is anchored in the earthly details of his overwhelming burden.

Eventually the silence soothes him, and he begins to droop into sleep, still seated in his chair, still formal in his appearance. He has a vision of Sidonia's fleet. He smells the sea and feels the pitch and roll of those lumbering ships. Facts and fantasies mingle. Nineteen thousand two hundred and ninety Castilian and Portuguese soldiers. Eight thousand three hundred and fifty sailors. One thousand gentlemen volunteers, from every household in Spain. Hundreds of monks and priests. Servants and surgeons. Thousands of Turks and Moors at the oars. A floating army. A hundred and thirty ships. Galleons and galleasses, merchantmen and carracks, Portuguese East Indiamen, pinnaces and supply ships. And above them all the standard of the fleet from the high altar of the Cathedral of Lisbon. All of Catholic Europe seems to be rolling toward him. He sees it as though from the shore—a huge tidal wave, white-crested and mountainous, foam flying heavenward, curling, rising, the wind that drives it howling obscenities. In his deeper sleep he is a child again, running on a rocky beach to escape the roaring wave. Chalky cliffs rise behind him and merge with the billowing clouds. He slips. He falls. He cries out and is answered only by a wailing gull that swoops on the currents of air and then rises in a shaft of sunlight to disappear in the sky.

He is startled out of his sleep and looks around the empty room, relieved to find himself in the security of his familiar home. He lectures himself in Laurence Tomson's voice: "You must rest, sir. You must rest." He rises slowly and goes to the window. He draws aside the drapes and looks out into the darkness, but he can see nothing. Before long the dawn will silhouette the noisy trees and the birds will announce another day.

He is halfway up the stairs to his room when there is a commotion in the courtyard. He hears the sound of a man on horseback and then voices. He waits, his pulse throbbing in his neck. He can almost guess what it is.

Doors open and close. Lights go on. Footsteps approach in the hallway leading to his study. He looks down from the staircase and sees Phelippes. "Here," he calls out, and his aide, still fully clothed, approaches with a letter in his hand. He pauses at the foot of the stairs, and Sir Francis comes down. Together they go into the study to find adequate light.

There Walsingham reads the letter while Phelippes stands by. "It's from Howard," he says. "The Spanish fleet is off the Lizard and prepared to move up the Channel. In spite of the weather he has gotten his ship out of Plymouth and moved to the windward of them. He says, 'The southerly wind that brought us back from the coast of Spain brought them out. God blessed us with turning us back. Sir, for the love of God and our country, let us have with some speed some great shot sent us of all bigness, for this service will continue long, and some powder with it.' "

He hands the letter to Phelippes, who reads it over. "Rouse Laurence and the others," says Sir Francis. "We have urgent messages to send."

ix

"I saw a ship a-sailing,
A-sailing on the sea,
And oh! it was all laden
With pretty things for thee!

There were comfits in the cabin,
And apples in the hold,
The sails were made of silk,
And the masts were made of gold.

The four-and-twenty sailors
That stood between the decks,
Were four-and-twenty white mice,
With chains about their necks.

The captain was a duck,
With a packet on his back;
And when the ship began to move,
The captain said, 'Quack! Quack!' "

On the road to Dover, Robert Greene sings this song about Sir Francis Drake, much to the amusement of his traveling companions, not one of which is absolutely sober. They are Tom Nashe, George Peele, Richard Tarleton, and Thomas Lodge.

"The Spanish call him El Dragoneta," says Peele, who is the same age as Roberto and easily matches him in dissipation if not rapidity of composition. Nevertheless, when his purse is panting for a shilling and his throat is dry, he can rattle off half an act a night by candlelight of what-you-will: biblical, historical, romantic or comical. And with considerable learning to boot, sporting as he does an M.A. from Oxford. In his more serious moments he has a genuine passion for poetry, but, as his friend and enemy Stephen Gosson has so aptly said of him, "His discipline is insufficient, though his gifts are great." There are puffs of flesh under his eyes, and he is a burden to his hired horse. He laughs from his belly and stops often to urinate.

The reformed and righteous Mr. Gosson has made his comment too on Thomas Lodge. He is, he has said, "haunted by the heavy hand of God." A graduate of Trinity College, Oxford, and Lincoln's Inn, he is as learned as his colleagues. His father was the Lord Mayor of London, and, were it not for the fact that he is a Catholic, he might have risen in arenas other than the precarium of the literary world. He falls periodically under suspicion and is asked, from time to time, to hold himself available for questioning by the Privy Council. He is not sure that it is wise for him to leave London in these crucial times, but he has been unable to resist the carnival atmosphere of the great trek to the coast to catch a glimpse of the Spanish fleet.

"Quack! Quack!" echoes Tarleton to Roberto's song.

"Our captain may be a duck," says Peele, "but he will tear to shreds those lumbering Spanish ships and put the poor fanatics to the sword."

"Quack! Quack!" says Greene.

"He's a bloated bladder and a Braggadocchio," says Lodge. "If he is pricked by a Spanish pike, God knows what foul things will be unleashed on the world."

"He's the best captain who ever put to sea," says Peele.

"I'll drink to that," says Roberto, helping himself from a wineskin without pausing to stop. The joggling of his horse makes

it almost impossible for him to drink. The wine runs down his face
and into his red beard.

They have come down the river from London to Gravesend,
where, after a night at an inn, they hired their horses. They are
near Dover now, but their progress has been slow and their needs
enormous. They have been three days en route, moving with
considerably less speed than the Spanish fleet.

Every young gentleman in London who can manage it, or who is
not otherwise engaged in military preparations, seems to have
joined the parade to the coast, with Dover as the principal gathering
place.

Dover! One of the cinque ports. A mere eighteen miles from the
European continent. The town is nestled in a valley through which
runs the Dour River, and rising on all sides are the high chalk cliffs,
one of which is dominated by the great Castle of Dover. There is no
better vantage point from which to view the drama that promises to
unfold. On a clear day, one can actually see the coast of France
across the Dover Straits.

But it is more than merely its geography that commends this
busy port; it is also its sufficiency of taverns, its mixture of peoples,
its shops, its ships, its merchants and sailors.

There is, of course, no room at any of the inns. Private homes
are thrown open—for a price. The cost of everything is double
what it was a week earlier. Normal schedules mean nothing. Lights
burn through the night. Bells ring. Troops are mustered, wagons
clatter in the narrow streets, artillery pieces are hauled up steep
hills, slip, stall, are hauled again by the thoroughly whipped horses.
And in the taverns, drunken laughter mingles with sober conversations and hot disputes about what the Spanish will do next, and in
which of a dozen ways they will be met, dispersed, and destroyed by
Howard and Seymour and Drake.

Among those who have come to Dover for the spectacle is Kit
Marlowe. With him is Tom Watson. Their problems are simplified
by the fact that Kit still has an aging grandmother in Dover.

They are welcomed cautiously by the old widow and her son,

Thomas Arthur, Kit's uncle, who has come out from Canterbury for the same reason as everyone else.

"Your father and I have volunteered as bowmen," says Thomas. He is a more serious version of his brother-in-law, John Marlowe. He offers this information in an accusative tone, as if to suggest that perhaps the younger Christopher should be doing something of the same sort.

"We are all doing our parts in London," says Kit, casting an amused glance at Tom Watson.

"And what parts might those be?" says Thomas Arthur.

"We listen to the sound of artillery all day long," says Kit. It is not really a lie, since there has been constant practice at the Artillery Grounds near Upper Moor Fields, not far from Holywell Lane and The Theatre.

"Have you gone into ordnance, then?" says Thomas Arthur.

"Oh, I can tell you everything you'd ever want to know about cannons," says Kit. "Not to mention demi-cannons, culverins, double cannons, basilisks, falcons, falconets, minions, sakers, and gambions."

"Amazing," says Thomas Arthur. "And I thought you was full of poetry and philosophics."

Kit assumes an air of patriotic devotion. "I would give up every one of my philosophics, Uncle," he says, "if the fate of my nation depended on it."

Tom Watson can barely keep himself from laughing. Instead he coughs and says, "I hope my coming along will not be too much of an intrusion upon your hospitality."

"Not at all," says Grandmother Arthur. She is a slight woman with small, sharp eyes who has not failed to appreciate the quality of the clothes that her grandson and his companion are wearing.

"Besides," says Thomas Arthur, "I've got to be back in Canterbury tomorrow. I had hoped that something significant would happen today, but they say the Spanish are miles away from the Straits and near the French shore. And, what's more, the weather's gone gray. John and I must stand ready to be called should there be a landing anywhere in Kent."

"That's unlikely, don't you think?" says Tom Watson.

"I wouldn't be too sure about that," says Thomas Arthur. "I wouldn't put it past them Spaniards to do the obvious thing. It's the shortest way across, and if Parma has his troops on barges they won't want to be on the water too long. There's rumors afoot that he might try to put across twenty thousand men all in one night. Not here, of course, against these cliffs; but farther up or farther down the coast. They say he could sail into the Medway River and try to take Rochester, but I hear there's been a great chain put across it."

"It's rather interesting, isn't it?" says Watson.

"Interesting!" says Thomas Arthur, frowning at the poet's cool detachment. "It's damned perilous, that's what it is."

It is not the Spaniards who invade Dover and Kent but an army of rumors. They gallop through the streets, fling open doors, shout into the taverns, visit insomniacs in the night, and put what little truth there is to the sword.

Anthony Munday, having eaten half of a rather large animal, lets escape some foul air and says, "On my way to the jakes I heard a man say there's been a landing on the Isle of Wight."

"Nonsense," says Stephen Gosson, whose eyes roam through the crowded room of The Dolphin. He has to lean forward to make himself heard. "You'll never guess who just came in," he says.

Munday looks toward the door. "Do my eyes deceive me, or is that Tom Watson and Christopher Marlowe?"

"Precisely," says Stephen Gosson. "They'll never find a place to sit down."

"Perhaps we should ask them to join us," says Munday.

"There isn't any room here," he says.

Less than a hundred yards away at The Anchor Inn, Robert Greene and his friends also listen to rumors. What's more, they invent a few of their own and send them like homing pigeons about the town and wait for them to return. "They say the great crescent has been broken somewhere between Eastbourne and Dieppe and that the Spanish fleet is routed." It is Thomas Lodge, pouring his imagination into the thirsty ears of a merchant at the next table.

"They say there are a thousand ships and that they will sail right up the Thames and with their great fifty-pounders destroy everything on both banks."

"They say that at this very moment the Duke of Parma is slipping out to sea in his troop barges under the cover of darkness."

"Medina Sidonia," they say, "has been visited by a vision of the Virgin Mary, who has promised him a great victory."

"Women were deceivers ever."

Roberto and an old sailor shout theoretical strategies into each other's faces, their noses but inches apart, their beards almost mingled, their breaths perfumed with rum. "I have seen those ships of Hawkins a-building," says the old salt. "The *White Bear*, the *Bonaventure*, the *Lion*, the *Revenge*. They are the fastest fighting ships in the world. They'll swoop at them Spaniards and let fly ten volleys to one. They'll sting the giant to death like a bunch of wasps. And there ain't nothing he can do about it."

"Sooner or later, though, they will have to come to grips," says Roberto. "Hand to hand and all that. You can't sink a Spanish galleon with a nine-pounder."

"They'll sink themselves with stupidity in the shallows of Dunkirk," says the sailor. "What do they know about those waters? What do they know about anything? And those little sea beggars, those Dutchmen, slipping in and out to nip them on the knees. You mark my words, young man . . ."

"Has it occurred to any of you military geniuses," says George Peele, "that we have no place to sleep tonight?"

"We don't plan to sleep," says Lodge. "We plan to stay up all night learning Spanish so that we may ingratiate ourselves to our new masters."

"Oh, treason! Treason!" shouts Dick Tarleton, and, from several tables away, Ingram Frizer and Nicholas Skeres break off their conversation to look in the direction of the theatrical noise.

"It's only those drunken play-makers from Shoreditch," says

Frizer, his hard face as expressionless as stone. "But mark it down! Mark it down!" and Skeres takes out a small black book and with a miniature pen records what he has heard of the conversation and who the speakers are. "The tallish one next to Dick Tarleton is Thomas Lodge," says Frizer. "He's been in trouble before."

"If it doesn't rain," says George Peele, "I suppose we can sleep on the beach or even in the streets."

"No need for that," says Tom Nashe. "I understand that Kit Marlowe is in town, staying with his old grandmother, Mary Arthur, in Mill Lane. He's trying to keep his good fortune all to himself—and his friend Tom Watson."

"That's downright unpatriotic," says Peele.

"I couldn't agree more," says Nashe. "We must pay him a visit and explain to him that desperate times call for desperate measures."

"He has a very mean temper," says Lodge. "Especially if he's been drinking."

"Ah, but on our side," says Nashe, "we have the strength of numbers and the weakness of wit."

"And he's got Tom Watson," says Lodge, "with whom I'd rather not cross swords."

"Or match wits," says Peele.

"Nevertheless," says Nashe, "friendship and proximity demand that we pay a call on our dear colleague. And, who knows—we may be met with compassion and an invitation to spend the night. Take along some bottles of manzanilla as a token of our affection for the young madman."

News reaches The Dolphin that the forty-six-gun *Rosario* has fallen into English hands. "They say it was carrying fifty-five thousand gold ducats and four hundred and eighteen sailors and soldiers. Ran afoul of its own neighbor. Broke its foremast and bowsprit." A great cheer goes up and cups are hoisted in the direction of the messenger, who is dusty and breathless enough to be convincing. True or not, it is the sort of thing that everyone hopes to hear.

"Do you suppose it's true?" says Tom Watson to Kit.

"I wasn't there," says Kit, "and I'm not about to believe anything I hear tonight."

"Would you believe that Tom Walsingham is at Dover Castle?"

"Oh? I thought he was up at Chatham, fiddling with his chain. What makes you think—?"

"When I was out this afternoon seeing about the horses," says Watson, "I came across a friend from Faversham. He says that Tom and his brother and some friends have ridden down for a few days to see things firsthand."

"Why didn't you say something earlier?" says Kit.

"I don't see that it matters. He'll be too busy to see us anyway."

"It's not *him* I want to see. It's the *war*. He could get us into the Castle grounds, I'm sure."

"And how exactly do you suggest we arrange it?"

Kit shrugs. "I don't know. Why don't we just walk up the hill in the morning and ask to see him?"

"It sounds too simple."

"We'll say that we have an urgent message for him from Chatham."

"That should do it," says Watson. "But what will the message be?"

"I don't know," says Kit. "We'll tell him that his chain has been tampered with during the night by a bunch of underwater Jesuits."

Their laughter is interrupted by the appearance of Stephen Gosson and Anthony Munday, who must pass their table as they leave. Awkward greetings are exchanged but very little conversation. When they are safely out the door, Tom Watson says, "Old Lazarus Piot himself in search of another pamphlet for the leeches of St. Paul's Churchyard. What do you suppose it will be this time?"

"Catholic lechery in the stews of Dover, no doubt," says Kit.

"The Theatre of the Misbegotten."

"A penny to a pound he's here on a government assignment."

"Speaking of which," says Tom, "I understand you were approached."

Kit smiles, the fire of wine dancing in his eyes. "Yes," he says, "by both sides."

"You're as bad as Robert Poley," says Tom. "Nobody knows for sure where his sympathies lie."

"He has no sympathies," says Kit. "He'll fiddle for anybody's penny. And what's more, he does his job well. He is the only honest man I know who is totally without principles."

"Well put, Mr. Machiavelli," says Tom, lifting his glass to his companion.

Outside the narrow house on Mill Lane, Roberto Greene and his cohorts lie in wait for Christopher Marlowe, alias Tamburlaine since his triumph in London. They have been told by Tom Arthur and his mother from an upper window that they cannot open the door to strangers in these dangerous times, "What with all the villainy, treason, and drunkenness afoot, we'll have our throats slit for our hospitality."

Thomas Lodge and George Peele are sitting on the ground against the wall. Dick Tarleton is rehearsing a jig and singing.

> "There was a maid came out of Kent,
>   Dainty love, dainty love;
> There was a maid came out of Kent,
>   Dangerous be;
> There was a maid came out of Kent,
> Fair, proper, small and gent,
> As ever upon the ground went,
>   For so should it be."

Roberto and Tom Nashe discuss with unsophisticated sophistry the problem of whether or not to open one of the three bottles of manzanilla that they, the Greeks bearing gifts, have brought with them. "Two's as good as three," says Greene, "to tempt our Trojan friend to fling wide his gates."

"No, no, no," says Nashe. "It's either one or three. One's a mere token, and as a symbol signifies much more. But three's that *more* and tangible and potable. Two's an awful compromise, the true pettiness that lies between genuine poverty and the grand gesture."

"You're too deep for me," says Roberto, leaning uncertainly toward Tom, who clutches the three bottles to his breast. "Politics was never my forte. Contemporary morality is my field and manzanilla is my drink. Crack open one of those little darlings before my devil strikes me dead."

Tom Lodge, speaking as though from a dream, says in a loud voice, "That which is gotten over the devil's back is spent under his belly; it comes running and departs flying with the wings of an eagle in the air." His head falls back onto his chest, and he is immune to argument.

The dispute over the manzanilla is abruptly halted by the appearance of Tom Watson and Kit Marlowe. They turn a corner arm in arm, and Kit calls out, "God's blood, the enemy has landed!" He tries to draw his sword but is restrained by Watson. But he is too far gone to be anything but congenial, especially at the sight of Tom Nashe and his little treasury of wine. He pounds on the door of his grandmother's house and announces himself boisterously. His uncle comes to an upstairs window and says, "Take your friends and yourself elsewhere. You can't come in."

"Open the door," shouts Kit, "or I'll burn the house down."

"Where do you think you're all going to sleep?" says Tom Arthur.

"It doesn't matter," says Kit. "The inns are full and the town is besieged. Give us one room. Just one."

Tom Arthur hurls a curse at his nephew and slams the window shut. But in another moment he is at the front door warning them in a loud whisper that his mother is asleep. "If you wake the poor woman, I'll toss the whole pack of you into the street for the night and report you to the constables to boot."

He lets them in reluctantly. Like naughty boys they shush each other elaborately and tiptoe clumsily into the dimly lighted house. Roberto sways, bows, and tries to kiss his hand, muttering something about honor and gratitude. "Take the downstairs room and mind your noise," Kit's uncle tells him and then retreats in his nightcap up the squeaky steps.

They are almost too exhausted to finish the three bottles of manzanilla, but they finally manage, falling one by one like swatted flies onto the bed, the chairs, and the rug.

x

The next day they discover that they have missed the most dramatic spectacle of the whole assault: the terrifying fire-ship attack on the anchored Armada off Calais. It panicked the Spaniards, scattered their ships, and left them open to the crucial battle that followed off Gravelines.

Tom Watson and Kit are the first to rise from the graveyard of a bedroom in the house on Mill Lane. They step across the corpses of their London friends and go to the window to see what all the commotion is about. The activities of the day before have resumed after what seems to Kit the shortest night in history. Everyone seems to be out of doors. There are wagons and horses and semi-uniformed, semi-armed troops. From the surrounding countryside, victuals pour into the town to repair the damage done in the inns and taverns the day before by hungry visitors, by hastily mustered military forces, and by shipworkers and sailors. Supply ships and pinnaces have put into the port to be replenished and to deliver information on the events of the early hours of August the eighth.

"Something seems to have happened while we were asleep," says Kit. His head is clogged as though with a small fog of its own, and there seems to be a drum beating behind his eyes. He goes to the washstand near the bed, across which lie Robert Greene and Dick Tarleton. He bends down, his face almost in the basin, and pours a pitcher of cold water over his head. He splutters and gasps and then sighs as the water drips back into the basin. The heat collected in his brains dissipates somewhat and the fog begins to lift. He dries himself vigorously, muttering, "That's better."

Tom Watson prefers the less drastic solution of a wet cloth, with which he wipes his face and the back of his neck. They pull their clothes together, comb out their hair, cough and spit and urinate into a nearly overflowing chamberpot and then agree that perhaps they are ready to face the world.

"But what about *them?*" says Tom as they are about to leave.

"My uncle will take care of them, I'm sure," says Kit, "before he leaves for Canterbury. He doesn't think much of writers or players or people from London or scholars or anybody else, as far as I can tell, except shopkeepers and clergymen. He'll have them out of here before long."

At a dockside tavern they force their way through the crowd that has gathered around two of the crewmen from one of the smaller ships that has been with the fleet since the beacons were lit in Cornwall and the English struggled against a perverse wind to get out of Plymouth. "We had heard they was off the Lizard," says one of the seamen, a middle-aged fellow, hard as oak and lean as a stray dog. His sun-wrinkled skin sinks into his cheeks, where his teeth are gone and his hairy brows and cheekbones almost meet to conceal his squinted eyes. He is treated to more ale and meat than he can consume in a month. When he breaks off his tale to drink or chew, his younger shipmate tosses in a brief comment. However, the younger man is always ready to defer to his more experienced, more articulate companion.

"But we didn't actually see them until they was off Dodman Point near Mevagissey. And, oh, what a sight it was, what with the sun goin' down behind them and all. They loomed there in the dying light, black as ghosts, a forest of masts, almost as far as the eye could see. It was a terrifyin' sight. We'd managed to put out some fifty ships all told, counting everything down to the last little pinnace. And them Spaniards looked in that light like two or three hundred—though we found out later on they was somewhat less. Well, we had all heard about their galleons and galleasses. Them four-foot-thick oaken sides and them thirty-pound culverins. We weren't about to get in close enough to be grappled by the likes of ships like the *San Marcos*, the *San Mateo*, and *Nuestra Señora del Rosario*. No, sir! We kept our distance, keepin' well to the leeward side of 'em. Around Eddystone we tested 'em with a few broadsides, our guns having the distance but not the impact. But they kept that crescent of theirs and just moved on up the Channel. It was like dogs nippin' at a bull. We wasn't sure exactly what we could do to 'em. If they kept that tight formation it looked as though they might get to Calais unharmed. On the other hand, our fleet was growing day by day as ships joined us out of the various Channel ports. We figured we could eventually count on Hawkins's eighteen galleons, some smaller galleons, and maybe a hundred and fifty merchantmen and another thirty or so pinnaces and frigates. But the problem always was how to hurt them without gettin' in too close. Like I say, it was a bit o' bull-baitin'. We annoyed the hell out of 'em but we didn't do much real damage. We circled 'em, we dogged 'em, we fired three or four volleys to their one. We wanted them to waste their ammunition. But they were smart—and patient. There was a lot of noise in them first few days, but nothing was decided, except maybe that we could tack into the wind and were faster and could generally take up any position on 'em we wanted.

"So we followed 'em and bothered 'em, followed 'em and bothered 'em. And then we took the *Rosario*, which ran afoul of its neighbor. And then there was an explosion on the *San Salvador*, and we took her too. But day after day they moved closer to Calais, and for a while there we were afraid they were goin' to succeed in meetin' up with the Duke of Parma over there. By the other day they was anchored off the Calais Roads, with old Parma no more than thirty miles away. But by this time we had the help of Lord Henry Seymour, who was patrolling the approaches to Dunkirk and Nieuport against the chance that Parma might make a dash for it across the Channel. And then, of course, there was the Dutch.

"Still, the problem was to break up that formation. Well, I had heard of fire ships, but I hadn't actually ever seen one, and I wasn't too sure how they managed it. And there was this Federigo Giambelli and his hell-burners what wrecked Parma's bridges at Antwerp; but I didn't know too much about that either. Anyhow, about midnight last night we knew somethin' was about to happen. Some ships joined us carryin' nothin' but barrels of pitch. And then they hauled in about eight empty frigates with spiked cannon aboard and covered them with this pitch. Then they hauled 'em in close toward Calais and waited until the tide was runnin' just right, which was about two o'clock in the morning or maybe a little earlier. They set those frigates on fire and just let 'em drift into that anchored formation. Now, every seaman knows that there ain't nothin' more terrifyin' at sea than a fire. And them Spaniards must've befouled their breeches when they seen them blazin' frigates rollin' down on them, spiked cannons blowin' up and blastin' iron all around. It wasn't that they couldn't have gotten away; they could've, had they kept their wits about them. But they didn't. And we didn't expect they would. They panicked. And, against orders, they cut their anchors loose and fled. When there was light enough, we couldn't see more than five Spanish ships in their original positions. The rest was scattered up and down the coast. And that gunfire you been hearin' all morning in the distance—well, that's the beginnin' of the end, as far as I'm concerned, unless Medina's been sent a miracle from heaven and pulled his fleet back together again. Unfortunate for us, we took a gash from floatin' debris and had to come on back into port for repairs. But we'll be out again in a day or two and we'll chase them heathen bastards clear up into Norway, 'cause there ain't no way they're goin' to go back the way they came—not with the wind and the English fleet at their backs."

The crowd gathered around the old seaman lets out a cheer, and the silence is broken into a score of noisy conversations as the ale once more begins to flow.

Later, with the skies overcast, and with rumbling coming from across the water that might be either thunder or guns or both, Tom Watson and Kit walk up the steep road to the Castle of Dover in search of Citizen Walsingham, the hero of the battle of Chislehurst, as Kit is already calling him. "I can't quite see him as the Terror of Kent, knee-deep in Spanish guts," he says. "The sight of blood, in fact, makes him ill."

"Now, now, be kind, Christopher," says Tom. "He has long and serious traditions to uphold. We who have inherited nothing have fewer responsibilities."

The road is crowded with traffic. People line the low rough walls and stare into the haze, hoping to catch sight of something, if only a firefly flash of light from the opposite shore, where the battle now rages off Gravelines. A gentleman goes by on horseback, a small fortune in plumage and armor on his rather insignificant body. He is surrounded by an entourage of half a dozen less colorful creatures. "Who in the world can that be?" says Tom Watson.

"Lord Bunghole of Barham, no doubt," says Kit. "Or perhaps the Sultan of Sandwich. Some wealthy piece of Kentish decadence, too wasted in the thighs to mount his horse without the help of half a dozen retainers. See how beautifully he rides, his bottom banging in the saddle. He'll get a medal for a bloody arse out of all this, even if the Spanish never set foot on English soil."

They pause to look out over the town of Dover and the treeless hills in the distance. And then again to watch a group of pikemen drilling in their glistening helmets and baggy breeches. "The second motion," shouts their commander. "The third motion!" They are infinitely more impressive than the trainbands they have watched learning the art of war in London, the fat and greasy citizens, huffing and puffing and out of step, with sticks for swords and not a musket among them.

At the first gate their way is blocked, but Kit steps forward with an air of authority and says something quietly to the guards, who step aside and let them pass. "How did you manage that?" asks Watson.

"Having been employed so recently by Sir Francis has certain advantages," says Kit. "It is merely a matter of using the right terminology. We will find our fearless leader conferring with certain captains not far from here, where that wall faces the sea."

In a few moments they come upon a colorful tableau: half a dozen gentlemen-captains gathered around a small table on which are spread some charts, the corners of which are held down by bottles of wine. Not far from them a group of horses snort and nod. And beyond them is the sea, gray-green and white-capped, stretching toward a horizon of low clouds. The men are fashionably dressed in military attire. One of them is pointing out to sea and seems to be explaining something to the others.

When they are less than a dozen yards away, Tom Walsingham sees them and breaks away from the others. He walks a bit stiffly in his new uniform. He seems genuinely glad to see them, though a little puzzled. "My dear, dear friends," he says. "I never expected to see you here. I thought you were both in London, making plays."

"Who can think of plays at a time like this?" says Watson.

"We didn't mean to interfere with your duties," says Kit, "but we heard you were here and dared not leave Dover without seeking you out."

"You came just in time," says Walsingham. "We are leaving within the hour—now that the fighting has broken out in earnest. Have you heard the latest news?"

"We've heard about the fire ships and the scattering of the Spanish fleet," says Watson.

"Well, come along and hear the rest," he says. "We have some very recent reports. And then we've got to see to our own defenses. It's been a very long night, and I'm fairly exhausted."

"Have you had no sleep at all?" Watson asks him.

"An hour or so, that's all."

He looks a bit ridiculous, thinks Kit, in his high boots, thick leather belt, and peascod breastplate.

"We've come down mainly to get the news firsthand," says Walsingham. "Now that the enemy is being driven northward, there's no telling where he will strike. But should he come into the Medway we are prepared to hold the line at Chatham. Leicester and Essex are at Tilbury with some twenty thousand men." He lowers his voice so that Tom Watson, walking on the other side of Kit, cannot hear him. "And how have you been, Kit?" he says with a tenderness that is inappropriate to his costume.

"Extremely well, thank you," says Kit. "And you?"

"Well, you see how it is with me," says Walsingham. "This Spanish affair has kept me totally preoccupied. But when it is over, you will come to see me at Scadbury, won't you? And catch me up on all the gossip."

Before he can answer, they have joined the others around the table, where a handsomely bearded officer is explaining the invisible action at sea. He does not pause for introductions. "Just this morning we also received news that Parma's barges are hopelessly pinned in at Dunkirk and that there is no way for them to carry out the rendezvous with Sidonia's fleet. We have, in fact, intercepted messages from Parma himself, describing his impossible situation. All that Sidonia can hope for now is some route of escape. They have felt the full force of our attack, and their losses are running high. Some portion of the Spanish fleet has been reassembled, we understand, but the wind is against them, and they have no choice but to move to the north. The weather is reportedly turning bad, which may be a stroke of good luck for the enemy, unless it drives them ashore in the shallows. If the wind favors them and we must cut off our action, they may still be able to move into deep water with a sizable force, but there is little question now, gentlemen, that the meeting between Sidonia and Parma will never take place." He traces the course of the battle at Gravelines on his chart as they all watch attentively. "How badly we've hurt them we won't know, of course, for some time."

"Isn't that marvelous?" whispers Walsingham to Kit. His brother Edmund turns to look at him. He is a pale, serious man, in an outfit not quite so glamorous as his younger brother's. He nods a silent greeting at Kit and Watson and then turns again to the charts.

The group breaks up. Walsingham is drawn into a conference with his brother Edmund, Henry Cobham, and Tom Leveson. Kit and Watson are more or less shunted aside. In a few moments Walsingham comes over to them and says, "There seems to be some concern about your presence here. Perhaps you ought to leave."

"Oh—well, by all means," says Watson, his instinctive diplomacy mingling with his embarrassment. "I mean, we were about to leave anyway, weren't we, Kit? Just stopped by to say hello. Didn't mean to intrude!" He takes Kit by the arm and starts to lead him away. Kit and Walsingham exchange glances but say nothing.

On the way down the hill, Tom says, "I hope you're not annoyed. We really had no business there, you know."

"It doesn't matter," says Kit.

"I thought Tom looked rather magnificent, didn't you?"

"I thought he looked like a silly ass!"

"And, what's more, I imagine he's doing a good job."

"Given the circumstances, I'd teach them a thing or two about war."

"If I didn't know you better, I'd say you were jealous."

"Jealous?" says Kit. "What's there to be jealous of?"

"Well, his military garb, if nothing else. Rather handsome!"

"For a masquerade ball, perhaps," says Kit.

When they get to the bottom of the hill, Kit says rather impulsively, "I think I'll go on to Canterbury and visit my family for a few days."

"Tomorrow morning?" says Watson.

"No, right now," says Kit. "As soon as I can get away."

"In that case," says Watson, "I guess I'll have to travel back with Roberto and the others."

"Travel with whomever you please," says Kit, and walks away.

xi

Elizabeth Tudor, Queen and mother and goddess of England, bald under her red wig, pale and pockmarked under the rouge and rice powder, thin to the point of boniness, too rheumatic in her joints to be comfortable on a horse, rides in triumph to Tilbury to address the troops assembled there to protect her person and the realm. In her white velvet gown and silver breastplate she is enormously impressive—especially from a distance. She speaks from her horse, the breeze playing in the white plumes in her false hair.

"My loving people, we have been persuaded by some who are careful of our safety to take heed how we commit ourselves to armed multitudes, for fear of treachery. But I assure you, I do not desire to live to distrust my faithful and loving people. Let tyrants fear. I have always so behaved myself that, under God, I have placed my chiefest strength and safeguard in the loyal hearts and goodwill of my subjects; and therefore I am come amongst you, as you see, at this time, not for my recreation and disport, but being resolved, in the midst and heat of the battle, to live or die amongst you all, to lay down for my God, and for my kingdom, and for my people, my honor and my blood, even in the dust. I know I have the body of a weak and feeble woman, but I have the heart and stomach of a king, and of a king of England too, and think foul scorn that Parma or Spain or any prince of Europe should dare to invade the borders of my realm; to which, rather than any dishonor shall grow by me, I myself will take up arms, I myself will be your general, judge, and rewarder of every one of your virtues in the field. I know already for your forwardness you have deserved rewards and crowns; and we do assure you, in the word of a prince, they shall be duly paid you."

xii

Matthew Roydon returns to London in the dead of winter after a trip to Scotland. He finds the city in the grip of January: days dying young, traces of snow in the fields, mud in the streets and lanes, and clouds made in the gloomy fjords of Norway that move across the English sky like Viking ships.

Like Marlowe he lives in Norton Folgate. He has a modest two rooms, the second floor of a small house on Lamb Street. Just across the road, where Primrose Street meets Norton Folgate, Ann and Tom Watson have leased a house. And just a stone's throw from them, in Moors Alley, Kit has leased a portion of an old house with sagging floors. He has one room up and one room down and a private entrance. On the other side of the wall lives his ancient and deaf landlord, who beats his dog and coughs a lot in the night.

Matthew Roydon is a quiet and serious man, a few years older than his good friend Kit. His stocky form and heavy hands are not what one might expect in a poet. He might more easily be taken for a farmer or an innkeeper. It is only the penetrating intelligence of his very blue eyes that gives him away. He is a handsome man, with his square jaw and black beard and soft, abundant hair. He is respected by an interesting variety of men, from Sir Francis Walsingham, who uses him as a government agent, to Ralegh and Harriot, who enjoy the presence of a first-rate mind. He is one of the few men in London for whom Kit Marlowe has developed a profound admiration.

On the very evening of his return, Matthew Roydon visits his good friends Ann and Tom Watson. He is eager for news and has no objection whatever to a hot meal and a warm fire.

"And how are our barbarian neighbors to the north?" Tom asks.

Ann brings in two cups of hot wine and serves the men, who are seated on low benches on either side of the fireplace.

"Oh, not quite so barbaric as you might imagine," says Matthew. "There's a considerable circle of rather interesting Englishmen there, you know. And getting larger all the time."

"You mean as things here get more difficult," says Tom.

"Yes," says Matthew. "And for all their odd ways, the Scots are rather congenial and tolerant."

"Perhaps it's because of their extraordinary illiteracy," says Tom. "I hear there are not ten books in all of Scotland, and half of those have never been read."

He laughs good-naturedly. "Those country squires are a bit rough in their ways. There's no denying that. And well fortified against the dreariness of the weather. If I had to live there all winter long, I'd choose their whiskey over the orations of Cicero myself."

"And what precisely were you doing there?" says Ann, standing in the small doorway between the kitchen and the living room.

"Discretion, my pet," says Tom. "One doesn't discuss these things."

"Oh, I don't mind," says Matthew. "Besides, it wasn't all that important. Nothing that you haven't done yourself from time to time. I took a small assignment from Robert Poley, who had it from Sir Francis. These agonizingly delicate negotiations with King

James. He's such a difficult man. A bit too much like his mother, I'm afraid."

"I thought the question of his sympathies was pretty much settled last August," says Tom, "when he ordered his nation to repel any attempt on the part of the Spaniards to invade his country."

"Unfortunately, that order was never put to the test," says Matthew. "Had there been a concerted effort to establish a foothold in Scotland, who knows what the outcome would have been? The Catholics are very strong there, you know, and not terribly reasonable."

"But surely, James knows that he is the logical successor to the English throne," says Tom.

"He also knows that before Elizabeth makes it official, he will have to make certain concessions. And he is not an easy man to deal with."

"But you don't believe for a moment, do you, that James really wants the French or the Spanish or anyone in Scotland? Such an alliance would virtually force the Queen to create a new line of succession. And what's more, most Englishmen would support her."

"I'm not so sure they would."

Ann intrudes. "If you gentlemen can put aside your politics for a while, there is some supper for you."

They go to a table at the other end of the room, where Ann has laid out a tureen of soup, a plate of meats, and a loaf of bread. "And how are all our friends?" Matthew asks. "Alive and well?"

"Most are alive," says Tom. "Not all are well. It's been a bad season."

"I suppose you know Roger Wiggins died," says Ann.

"No, I didn't," says Matthew.

"And pretty Jane Newell," says Tom.

Matthew shakes his head. "What a nasty game death plays with us, so often picking the most unlikely. I suppose his friends are still mourning poor old Dick Tarleton."

"They're turning him into a legend with all their talk," says

Tom. "And not all of it good. If only he hadn't taken ill and died at the house of Em Ball. It stirred such gossip."

"All of it true, I'm sure," says Matthew. "There isn't anything I wouldn't believe of Roberto and his Shoreditch mob. She may have been his mistress, but I wouldn't put it past him to have lent her around. Before they moved in together, they say her own brother Cutting Ball pandered for her."

"I heard the other day that Kit was not well," says Tom.

"Anything serious?"

"I don't know. I tried to go around to see him, but he's got the door locked and says he doesn't want to see anyone until his play is done."

"What play is that?" says Matthew.

"Something about a notorious Dr. Faustus," says Tom.

"You mean from that awful ballad of Faust the Conjurer, or whatever it was, that we saw at St. Paul's Churchyard just before I left?"

"No, from a German book, Englished by my friend Peter Forman," says Tom. "I had a copy made and agreed to find him a publisher. It's quite fascinating. Peter's a merchant, you know, who's spent some time in Germany. And his brother is that peculiar gentleman Dr. Simon Forman, who some claim is a conjurer himself."

"Kit was always rather interested in magic, wasn't he?" says Matthew.

"It's difficult to say what Kit is really interested in," says Tom. "He has such sudden passions for things. Sometimes he worries me."

"Don't you think we should try to see him?"

"I don't think it will do any good," says Tom. "He'll come out when he's ready."

"But suppose he's really sick?" says Matthew.

"Why don't you both go around after supper," says Ann, putting her hand on Tom's and in this gentle way persuading him that it's the right thing to do.

There are no lights in Moors Alley and there is no moon. Fortunately, it's a very short distance from Primrose Street, and Tom and Matthew make their way by whatever light escapes from the curtained and shuttered windows. Invisible cats lurk in the gutters, and there is the smell of smoke in the damp air from all the chimneys. The only sounds are the rush of wind and the distant voices from The White Lion.

"This is it," says Tom, feeling the door that he can barely see in the darkness. "Yes, this is it. I recognize the shape of the knocker."

"The lights are all out," says Matthew. "Perhaps he's asleep."

"Perhaps he's dead," says Tom.

"I wouldn't jest if I were you," says Matthew.

Tom lifts the knocker and lets it fall gently. "I was quite serious," he says.

They listen. Then Tom uses the knocker again—once, twice, three times. There is no answer.

"Is it possible he's gone away?" says Matthew.

"I don't think it's likely," says Tom. "I saw George Chapman at The Nag's Head yesterday. He said he also tried to see him but was turned away."

"Then he's probably asleep."

"Or drunk."

Matthew tries to force the door, but it is firmly locked. "What about the old man next door?" he says. "Doesn't he have a key?"

"The old bastard's deaf as rocks," says Tom, exasperated. But no sooner does he say this than the landlord's door opens and an old man steps out leading a dog on a rope and wielding a stick. He doesn't see them at first. He's muttering curses at his dog. When he notices the shadowy figures not far from him, he is startled. "Hey, what's this? What's this?" he says. "Who are you?"

"Friends of Mr. Marlowe," says Tom, but the old man doesn't hear. He comes up closer, his stick in the air.

Matthew raps again at the door and gestures. The dog growls and tugs at its rope. "Quiet, you diseased mongrel," says the old man, whacking the poor creature with his stick. "Damned bitch is in heat," he says. "It won't do you no good to knock at that door.

He's in there, all right, but he won't answer. Tried to throw Mistress Cowley out the upper window, he did. Mad as ghosts, he is, and talking with devils. Good thing for him his rent is paid up. I'd have him out of there in a minute. God knows what damage he's done, tossing things about. And Widow Halle, she comes with her charms, her *In verbis, et in herbis,* and all that, and gives him her *aqua mirabilis,* but it only makes him worse, and he sends her screaming from the house."

With his heavy hand, Matthew grips the latch. He feels it slip its notch, and then with a heave of his broad shoulder he opens the door.

All three men go in and light candles. And there, sprawled on the floor, fully clothed, in the debris of what was his furniture, they find Kit Marlowe, his arms spread out as though he imagines he is flying or has been crucified against the uncarpeted boards of the floor. The old man, who was raised a Catholic, instinctively crosses himself and says, "God help us, he's dead!" But Kit lets out a moan to give him the lie, and his head rolls to one side.

Matthew is on his knees in an instant and has Kit in his arms. "He's in a raging fever," he says. "Light a fire, Tom. We've got to put him to bed."

Unable to communicate in any other way, Tom takes the old man firmly by the arm, leads him to the door, and shoves him out.

Through the long night, Tom and Matthew sit with Kit and listen to his feverish ravings. They cover him well and keep the fire going. He shivers and sweats all at once. Sometimes he lapses into sleep. Sometimes he talks, as though from a coma or the grave, his eyes closed. Sometimes he is startled. His eyes open with fear and he struggles to sit up and cannot seem to catch his breath. And sometimes he is lucid and logical and even calm. "There's nothing to be done but wait," says Tom. "The fever will either kill him or cure him."

"I could try to fetch Dr. Morton from Whitechapel," says Matthew. "They say he's quite good."

"He won't come at this hour," says Tom. "Not for a fever. And if he does, he's liable to bleed him and leech him and bathe him in cold water and kill him. No, Matthew, there's a better physician than Dr. Morton or any of them—and that's Nature. Let her have her way."

Outside it begins to rain, and there is the rumble of thunder. Kit stirs and then falls off again. "Why don't you go on home to Ann?" says Matthew. "I'll sit with him the rest of the night."

"Ann's not afraid of a little thunder and lightning," says Tom. He's poking at the fire. "And besides, we should bring a little order out of this chaos." They are in the upstairs room, where they have put Kit to bed. Like the room downstairs, it is not merely neglected; it is ravaged—as though a caged animal had been trying to break out of it.

"Do you suppose these are the pages of his new play?" says Tom, picking up the scattered sheets of a manuscript. "It looks as though he flung them across the room in disgust."

"Can you put it together?" Matthew asks.

"Fortunately, they are numbered," says Tom. He sorts them out, noting the missing numbers and hunting here and there for them. "It *is* the Dr. Faustus play, after all," he says. He lingers over one of the pages. As he reads, a loud voice seems to leap at him from the manuscript, the kind of voice one might hear on the stage. But it is actually coming from Kit, whose eyes remain closed, and whose face glistens with perspiration: "May the Gods of Acheron be favorable to me! Away with the triple deity of Jehovah! Spirits of fire, air, water, earth, hail! Prince of the East, Beelzebub, monarch of burning hell, and demigorgon, we ask your grace that Mephistophilis may appear and rise." He pauses, as though waiting for someone or something to appear, and then he shouts impatiently, "*Quid tu moraris?* By Jehovah, hell, and the holy water which I now sprinkle, and the sign of the cross which I now make, and by our vows, may Mephistophilis himself now rise to do us service."

Matthew lays his hand against Kit's burning cheek and tries to calm him. His voice trails off. His head rolls to one side and he breathes heavily, as though he has been running a long way.

They all sit quietly for a while. The fire hisses. The wind and rain blow against the shuttered window. Tom, having assembled the manuscript, reads to himself.

"Who exactly was this Dr. Faustus?" says Matthew. "Was he real or imaginary?"

"Some say real," says Tom. "A man of Simmern named Johannes Faust, who took degrees at Heidelberg University and then turned his talents to astrology and black magic, denouncing divinity and binding himself to the devil by a contract drawn in blood. They say he could perform such extraordinary feats that he must needs have had the devil's help. And all of this less than a hundred years ago in Germany."

"Time enough for a legend to grow," says Matthew.

"Unless the devil's more than metaphor, after all," says Tom, "diffused throughout the world as universally as God, and bodying forth himself through certain avenues of the mind."

"The devil's a myth," says Matthew, "and you're as much a fool as this Dr. Faustus if you believe otherwise. I do not pretend to understand all the complexities of this world, but unless my reason's but a toy, I see no sense at all in magic of any kind, whether it's performed by a wayward student of theology or a carpenter's son out of Nazareth."

"If our friend is merely sick," says Tom, "where are the other signs of his sickness? No rheum, no cough, no rash. Nothing but this consuming fire. You must admit he seems a man possessed."

The storm moves closer. Lightning breaks the darkness, flashes at the window, and is followed by a peal of thunder. Kit stirs under his blankets. Matthew wipes the perspiration from his forehead but is halted in mid-motion by Kit's loud voice. "I know you, Death," he says, still lost in his dream. "I have seen your work in the narrow rooms of Canterbury and the vasty vaults of the cathedrals of this world. You sit there smiling, confident, and indestructible. But I will learn a way to cut your throat and rid the world of your annoying arrogance." He struggles to rise, though his eyes are still closed.

"Will he walk in his sleep?" says Matthew. "Perhaps we ought to tie him to his bed."

"He's too weak to do much harm, even to himself," says Tom.

It takes only a firm touch of Matthew's heavy hand for Kit to fall back against his pillow with a sigh. "The key," he says. "Where is the key?"

Matthew's face is close to his. "What key, Christopher?" he whispers.

"The key to unlock the final thousand doors between me and my God," says Kit. He seems to have heard his friend, but it was another voice that made him respond, one that neither Tom nor Matthew could hear. "Not under the bishop's skirt, I pray. No, I'll not take holy orders, not feast on ignorance. Divinity *adieu!* They're burning Kett in Norfolk with all his brains so full of books. See how he leaps about in the fire, washes himself in it, nay, kisses it, dances like devils to be consumed, screaming, 'Blessed be God.' And I say blessed be the angel of Satan. Is he not also a God? And am I not also a God? I who have created worlds in my mind and made light where before was only darkness on the inky waters of the word—*per accidens.*"

"He almost speaks sense," says Matthew. "Perhaps his fever has in fact made him sane."

"It's not Kit Marlowe who is speaking," says Tom excitedly. "It's his damned Dr. Faustus. He's written himself clear into his play. Listen! Listen to what he has written here:

> "If we say that we have no sin,
> We deceive ourselves, and there is no truth in us.
> Why, then, belike we must sin,
> And so consequently die:
> Ay, we must die an everlasting death.
> What doctrine call you this, *Che sera, sera:*
> What will be, shall be? Divinity adieu!
> These metaphysics of magicians,
> And necromantic books are heavenly;
> Lines, circles, letters, and characters;

> Ay, these are those that Faustus most desires.
> O, what a world of profit and delight,
> Of power, of honour, and omnipotence,
> Is promised to the studious artizan!
> All things that move between the quiet poles
> Shall be at my command: emperors and kings
> Are but obey'd in their several provinces,
> Nor can they raise the wind, or rend the clouds;
> But his dominion that exceeds in this,
> Stretcheth as far as doth the mind of man;
> A sound magician is a demi-god . . ."

"Is the play done?" says Matthew.

"On paper it's done, but not in his mind."

Matthew rises from the foot of the bed, wrings out a rag in cold water, and returns to lay it once again against Kit's face.

Kit moves toward the coolness as toward a lover's hand. "In Elysium have I dwelt," he says, "beyond the power of the Christian God and bathed in waterfalls of wisdom with the grand old men of Greece. There we have played among the naked boys of truth and linked our tongues in juicy dialogues of love."

"How fantastic that he should speak this way out of his dreams," says Matthew.

Kit's voice lowers into a chant. "Holy Mary, Mother of God, that was a whore in Bethlehem and kissed me in the mouth under the bells of St. George the night the bats of death sucked forth my soul—see where it flies!"

"Ah, it's here, it's here," says Tom, turning the pages of the manuscript.

> "Was this the face that launch'd a thousand ships,
> And burnt the topless towers of Ilium?—
> Sweet Helen, make me immortal with a kiss.—
> Her lips suck forth my soul: see where it flies!—
> Come, Helen, come, give me my soul again.
> Here will I dwell, for heaven is in these lips,
> And all is dross that is not Helena."

"I'd give my soul to put together words like that," says Matthew.

"Perhaps that's exactly what he's done," says Tom.

"See how he shivers," says Matthew. "His wasted body cannot stand much more of this. There must be a cure for such a malady."

"The cure is death," says Tom, "unless he purge himself through recitation of these fantastic things."

Kit grinds his teeth and speaks in a low growl. "Is there nothing that I can do to crack the axle-tree of this relentless world and break all the wheels of the sun's galloping chariot? Come, gentle moon. Fall into my arms that I might lull the heavens to sleep and kill all time that murders my sweet life and boyish joy!"

Thunder and lightning silence him for a moment; then he goes on in a quavering, startled voice: "What canons of lust roar in the lions of my heart and break the bones of innocent babes against the walls of Samarkand!"

"These must be lines discarded from his plays," says Matthew.

"But lodged in the nether regions of his mind," says Tom. "The deep wells from which all poetry springs."

"Be done with all this boiling noise," says Kit, "this leaping heart. Blood, congeal! Spirit, dissolve! Cool Earth, receive my elements that I may bark no more in the haunted halls of all my echoes and disappear forever into sweet silence and black oblivion."

"He would go one way or the other," says Matthew, "into the world forever or out of it absolutely."

Kit's head rolls from side to side, as though he is trying to avoid an agonizing thought. "These gardens of delight, hung with the fruits of lunacy, make lechers of us all—that we would rape the world and kiss the sky to learn the way to immortality. *Veni, veni, Mephistophile!*"

"Thank God we have no other witnesses to this heresy," says Tom.

Kit mutters incoherently for a moment and then turns lucid again: "Cull me out some courtesans, some wanton boys, and all the wines of Portugal that I may bathe my lust and drown my thirst in revelries, and kiss my joy to death and sleep for all eternity."

He pauses and stutters, as though the next words will not come, and then he seems to give in to whatever he is wrestling with. In a subdued voice, he says, "I, Christopher Marlowe, of Canterbury, Master of Arts, by these presents do give both body and soul to Lucifer, Prince of the East, and his minister Mephistophilis; and furthermore grant unto them that, four and twenty years being expired, and these articles above written being inviolate, full power to fetch or carry the said Christopher Marlowe, body and soul, flesh, blood, or goods, into their habitation wheresoever . . ." His voice trails off, and he falls into a deeper sleep.

"God help the wretched fool," says Tom. "His hell is here, and he is in it. He and Dr. Faustus are one. Listen:

"Ah, Faustus,
    Now hast thou but one bare hour to live,
    And then thou must be damn'd perpetually!
    Stand still, you ever-moving spheres of heaven,
    That time may cease, and midnight never come;
    Fair Nature's eye, rise, rise again, and make
    Perpetual day; or let this hour be but
    A year, a month, a week, a natural day,
    That Faustus may repent and save his soul!
    O lente, lente currite, noctis equi!
    The stars move still, time runs, the clock will strike,
    The devil will come, and Faustus must be damn'd.
    O, I'll leap up to my God!—Who pulls me down?—
    See, see, where Christ's blood streams in the firmament!
    One drop would save my soul, half a drop: ah, my Christ!—
    Ah, rend not my heart for naming of my Christ!
    Yet will I call on him: O, spare me, Lucifer!—
    Where is it now? 'tis gone: and see, where God
    Stretcheth out his arm, and bends his ireful brows!
    Mountains and hills, come, come, and fall on me,
    And hide me from the heavy wrath of God!
    No, no!
    Then will I headlong run into the earth:

Earth, gape! O, no, it will not harbour me!
You stars that reign'd at my nativity,
Whose influence hath allotted death and hell,
Now draw up Faustus, like a foggy mist,
Into the entrails of yon lab'ring cloud
That, when you vomit forth into the air,
My limbs may issue from your smoky mouths,
So that my soul may but ascend to heaven!
Ah, half the hour is past! 'twill all be passed anon.
O God,
If thou wilt not have mercy on my soul,
Yet for Christ's sake, whose blood hath ransom'd me,
Impose some end to my incessant pain;
Let Faustus live in hell a thousand years,
A hundred thousand, and at last be sav'd!
O, no end is limited to damned souls!
Why wert thou not a creature wanting soul?
Or why is this immortal that thou hast?
Ah, Pythagoras' *metempsychosis*, were that true,
This soul should fly from me, and I be changed
Unto some brutish beast! all beasts are happy,
For, when they die,
Their souls are soon dissolved in elements;
But mine must live still to be plagu'd in hell.
Curs'd be the parents that engender'd me!
No, Faustus, curse thyself, curse Lucifer
That hath depriv'd thee of the joys of heaven.
                    The clock strikes twelve.
O, it strikes, it strikes! Now, body, turn to air,
Or Lucifer will bear thee quick to hell!
O soul, be changed into little water-drops,
And fall into the ocean, ne'er be found!
        Thunder and enter the Devils.
My God, my God look not so fierce on me!
Adders and serpents, let me breathe awhile!
Ugly hell, gape not! Come not, Lucifer!
I'll burn my books!—Ah, Mephistophilis!"

Tom sits very still with the manuscript heaped on his knees. Matthew is standing by the window, his face half-silhouetted from a candle on the bureau. Neither one speaks. They seem embarrassed, as though they've stripped their friend clean naked or assaulted his privacy. They both look toward him.

"He's breathing easier," says Matthew. "Perhaps the fever's broken at last."

"Perhaps!" says Tom, his eyes heavy with sadness and fatigue. "Go if you want. I'll stay with him and perhaps sleep a bit in this chair."

"No," says Matthew. "I'll stay. It won't be long now before the dawn."

xiii

Scadbury in the summer is full of birds. They sharpen one's sense of silence as one sits in the garden and contemplates the flowers, the slope of the lawn, the indifference of Nature and her relentless lushness. So it has all come around again, thinks Kit: the horrible winter, the spring in which *Dr. Faustus* has leapt upon London like a tiger, and now the summer again. Everything is different, and yet everything is the same.

He watches Tom Walsingham come out of the house and walk along a path toward where he is sitting. It's like a dream. He sees Tom, his graceful step, his slender neck. He hears birds sing among the tall bushes and in the leafy trees. He feels the sunlight on his hands and face. He expects this moment to go on and on forever, Tom forever walking toward him, his mind forever locked in, suspended.

Tom's brother Edmund has died, and all the Walsingham estates have fallen to Tom. In the language of his father's will they are: "My manor at Scadbury in Chislehurst, Pauliscray, Footescray, St. Marye Cray, Northcray, Eltham, Motingham, Lee, Orpington, Bromley, and Bexley . . ."

"How rich you are," says Kit, when Tom is once again standing in the garden with him.

"Ah, but think of all the work," says Tom. "Think of the decisions, of the people cheating you in Orpington or Eltham, because you cannot be there to watch them, conspiring over the price of wool or selling off your cow and claiming it was diseased and had to be destroyed. And then all those nasty little people talking about you because you are the absentee landlord, exploiter of the common folk, rich and decadent."

"But, Tom," says Kit, "you *are* rich and decadent."

"My dear Christopher. Far from being decadent, I am forced to grow more and more respectable every day. Before I know it, someone will arrange for the Queen herself to visit here on one of her progresses. And then I shall have all the expense and fuss and people descending from all over. And everybody gossiping about how I am not married and should be, if only to have an heir, but winking and hinting at all sorts of things."

"Is there much to wink and hint at?" says Kit. They are walking now under the brick archway toward the outer court and the moat.

"Life, my dear friend," Tom says, "is infinitely more complicated than either one of us could have guessed when we took it on."

"You mean when it was thrust upon us."

"You spend too much time with those quibblers at Durham House," says Tom. "I don't know whether I came upon it or it came upon me. All I know is that I am here."

"Not only are you rich and decadent," says Kit, "you're a heretic and a hedonist. You'll never get to heaven."

"It's very hard to think about getting to heaven when one has so many earthly responsibilities."

"Perhaps you should take vows of poverty and go into the desert with a hair shirt on and talk with God."

"Good heavens!" says Tom. "Whatever would we have to say to each other? I mean, it's difficult enough talking with the Cobhams and the Sheltons and the Levesons. How could I possibly carry on a sociable conversation with someone as significant as God?"

"Well, He's not *that* much more important than most of your friends, is He?"

"As nasty as ever, aren't you? And just as charming."

"Begging your pardon, sir, Your Lordship," says Kit, "but is it possible? I mean—how shall I put it?—you know how difficult it is for me to express myself. But are you glad your brother is dead?"

"You horrible little cutpurse of the mind!" says Tom. "How can you talk like that?"

"There are two things I do extremely well," says Kit. "Tell the truth and lie."

"And which are you doing now?"

"Frankly," he says, "I think you're glad he's dead, and, what's more, I don't blame you."

Tom says nothing. They cross the drawbridge and continue down the road. "It's been a rather awkward relationship," he says, "but I've always had a great deal of respect for my brother." He hesitates and then adds, "In spite of the fact that he was perhaps one of the most boring men in the world."

"I won't argue with you," says Kit. "I never liked him very much."

"But let's not talk about Edmund," says Tom. "It's all too sad. And let's not talk about me. It's a subject I know very little about. Let's talk about you. I hear that you're back with Ann and Tom Watson and sharing a place in Holywell Street."

"Yes, it's a whole house, for a change. I have the rooms upstairs. Three of them. Imagine that! A small mansion, as things go in Shoreditch."

"Hardly a substitute for a real mansion."

"What do you mean?"

"I mean, why don't you move in here as my secretary?" says Tom. "Now that Edmund's gone—"

"I wouldn't be a very good secretary," says Kit.

"That doesn't matter. As long as you behave yourself."

"I'm not sure I want to behave myself, as you put it. And, in the long run, I think I would be an embarrassment to you. You need your respectability."

"But there are other things I need, too," says Tom. "I'm not a simple person."

"I'm well aware of that, but we can't have everything, can we?

And yet, I am tempted. Sorely tempted. It's very lovely here. And London can be terribly grim at times. Confusing. Exhausting. One has to get away from time to time. These trips are good for me. And you've been more kind than you have any reason to be."

"I have my reasons," says Tom.

Kit turns away from him and stands in the middle of the tree-lined road. "Oh, God, it's so damned difficult," he says.

Tom tears a branch from a bush beside the road and, peeling the leaves off one by one, says, "I suppose you've got—other friends in London."

Kit turns on him angrily. "Of course I have other friends in London! What do you expect?"

He tosses the denuded branch away. "I don't expect anything, Kit. Nothing at all, except—"

"For the love of Christ, don't say *appreciation!*"

"That's not exactly what I had in mind. It was something more fundamental, but I'm afraid I can't find a word for it. In any case, if there is a word for it, I'm sure it's not in your vocabulary."

"You're probably right," says Kit. "Even now, I'm not sure I know what you're talking about."

"Oh, it doesn't matter," he says, forcing a smile.

On the way back to the house, their conversation is strained. And after dinner that evening Kit says that he will probably return to London in the morning. Tom expresses polite disappointment but does not try to keep him from going.

xiv

Ann Watson returns from a visit to her brother's house in Holborn. She, who can ordinarily weather the usual crises of life, is visibly shaken by something. Tom takes her in his arms and comforts her. "What is it, my love?" he says. "You look so pale."

She draws away and collects herself. "It's all that nasty business with William Bradley."

"You mean that young tough whose father runs The Bishop's Head in Gray's Inn Lane?"

"Yes," she says. "He's causing my brother Hugh a great deal of trouble."

"What's this all about?" says Kit.

"You may remember," says Tom, "that some time ago John Alleyn was stupid enough to lend this Bradley fellow fourteen pounds. Well, he has steadfastly refused to repay it. John hired Hugh as his lawyer and has threatened to take him into the Court of Common Pleas to force Bradley to pay up. What's happened now I don't know."

"Well, he sent around a very nasty friend of his," says Ann, "one George Orrell, to threaten Hugh with bodily harm. They say he's a murderer, though it can't be proved, and that, for a fee or a friend, he'd gladly cut somebody's throat. A burly, ugly fellow, he is. Naturally, Hugh is all upset. And his wife is in such a panic she's liable to miscarry. He's gone to the bench to seek securities against the man, but that's not likely to stop his sort."

Tom is furious. He paces across the floor and then turns as though prepared to fight. "Damn that Holborn crowd!" he says. "Bradley and his bully friends have finally gone too far. I think it's time they were taught a lesson."

"What are you going to do?" says Ann.

"Two can play at the game of force," he says. "I think perhaps John and Hugh and I might just go around and have a little talk with Mr. William Bradley."

"Good," says Kit. "I'll go with you."

"No," says Tom. "It's not your affair. Stay out of it." He goes into another room and comes out with his rapier and dagger.

"Tom, there must be another way," says Ann.

"Don't worry," says Tom. "We won't do anything drastic. Just a sharp word or two to let the bastard know that he can't level threats against our friends. It's the only language they understand." With that he goes off, leaving Ann and Kit alone.

"Do you think he'll be all right?" says Ann.

"I wouldn't want to face Tom with a sword in his hand," says Kit. "He learned his lessons in France and won't be easily outdone by the likes of William Bradley."

XV

The drama at The Bishop's Head is brief but satisfying. The three men, all fit and in their thirties, decorated for action, make their way with marvelous strides and angry silence across Hog Lane to the Artillery Ground, and from there to Long Lane, which takes them to West Smith Field. From there it is but a short way down Cow Lane to Holborn Hill and then Gray's Inn Lane. They have agreed already that their best strategy is to burst right into the place and take Bradley by surprise. They will make it clear to the thick-headed bully that he is in no position to threaten a gentleman like Hugh Swift, and, what's more, that he must repay the amount owed to John Alleyn while he's still got an unbroken arm with which to open his purse.

On their long march to the Battle of Holborn they receive many an admiring glance, especially from certain young ladies along the route. They cannot imagine what forces move these three handsome men along in this military fashion, but their everyday hearts leap at the sight of such graceful and muscular legs, such belts, such shoulders, such plumes.

They do not slow their pace at all until they are standing in front of Bradley's inn. It is mid-afternoon, and only two of the tables are occupied in the taproom. There are three men at each table, and a woman in a red apron is waiting on them. Probably William Bradley's mother, since the inn is a family affair.

The three heroes of Shoreditch pass from afternoon sunlight into the cool interior of the inn. Several curious people wait outside to see what this is all about. Tom and his friends pause inside the door and survey the situation. The six men at the two tables and the red-aproned woman all stop what they are doing and stare at this sudden apparition.

Undaunted, the portly woman approaches them, her thick arms akimbo, her fists at her hips. "Well, now, what do we have here?" she says, as tough and as ugly as her son.

"We want a word with William Bradley," says Tom.

"Me son's not here," she says. "He's gone to the West Country and won't be back for a month of Sundays."

But at that very moment young Bradley comes through the door at the rear and says, before he can see what is happening, "Hey, what's all the shoutin' about?" When he sees the three men, he stops dead in his tracks and takes a step backward. He is a broad-shouldered man with a jutting jaw. His receding hairline and his bulk make him look considerably older than his twenty-six years.

"Don't run away, Will Bradley," says John Alleyn. "We've come to talk business, not to do you any harm."

Bradley holds his ground, putting the wooden counter between him and the intruders. "Well, say what you have to say and get out."

"I understand," says John, "that you have put one of your mongrel friends onto my attorney, Hugh Swift, and threatened to beat his brains out if he pursues my case against you for the fourteen pounds you owe me."

"I've done no such thing," says Bradley.

"You're a liar," says Tom. "Your flunky George Orrell has made these threats on your behalf, and we're having him up for securities against a breach of the peace. And what's more, should he or you or anyone else lay so much as a finger on Mr. Swift, he'll have a bit of fury to contend with. Is that clear, Will Bradley?"

"I ain't responsible for what George Orrell does," says Bradley.

Tom approaches the wooden counter menacingly, half-drawing his rapier. Over his shoulder he says to his companions, "I don't believe Mr. Bradley understands the Queen's English. We may have to write him a grammar lesson in his own blood."

"Hey, now, wait a moment," says Bradley. The arrogance has gone out of his voice. "John and I can settle this between us."

"The matter is settled as far as John is concerned," says Tom. "You keep your butcher's hands off Mr. Swift and you pay him his fourteen pounds before the month is out."

"It ain't your quarrel, Tom Watson," says Bradley.

"Hugh Swift is my wife's brother," says Tom. "That makes it my quarrel as much as his. Do you understand?"

"Throw them out, Will," shouts Mistress Bradley. Someone at one of the tables laughs.

"All right, all right," says Bradley. "You'll have what's comin' to you before the end of the month." Another man laughs. "But you didn't have to come bargin' in here like a bunch of cutthroats, disturbin' my customers at their meals."

"Oh, we don't mind, Will," shouts one man. They are all amused, but no one dares interfere."

"We won't ask for your word," says John, "because it's no damn good. Just deliver by the last day of September and there will be no more trouble."

Bradley nods, his face flushed with fear and rage. "I think we've made our point," says Tom, shoving his rapier back into place. "We'll be off now." He turns to the men at the tables. "Our profoundest apologies, gentlemen. And to help your digestion, have a drink on us." He tosses a coin in Bradley's direction. It hits the counter, bounces once against the wood, then again against Bradley's belly, and lands on the floor at his feet.

When the three men are gone, Bradley says between clenched teeth, "He'll pay for this, by God!"

His mother picks up the coin from the floor and pockets it. "You can draw me an ale out of that," calls out one of the men.

"I'll draw you a bloody ale," shouts Bradley and hurls a tankard across the room at the man.

xvi

It is the eighteenth of September, and Kit Marlowe has been at The White Lion since before noon. He has been reading and sipping wine and thinking about his new play, a play about a rich Jewish merchant. But it has not all come together in his mind, and he cannot quite begin to put it down on paper.

It is early afternoon when he leaves. He turns the corner out of

White Lion Yard and heads up Norton Folgate toward The Theatre. There he has agreed to meet Tom Watson, who has a play in rehearsal, a trivial thing called *Fair Em*, not designed to win the affection of Robert Greene.

As Kit approaches Hog Lane, he is so deep in literary calculation that he does not see the man standing against the wall, just off the main road. As he passes him, the man leaps out at him and blocks his way. It is William Bradley, his sword and dagger ready, his eyes ablaze with fury and liquor. Kit, who has seen him only once or twice before, is slow to recognize him. But when he does, he steps forward, not backward, and says, "Out of my way, you son of Sodom, before I knock you down!"

"It's not you I want," says Bradley. "It's your friend Tom Watson. I owe him a pretty penny for his pretty speech, and we'll have it out on Windmill Hill, if he's got the courage to face me man to man."

"He'll quarter you in a trice, you clumsy ass," says Kit.

"Ho," says Bradley. "That effeminate fop. Without his mob—"

Kit grabs the handle of his rapier. "You call my friend a coward?"

Bradley closes on him until their faces almost meet. "I call him a coward and more: a jackal, a peacock, and your little Audrey. Disgustin' bunch of degenerates." He spits at Marlowe's feet.

"Would you do me the honor, sir, of drawing your sword," says Kit, "so that I might spill your ugly guts in the street?"

Bradley obliges, springing back with more agility than his bulk should logically allow and jutting forward his jaw. He draws both sword and dagger and shouts, "Come on, then, you braggin' scribbler. Let's see what you can do. I'll have your blood *and* his before my work is done today."

Kit draws quickly and faces him with similar weapons. They circle cautiously at first, then lunge, then parry. Their swords clank off each other. They swipe and hold with their daggers. They push away, cursing. "Swift as a rabbit, you are," says Bradley. "But we'll skin you yet!"

His anger blinds him to all logic, and Kit can see nothing else but the grimacing face of his sweating opponent. He wants to cut him, but he's as cautious as a cat. The excitement brings a smile to his face. And then, as Bradley lunges again and falls off balance, almost into the ditch along Hog Lane, Kit breaks into a cruel laugh. "Into the ditch with the other turds," he calls out. But Bradley recovers and charges at him in a blind rage. Kit backs away; he dodges, but not quite in time. Bradley's thrust misses, but his bulk bangs Kit against the stone wall behind him and bruises his back.

By this time a sizable crowd has gathered. Some urge the fighters on; some shout, "Call the constables!" And then one man, who seems to know what the fight is all about, says, "Here comes Tom Watson!"

Bradley, still defending himself, calls out, "Have you come, then? My bout's with you."

"All right!" Tom says, drawing his weapons. "Christopher!" he calls out. "I'll handle this."

"Then handle this," says Bradley, rushing at him before he is fully set to fight. He cuts his arm and the blood oozes through his shirt. A gasp goes through the crowd. But Tom ignores the wound to his left arm and fights on. They parry and thrust, step and jab, taunt and curse.

Watson is clearly the better of the two swordsmen, but the wound has weakened his dagger hand, and the blood runs down his arm. He is driven down Hog Lane, the circling crowd giving way as a rough voice cries, "Give 'em room. Give 'em room." Another man says, "He's done for, that one is." And indeed, Watson is in a bad way. He is forced to the ditch at the north end of the lane. His retreat is cut off. Bradley increases the fury of his attack and seems about to cut him to pieces or force him over backwards into the deep ditch, where he will be helpless.

But just as it seems as though it is all up for Watson, there is a bellow that fills the neighborhood. Bradley is stopped in his tracks by a desperate thrust that strikes home. Watson drives his sword six inches into the man's right breast. The weapons fall from his hands. His scream dissolves into a gurgling growl. He clutches the spurting wound, staggers, and then falls over on his back. His head and legs give a final twitch, and then he goes limp. In a few moments he is dead. A deathly hush falls over the crowd, as though they can hardly believe what they have seen.

And then there is a great bustle of activity. Some men kneel over the corpse. Marlowe rushes to his friend's side and holds him around the waist, lest he collapse. And the crowd parts to admit the constable, Stephen Wylde, who has arrived a minute too late.

He takes charge, jots down the names of several witnesses and asks the name of the deceased. "He's William Bradley of Holborn," says Kit. "He came all the way up here to lie in wait for Tom." Some members of the crowd mumble their confirmation, but the constable takes both Kit and Tom into custody. "That may be," he says, "but we'll see about it when we come before the justice, Sir Owen Hopton. Here, bandage this man's arm, and cover up the corpse. We'll post a guard on him until the coroner can make his inquest."

Tom and Kit are escorted to the home of Sir Owen by the constable and two other men. There they make their statement, after which a routine warrant for their arrest is drawn up, and they are sent off to be lodged in Newgate Gaol, pending investigation into the matter. "If it's all as you say," explains the justice, who knows both men, "you have nothing to fear, but the law's the law, and there are certain procedures that we have to follow."

"Will someone be sent around to explain to my wife?" asks Tom before they leave.

"We'll take care of that," says Sir Owen.

A cart is drawn up outside of Sir Owen's house to carry the men off to Newgate, and Kit and Tom brace themselves to endure the humiliation of imprisonment.

xvii

The arrest of Kit Marlowe and Tom Watson on a charge of homicide is the most attractive piece of news in London for the next several days. Gossip and rumor, as usual, distort the actual event. New motives for the murder are invented. Links with political conspiracies are suggested. Even the mysterious Marprelate is mentioned. The suggestion is not outside the realm of possibility, since both men are quite well acquainted with John Penry, the chief suspect in this outrageous attack on the Established Church.

While briefly in London, Penry himself hears of the arrest of Marlowe and Watson and wishes that there is something he can do to help, but he is in deep trouble and preparing for his flight to Scotland. There he hopes to find refuge among the Calvinists and to continue his underground activities. He has attacked every major figure in the Church from Whitgift to Aylmer to Cooper and Bancroft, accusing them of misusing funds, of carrying out Romish inquisitions, of domestic irregularities and sexual perversions. His aptly named Pilgrim Press had been forced to move from place to place as Whitgift's pursuivants sniffed him out. He and his cohorts took the cumbersome equipment from Kingston-on-Thames to Fawsley in Northamptonshire, to Coventry, and finally to Hazely in Warwickshire, where it was finally seized.

When news of the Bradley affair reaches Stephen Gosson, he is so filled with un-Christian delight that he rushes about London, spreading exaggerated tales of Marlowe's drunkenness and atheism.

Matthew Roydon takes the news to Thomas Walsingham in Chislehurst and fully expects that Tom will return with him to London and do his best to free both men. But Tom hesitates. "You say it is a clear-cut case of self-defense?"

"Yes," says Roydon. "There were plenty of witnesses—"

"Well, then, there's not much to worry about, is there?" says Tom. "Except perhaps arranging a bail for Christopher. It's not likely that Tom will be granted bail, but in due time he'll be let go."

"But your personal appearance at this time might make things considerably easier."

"But, my dear fellow, I'm not sure I can afford to make a personal appearance in a matter of this sort. I hope you will understand."

"All too well," says Roydon.

"I mean, I must keep my name out of it. But I will send Ingram Frizer to attend to the matter. He will have with him sufficient funds to see to it that they receive the best possible treatment at Newgate and are given the best of legal attention. Now, is there anyone you know who might be willing to stand surety for Kit, so that he might be released as soon as possible?"

"Hugh Swift has suggested a certain Richard Kitchen, and possibly his friend Humphrey Rowland. But it will be a matter of money, of course."

"Don't worry about the money," says Tom. "Hugh Swift is Tom's brother-in-law, is he not?"

"Yes," says Roydon. "Ann's brother."

"Good," says Walsingham. "I'll put Ingram in touch with him immediately and we'll have this whole affair settled as quickly as possible."

xviii

Kit and Tom Watson have heard of the horrors of Newgate, but nothing they have heard can compare with what they now see with their own eyes.

They are brought in and recorded and spend the first night in irons in a cell known as Limbo. It is a routine piece of terror to which all newcomers are treated, a kind of initiation. Their arguments are brushed aside. "It says here 'suspicion of murder,' with an inquest to be held tomorrow," says one of the guards, who leads them up a narrow staircase, across the main gate, to a trapdoor. They are ordered down the hatch into a windowless room. On a black stone a single candle burns. The hatch slams shut and they stand there silently in the dim light, feeling as though they are underground, though they know they are not.

"What a stinking hole," says Kit. "We'll suffocate before morning."

"I'm sure it's only for one night," says Tom. "I'm sure we'll be cleared at the inquest tomorrow."

"And what if we're not?"

"Well, then," says Tom, trying to laugh, "I suppose we'll have to become accustomed to the smell of excrement for the rest of our brief lives."

"How's your wound?" says Kit.

"The bleeding has stopped, thank God." He shuffles around in the confined space, kicking at the straw, only to turn up a dead rat. "Oh, Christ!" he says, and retreats to the small circle of light thrown by the stump of a candle.

"It'll never last through the night," says Kit.

"What night? What day?" says Tom. "It's all the same in here. If we only had some wine, we could drink ourselves to sleep."

"I would gladly try to sleep," says Kit, "if I knew that the coroner's verdict was going to be favorable."

Tom suddenly slumps to the floor, overcome by dizziness. Kit comes to his side. "Are you all right, Tom?"

"I'm not sure," says Tom in a weak voice. "I'm shaking like a leaf and I'm suddenly cold all over."

"The shock is just beginning to reach you," says Kit. "Or perhaps you've lost too much blood."

"I think I'm going to be sick," he says, and tosses forward onto all fours. Kit holds him while he vomits, stroking his back and steadying him. When his spasms have subsided, Kit scrapes together a heap of straw and tries to make him comfortable. "I'm sorry!" Tom manages to whisper. His breathing is labored. "It's foul enough in here already without that."

"Never mind," says Kit. "Lie here. Try to rest. Try not to think about it."

Tom collapses onto the heap of dirty straw. The room seems to be slipping to one side. He shuts his eyes, but it does not help. "I've never killed a man before," he says. "I didn't want to kill him. Oh, what an awful feeling—that steel going into his flesh. Oh, my God! And the blood spurting."

"He deserved it," says Kit. "Put it out of your mind. Try to sleep." He holds his hand against his friend's cheek.

Tom's breathing becomes more regular. His body seems to relax, and soon he is either unconscious or asleep, and Kit lies down beside him.

In the night, scurrying and scratching sounds startle Kit from his restless sleep. There are rats in the place. He sits up, his heart pounding, his eyes trying to penetrate the darkness. The candle has gone out. The darkness is as complete as if he were blind. Terror grips him. He feels the hair rise on the back of his neck and the cold dampness of his hands. In this excited state he waits and waits for some sign that the long night is over.

The next day the jailer removes them, blinking and staggering, into midday sunlight. The coroner, Ion Chakhill, holds his inquest with a jury of twelve men and finds that the murder has in fact been in self-defense. "You'll be needing a drink and some decent lodgings, now," says the jailer, "providing you've got the where-withal to pay for it. But I imagine a fine-lookin' pair of gentlemen like you will be able to afford the very best."

"When can we leave this rathole?" Kit asks.

"Oh, it's not that simple, lad," says the jailer. "The next session's not until early December. And this one here's not allowed a surety in any case. As for you, well, we'll have to see who comes forth with the pledges to bail you out. These things take time. For now you've got your choice. What will it be? The Master's side, the Middle Ward or the Stone Hold?" He laughs, revealing a few yellow teeth and black spaces.

"Give us whatever money will buy," says Tom. With his wounded arm he indicates his purse. Kit opens it and takes out some coins.

The jailer scratches his head and squints his eyes to see how much money is available. "Well, now," he says, "ten shillings will take you a long way toward a good night's rest and some food and drink for a few days." It is exorbitant, even by prison standards, but Kit hands him the money. Their shackles are removed, and they are led down a long corridor.

Later that day they are allowed a visit by Hugh Swift, who explains that he is their lawyer. He sits with them in their small but comparatively civilized cell and explains what is happening on their behalf. "Your bail has been set at forty pounds," he says to Kit. "I'm going to speak with Richard Kitchen, a lawyer at Clifford's Inn. He's gone surety before for one of my friends. But it's a large amount, and he will want some assurances about you, and he may want to share the burden with someone else. Of course, there will be a good fee in it for him. Matthew has been out to Chislehurst to speak with Tom Walsingham, who says he will send his man Ingram Frizer up to assist us in the arrangements."

"Ingram Frizer!" says Kit. "Why couldn't he come himself?"

"It seems he doesn't want to get personally involved," says Hugh.

"No, of course not," says Kit, "not dear old Tom Walsingham, Lord of the Manor. Why should he dirty his hands with the likes of us? I mean, after all, who are we? A pair of writers—a poet and a cobbler's son."

"Easy, Kit," says Tom. "He's got his reasons."

"Frizer will have money with him," says Hugh. "We'll have you out of here before you know it."

"It's wonderful, isn't it, what money can buy?" says Kit.

"And how is Ann taking all this?" Tom asks.

"Better than most women might," he says.

Before he leaves, Hugh says again how sorry he is to have brought on all this trouble. The men embrace, and Hugh leaves, full of encouraging words.

xix

As soon as his bail is arranged, Kit hires a horse and rides out to Scadbury to see Tom Walsingham. He has been in Newgate for some thirteen days. When he arrives, he discovers that Robert Poley is there. He is given an affectionate greeting by both men. They rise to meet him halfway across the rug. Kit does not at first recognize Poley with his new beard, but his voice and manner are familiar. "An awful business," he says. "You must feel dreadful." He is holding Kit's hand overly long and touching his arm. It is a political gesture, not a sexual one. His hands are like his tongue—ambiguous. Kit draws away slightly and turns to Tom, who is about to embrace him. Kit's cold stare modifies his motion and Tom merely puts his arm across his friend's shoulders and says, "So good to see you again. Was it awful in there? In Newgate, I mean?"

"More awful for Tom than for me," he says.

"Come, sit down. What will you have?"

"Whiskey!" says Kit. "Scottish whiskey."

"How appropriate," says Poley. "We were just talking about Scotland."

"Well, don't let me interrupt," says Kit.

"It's all very fascinating," says Tom. "You must hear what Robert has to say. Do go on, Robert, but back up a bit and tell him what you've been telling me."

"The latest rumor," says Poley, "is that King James has entered into a secret agreement with the earls of Huntly, Errol, and Angus to provide the Spaniards with a foothold in Scotland. But, mind you, this is only a rumor, and it, in turn, is explained by other rumors—wheels within wheels. There are those who say that nothing of the sort is about to take place; that James is letting out the rumor in order to put pressure on Elizabeth to name him her successor. Still others say that the rumor has been started by the Catholic earls themselves in order to undermine James's position in relation to Elizabeth. In the meantime, much refugee Catholic activity has shifted from France to Scotland. Since it seems inevitable now that Navarre will be the next king of France, with our backing, of course, the situation there has polarized a bit more clearly. The assassination of Henry the Third, though unfortunate for him, was rather fortunate for England. There is considerable dissension and disenchantment among the English Catholics in France. Many of them have chosen to go to Scotland, where they have generally been given a good reception. Besides, after the debacle of the Spanish Armada, it is now apparent to everyone that a land invasion of England stands a much better chance of success than an invasion by sea."

"But you don't seriously think there will be an invasion, do you?" Walsingham asks.

"That's not an easy question to answer," says Poley. "Should the Queen die suddenly, and should James's claim to the throne be challenged—well, there's no telling what would happen at that point. Almost everyone in Scotland wants to be prepared for this possibility. James is playing both sides at this point, catering to Protestants and Catholics alike. On the one hand, he has just married, by proxy, Princess Anne of Denmark, a Catholic. On the other hand, he is harboring Puritan malcontents, such as John Penry. He is also cultivating good relationships with a number of English noblemen, who hope to thrive under his rule—should he come to the throne. The Sheltons, for instance."

Kit glances at Tom Walsingham, who catches his look but says nothing. "Does that explain your interest in Audrey Shelton?" says Kit.

"I never said I was interested in Audrey Shelton," says Tom.

"But what a nice piece of insurance that would be," says Kit. "I mean, to be married into a family that is in such favor with the new king."

"He's not the king yet and may not be for many years to come, if ever," says Tom. He looks accused.

Poley rescues him. "My dear Christopher, don't be simplistic. It's a two-way street, this business of courting the court of Scotland. You see, we know which families have some leanings toward James, and which families he tends to favor. The Queen is fully aware that these are precisely the people who might be used to exert some influence on James. And that's why Tom here will soon be making a trip to Edinburgh."

Kit is taken by surprise. "Tom?" he says. "Going to Scotland? What in the world for?"

"Oh, all very straightforward," says Poley. "He will be one of several personal emissaries to the court of James, carrying with him official messages from Her Majesty. Communications between the two principals must be constant, competent, and diplomatic. It wouldn't do to send just anyone. There are, after all, certain

factions in this country who would hate to see the son of Mary
Stuart sitting on the English throne. They will do everything in
their power to prevent it."

"Does that mean you're allowing yourself to be *used?*" says Kit.

"No," says Tom. "All it means is that I must give James the
impression that I favor his succession."

"And do you?" says Kit.

"As a matter of fact, I do," he says. "I understand he's quite an
intelligent man."

"And I've heard that he's a slobbering, shuffling idiot and a
sexual pervert," says Kit.

"Do my ears deceive me?" says Poley with a smile. "Aren't you
the Christopher Marlowe who was supposed to have said in public
one day that all those who do not love tobacco and boys are fools?"

"I don't plan to be the king of England," says Kit.

"But surely the man's personal tastes don't disqualify him," says
Poley.

"Does that mean that you, too, support his succession?" says Kit.

"I didn't say that. Nor was I really defending the man," says
Poley. "I admit that he probably drinks too much. Everybody in
Scotland does. And his sexual leanings are the subject of some
amusing gossip. He's also fascinated with witchcraft, if that's of any
interest to you. But you'll be disappointed to discover that he hates
tobacco. But all of this is beside the point. And as far as my personal
preferences are concerned—well, you should know by this time that
I have none. I am in the service. I have very specific problems to
deal with, and I take my assignments very seriously."

"And what exactly is your assignment this time?" says Kit.

"Can't you guess?" says Poley.

"I'm afraid not," says Kit. "I have no mind for this sort of
thing."

Poley laughs, a bit too theatrically. "Now, really, Mr. Machiavelli. You're much too modest. I think you have an excellent mind
for all sorts of things."

Tom interrupts. "What exactly will you be doing?" he says.

"Why, simply discovering the truth, that's all." His eyebrows are raised, and he has a look of smug innocence on his face. "We must discover the true intentions of the Catholic earls. And there is only one way to do that. We must do with them what we did in the Babington affair: set up a system of communications for them so that what they have to say to each other and to their friends in England will pass through our hands. We must go to them as sympathizers, which, for me, is not very difficult. I don't have to tell you how much time I have spent in prison establishing my reputation as a Catholic sympathizer and courier."

"Ah, it all becomes clear now," says Tom.

"And you, too, Kit, have something of a reputation," says Poley. "You would be very useful in this enterprise."

"In what way?" says Kit.

"Well, for one thing," says Poley, "some of your friends from Rheims are now in Scotland. It would not be very difficult to insinuate you into Catholic circles. You could explain that you are considering Scotland as a refuge from persecution at home. And that's not so far from the truth as you might imagine. To be brutally realistic for a moment, the time may come, my friend, when your lie will prove to be the truth. You are very outspoken. You are probably being watched. If you don't stop attacking the Established Church and calling Moses a juggler and Jesus Christ a homosexual, you're going to be in very serious trouble."

"It's all tavern talk," says Kit. "A man's not responsible for what he says when he's drunk."

"*In vino veritas!*" says Poley.

XX

It is not until the next day that Tom and Kit are left alone to talk about more personal matters. Robert Poley has gone off early in the morning, taking with him a promise from Kit that he will consider a trip to Scotland, but not until after December third, since he has been bound over until the next sessions of Newgate and must live a proper and quiet life until then. And, what's more, he's got a play to finish.

They watch Poley ride off. The morning is chilly, but the sun has just risen and the sky is a brightening ocean of blue in which puffs of white islands are tinted with yellow light. The ground is damp with dew, and birds chatter like. schoolboys in the choirs of the greenery.

"I hope you're not angry with me," says Tom as they stroll back toward the house.

"What makes you think I'm angry?" says Kit.

"I had that feeling when you first arrived yesterday," says Tom.

There is a long pause. "Well, perhaps I am—or was," says Kit.

"It was because of Frizer, wasn't it?" says Tom. "I mean, because I sent him to take care of things."

"Well, damn it," says Kit, stopping in front of the house, "I don't see why you couldn't come yourself. It wasn't just a matter of money."

"I'm sorry," says Tom. "I didn't think it would make that much difference."

"What you mean is that you didn't want to get involved. Why don't you tell the truth?"

"All right, then, I didn't want to get involved. Is that what you wanted to hear? Listen, Christopher, I love you dearly. You can't deny that. But don't drag me into your sordid London brawls."

"Good lord, Mr. Walsingham," Kit shouts, "what are you talking about? Your good friend and mine Tom Watson gets attacked on the street, defends himself to save his life, and you call it a sordid brawl. Do you have any idea what we have been through in the past fortnight, and what poor Tom still must face, locked up in that filthy prison? Have you ever slept in the company of rats and gotten drunk in the Boozing Ken with cutthroats and counterfeiters? Have you ever listened in the night to desperate men huddled together, starving to death, sleeping in their own excrement?"

"I'm sorry," he says in a barely audible whisper, his eyes averted. "Perhaps I should have come to see you, after all."

"Yes," says Kit. "I think you should have. We are not common criminals, you know. And we were not in prison through any fault of our own."

They are back in the house now. They have gone into the study and closed the door. "Afraid of the servants?" says Kit, unable to conceal his contempt.

Tom goes all limp and apologetic. "Look, Christopher," he says. "I can't tell you how sorry I am about all this. I did the wrong thing. I know it now. But I'll make it up to you. Just tell me what it is that you want."

Kit walks back and forth, agitated, rubbing his hands, then his chin, then brushing his hair back. He stops in front of Tom, who is sitting down, his hands folded in front of his mouth as though he is praying or deep in thought. "I'll tell you what I want," he says. "I want to live my life honestly and truly. I want to be whatever it is I am and not somebody else's idea of me—whether it's yours or the Church's or the government's. I will not act a part for anyone. God knows, it's small enough a thing—one stinking human life. It's gone in a moment. I don't even know for sure where. Oblivion, perhaps. Or some undiscovered country. It doesn't matter. That's business for the soul—*if* there is a soul. I'm talking about this life of ours, of mine! I am in my twenty-sixth year. Before long I'll be thirty. And before much longer I'll be dead. I want to do what I please, say what I please, write what I please, make love when I feel like it, get drunk when I want to and tell my friends I love them and my enemies I hate them. I am not devious. I am not a coward."

"You expect too much out of life," says Tom. "You'll be disappointed."

"But how else can I live?" says Kit. "What am I to do? Fawn and cater and simulate? Flatter important men? Speak lies? Write frivolous, harmless nonsense? And what for? To rise in the world? Where do you think I am going to rise? Me, a cobbler's son! I will never be more than a writer. All I can hope for is to be the best writer who ever lived. You see, I believe there is magic in the written word—and that's another kind of success. I will never have what you have, Tom, because I was not born into it. Therefore, I don't have to protect it or long for it. I simply will never have it: noble family traditions, social position, estates, money. I will never even be rich. With luck, a merchant can get rich. And many a Jew has been rich. But how can a writer get rich? I rely on the fees I make from my plays and from gifts. Gifts! I hate the word. And yet, Tom, I take your gifts. You have no idea how much I want to be the giver of gifts and not the receiver. It's not quite the same to play king of the tavern and give a shilling-token gift to a pretty young actor or a boy of the streets, as you call them. That's a pathetic piece of play-acting, a poor imitation of our more real lords and ladies."

"If you don't like my gifts, why do you take them?" says Tom.

"I take them because I like nice things," says Kit. "It's not the gifts I dislike, you fool; it's the act of receiving them. I feel I should fall on my knees and kiss your royal ring. And that makes me furious."

"You know I don't expect anything of the sort," says Tom.

"But do you understand what I'm talking about?" says Kit.

"Of course I do," says Tom. "I've been aware of the tension between us for a long time. I love you, Christopher, but you also frighten me, and I must confess that I am something of a coward. I can't help it that I was born to certain responsibilities and to a certain social position. I would love to join you from time to time in your—your *freer* way of life, but I hate gossip and scandal. I know you despise the word, but I want my respectability and I like my position. I would not trade it for yours. And yet I envy you. I envy you because you have something that I will never have—the courage to be yourself. Forgive me, Kit, if I am not as brave. I can't go around confessing to the world that I have strange longings; that I am in love with a poet who lives in Holywell Lane, that I would prefer not to marry; that, given a better world than this, I would sweep you away to some Grecian isle and there, amidst nymphs and satyrs, we would while away our lives in sweet pleasures in the orchards and vineyards of our wildest imaginations. But that's a dream, Kit. A myth. It doesn't exist. What exists is the dreary day-to-day cannibalism of English politics and English society. Thank God for this place in the country! I would go mad if I could not get away from London as often as I do. I love it here at

Scadbury. And I would love it infinitely more were you to come live here with me in some acceptable capacity."

Kit seems to have spent himself. He sits down at Tom's desk and toys with a crystal ornament. "I love it here, too," he says. "I've been tempted a thousand times to give up the noise and confusion of London. Unfortunately, it is my arena, and in it I must play out my life."

"You don't have to live in London to be a writer," says Tom. "Look at Edmund Spenser. All those years in Ireland. Even among the barbarians one can be civilized." He gets up and goes to the desk. He leans across it—their roles reversed, as though Kit were now the lord of the manor, sitting there in Tom's place. "Come, dear Kit," he says. "Come live with me and be my friend. Stay away from those drunken rebels, those atheists you call your friends. They'll bring you down. And all for what?"

"For truth," says Kit, transfixed by the crystal form.

Tom tosses up his arms. "Ah, the miserable ghost of truth. You can pursue that phantom right into the teeth of hell. It's all a myth, I tell you!"

Kit bursts out laughing. "Can you stand there, Tom, and tell me that the truth's a myth? Where's your logic, man?"

"I say the blind pursuit of the truth absolute is the shortest way to hell. It is the oldest sin, Christopher. Pride. That's what it is. Prometheus. Icarus. The Tower of Babel. You are a scholar. Don't you know these things? You will fly to hell on the wings of pride!"

Kit is reduced to a near whisper. "You sound like a preacher, Mr. Walsingham. Spare me the fire and brimstone."

"It would do you no harm to go to church a bit more often," says Tom.

"Perhaps," he says, "I should have taken holy orders, after all. Then I, rather than Richard Harvey, could have been the rector of Chislehurst, as you have so often pointed out."

"It might have kept you out of trouble," says Tom.

"Perhaps I don't want to be out of trouble that badly," says Kit. "And yet, what marvelous sermons I could have preached—full of the blood of the Lamb of God, the miracle of salvation, and the evils of the public theatre. I would have had them all on their knees, weeping for their sins. And I could have published my collected sermons in forty volumes and written treatises on the true enemies of the Holy Ghost. And meanwhile, you and I could have proven in the virgin woods of Chislehurst that it was all a pack of lies."

Tom turns away from the desk and walks across the room. He stops in front of a window, where he is a silhouette against the morning light. "I can't match wits with you for long, Kit. And it seems there's not much more to discuss."

"Shall I leave, then?" he says.

There is a long pause, a silence broken only by the sound of birds. "No," says Tom. "I can't send you away. Stay awhile, at least until your appearance at the next sessions of Newgate. That will give us two months. We can talk about it again after that."

He considers for a moment and then says, "All right. I'll stay, but on one condition only."

"What's that?" says Tom, a note of apprehension in his voice.

"That you send Ingram Frizer away as long as I am here," says Kit.

"Send him where?" Tom asks.

Kit stands up suddenly and strides across the room toward Tom. "I don't give a damn where you send him, just get rid of him. I can't stand the man. He's—he's sinister. And besides—"

"Please don't suggest again, Kit, that there is anything between me and Ingram, because there isn't."

"Isn't there?"

They are standing face to face now. Tom allows their eyes to meet. "No," he says, "nothing at all!"

"But you will send him away, won't you?"

"If you insist—yes. I will send him to—I don't know. Scotland, perhaps."

"You can send him to hell, for all I care," says Kit. "As long as he's not slinking around here, watching us with those snake's eyes of his."

"All right, all right," says Tom. "Consider it done, and let's not talk about it anymore. Come, give me your hand."

xxi

"Come live with me, and be my love,
And we will all the pleasures prove
That hills and valleys, dales and fields,
And all the craggy mountains yields.

And we will sit upon the rocks,
Seeing the shepherds feed their flocks
By shallow rivers, to whose falls
Melodious birds sing madrigals.

And I will make thee beds of roses,
And a thousand fragrant posies,
A cap of flowers and a kirtle
Embroider'd all with leaves of myrtle.

A gown made of the finest wool
Which from our pretty lambs we pull,
Fair lined slippers for the cold,
With buckles of the purest gold;

A belt of straw and ivy-buds,
With coral clasps and amber studs,
And if these pleasures may thee move,
Come live with me, and be my love.

Thy silver dishes for thy meat,
As precious as the gods do eat,
Shall on an ivory table be
Prepar'd each day for thee and me.

The shepherd swains shall dance and sing
For thy delight each May-morning;

If these delights thy mind may move,
Then live with me, and be my love."

In the cool, bright air of October, they lie in a small clearing on the slope of a hill that looks out over fields and hedges toward a lake. Heavy summer has come around to fall and given up its harvest. In the checkered fields in the distance they see the men moving up and down the rows, cutting and bundling, their bent forms and slow movements echoing the movements of the grazing sheep. Beyond a cluster of low houses with thatched roofs are orchards rich with apples and pears and, beyond them, still-uncut fields of wheat that move like blond hair in the mild breeze.

"It's a marvelous poem," says Tom. He lies on his back, his head against Kit's thigh. And Kit leans against the smooth bark of an ancient beech tree, a sheet of paper in his hand. "It should be set to music."

"It's as much your poem as mine," says Kit.

"I had nothing to do with it," says Tom.

"Yes, you did," says Kit. "You gave me the first line."

"I don't remember," says Tom.

"It doesn't matter," says Kit. "What we need now is a title."

"Make it something simple, please," says Tom. "Nothing Latin or cumbersome."

Kit's eyes sweep slowly across the landscape. In the distance the white steeple of a church catches the early sun. Down a narrow red-brown path a man is driving a herd of pigs. Hills of creamy clouds crown the fruity earth near the horizon, but all the rest of heaven's vault is delicately blue, whitening toward the sun. Amidst the grazing sheep stands an isolated shepherd. He is bearded and long-haired, and his rags are belted tightly around his waist. From this distance Kit cannot tell whether he is old or young. A child with golden hair runs across the rolling pasture. The shepherd turns. The child flings himself about his waist, and the thin shrillness of his innocent voice carries across the fields and mingles with the music of the birds. Perhaps he's another Christ, thinks Kit, and this is the last of all our days on earth.

"Well?" says Tom, interrupting his reverie. "What are you going to call it?"

"How about 'The Passionate Shepherd to His Love,' in honor of this pastoral paradise?"

"Yes, I like that," says Tom, "I like it very much. Did you write it for me?"

"I wrote it for poetry," says Kit. "And for you."

"Then I want it," he says, sitting up and reaching for the sheet of paper.

Kit holds it out of his reach. "Not until I've made a copy," he says. "You can't expect me to remember my own poetry."

"I'll make a copy for you," says Tom.

"Your writing is unreadable," says Kit. "I'll get Tom Kyd to do it for me. His father was a scrivener. He's got a good hand."

"A good hand for what?" says Tom.

"Oh, for this and that," says Kit, teasingly.

"Then I'll chain you here in Chislehurst, and you'll never see him again," says Tom.

"Poor fellow! He feels somewhat out of things, not having gone to the University and all. But he has a modicum of talent. We've done some work together."

"On what?"

"We were working together on a play called *Prince Hamlet*, based on a tale out of *The Danish History* of Saxo Grammaticus. Something Tom dug up. He's full of ideas, most of them ridiculous. But this story seemed to have possibilities. Do you know it?"

"No," says Tom.

"It's fairly marvelous," says Kit. "Full of madness and slaughter. A real opportunity for the stage; though, artistically, I don't think it has much point. Another one of those Senecan revenge plays— that's all it was good for. And since Tom had had such good luck with his *Spanish Tragedy*, I suppose he was looking to duplicate his success."

"Did you ever finish it?"

"I'm afraid we had some disagreement about it," says Kit. "And in the end, I gave it all over to Tom and told him to do it his own way. You see, I would have made the hero a much more complicated person, but Tom didn't know what I was talking about."

"And did he have it acted?" says Tom.

"Yes, but only several times," says Kit, "and it was not well received. Too bad, in a way. It could have been something better!"

xxii

In the weeks that follow, Tom and Kit have a great deal of fun with *The Rich Jew of Malta*. They dress themselves up as theatrical Jews, cutting up old drapery and fashioning wigs and false noses. They tint their skin and put on long Semitic beards. They hunch their backs. They rub their hands.

Halfway through the play, Marlowe has an inspiration. "I'll put old Machiavelli on the stage. I'll give him a prologue to speak. He will be himself, but in the extreme."

"Oh, they'll love it, all those vulgar shopkeepers," says Tom. "It will be more clapper-clau'd than anything of Robert Greene or Robert Wilson."

And when the prologue is done, Kit puts on a borrowed suit of black and oils his beard to a tiny black point. He surprises Tom in his bedroom and forces him to listen:

> "To some perhaps my name is odious;
>   But such as love me, guard me from their tongues,
>   And let them know that I am Machevill,
>   And weigh not men, and therefore not men's words.
>   Admir'd I am of those that hate me most . . ."

"Oh, that's hard language," says Tom, "even in the mouth of a villain. 'I count religion but a childish toy.' Is that what he says? And, 'Might first made kings.' How will that sit with the Master of the Revels?"

"He is no ordinary villain," says Kit. "He is the arch villain of all times. And the Jew, who follows his philosophy, will be given a horrible death—I don't know yet what it shall be, but it shall be horrible indeed. Think me up something gruesome, Tom. I want all the women to faint, every one of them. Come, what shall we do at last to this awful Jew?"

"What a pity we were born with a Christian conscience," says Tom. "We would have made a marvelous pair of wandering thieves, adventurers or pirates. Can't you see us now, preying on Spanish ships loaded with gold from America, or raiding the merchantmen of the Mediterranean and escaping to the secret coves of Corsica or Libya?"

"Oh, it's all very convincing in books and plays," says Kit, "but reality—ah, that's another matter. Think of the heat, the scabs, the lack of food. Think of scorpions, the pursuivants, the navies of Venice and Italy. And think of the ultimate executioner, when the game is up—the rope around your neck, the cold blade against your belly and your chest."

"Oh, stop! Stop!" says Tom. "I'll give it all up. I'll stay honest and live out my life in dreary Kent and ordinary London."

"Not to mention sunny Scotland," says Kit, "where once, I heard, it did not rain one day a thousand years ago. When is it that you are due to make this trip?"

"Not until the end of the month," says Tom, "but before your appearance in court. You're welcome to stay here, of course, while I'm gone. Come back after the December third sessions."

"Providing I am found totally innocent and let go," says Kit.

"Can there be any question about it?" says Tom. "It's an entirely routine matter."

They are seated by the fire. The night is cold, October having given way to November. The farmers have cut and stacked their wood for the winter. There has been a good deal of rain, and the harvested fields have turned to mud.

"So our little holiday draws to a close soon," says Kit.

"Inevitably," says Tom, "but there will be others, I hope, unless I can persuade you to retire to the country."

"Not just now," he says. "The play is done, and I am rather eager to try it out on the amoral mob."

"You miss London, then?" says Tom.

"In many ways—yes," says Kit. "But these have been good days, and I may be back more often than I am welcome. Besides, you have an excellent wine cellar, among other virtues." He raises his glass to Tom. They smile and drink.

xxiii

After five months in Newgate, Tom Watson is finally released with a formal pardon from the Queen. The law's cruel and ridiculous delay leaves him bitter. The dampness, the boredom, the debilitating consolations of the Boozing Ken leave him pale, rheumatic, and emaciated. Only in his thirty-third year, he looks considerably older. It is the twelfth of February, 1590. His homecoming is celebrated by all the literary dignitaries and theatrical lowlife of Shoreditch and Norton Folgate. He is a hero in their eyes—a man as swift with his sword as he is deft with his pen. Their gathering place is The Nag's Head, not far from Primrose Lane.

Watson sits with Matthew Roydon and George Chapman and Kit, but they are soon joined by Robert Greene and Tom Nashe. "We drink to your return from the jungles of Newgate," says Roberto. "And welcome you once more into these Arcadian forests of iambic swains and bubbling bawds. Oh, what a gaping vacuum your terrible absence has been to us. What tears we've shed, what tales we've told in the cups of our despair."

"Sit down, you bag of booze," says Kit, "and let the poor man speak."

With an elaborate burp he lowers himself onto the bench. The silent, smiling, wiry Nashe joins him. "They say that whole educations can be had in Marshalsea and Newgate," says Matthew, who has been drinking with Kit since before Tom's arrival.

"They teach us something about the darker side of things, that's for sure," says Tom. "Man's capacity for cruelty and corruption is appalling."

He recites a long list of abuses and describes a cast of Newgate characters. "There was a man, one William Reid, who murdered his wife and child for no reason that he could explain. And Henry Hopkins, who was a grave-robber and morbidly fascinated with dead bodies. And Richard Gray, whose habit it was to marry old women for their money and then dispose of them by various poisons and accidents. And George Cockcroft, printer of vile and immoral literature, as lewd as the mind can imagine, a whole hell of sexual perversions. And one John Poole, a maker of counterfeit coins."

"I remember him well," says Kit. "He had a great skill in the mixing of metals, as much as any scholar or alchemist. And he taught me enough so that I, too, might make my own coins. For, as he says, by what right can one man stamp a coin and not another, since it is only the shaping and imprinting of metal? And Richard Chomley and his band of atheists have said the same, claiming that when they take over the country and select a king from among the people, they will banish the Church and govern themselves and strike new coins, but as real currency for their godless utopia and not as symbols of God's granting this or that man divine privileges."

As Kit talks, an inconspicuous man, sitting at a table nearby, scribbles notes on a piece of paper with a book open before him, as though he might be a scholar or a merchant catching up on his work over a glass of wine and a late supper. His name is Richard Baines. He is employed by the government and is a professional informer. His employment is kept confidential. When he appears as a witness, it is as a private citizen, concerned with the security of the state and the sacredness of the established religion. He listens and writes: *That he had as good right to coin as the Queen of England, and that he was acquainted with one Poole, a prisoner in Newgate, who had great skill in mixture of metals, and having learned some things of him, he intended, through help of a cunning stampmaker, to coin French crowns, pistolets, and English shillings . . ."*

"I understand it was you," says Robert Greene to Kit, "who persuaded this Richard Chomley to atheism and revolution and that he and his followers will show you their gratitude by making you king of the churchless state. Is that right?"

"We have had some discussions, that's all," says Kit. "He and I and Richard Strong and George Collins and William Greene."

"Men with small enough educations to be persuaded by the likes of you," says Nashe. "You'll all be swinging to the tune of Walsingham before long."

"You misunderstand me," says Kit, his face flushed, his eyes wide. "I am not a revolutionary. I am a professional drinker, though I make my living by my pen. And my interest in religious atrocities is a kind of amusement. I am amused by the ordinary man's inability to understand anything objectively. He is appallingly ignorant, selfish, frightened, gullible, and illogical. Naturally, he is devout. The truth is, after all, negotiable—ask Tom Watson. And what better bargain with life can one strike than to live with the promise of immortality?"

John Lyly has joined the discussion. "Since the truth is absolute and will out," he says, "there are no bargains to be made."

"Except with the devil," says Robert Greene. "Witness one Dr. Faustus, that lecherous conjurer. Though any man who would have Helen of Troy for his paramour can't be all bad."

"A bargain with the devil is only a bargain with oneself," says Kit.

"Then you deny magic," says John Lyly.

"It goes against reason," says Kit. "A magician can only create illusions, whether he is Faustus or Moses or Jesus Christ. They were all magicians, all conjurers. Do you think for a moment that Christ could actually bring a man back from the dead? Nobody ever comes back from the dead."

"You say such things are fantastic, and yet you write plays about them," says Lyly.

"Why not?" says Kit. "The poet's vision goes beyond the possible, and his craft is often merely a tool for entertainment. Surely you, of all people—and Tom Nashe and Roberto—know what I mean. Three fine tools for official hypocrisy!"

"What do you mean by that?" shouts Tom Nashe.

"Oh, come now, little Tom prick-pen," says Kit. "Don't tell us that you and Lyly-white John here are not composing magnificent lies for old Whitgift to answer Martin Marprelate for his attacks on the 'cursed uncircumcised murdering generation' of the clergy and 'the horned monsters of the Conspiration House.' And you dare talk about *truth absolute.*"

"It's not the same thing at all," says Lyly.

"Is it true that Martin Marprelate is really John Penry?" asks John Alleyn from the fringe of the gathering.

"Ask Kit here," says Roberto. "They say he's been to Scotland to spy out conspiracies."

"Actually, I went to Scotland," says Kit, "to speak with King James. I felt he needed my advice in these trying times."

"And what did you speak about?" asks Robert Greene.

"Why, bugbears and buggery, of course," says Kit. "That is to say, superstition, witchcraft, Christianity, and sodomy—a happy combination of corruptions. Unfortunately, our conversation was not consummated, and I have returned empty-handed. I think I shall advise the Queen against a Scottish succession."

The wit of the conversation rises in direct proportion to its decline into illogic and irreverence. The wine goes around. Toasts are drunk to this and that—to Tom Watson's return, to Kit Marlowe's *Rich Jew*, to Martin Marprelate, and to the ghost of Dick Tarleton.

The humorless informer Richard Baines scribbles furiously and struggles to find some coherence in the boisterous and drunken conversation. *"That the Indians and many authors of antiquity have assuredly written above six thousand years ago, whereas Adam is said to have lived within six thousand years . . .*

"That Moses was but a juggler and that Thomas Harriot, Sir Walter Ralegh's man, can do more than he can.

"That the first beginning of religion was only to keep men in awe . . .

"That Christ was a bastard and his mother dishonest . . .

"That Christ deserved better to die than Barrabas and that the Jews made a good choice, though Barrabas was both a thief and a murderer.

"That if there be any God or any good religion, then it is the papists, because the service of God is performed with more ceremonies, such as

elevation of the mass, organs, singing men, shaven crowns, and so on.
And that all Protestants are hypocritical asses . . .

"*That all the New Testament is filthily written . . .*

"*That the angel Gabriel was bawd to the Holy Ghost, because he*
brought the salutation to Mary.

"*That one Richard Chomley has confessed that he was persuaded by*
Marlowe's reasons to become an atheist."

Richard Baines pauses, takes out his handkerchief, wipes his
sweating hands and his forehead, and then begins again. It is late.
The crowd begins to thin out at The Nag's Head. Baines notes it
down that Marlowe and Watson, among others, are in a state of
serious intoxication. They leave, supporting one another and
singing:

> "Now that the truth is tried
> Of things that be late past,
> I see, when all is spied,
> That words are but a blast,
> And promise
> Is but a heat
> If not performed at last."

xxiv

By the spring of 1590, Christopher is a regular member of the
group that meets at Ralegh's Durham House. Though Ralegh's
star shines with sufficient brightness in Cynthia's sky, there is
another star rising to rival it—the broad-shouldered, handsome,
brash, unruly stepson of the Earl of Leicester—Robert Devereux,
second Earl of Essex. His erratic behavior and his influence over
the Queen are frequent subjects of discussion at Durham House,
along with things more scientific and poetic.

Two important events have occurred in recent days to heighten
political speculations and to lure these free-thinkers of Durham
House away from their more usual preoccupations: the nature of
Nature, perception, astrology, mathematics and cosmology. "What

an incredibly foolish thing to do," says William Warner. He is referring to the recent marriage between the Earl of Essex and Frances Walsingham, the widow of Philip Sidney. This is one of the important events that they cannot keep from discussing. The other, less surprising and less recent, is the death of Sir Francis Walsingham. All of London is busy trying to determine how these two events will affect the state of things in England. Who will succeed the remarkable Sir Francis as Secretary of State? (Poor man, he died so miserably in debt that he had to be buried at night to prevent his creditors from seizing his coffin.) And how severely will Elizabeth punish Essex for marrying beneath him and without her permission?

"Though she rages now," says George Carey, "I understand that there are already indications that she will forgive him. She is not so young as she once was and is somewhat hardened to these disappointments. Robert Devereux is twenty-four. Elizabeth is fifty-seven. It was all very different with you, Walter, and certainly with Robert Dudley. She was a girl, then, and might easily have married Robert. But I don't think there was ever any real likelihood that she would marry you."

"Oh, don't you?" says Sir Walter.

"Well, I always assumed it was highly unlikely," says George Carey. At forty-three he is the oldest one in the room. He sits comfortably with a glass in his hand, a bearded, ordinary-looking man next to Ralegh. And next to him is the so-called master of the school, Thomas Harriot. Through these political discussions he usually sits aloof and indifferent, eyebrows arched, a patient young schoolmaster waiting for his scholars to come to attention.

The other men present on this particular spring evening at Durham House are Ferdinando Stanley, Walter Warner and Robert Hughes; and three poets, George Chapman, Matthew Roydon, and Christopher Marlowe.

Having discussed, nearly to extinction, the death of Sir Francis Walsingham and the marriage of Essex to his widowed daughter, they move on to other matters. "I understand," says Ralegh, "that Kit Marlowe has prepared a little lecture of some sort for us. I have no idea what it's all about, so I can give it no further introduction than that." He nods in Kit's direction.

"I had hoped to make certain observations about religion," says Kit, "with special reference to the Old and New Testaments. In our rambles here we have touched on many of these points, but we have not looked at them in an organized way." He goes on to point out that there is very little convincing evidence that the Scriptures are anything but the scribblings of ordinary men, and not very literary men at that. "There are discrepancies and contradictions that one would hardly want to attribute to God. And the whole thing is badly put together." He denies that God can speak through mere mortals or that there is any way, in fact, for communication to take place between man and God. He does not deny the existence of God but defines the force that binds and runs the universe as something other than the God of the Scriptures. "God is not a man, nor does He have the body of a man or the tongue of a man. If there is a God at all, it is merely a concept in terms of forces and causes—that's all. Without a personality and perhaps without compassion. This first cause of things, whatever it is, is probably indifferent to human problems and human suffering. Hence, it is ridiculous to pray to it." He attacks the Holy Trinity as nonsense. "As history," he says, "the Bible is grossly inaccurate." He sees no evidence for the deification of Christ. And if, through what we call the soul, we participate in some fashion in those mysterious forces we call God, it is more than likely that soul is part of body and dies when the body dies. The gist of his whole argument is that the basis of all Christianity is the Bible and that the Bible is not reliable. "If we expose Moses, the Lawgiver, as a mere juggler, that is to say, a man who deceived his people in order to establish his power over them; and if we expose Christ, the Redeemer, as a mere conjurer who misled people into believing that he was the Son of God by certain magic tricks—well, then, what do we have? We have the enormous superstructure of the Church, built on a swamp of fiction. After the first lies, the rest was all politics, all organization, all quibbling and ecclesiastical law. An enormous debate over something that doesn't exist."

Kit's "lecture" is followed by a long silence. Finally Ralegh clears his throat and says, "Well, now, who will venture a refutation?"

XXV

Archbishop Whitgift is invited to a quiet supper with Lord Burghley and his son, Robert Cecil. They talk inevitably about the subjects that preoccupy them all: the continuing war with Spain, the arrival in Brittany of new Spanish troops under Don John D'Aquila, the delicate business of persuading King James of Scotland to deal more harshly with his Catholic factions, the eternal troubles in Ireland, and the still unresolved question of who should assume permanently the position left vacant by the death of Sir Francis Walsingham. His duties have fallen for the moment to Lord Burghley, who is assisted by his son.

Among the lesser matters discussed on this perfectly ordinary occasion is an incident at The Theatre. "Quite a scuffle, I hear," says Robert Cecil. "They say old Burbage bashed a fellow in the nose and made him bleed."

"A totally unreliable bunch of people," says Lord Burghley, adding water to his wine. "And if you will forgive me, John, for saying it once more, it was a dreadful mistake on your part to involve such people in political matters."

"You needn't labor the point, William," says Whitgift. "I have made my confession a thousand times."

"I mean," says Burghley, "that they are already too much involved in politics and religion. Some represent their own views, but many are hired or bribed or urged by this or that group or this or that aspiring individual. We can't have this sort of thing. It is a potential source of civil disturbance. If we are to have plays at all, they must be severely restricted to innocent entertainments. I would rather see the groundlings laugh at a touch of ordinary obscenity than to see them stirred to riot by a piece of propaganda concocted and paid for by Essex or Ralegh or anyone else."

"Our new regulations, William, will go a long way in this direction," says Whitgift.

"Provided they are carried out and enforced," says Burghley.

"Our Master of the Revels, Sir Edmund Tilney, has specific instructions to be as severe as the law will allow him to be," says Whitgift.

"And, speaking of literary propagandists," says Burghley, "has Thomas Bancroft found out anything further about this Marprelate fellow?"

"Whoever he is," says Whitgift, "he seems to have been accommodated in Scotland."

"I thought you knew his identity," says Burghley. "I thought he was a certain John Penry."

"Let us say that he is *at least* John Penry," says Whitgift. "He may be considerably more people than that. He may, in fact, be an entire organization. And certain members of that organization are undoubtedly still here in London."

"Well, good lord, man, why can't you discover them?" says Burghley.

"Because there are a quarter of a million people in London," says Whitgift, "and most of them are dishonest and irreligious, if not downright criminal. The only way that we could possibly put an end to sedition and heretical literature is to close down all the stationers and all the theatres and put all the scribblers instantly into prison. In which case, we would probably have a revolution on our hands."

"It would be helpful, wouldn't it," says Robert Cecil, "if King James were a little more cooperative."

Lord Burghley pulls at his beard meditatively and then puts his hand on his son's arm. "Robert, weren't you at Cambridge with this Christopher Marlowe fellow?"

"For a while, yes," he says.

"Do you think he has anything to do with these Marprelate attacks? I mean, he has something of a reputation, doesn't he, for being rather outspoken against the Church?"

"It's very difficult to tell about Christopher," says Robert. "He's quite erratic. Oh, but brilliant! Brilliant! I've heard him called a papist and I've heard him called a Puritan. I've even heard him called an atheist. But, quite honestly, I don't think he's really interested in politics or religion. I think he's interested in poetry."

"He was one of Sir Francis's confidential couriers or something, wasn't he?" says Lord Burghley. "I remember the Council had to make excuses for him so that he could be granted his M.A. at Cambridge."

"Yes," says Robert, "he's had some assignments abroad, most recently in Scotland, but on perfectly routine matters. His behavior has been partly cultivated, you know. I mean, he was supposed to give out the impression that he was pro-Catholic, in order to be a more effective agent. He seems, on occasion, to have been trusted by the Catholics, but in any case, his involvement in these things is quite limited."

Burghley turns to Whitgift and says, "What do you think, John?"

"He is already being watched," says the Archbishop, "along with one Matthew Roydon and quite a few other people in that circle—if you know what I mean."

They clear their throats, refill their glasses, and go back to the more comfortable question of the Scottish succession. Robert Cecil is relieved, but he promises himself that as soon as possible he should have a confidential talk with Sir Walter.

xxvi

Robert Poley's sudden appearance at The White Lion one morning is no mere coincidence. He has traced Kit to this little seclusion of his and intrudes on his reading, his wine, and his meditations.

He comes directly to the point, without his usual deceptive sociability. "Will you kindly explain to me," he says, "what all this business with William Bray is?"

"William Bray?" says Kit. "Why, what's so important about William Bray?"

"You brought him certain books from Scotland when I sent you there last winter, didn't you?"

"Is there any harm in that? After all, the man is a dealer in St. Paul's and a fancier of books."

"Do you have any idea what sort of books they were?"

"I personally don't care what sort of books they were," says Kit. "As far as I'm concerned, what a man reads is his own business."

Poley heaves a sigh of impatience. "It so happens, Christopher, that Mr. Bray is perhaps the chief conveyor of Catholic literature into England—illegal literature! And it seems that you have participated, knowingly or unknowingly, in this traffic."

"If he's such a notorious peddler of papist propaganda," says Kit, "then why hasn't he been arrested?"

"Because he is more useful precisely where he is," says Poley. "We have drawn up a considerable list of his customers."

"Then what does it matter that I brought him in a few books?" says Kit.

"Because, you fool," says Poley, "you were not authorized to do so, and if this fact is discovered by anyone else, you are liable to fall under suspicion."

"I thought I was *supposed* to fall under suspicion," says Kit.

"Publicly, yes!" he says. "But not within the organization. I am having a difficult enough time myself persuading my superiors that I am not a double agent—especially now that Sir Francis is dead. Don't you understand anything?"

"I'm not as sophisticated in these matters as you are, Robert," says Kit. "I wish you would explain."

"I have this information through Berden, who himself now is beginning to wonder. You see, someone might imagine that you and I were working together in this matter."

"But it was an accident," says Kit. "William asked for a few books, and I brought them in for him. I never gave it much thought."

Poley has a long, penetrating look at him, his jaws working. "Are you sure?" he says. "Are you absolutely sure? You must be honest with me, Kit. This is a very dangerous game."

Kit puts his hand over his heart. "My word of honor as a cobbler's son," he says.

Poley brings down his fist in exasperation on the table, shaking the glass of wine. "I warn you, Christopher, if you have made any foolish private arrangements, you will find yourself in profound trouble. And that goes for your friend Matthew Roydon as well. You can't feather yourself a Scottish bed at our expense. And especially at my expense. Don't embarrass me, Christopher. You'll be a very sorry young man if you do."

Kit's levity turns into a frown, but before he can say anything else Poley gets up and stalks out of The White Lion into the early winter gloom.

xxvii

A few days later Kit receives a letter from Tom Walsingham. Its arrival is a surprise and its contents disturbing.

"You will accuse me," writes Tom, "of excessive formality and perhaps of cowardice for putting my thoughts on paper instead of speaking my mind to you in person, but I find it very difficult to be harsh with you when we are together. I cannot maintain my firmness of purpose. You have a weakening effect on me that grows, no doubt, out of my enormous affection for you. Well, accuse me of what you will, but there are a few things I must say to you—calmly and clearly. I trust that you will not take them amiss and that my honesty will strengthen and not destroy the bond of love that exists between us.

"Some several pieces of news have reached me about your recent behavior that puzzle me to distraction. I have heard, in the language of one of our mutual friends, that you have become a sort of tavern clown; that you perform daily for an audience of spiritual spendthrifts and intellectual wastrels; that you squander yourself and deaden your talents in bacchanalian bouts. But worse than all this, I have heard that you continue to talk so irresponsibly about certain delicate matters that your views are now commonly referred to as 'Marlowe's monstrous opinions,' and that you yourself are known as Mr. Machiavelli. I understand that you now regularly attack Her Majesty's government, the Privy Council, the Church of England, and Christianity in general, labeling practically every man in a position of authority either a hypocrite, a hedonist, or a sodomite.

"Furthermore, you seem obsessed, they say, with a need to talk about your sexual proclivities and to defend the classical loves of men and boys, while at the same time you revile women and dismiss as disgusting nonsense the romantic feelings that pass between the members of the opposite sexes. If you were content to keep your arguments theoretical the damage would not be quite so serious, but apparently you prefer to involve the names of specific people, including my own at times.

"In matters political and confidential you seem also to have caused considerable consternation, speaking too freely of your services for Sir Francis Walsingham and of your recent trip to Scotland. You have earned the reputation of being unreliable, and, worse still, you have brought upon yourself considerable suspicion, some of this having to do with one William Bray, according to Robert Poley.

"Needless to say, I am deeply disturbed by all this and find myself at a loss as to what course of action to take. I cannot dismiss you abruptly or disassociate myself from you. And yet, can I afford to embrace you publicly? Can I afford to let the world assume that I condone all that you do and say? I think you know the answer to that. This difficulty between us has been growing for some time, and I have already suffered considerable criticism for my defenses of your behavior. I'm afraid I can no longer defend you. Nor can I offer you the same degree of intimacy to which, over the years, we have both become accustomed. For the moment, allow me to withdraw a bit.

"In the meantime, I hope with all my heart that you will consider seriously the predicament you are weaving for yourself as well as the difficulties you are creating for me. Do not force me to flee from the only person I have ever been able to love in my entire life. I beg you to retire into your work and into yourself for a while. And when the terrible storm of your mysterious rebellion has passed, I fervently hope that you will come to me so that we may once again enjoy sensibly the pleasures of this world."

Kit reads the letter through several times in the privacy of his room, lying across his bed. Then he flings it roughly away from him and buries his head in his arms. It is not sadness with which he is overwhelmed, but rage. He rises suddenly, stalks about the room, kicks at the furniture, curses aloud, and, finding the crumpled letter on the rug, picks it up and tears it into a hundred pieces.

xxviii

The whole next day he walks the streets of London, shapeless revenge and fury in his heart. He wants to hurt somebody or something: Tom Walsingham, Robert Poley, William Bray, and a thousand other nameless people who have conspired to make his life difficult.

Gradually a plan of sorts emerges. He turns it over, refines it, wonders if it is indeed possible, after all. At St. Paul's Churchyard he searches for a copy of Holinshed's *Chronicles*. He finds it at last at The Green Dragon. It is expensive, but he does not argue over the price. He stops at the nearest tavern, which happens to be The Spire, and searches the pages of this popular history book for a piece of reality that he might translate into drama. He wants to write a history play. He wants to write a play for the Earl of Southampton.

He tuns the pages slowly, hunting for a king. Occasionally he pauses to sip at his wine. The light is failing early, and there is a winter wind playing at the panes of glass behind him. The fire roars. Half a dozen people eat and drink quietly at other tables. When he finds it difficult to read, he calls for a candle and orders another glass of wine.

He discards kings as one might tear away the pages of a calendar. Each sits for a brief moment under the burden of his earthly crown and under the scrutiny of his raging eye, and then is gone, shoved back into his grave, into time, into the giant folio, fourteen pounds of royal tombstones—the 1587 edition, complete with marginal glosses. How Tom Watson will laugh at this extravagance! Will he laugh also, Kit wonders, at his grand design? After all, this William Shakespeare of Stratford, a man of ordinary talent, seems to have aroused Southampton's interest with a group of plays on the reign of Henry the Sixth, two of which are merely revisions of poor Thomas Kyd's *Contention of York and Lancaster.* How tedious! Of course, he has not seen Shakespeare's recently completed version, but he is familiar with Kyd's and cannot really understand why anyone would want to bother with all that complicated controversy, except, of course, to justify the Tudor version of history. Now Richard the Third! There is a character with possibilities, the only character in the whole Lancaster-York mess worth considering. A Machiavellian crookback. That's more like it!

He scans the long, dense double columns, stumbling here and there over an odd spelling, going back occasionally to consider the possibilities of, say, Henry the Second or Richard Coeur-de-lion. There was Thomas à Becket, of course. He is momentarily fascinated. He begins to plot. Something of the relationship between Henry and Thomas emerges. But then the vision is incomplete. It slips away, and he moves on.

After several hours he comes upon the story of Edward the Second. He knows from the very first that this will be his history play, his introduction to the Earl of Southampton, his revenge against Tom Walsingham, and his vehicle for giving expression to the truest part of himself. His heart races. He finishes in one gulp a large glass of wine. It's all there. Piers Gaveston and Edward. How much clearer can it be? They were lovers. But how diplomatically it is all presented by these chroniclers. And a king deposed. Marvelous. And, what, adultery to boot! Oh, shameless Isabella! Oh, sinful Queen. Daughter of France. Whoring it up with young Mortimer. And then poor Edward in his dungeon. And then the awful murder, the red-hot spit, the excruciation.

He cannot wait to begin. He staggers from The Spire, his monstrous book under his arm. He half-walks, half-runs through the dim streets, ducking his head into the wind, avoiding the sting of winter, turning a corner, hugging the wall. Cheapside, Poultry, Threadneedle, Bishopsgate. And at last, his arm about to fall off, he is home, and the house is warm and full of Ann's cooking and Tom's tobacco. He goes by them and up the stairs to his rooms. Tom and Ann glance at each other in confusion. "What do you suppose he's up to now?" says Ann.

"God only knows!" says Tom, his pen poised above the page on which he is working.

xxix

It is a full month later before the work is done. But this time Kit has worked as a scholar might work, not as a poet possessed. Oh, there is passion in his play, all right, but there is also structure and history and erudition. Not that he allows for a moment the mouse of history to stand in the way of the tiger of art. But he has what facts are available to him, and he bends them vengefully, pointedly, to his purpose. He uses not only Holinshed but also *Fabyan's Chronicle* and the *Chronicle* of Thomas de la Moor. And in the end, he has not written himself into a trance, as he did with *Dr. Faustus*, but into a state of exhilaration. It is good, he thinks, reading once more through the completed manuscript, before beginning the copy that he will send to Southampton. It is so good, in fact, that he is brought to the brink of tears at times by his own language.

> I must have wanton poets, pleasant wits,
> Musicians, that with touching of a string
> May draw the pliant king which way I please:
> Music and poetry is his delight;
> Therefore I'll have Italian masques by night,
> Sweet speeches, comedies, and pleasing shows;
> And in the day, when he shall walk abroad,
> Like sylvan nymphs my pages shall be clad;
> My men, like satyrs grazing on the lawns,
> Shall with their goat-feet dance an antic hay;
> Sometime a lovely boy in Dian's shape,

With hair that gilds the water as it glides,
Crownets of pearl about his naked arms,
And in his sportful hands an olive-tree,
To hide those parts which men delight to see,
Shall bathe him in a spring; and there, hard by,
One like Actaeon, peeping through the grove,
Shall by the angry goddess be transform'd,
And running in the likeness of an hart,
By helping hounds pull'd down, and seem to die:
Such things as these best please His Majesty.

He expects his audience to know their history and has decided not to translate into poetry Holinshed's description of Edward's murder, but only to suggest it with certain props. The chronicler can afford to be more blunt: "Whereupon when they saw that such practices would not serve their turn, they came suddenly one night into the chamber where he lay in bed fast asleep, and with heavy featherbeds or a table (as some write) being cast upon him, they kept him down and withal put into his fundament an horn, and through the same they thrust up into his body a hot spit, the which passing up into his entrails, and being rolled to and fro, burnt the same, but so as no appearance of any wound or hurt outwardly might be once perceived."

xxx

Christopher waits for a response from the Earl of Southampton. He is prepared to wait an eternity of days for his answer—a whole week, if necessary. But he is naïve and overreaching. It is a fortnight before he receives, not from Southampton, but from Lord Burghley, the following letter:

"It has come to our attention that you have sent to His Lordship, the Earl of Southampton, a copy of a play about King Edward the Second. Your request, I gather, is that you be allowed to dedicate this play to him. Inasmuch as he has not yet reached his majority and is a royal ward, and since I am his guardian, it is incumbent upon me to look into such matters. Literary patronage is a most complex matter these days, and must not be granted in a random way, lest such patronage suggest approval of all the works thus dedicated.

"I must confess that I have read only the first act of your play. But I think that much is sufficient. I do not think that this is the sort of literary accomplishment to which His Lordship would want to attach his name. As you know, it is most unusual, in any case, to dedicate a play to anyone. A poem, perhaps, would be more appropriate. However, lest I encourage you beyond the facts, let me hasten to say, Mr. Marlowe, that I do not really think it worth your while to approach young Southampton again on this matter. It is part of my duty to see that his innocent taste is not corrupted by the kinds of ideas that you are inclined to deal with.

"About the play itself, let me add, that you seem to have done an injustice to history to satisfy certain preoccupations of your own. It offends my sensibilities to see such a cripple of a subject dressed in such gorgeous poetry."

At first he is angry. Then he is fatalistic, reminding himself that it was not a very likely possibility to begin with. If he can find a way to do it, he thinks he may try to approach the Countess of Pembroke. And then, of course, there is always Tom Walsingham. They have not really broken off their relationship, and it would not be very difficult to bring about a full reconciliation. In the meantime, he is sure that the Admiral's Men will want to do the play. The part is perfect for Ned Alleyn.

xxxi

The very next day, news reaches the gossip mills of London that the young Earl of Southampton, still only seventeen, has run off secretly, without license or permission, to join Essex in France. Kit goes from tavern to tavern, hoping to hear more of this daring adventure. He goes to The White Lion, The Unicorn, The Nag's Head, and finally The Mermaid. There he finds Will Shakespeare, sitting alone, enjoying a pipe of tobacco. "May I join you?" he says.

Will looks up at him through soft, heavy-lidded eyes, and nods without saying anything. They move in somewhat different circles and are not great friends. Shakespeare, in fact, is something of a loner and cannot be accurately described as moving in any circle at all. He does not drink much, nor does he keep late hours. He lives alone in a single room and spends a good deal of time reading. He has a high forehead and a sensuous mouth. His beard is neatly trimmed to a point, and his hair is long and kept in much the same style as Kit's, though, like his whole demeanor, it seems more collected. His calm expression, in fact, makes Kit rather nervous and forces him to talk more than he would like to. Will proves to be an exasperatingly good listener.

"I understand Lord Burghley is very upset," says Kit. "He takes it as a personal injury."

"He's an old man," says Will. "He's been very good to the lad."

Kit imagines an indication of familiarity in his tone. "Do you know him, then?"

"Oh, no, not really."

"It has been rumored for some time that you know him quite well."

"A very flattering rumor."

"Then you don't know him?"

Will fixes his eyes on his inquisitive acquaintance. "How much does it matter to you whether or not I know him?" he says.

"A natural curiosity at a time like this, don't you think?"

Will pauses and then says simply, "I had the honor of meeting him just once. But I have had some conversations with Lord Burghley and his son Robert."

"Oh?" says Kit, and waits for elaboration. When it does not come, he adds, "I can't imagine about what."

"But surely you must know," says Will.

"I'm afraid I don't," says Kit.

"They are trying to encourage the creation of certain plays and pageants that will give the public a sense of English history."

"You mean a favorable sense of Tudor history."

"It wasn't put to me quite that way," says Will, "but perhaps you're right."

"Does that explain your interest in Henry the Sixth and the Lancaster-York material?"

"I am interested in the theatre," says Will. "I have a family in Stratford, a wife and children, and I have to make a living. That should answer most of your questions."

"At the risk of annoying you still further, let me say that you are something of an enigma to the rest of us. We don't quite understand you. You don't seem to have the—the background for this sort of life."

"You mean, I haven't been to the University," says Will with a smile. "Well, you are quite right, Mr. Marlowe, I have not been to either of those marvelous institutions of learning. Nor have I ever been to any other school of any reputation. Still, I am familiar with the English language and can put three or four words together so that they add up to more than gibberish, which is more than I can say for some of your University friends."

"And now, having discovered that you will never be more than a mediocre actor," says Kit, "you have decided to try your hand at poetry and the making of plays."

"Your quickness of mind astounds me, sir. What else can you tell me about myself?"

Kit turns more serious. "I can tell you that it is common knowledge that you would like to have the Earl of Southampton as your patron."

Will laughs. "A common enough ambition these days—to want a patron, I mean."

"But uncommonly difficult to achieve."

"You seem to have done extremely well. They say you are quite thoroughly patronized by Thomas Walsingham."

Kit frowns. He catches the cool cruelty of the remark. "How do you mean that?" he says.

"Only in the most literal sense, Christopher," says Will. "You have your patron; would you deny me mine?"

"It's not up to me to deny you anything," says Kit. "It's Lord Burghley you must deal with—at least until Southampton reaches his majority in October."

"Ah, yes. We come back to Lord Burghley. I'm not the only one who must deal with him, am I?"

"What are you trying to say?"

Will sighs, then sips at his wine. "I had occasion to read a play of yours about Edward the Second," he says. His tone is quite matter-of-fact.

"You what?" says Kit. "I don't understand."

"It's really quite simple, Christopher. You sent it to Southampton. It came into the hands of Lord Burghley. Since he and I were discussing history plays, he handed it to me to read. That's all. I gave it back to him and told him what I thought."

"And what did you think?"

"I thought it was quite brilliant, a little mad, and very indiscreet."

"The indiscretions were King Edward's, not mine," says Kit.

"You might have chosen a more diplomatic subject."

"I was not trying to be undiplomatic."

"Then you succeeded without even trying," says Will. "Perhaps it comes naturally to you. I mean, these unnatural themes."

"Is it so unnatural for a man to love another man?"

"There are all kinds of love. But I was thinking more of certain parallels that might be drawn between your character and the Scottish king. His private life, his religion, and his difficulties with his noblemen. I'm sure you had none of this in mind, but your play might easily be misconstrued."

"It never occurred to me," says Kit. "I saw only the dramatic possibilities."

"I find that hard to believe," says Will, "but that's neither here nor there. What I really don't understand is why you sent it to Southampton."

Kit cannot answer for a moment, but then he says, "I take it you're annoyed. I mean, we seem to have fallen into a bit of a competition."

"Oh, hardly," says Will. "With your reputation, it's not very likely that you will get very far with Southampton—or Lord Burghley."

"And what, exactly, is my reputation?"

"Oh, come now, Christopher, don't play naïve," says Will. "You are generally acknowledged to be the most talented poet in England, aside, perhaps, from Spenser. Surely the most talented and most successful playwright. But also unstable. Also a religious rebel. A friend of Ralegh and his associates, a wit, a scoundrel, and—what shall I say?—a man with certain exotic sexual tastes."

"And you, Mr. William Shakespeare of Stratford-on-Avon," says Kit. "I suppose you are a model of decorum, good sense and orthodoxy."

"I am, in fact," says Will, "a much simpler man than you are. That's as much a confession as a boast, though I would not have it otherwise. I enjoy the theatre and I think I will, sooner or later, find my place in it. And yes, I do want the Earl of Southampton as my patron, and must admit I was annoyed to discover you making flirtations in this direction. So there, you have it all. There's not much more to be said, is there? You can have your drunken battle of wits with your tavern friends, and you can have your atheistic speculations at Durham House. Give me a pot of ink and a pen in a quiet room. That's all I really want—and time to spin all the threads of my imagination into dreams that come alive to walk and strut upon the stage with all the brief reality of life."

Kit is silenced by the man's integrity. He wants to apologize and curse all at once. A little arrow of truth has caught him in the throat, and he cannot speak. Before he knows what is happening, he sees his own arm strike out and sweep his glass of wine from the table. At the same time he stands up, stares into Shakespeare's collected countenance, and then stalks out into the gasping light of the dying day.

xxxii

Once again he strikes home with the public. *Edward the Second* has proved an enormous success. Kit has searched out the secret longings and lusts, the malformations of spirit of the ordinary man, and satisfied them. He has given the public violence. He has given them love. He has given them monstrous corruption. And then, at the end, as inevitably as the gathering in of taxes, he has given them justice. It is only from certain individuals that criticism comes. He hears that Gabriel Harvey hates the play, but he is not surprised. Robert Greene has reservations, but must admire its structure. George Peele says more emphasis should be placed on the problem of incompetence and abdication, and less on Edward's passion for Gaveston. Tom Watson agrees, adding, however, in confidence, "Everybody knows that these things are fairly common, but nobody talks about them very openly. I think it's a mistake to force the issue this way. Discretion, Christopher! Discretion!"

Rumors grow like delicious tumors in the brains of literary London. Truths are discovered about Kit's nocturnal habits, and stories are invented out of thin air about orgies with young boys, about a pander in Pearl Street, about the School of Night at Durham House. "Buggery, magic, and atheism—that's what they're up to. They conjure up the bodies of dead ladies and spell the name of God backwards. And then they take off all their clothes and celebrate the devil's mass. Everything unnaturally reversed."

Southampton has returned from his adventures in France. Will Shakespeare has wormed his way into the young man's confidence and is encouraged by Lord Burghley to help promote the match between Southampton and Elizabeth Vere, Burghley's granddaughter. Kit's jealousy is undisguised. In The Anchor, ranting among pirates and actors, in the lowest circles of smoky, drunken company, he says, "I know what the pretty lad needs, and it's not some smelly little fish of a girl, some inbred idiot piece of old English aristocracy, congealing like cold mutton between the silken sheets of the earl's bed. You boys who have been to sea for too many years know what I mean." And then, drunker still, he accuses Will Shakespeare of being the lad's lover and says that it's Lord Burghley himself who arranged it all. He falls asleep in an incoherence of obscenities, is carried home, robbed of his purse and dropped in the mud in front of his house.

Dissipation is followed by remorse and a kind of lethargy, which is followed, in turn, by an effort to get back to work. When he is approached by Thomas Kyd to work with him on a play for the Admiral's Men called *Lust's Dominion, or The Lascivious Queen,* he does not refuse, though he has little enthusiasm for either the subject or his co-author. Nevertheless, it is something to do and a chance to get out of the house in Holywell Lane for a while. He moves in temporarily with Kyd, and they struggle through the thing, arguing repeatedly, disagreeing about everything. Kit cannot conceal his contempt for his collaborator. And once, when Kyd dares to use some words of endearment, Kit knocks him down with the back of his hand and tells him to save his romantic nonsense for his stupid plays.

It is after this incident that he decides that it is stubborn and foolish for him to wait any longer for word from Tom Walsingham. It is an accidental meeting with Robert Poley that brings him around. They meet one afternoon at The Spire, and Robert says that Tom is extremely concerned and that his feelings are deeply hurt by this prolonged silence. "The least you could do is to write him a letter," says Robert.

But Kit decides to do more than that. He has heard that Tom is in London for a few days. He will surprise him. He will go around and see him—unannounced.

Dressed in his best clothes, bought for him by Tom, and fortified with a small amount of brandywine, Kit sets out late one afternoon in the spring of 1592 to reestablish himself in the bosom of his patron.

He lifts the heavy brass knocker and lets it fall. In a moment a man comes to the door. Kit recognizes him as Peter Wickes from the house at Chislehurst. The immaculately dressed Wickes plays the perfect servant and allows Christopher only the barest sign of recognition. "I'm afraid the master is entertaining guests," he says.

"Tell him Mr. Marlowe would have a word with him," says Kit.

"Yes, sir," says Wickes, indicating that he should wait just inside the door. As he waits he hears polite laughter from a farther room,

the main parlor, he assumes, remembering the house as though it
once were his own.

It is not Wickes who returns but Walsingham himself. He rushes
across the polished hall, his hands outstretched. "Christopher!" says
Tom. "How good it is to see you, after all these months. I was
afraid that your success had gone to your head and that you had
given up your old friend. You look a bit pale. You're not unwell, I
hope. So much illness going around these days! I wouldn't have
come to London unless it was absolutely necessary. And as soon as I
can get away, I'm going back to Scadbury."

"When are you leaving?" Kit asks, finding it more difficult to
speak to Tom than he had imagined he would.

"Tomorrow or the next day, if possible," says Tom, "but
certainly not before you and I have had a long talk."

"I gather you're busy this evening," says Kit. They are still
standing, rather awkwardly, in the hallway.

"Yes, I am rather, though it's nothing special," says Tom. "A
very small dinner party. A few friends." He hesitates, examines Kit
carefully, and then says enthusiastically, as though he has not
weighed the matter, "Oh, but you must join us for a few
minutes—at least for a little refreshment before we go in to dinner.
And then perhaps you can stop by another time when we can be
alone." They go side by side down the hall, and, just before they
enter the room where people are talking, Tom touches Kit's hand
and says, "I've missed you."

In the parlor, Tom introduces Kit to John Thornborough and his
wife and to Audrey Shelton and her uncle, Sir John Shelton. "I
think I've already had the pleasure of meeting your friend," says
Audrey. "It was several years ago. A masquerade of some sort,
wasn't it? Right here in this very house."

Her large eyes absorb him with a smile. He remembers her dark
hair and very white skin and her delicate beauty.

When the conversation begins again, Kit has the feeling that
small talk has taken the place of something far more significant. He
tries to discover what these five people have in common and why

they are gathered here this way. It could be sheer coincidence, of course. But there is something odd in the air, and it makes him extremely uncomfortable. It is clear after a few minutes that he does not belong there—and yet, in some strange way he *does* belong there. He has heard of John Thornborough, but he has never met him, or his very handsome wife. What he has heard of the man has not been altogether flattering. He is about forty years old, and left behind him at Oxford a reputation rarely rivaled for undergraduate debauchery. Tales still linger about him and Robert Pinkney of St. Mary's Hall and the notorious Simon Forman, who, they say, was the minister of his pleasures. It takes only a few minutes of totally trivial conversation with him for Kit to decide that he is a man of very complicated corruptions, in spite of the fact that he is chaplain to Henry Herbert, the Earl of Pembroke. And yet, he has a certain charm and even—he hesitates—a certain flirtatiousness. He allows himself to laugh a bit too easily and reaches out to touch Kit's arm as he does so.

Kit dimly remembers also a bit of gossip about Mrs. Thornborough and Audrey Shelton. Now he sees them sitting side by side, talking quietly, their faces close together, and before very long he is convinced that theirs is no ordinary relationship.

Only Sir John Shelton, Audrey's elegant uncle, seems untainted by these subtle (and yet familiar) vibrations. He is the staunch representative of one of England's leading families, representatives of which have served the country since Crécy and Agincourt. Sir John himself has played a distinguished role in the war against Spain and is full of stories and military stratagems. But why is he here this evening? wonders Kit. Perhaps he is helping to arrange the rumored marriage between Tom and Audrey. That might very well be, he decides, but there is more to the gathering than that. On a gamble with himself he ventures to mention his trip to Scotland. Their reactions make it clear that that was indeed what they were talking about before his intrusion. His bluntness is greeted with diplomatic evasiveness, and the conversation never quite comes around to the Scottish succession. It is Tom who changes

Christopher's probing course by reminding his other guests that they are in the presence of the brilliant young man who is the author of such marvelous plays as *Tamburlaine* and *Dr. Faustus.*

"How very interesting," says Sir John Shelton, who hates plays. "We had quite a discussion of your *Dr. Faustus* one evening," says Thornborough. "The Countess of Pembroke said you should have written it as a comedy. She thought your *Rich Jew of Malta* was infinitely more entertaining, though terribly vulgar."

They all laugh in their slightly exhausted way and refuse to pursue the matter. They seem determined to maintain an appropriate gulf between themselves and Kit.

The ordeal is ended by the appearance of Peter Wickes, who announces that dinner is served. They rise and move toward the door. Tom takes Kit aside and says, "I'm sorry!"

"For what?" says Kit.

But there is no time to explain. He leads him to the hall and quickly says good-bye. "Can you come around tomorrow morning?"

"I suppose so," says Kit, "if you think there's any point in it."

"You know there is," says Tom, taking him briefly by the hand, before turning away to rejoin his guests. As he does so, he is startled to find Audrey standing there. She has a hint of a smile on her face, and her eyebrows are arched thinly over her large eyes. She nods to Kit and allows Tom to offer her his arm. For a moment Kit is transfixed. He watches them walk slowly away and then turns to find Peter Wickes holding the door open for him.

xxxiii

The days are growing longer, and light still lingers in the sky as Kit makes his way back along the Strand, past the Inner Temple to Fleet and Ludgate and then to St. Paul's. The gathering at Tom's house is an undigested irritation in his mind. As he walks, he spins a little web of anger around it. There they were, all cozy and intimate, full of the privileges of their class, their confidential plans, and their dirty little secrets. Maneuvering, no doubt, for a happy union of Scotland and England. Hadn't Thornborough made his views clear on this subject publicly? He's not sure. But surely now it is evident what Tom and Audrey and all the Walsinghams and Sheltons are up to. He feels as though an iron gate has been slammed in his face. But not before he has had a glimpse into the real relationships that bind such people. So what is he to Tom, after all—a potential scandal? An incidental indulgence? He conjures up in his mind a whole circle of intimate friends, a kind of inner circle of aristocratic initiates into pleasures generally not acceptable, but most delightful. What polite little orgies they must have, he thinks, and sees, suddenly, Audrey Shelton and Mrs. Thornborough in a naked embrace.

He has been heading, perhaps out of force of habit, toward The Mitre or The Mermaid, but suddenly he turns north and seeks out a shabby tavern in Cock Lane, where occasionally he goes to be away from all the familiar faces, all the wits and actors, the poets and poseurs. He's sick of them all, sick of their greedy calculations and their petty competitions.

In his loneliness he longs for strangers, for simple people: shopkeepers and sailors, cobblers and tapsters, and honest whores. He finds them all at The Black Swan in Cock Lane. It doesn't take many people to make a crowd in such a small place, nor does it take much time to make friends. Before long he is learning dirty ditties from a pair of young sailors who have no objection whatever to his buying them drinks. Soon their table is a clutter of bottles, and they have an audience for their bawdy performance.

> "Who e'er would marry pretty Kate
> Would have himself a handsome mate,
> For she has been for one and all
> A cunning little port of call."

"You've got a really fine voice," says the red-headed seaman from Torquay.

"Hey, do you know 'A Minion Wife'?" asks his fair-haired friend. And they launch into it, leaning together, Kit in the middle, the others holding him around the shoulders.

Kit keeps the ale and wine and rum flowing, much to the delight of the Cock Lane crowd. "Oooh! He's a fine gentleman, he is," says an aging whore, her market value somewhat diminished by the loss of her teeth.

"Do you suppose he's somebody what's really important?" says her plump friend. "Or the son of somebody? Don't suppose he'd relish the likes of us."

"Speak for yourself, dearie," says the other. "If I had me teeth or somethin' to keep me lips from cavin' in, he'd give me a look over, he would."

"Maybe he'll buy his sailor boys a tumble in the hay," says the plump one.

"I don't know," she says. "P'raps he fancies them hisself." And she cackles as though she's just laid an enormous egg.

Kit and his new friends, deep in their cups, fall to telling tales. No one really cares where the truth ends and the lies begin. The red-haired lad, to hear him tell it, was the hero of the Battle of Gravelines. And the other has boarded Spanish ships in the Indies and scooped up pearls in Florida. "And what have you done?" he says, just slightly belligerent.

"Oh, I've killed a few kings in my time," says Kit. "And burnt the topless towers of Ilium."

"What in bloody hell is he talkin' about?" says the red-haired one.

"Drink up! Drink up!" roars Kit. "It doesn't matter what we've done, but what we have still to do. The night is young, and the ravens of pleasure are all the nightingales we'll ever need. Let's bid farewell to this cocky place, whatever it is, and be on our way. We'll visit all the bawdy houses in London and stand the ladies on their heads to see if what they say is true that upside down they all look alike. Come on! Come on! See if you can stand. The seas are high, but you boys have got the legs for it. It's up to St. John's Street to Lucy Negro, and then to Bouncing Bess and Lusty Kate. We'll give their girls a scream or two before the night is out."

"Yo, ho, and up she rises," they sing out, staggering to their feet and knocking the bottles about. And soon they are making a zigzag path across West Smith Field under a fat and flying moon that's almost as good as daylight, only ghostlier.

Lucy Morgan has had a very slow evening or else she might not let in such a crew. But she is impressed by Kit's clothes and his elegant speech. She takes him for a gentleman or even better. "A little party for my friends," says Kit. "Forty months at sea they've had and can't tell boys from girls. You've got to set them straight, Lucy Morgan, Black Lucy. Bring on a brace of birds and a bottle of manzanilla and give us the biggest bed in the house."

"What! All in one room?" says Lucy, an elegant woman once, they say, a gentlewoman attendant on the Queen.

"And why not?" says Kit. "We're not here to whisper sweet nothings and love me till death. We're here for sport—a pair of sea dogs to bait your cows."

She laughs good-naturedly. "Have it your way, my lads, but mind you, don't get nasty with my girls. I'll have no marks on them for the next guests to wonder about. And see to yourselves if you've got a touch of the pox."

"My boys are as clean as the Arctic snow," says Kit, "and as innocent as Hyrcanian tigers."

"And you," says Lucy. "Won't you have a girl?"

"Two will do for three," he says. "I am, madam, only the master of the revels. I must see to it that my little pets are properly fed. I'll pay for their fare and we'll dine together over the devil's back, until the witch of morning sucks forth our souls." He holds his head and frowns and sways toward Lucy Morgan.

"Are you all right?" she says.

"If God's in His heaven and Tom's in his house, what can possibly be wrong?" he says. "Show us to our room."

The girls are young, and the boys prove shy at first, but Kit urges them on, helps them to undress, and taunts them for their inability to rise to the occasion. "Shall I give you lessons?" he says, tearing off the clothes of one of the girls, a bony thing of seventeen or so who is more amused than frightened by this rough treatment.

"She likes a firm hand," says her rosy-faced friend. "She's small, but she likes the big ones. You can hurt her a bit, but don't mark her up." As she speaks, she is dropping away her clothes.

The more naked things become, the braver the sailors are, until at last they are rolling about on the floor and the bed, doing whatever they please and to whomever. "Oooh, look at that," says Miss Rosy Cheeks. "Just like a pair of dogs, they are." And then she's knocked on her back and rammed hard by the red-haired lad, who has come to life with a vengeance and spends himself in a gale of obscenities as they all look on in a huddle of bundling flesh.

By dawn the battlefield is strewn with corpses. The bottles are empty, the sheets are torn. The sailors lie on the bed with the girls in a tangle of arms and legs, and Christopher is naked on the floor. As morning sounds rise from the street and sunlight peeks through the shutters, he stirs. He lifts his head and then falls back in an agony of dizziness and nausea.

It takes him a full five minutes to struggle to his feet. He finds a pitcher of water and pours it over his head. The others don't even so much as move. They might be a grotesque piece of statuary for an Oriental prince. He looks at them for a while, unable at first to remember how they all came to be here. And then he laughs and makes over them the sign of the cross.

Quietly he puts on his clothes, and quietly he leaves.

xxxiv

During the spring and summer, tensions mount throughout England. The war goes on in France. Rouen is besieged, but the English and French are forced to retreat when news is received that the Duke of Parma is approaching with twelve thousand foot and four thousand horse. There are other setbacks and rumors of a major disaster for the English in Brittany.

The war is a drain. Reinforcements are sent from time to time to France and the Lowlands. Certain gentlemen are severely reprimanded for willfully refusing to make their contributions in the levy of sums for soldiers and other public services. Desertions from the army rise at an alarming rate. They cross the Channel by the hundreds around Dover, along with legitimate veterans wounded in the wars. The laws are tightened against the deserters themselves and those who would aid them. Such a proclamation is made throughout the City of London and its suburbs.

Rumors of a Spanish invasion are as common as flies. They are said to have a fleet of sixteen great ships assembled, together with twenty thousand men. They are said to be prepared to land in Ireland, in Scotland, on the Isle of Wight, in Sussex. In the name of self-defense and the preservation of the kingdom, severe measures are taken.

Sir John Perrot is brought to trial after spending a year in the Tower. He is accused of having raised a rebellion against the Queen in Ireland, of having made offers of help to the Spaniards, and of inciting Sir Brian O'Rourke to rebellion. He is condemned to death by hanging, drawing and quartering, his traitor's heart to be shown to the crowd.

Recusancy in the north, especially throughout Lancashire, is so widespread that the churches are virtually empty and the preachers preach to themselves while the obstinate congregations make a mockery of the sabbath by playing at games and indulging in holiday merriments. All this by way of protest against the Established Church and the rule of the bishops.

In Wales, also, recusancy is rampant, and many people are reported to secretly practice papist rituals and to go in great numbers to old holy places where certain Catholic images are preserved. Because the enforcement of the law has been more difficult in Wales, many recusants have sought refuge there. But now the Privy Council is moving to establish a commission for inquiries into the activities of Jesuits and seminaries and other subversive people, similar to the commissions at work in other parts of England.

Proclamations have been issued from time to time against the large number of masterless men and vagrants, some of whom are deported to Ireland, and some of whom are taken forcibly into the army.

In Southwark there are riots following the arrest of a feltmaker's servant for no apparent reason. One of the Knight Marshal's men served his summons upon the poor man and had him taken off to Marshalsea. This provoked to riot a multitude of people in the neighborhood, led by apprentices of the feltmakers out of Barmsey Street and Blackfriars, and joined by many loose and masterless men. Charges of brutality are leveled against the Knight Marshal's men, who used daggers and clubs to quell the riot.

The problem of foreign artisans in England grows daily more serious and dangerous. The freemen and apprentices are brought to the brink of violence. Certain pleas are made on the foreigners' behalf by M. Caron, agent for the States, but nothing is resolved. The Privy Council undertakes a confidential survey of the numbers of foreigners now working at handicrafts in London and looks into charges that some of them have grown wealthy and send goods abroad and avoid Her Majesty's customs. There is a general fear and conviction that the Southwark riots will spread to other parts of London. Plays are forbidden as well as all public gatherings that bring together potential mobs.

Several priests are hanged on charges of treason, and the Jesuit Southwell is sent to the Tower to be closely guarded by Mr. Topcliffe himself.

To add to the political confusion, a rumor sweeps London and the rest of England that Sir Walter Ralegh himself has been thrown in the Tower because of a secret marriage to Elizabeth Throckmorton, who has already borne his child. His enemies are delighted, but his friends set to work to bring about a reconciliation between Sir Walter and the Queen, if only to restore the balance of power internally. They are dreadfully afraid that the Essex faction will get a disastrous grip on the nation and that the erratic, hot-blooded earl will firmly establish himself as the heir to Leicester.

Through all of this, Christopher Marlowe is uncertain as to what his personal course of action should be. He has been repeatedly advised by his friends to find some way to ingratiate himself to the authorities, through whatever high connections he can use, and to do whatever he can to repair his bad reputation.

When he receives a brief and formal invitation to meet with Robert Cecil "on certain matters of extreme importance to the state," he does not know whether to respond with hope or trepidation. "Be a good listener," says Tom Watson, "and reveal as little as possible. Cecil is an old friend of Sir Walter's and will do what he can. On the other hand, he may want Ralegh's power diminished, though not destroyed, since he must use him against Essex. He will probably want to ask you about the meetings at Durham House and the accusations of atheism leveled against the whole Ralegh circle. Keep your temper, and avoid, if possible, any discussion of the Scottish succession. It is pretty well understood that King James and Ralegh are natural enemies. And Robert Cecil knows where his bread can be buttered."

They meet at Cecil's house, in the privacy of the young Privy Councilor's study. But there is none of the ease and informality of their Cambridge days. Robert has grown too wily and successful. Suspicion has sharpened his eyes. Hard work has aged him prematurely. There is a touch of gray in his hair and beard, though he is not yet thirty years old.

"I regret that we have seen so little of each other in these past several years," he says, "but the nature of my involvements is such that I have little time for leisure or literature or anything else. Though I must confess that I made it my business to see a performance of your much discussed *Edward the Second*. In fact, it is this play, among other things, that prompted me to invite you here. Tell me about it, will you?"

"I don't quite know what you mean," says Kit. "It's a piece of history—as far as I know, true to the chronicles, especially Holinshed."

"Was the choice of subject your own, or were you—what shall I say—encouraged in this direction by anyone?"

"The choice was entirely my own. Why do you ask?"

"Someone has suggested," says Robert Cecil, "that perhaps, since you are somewhat close to him, Sir Walter Ralegh put the idea in your head. And, as I am sure you have already heard, the play has been taken by some people to be an indirect commentary on James the Sixth of Scotland."

Kit laughs nervously. "It was nothing of the sort," he says. "I chose the subject for purely dramatic reasons. I was interested not in the politics of the play but in the human relationships. I had considered, for instance, Henry the Second and Thomas à Becket before deciding on this material."

"That might not have been a much wiser choice," says Cecil. "I realize it's not your fault and that you have an inquiring mind, but almost any dramatization of history these days is risky. Everyone is looking for contemporary parallels. They find sedition in literature where none was intended."

"I assure you, I intended nothing of the sort," says Marlowe.

"Christopher, I believe you," says Cecil with exaggerated assurance, "but you must understand my position. To put it mildly, we are in the midst of a very delicate situation right now. Both of us, I am sure, would like to help Sir Walter in whatever way we can, but his enemies are numerous and his position is rapidly deteriorating. If we are to do anything at all for him, you must be as honest as possible with me."

"What exactly would you like to know?" Kit asks. "I personally have nothing to hide."

Cecil smiles. "Perhaps it would be more accurate to say that you have, thus far, been unable to hide anything. Your public conversations have been a little less than cautious. But let's not get into all that right now. I have some specific matters to put to you."

Marlowe visibly contains his embarrassment and anger and nods his willingness to cooperate.

"First of all, there has been a steady supply of seditious books arriving from abroad," he says. "Do you know anything about this illegal traffic?"

"Nothing at all. As you know, my involvements abroad have been limited to a few assignments as an ordinary courier in Rheims and Scotland."

"You know nothing, then, of a certain Jesuit pamphlet circulated in English under the pseudonym Andreas Philopater? The true author is almost certainly Robert Parsons. It answers rather vigorously the recent proclamation against Jesuits and seminary priests."

"I have heard that there was such a pamphlet, but I have not seen it, nor do I know what it contains."

"Well, among other things," Cecil says, "it suggests that Sir Christopher Hatton was murdered for his moderate views, and that my father and I are sympathetic to the Puritan cause. The attack against my father is particularly vicious. He is accused of keeping to himself the power that was Sir Francis Walsingham's and trying to control entirely the affairs of England with my help. We are made the villains of a Catholic persecution. Furthermore, Sir Walter Ralegh is accused of running a school of atheism with the participation of certain conjuring mathematicians and astrologers who deny the truth of the Scriptures and ridicule Christ. Now, certainly, this touches you a bit more closely, doesn't it?"

"Surely you are not going to allow Robert Parsons to shape your judgment of these things," says Kit. "You know as well as I do that our gatherings at Durham House have been devoted purely to informal discussions and to the quest for broader knowledge and understanding. There has been nothing at all political about them."

Cecil pauses, tapping the tips of his fingers together. Behind his large desk he seems diminutive, as though he is sitting on a low stool. "Oh, have you heard, incidentally," he says, "that Giordano Bruno has been arrested and is in prison in Rome? It was foolish of him, of course, to go back to Venice. But then he has always been a rather reckless man, hasn't he? What you might call a 'seeker after truth.' "

Kit has gone pale. Robert's tone and the implied parallel does not escape him. After a moment he says, "The man is a great genius. He should be free to pursue his inquiries wherever they lead. The suppression of scholarship and intellectual pursuits is the worst kind of tyranny."

"Oh, I couldn't agree more," says Robert unconvincingly. "But it's not that simple, is it?"

"Why not?"

"Because these matters are not entirely up to you or me or Sir Walter, or anyone. Religious matters are inextricably bound up with political matters. And there is nothing we can do about it. In another life, in another world, perhaps it would be different. But, Christopher, we are here and now, and we must be practical, mustn't we?"

"Sometimes I'm not sure it's worth it."

"Many a rebel has felt that way, only to lose his conviction at the sight of the executioner. But by then, of course, it's too late, isn't it? Think for a minute of the sweetest things you've known: fine wine, intelligent intercourse, a spring day at Scadbury. Good friends, such as Tom Walsingham. Certain pleasures of the flesh. And then think of the awfulness of death, the hangman's rope, the executioner's knife. Your lovely members carved away that might be employed in more pleasant ways. Your heart held high for the vulgar mob, that might otherwise palpitate at beauty's sight."

"What exactly are you trying to tell me, Robert?"

Cecil turns suddenly very serious and leans forward on his desk. "I am trying to tell you, Christopher Marlowe, that you and Sir Walter and quite a few other people are in greater jeopardy than you might imagine. There are people in the Privy Council who would put an end to our riots, our Catholic problems, our Puritan problems, the circulation of seditious literature—all those things they consider a menace to the state—by terrible and ruthless means. If they have their way, these times that you think of as so oppressive will seem like halcyon days to you, as you think back on them from some rat-infested dungeon, should you be so lucky as to be merely tossed in prison.

"You must listen very carefully to what I have to say, Kit. I am not determined to destroy Sir Walter or any of his circle of friends. I am, in fact, committed to restoring him to his earlier position of power and influence. I don't think I have to explain why. I am also opposed to reckless persecution. I think our nation can better be served by level-headedness at this point, and by domestic diplomacy."

"And what exactly would you have me do?" Kit asks.

"I am going to intercede in whatever way I can for Sir Walter," Cecil says. "I suggest these meetings at Durham House be discontinued. I suggest you restrain yourself in public and keep your opinions to yourself. I suggest you choose for your plays subjects less controversial, and perhaps even more consistent with the official policies of the government."

"Such as what?" asks Kit.

"Oh, I don't know. I'm not a writer. Something obviously anti-Catholic, for instance. Surely there is material enough around from the past several decades to draw upon. Since we are fighting in France and supporting the Huguenots, why not something French? The St. Bartholomew's Day massacre, perhaps. Surely there's enough blood in an event like that to satisfy the mob. Besides, we must remind our subjects why we are in France. Too many of them seem reluctant to fight. Too many of them don't know what it's all about."

"I'll think about it," says Kit.

"And while you're at it," says Cecil, "think about the other things we talked about—and don't leave out those luscious forests and fields of Scadbury."

xxxv

The result of this interview with Robert Cecil is a hastily written play called *The Massacre at Paris*. If nothing else, it should put to rest any official suspicions that his leanings are Catholic.

Put together from news sheets and broadsides, it is, from an artistic point of view, an atrocious piece of work both in its structure and in its poetry, but from the commercial point of view it is destined to be an enormous success.

The action of the play rambles over seventeen years of bloody French history, beginning with the marriage of Henry of Navarre to Margaret of Valois, and ending with the assassination of Henry the Third. The audience is treated to the poisoning of the old Queen of Navarre, Catherine de'Medici's council before the massacre, and the massacre itself, in excruciating detail, including the murders of Admiral Coligny and Peter Ramus, the scholar. Included also are the crowning of Henry the Third and the murder of the Duc de Guise.

Though his heart is not in the writing of this play, he cannot help but seize upon the character of the Duke of Guise as still another mad dreamer in his catalogue of overreachers, those obsessed with unattainable goals, aspiring toward the impossible.

It is a slaughterhouse of blood and gore, a body for every other line, assassinations, mutilations, and massacres: the murderous hordes of Catholics let loose on the innocent Protestants of France. Unfortunately, the theatres are closed because of the plague, and the hungry public will have to wait awhile for this delicious fare.

xxxvi

The death of Robert Greene comes as no surprise to anyone who ever knew him. The miracle was that, given his habits, he lived so long. Nevertheless, it is a sad story and an important piece of news in the literary quarters of London. Several versions of his last days circulate. Some of them are kinder than others. Gabriel Harvey's is downright cruel.

Roberto, it seems, fell sick after a bout of heavy drinking and eating. The nature of his disease was never fully discovered, but he suffered a general swelling of the body and for a month lay at the house of a shoemaker in Dowgate, unable to make the journey to Em Ball's house. His mistress came to see him, and certain other friends called, but none had the wherewithal to help. It was obvious that he was dying, and there wasn't much to be done. During this time, they say, he was most penitent, turning to God, and asking forgiveness for the life he had led. He spoke no obscenities, as was his custom, and did not rage at the approach of death, but gave himself back to God, recalling the innocent days of his childhood and the comforts of prayer. He continued his work as best he could, putting together a book which he called *Greene's Groat's-worth of Wit, bought with a million of repentance.* And since he had no money

at all, he appealed to his wife, the woman he had abandoned for Em
Ball, to settle his debt to his humble host:

Sweet Wife,
   As ever there was any good will or friendship between me
and thee, see this bearer, my host, satisfied of his debt. I owe
him ten pound, and but for him I had perished in the streets.
Forget and forgive my wrongs done unto thee, and Almighty
God have mercy on my soul. Farewell, till we meet in heaven,
for on earth thou shalt never see me more. This Second of
September, 1592.
                                  Written by thy dying husband,
                                            Robert Greene

   Kit Marlowe and his friends hear the account for the first time
from Gabriel Harvey, who goes up and down London like a
vulture, picking at the dead man's bones. They are in The
Mermaid. Pompous Harvey is seated at a table, dressed in his
foppish best, surrounded by curious listeners. "Well," he says, "as
you know, I was in London to challenge Mr. Greene in the courts
for the libels he published in *The Quip for an Upstart Courtier*, in
which he attacks my entire family. When I heard he was dead I was
rather disappointed. I had hoped to force him to admit to the world
that he was a liar.
   "In any case, I went around to this shoemaker's house in
Dowgate to find out what I could about his death. I spoke with the
shoemaker's wife, Mrs. Isam, and learned that the man died as he
lived, poverty-stricken, drunk, and obscene. No one came to see
him, she said, except a Mistress Appleby and Em Ball, about whom
you all know." He gives an aristocratic sniff, as though there is a
foul smell in the room. "Through her he gave the world his only
heritage, a bastard son named Fortunatus.
   "As to the cause of his death, I was told that he and his
companion Tom Nashe indulged excessively a month or so earlier
on a banquet of pickled herring and Rhenish wine, after which he
fell sick. He had with him only the clothes on his back and his

sword. This sword, along with his doublet and hose, was sold for three shillings. And, says Mrs. Isam, while she was having Mr. Greene's shirt washed, he had to borrow one of her husband's to wear. In spite of his illness, he went on drinking—when he could get it. He would beg from his host a penny pot of malmsey to see him through his pain.

"The good shoemaker and his wife did more for him than he was worth, and I doubt that they will ever recover the money they put out in his behalf—and him but a stranger off the streets. Four shillings for his winding sheet, six shillings and fourpence for his burial in the new churchyard near Bedlam, and ten pounds otherwise of indebtedness to Mr. Isam. But even so, the kind Mrs. Isam made for his head a garland of bays to wish him farewell on his journey out of this life."

The death of Robert Greene is followed by a wave of private promises to reform. Most of them last as long as an hour or so, and that very evening they are flushing their old devil down to hell in a small ocean of toasts at The White Lion, The Spire, The Unicorn, and The Nag's Head.

A fortnight later Henry Chettle rushes *A Groat's-Worth of Wit* to the press and feeds the furnace of literary controversy and gossip, for, in this testament of a dying sinner, there are attacks on such people as Nashe and Peele and Shakespeare and Kit Marlowe. The attack on Kit is especially vicious. Greene exhorts him to give up his atheism and his Machiavellianism.

As bitter as Greene is against his fellow playwrights, he is even more bitter against those actors and actor-managers who turned their backs on him in his hour of need, though it was he and people like him who put the words in their mouths that made them rich. Among the more obnoxious of this breed is a new arrival on the scene, "an upstart crow, beautified with our feathers, that with his tiger's heart wrapped in a player's hide, supposes he is as well able to bombast out a blank verse as the best of you: and, being an absolute Johannes factotum, is in his own conceit the only Shake-scene in a country." Those who know him readily recognize "the upstart crow" as Will Shakespeare, a man with the mind of a businessman and the soul of a poet.

With the death of Greene and all the bitterness that follows, and with London in the grip of the plague and the theatres closed indefinitely, Kit feels that his little world is beginning to fall apart. As gloomy as he is, he is not prepared for the next and cruelest shock of all: the sudden death of Tom Watson.

xxxvii

After the modest funeral, attended mainly by Tom's friends and a few relatives, Ann and Kit return to the house in Holywell Lane to pick up the last of her things. She has already moved in with her brother and his wife, who have recently bought a house on Broad Street near Bishopsgate.

They stand in the living room of the dead house. It has been scrubbed and packed away, as sure as Tom Watson was. Its soul has escaped through the windows and fled to places that are still warm with life and laughter, where the fire still burns in the fireplace, and the plates are handed around for beef stew and kidney pie.

Ann is very pale against the black clothes she is unaccustomed to wearing. No one has seen her cry. She has kept all that to herself. On the floor, from which the rug has been removed, there are two boxes tied with rope. "I suppose that's all there is," she says. She looks around the bare room. There are rectangular marks on the walls where pictures or mirrors stood. "It was all so predictable and yet such a shock. I mean, all along we think we know what death is, but we don't. Really, Kit! We don't. We don't know."

He stands beside her, afraid to touch her, afraid not to. "Nothing will ever be the same without Tom," he says.

"Nothing was ever the same with him," she says with a wistful smile that brings a hint of color back to her face and gives her such a sudden saintly beauty that Kit wants to hurl himself at her, fall at her feet, kiss the hem of her widow's weeds and confess his eternal love. Instead, he puts his arm gently about her waist and draws her to him. "He was so full of new ideas," she says, "new things to do. And he made me laugh. He made us all laugh. Each day with him was like a whole lifetime."

"He was more alive in his few years than ten people living to four score each," says Kit. "He'll be missed in the taverns and theatres of this town and in our broken hearts." He sighs and lets go of Ann to pace around the wooden boxes, as though they are a pair of little coffins. "Oh, God, it's an awful world."

"I suppose we ought to be going," she says. "They've all gone back to Hugh's house, and they'll be expecting us."

"The epilogue to a sad little comedy," says Kit. "A few cakes and wine and a eulogy or two. There is not much really that one can say. I wish there were something left to drink in the house. We could give him a last private toast. Just you and I, who loved him in special ways. You as his wife, and I—"

"And you," she says, "you, dear Kit, as more than brother. You've been a part of us." She kneels suddenly, as though she is about to pray over one of the boxes, but she starts to undo the rope. "I think there is something in here with these books," she says. "A small flask of brandy. He kept it on the shelf, between Plato and Plutarch." She laughs. "Imagine that!"

"Plato and Plutarch would have approved," says Kit. He kneels beside her and helps to open the box.

In a moment they are sitting side by side, each on one of the boxes in the empty room. Ann raises the flask to the ghost of Tom and says with glistening eyes, "Good-bye, dear man. Take all my love with you on your far journey." She drinks and then hands the leather-covered flask to Kit.

"I'll steal a line or two from myself to bid our boy farewell," he says. He raises the flask. "Life is a golden bubble full of dreams, that waking breaks and—" He hesitates, as though he has forgotten what he was going to say.

"And what?" she says.

His distracted eyes move from empty wall to empty wall and then back to her face. "And nothing!" he says.

"Nothing?"

"Yes, nothing! Nothing, nothing, nothing! What is a bubble when it's burst?" He tilts his head and takes a long drink of brandy.

"Kit, hold my hand," she says. And he puts his hand on hers. Her long, delicate fingers are cold. She grips him, opening and closing her hand as though she is not sure she has gotten hold of anything. She takes another sip of brandy. "Do you think that he is *all* dead, Kit?"

"What do you mean?"

"You know what I mean," she says. "The way you two would sit up all night talking about the soul and what it is and what it isn't, and how when a man is dead he is all dead—absolutely. And how it is nonsense to think of his spirit flying around in the air somewhere."

"That was just talk."

"But you believe it, don't you? You believe that Tom is all dead. That his soul is dead too. With him in the ground. Don't you?" She forces him to look her in the face.

"Yes," he says. "But you needn't believe that way. Believe what your heart tells you to believe."

She leans against him. They share the brandy. "God," she says, "how I wish it were another time. One of those ordinary sunny days ages and ages ago when the cat warmed himself by the fire and Tom scribbled at his desk and horses went by the window and the old widow complained about her back."

"There will be ordinary days again."

"Do you think so?" she says. A small pale laugh escapes from her trembling lips. "I don't see how there can be any days at all after this one."

Her face is very close to his. He kisses her and holds her. He touches her hair, her cheek, her eyes. Gently he wipes away the tears that she can no longer contain. She is crying. Giving in. Almost collapsing against him and into his arms.

"He shouldn't have died in September," she says. "It was his favorite month. He loved this time of year."

"I know," says Kit.

"Do you remember how we rode up to Kingsland one day—the

three of us—to steal vegetables and fruit because we had spent all our money on wine the day before?"

"It was a good adventure, wasn't it?" says Kit.

"There was an enormous turnip that looked surprisingly like a man's head. Do you remember that?"

"Yes. And Tom called it Sir Gabriel and chatted with it all the way home."

"And then we made love. Tom and I, I mean."

They fall silent for a moment, and the empty room seems more empty than ever. "Ann," says Kit, after a while, a note of urgency in his voice that makes her lift her head to look at his face. She sees that he too has been crying. "Ann, why don't we stay here?"

"Stay here? You mean, in this house?"

"Yes. You and me."

She looks puzzled. "How can we do that? I mean—"

"We can do it. We can live here together."

She shakes her head. "They wouldn't let us, Kit. My family. You know how they are."

"All right, then, we'll get married," he says.

She puts her hand lovingly against his cheek. "Kit," she says, "you don't want to be married."

"I want to be with you, Ann. Tom would have understood."

"For now you feel that way," she says. "For the moment. But it wouldn't work. You know it wouldn't work."

"Why not? I've got to do something with my life. I'm almost thirty years old. You would be good for me, Ann. You would—you would take care of me. I need looking after. I'm too—too restless."

"You would go on being restless, Kit."

"But perhaps together things would be different."

"Perhaps. But I know you very well, Kit. You need your freedom. And besides . . ."

"You needn't love me, Ann. It's not a matter of love."

"Oh, but I do love you, Kit," she says. "Not as you might imagine, but I do love you."

"Then marry me, Ann, and let's make some kind of a life together."

"You have a life. You have your friends, your work. You have Tom Walsingham."

"I have less than you might imagine," he says. "My privacy is painful, and I am sometimes afraid of the dark. I need somebody to scold me. Somebody to tell me I am ridiculous. Somebody to argue with and to make love with."

"We would never argue, Kit," she says.

"Then we could make love."

"Would you like to make love to me?"

"Yes," he says.

"I mean, right now. Here."

"Right here?" he says.

She takes the flask from his hand and finishes the last drop. "Yes," she says. "I want you to."

"But we have to go. They're waiting for us at your brother's."

"They can wait." She stands up and takes him by the hand. "Come, Kit. Tell me you are Tom and make love to me. And I will call you Tom and you will call me Ann. Don't think about it. You know how he was."

They embrace in the middle of the room. Her moist mouth finds his, and the tension of his lips melts. Her eyes are closed. She kisses him again and again. She feels his neck and his shoulders and his arms. She is slipping into a dream. She takes Kit's hand and places it on her breast and holds it there. "He would make love to me standing up sometimes. And sometimes on a chair. What naughty children we were! At my mother's house, with people in the next room and all. With all our clothes on, looking so innocent as soon as anyone came to the door. How quick he was. How devilish." Her hand moves to Kit's arm, then down to his side, his hips. She draws him on.

"There is still a bed in my room," says Kit quietly. "Shall we go there?"

"No," she says. "Here! Right here in this bare place. Our place." She sinks to her knees and then lies down, inviting Kit to lie beside her. "In our minds we'll light a fire in the fireplace and put down the rug. Close your eyes. Kiss me."

He kisses her for a long time. Her breathing grows heavier, her mouth more desperate. He undoes some buttons to bare her breast. She draws up her black skirt and boldly removes some undergarments. She was always fond of simple clothes. Her long white legs are incongruously naked against the bunched black fabric. She spreads them longingly. He sees the light patch of hair and the soft place where her thighs round into hips.

Kit hovers over her, holding his weight away from her, finding his place between her legs. She receives him with a gasp, then again, and again. "Oh, God! Oh, Tom! Don't leave me!"

Kit's arms give way. He falls into her, on her. Their bodies entwine. Her hands grab desperately at him, as though he might disappear any moment. Kit feels himself falling with her into a deep abyss. They are falling, falling. She is whispering in his ear, biting him, clawing at his clothes and his back. And then a great ocean of a sky opens beneath them, and they are flying downward amidst downy clouds, and streaks of sunlight are piercing them as they sigh away their impossible union. It is an ecstasy and a terror for her. The beginning and the end. She wants it but struggles against it. And then she swoons in the crisis of her pleasure, her body arching, stiffening, and then going suddenly limp.

But it is only for a few moments. And then slowly she opens her eyes to find that she is looking into Kit's face and that he is beside her, holding her, kissing her gently.

Silently they put their clothes together. Silently they stand and move about the room. Kit ties up the wooden box. Ann touches his hair as he kneels. When he is done, he takes her by the hand and says, "They're waiting for us."

"I should marry you, Kit," she says. "But without Tom, it wouldn't be any good. But don't marry anyone else. Stay free and come to see me."

"You know I will, whatever else I do."

She takes a deep breath, as if to face the world. "I wish we could stay here in this empty room forever. I don't want to face all those people. Everybody saying how sorry they are."

"We could go somewhere alone," says Kit. "We could run off to the country. We could find a cottage somewhere."

She laughs. "Such a silly dream. You would be back in London in a week. It's not what you want."

"I'm sick of London," he says. "I hate London. And all those drunken clever people."

"You may hate it, but you love it," she says. "And you need it. Go back to your books. Write your plays. Come, we are very late. If we don't go, they will come for us, and it won't seem right."

She leads him to the door. She kisses him tenderly and waits for him to undo the latch.

xxxviii

All through the fall and into the winter the plague grows worse in London. From March to December, 11,503 deaths are recorded. All business before the Courts of Chancery, the Star Chamber, Exchequer, Wards and Liveries, the Duchy of Lancaster, and the Court of Requests is moved to Hertford, and no person whose house has been visited by the plague is allowed access to the town. A proclamation is issued forbidding anyone to approach within two miles of the Queen's court without special permission; nor is anyone who attends the Queen allowed to go into London or its suburbs. Announcements are made at Paul's Cross that the various feasts of the city have been canceled. Those who can get out of the city do so, but many cannot, and in the poorer quarters and in the prisons they die by the thousands, and those who survive endure a hell far worse than ordinary death.

Through all these months, nothing is heard of Christopher Marlowe. Some of his friends assume that he has gone to stay with Tom Walsingham at Chislehurst; others think that surely he is in Canterbury with his family. But none knows for sure, and most are too concerned with their own fates to make careful inquiries.

It is Matthew Roydon who finally makes the trip to Scadbury to try to discover what has become of his friend. When he finds that he has not been there, and when he tells Tom Walsingham that he has not been seen in London for some time, they both become deeply concerned. Tom pleads with Matthew to do what he can to find him and arms him with an affectionate invitation and some money. "As soon as you find him, bring him here," says Tom. "I am afraid that he is not in a healthy state of mind."

"The death of Tom Watson was a heavy blow for him," says Matthew. "We had hoped that he would stay on in the house, with or without Ann, but it has been closed down now for several months, and Ann, they say, has gone to live with her brother Hugh Swift."

Matthew returns to London and, at the risk of his own life, makes inquiries that lead him into quarters where funeral pyres burn and bodies are carted through the narrow streets. Infected houses are locked shut from the outside, and those still alive inside are not permitted to leave but are supplied with food and water.

Still, life goes on, and the taverns remain open. It is a common if desperate joke that much drinking will keep away the plague—and, in any case, will make the victim insensible to its torments. In one such place in Southwark, Matthew questions an innkeeper, describing the man for whom he is looking. "He is twenty-eight years old, well dressed, with black hair and a closely trimmed beard."

The innkeeper laughs. "London is full of young men with beards. And besides, whoever he is and whatever he's wanted for, it's none of my business."

Matthew persuades him with sincerity and money that he is not a pursuivant and that the man is not an outlaw of any sort. "He is a personal friend of mine and a man of some importance. You would have noticed his educated speech, I'm sure. His name is Marlowe— Christopher Marlowe."

The innkeeper scratches his head. "There's a fellow," he says, "that comes here almost every evening after dark and sits at that table there and drinks himself into insensibility and talks religion. We take him here for a renegade priest and a lunatic, but what does it matter these days? We'll all be dead in a week or two."

Matthew waits for several hours at the designated table, and eventually Christopher appears—or is it the ghost of Christopher? He moves unsteadily across the room. His face is drawn, and there are deep shadows under his eyes. He has grown so thin that the skeleton beneath his skin is almost visible. His clothes, while not ragged, are hopelessly disheveled, as though he has slept in them for a month.

He comes face to face with Matthew and does not recognize him at first. "Oh, my God," says Roydon, "what have you done to yourself?"

And then a weak smile comes across Kit's face. "Is it you, Matthew?" he says. "I thought you were dead. I thought everybody was dead. Are Tom and Robert and John and Edmund all alive too, and Dick Tarleton and Sir Francis and Campion and all the spirits that used to walk the world? Have I been dreaming all these years? Say I have been dreaming, Matthew, and that you have come to wake me up."

"I've come to take you down to Scadbury," says Matthew. "Tom Walsingham has been very worried about you and wants you there right away."

"I don't believe you," says Kit. "Tom Walsingham is a Scottish spy and a Catholic pervert. And besides, I'm terribly busy, as you can plainly see. I'm working on a cure for the plague. And if it doesn't work, I can always bring them back from the dead by the application of certain numbers. There's magic in numbers, you know. Hobberdidance, flibbertigibbet, modo mahu."

Matthew forces the letter from Tom onto Kit. "Here," he says, "read this. Sit down and read it, man! And pull yourself together."

Whatever the letter says, it seems to bring Kit to his senses. He agrees to go. "But not before we share a bottle of wine," he says.

"There will be plenty of time for that in another place," says Matthew. "It's a wonder you're still alive, hanging about ratholes like this."

"I'm somewhat surprised myself," says Kit. "I gave God every chance to strike me dead, short of climbing a church steeple in a lightning storm. And here I am, still more or less moving about. Do with me what you will. I don't much care!"

IV

SCADBURY

i

THE mild dampness of February brings an early spring to Chislehurst. By the beginning of March the land is alive again. It does not take Kit long to recover in such surroundings. He moves, much like the seasons, from death to life. Small leaves sprout, the grass grows thick, fields are planted, and the birds announce the resurrection of the earth. He has put London out of his mind, and not much news of it comes, anyway. He rises early. He reads. He takes long walks and returns with damp shoes, ruddy cheeks and an appetite. Tom is attentive, but not oppressively so. There seems a change in him, thinks Kit. But then he has had his thirtieth birthday and is, after all, the responsible heir of an old and responsible family.

After several days of rain, the sun rises like a revelation and lords it over a morning as perfect as the first day of creation. Colors leap out of the mossy walls, the frog-infested moat, and the still-damp woods. Lying in bed, Christopher hears the delicate voice of a girl singing in the courtyard—one of the servants doing her chores:

> "I mun be married a Sunday;
> I mun be married a Sunday;
> Whoever shall come that way,
> I mun be married a Sunday."

Her voice trails off into humming. He can almost see her moving across the cobbled court, bending and lifting and dreaming herself into womanhood.

When he comes down he finds that Tom is already up and dressed for riding. He wears long boots, a handsome coat belted about the middle, and a green cap with a yellow feather that might be from a golden bird out of the fictions of Greece. "Come on, you lazy fellow," he says. "You can't waste a day like this. I've got a horse all saddled up for you. We're riding out to St. Marye Cray."

"And pray tell, my lord," says Kit, "what will we do in St. Marye Cray?"

"We must tend to some business of the utmost importance."

"Ah, matters touching the benefit of the country, no doubt."

"A matter of pigs, in fact," says Tom, "than which nothing could benefit more a country so fond of meat."

On a pair of handsome geldings they ride out, cockily dressed. They pass through the arch, drum their way across the drawbridge, and ride down the gritty road to discuss with the steward of St. Marye Cray the sale of a herd of swine.

They trot, they gallop, they revel in the sudden gorgeousness of life. It is impossible to imagine that only a dozen miles away Death lays siege to the City of London.

They turn off the road and cut across a field. The ground is soft under the horses' feet. They go leisurely side by side, talking of ordinary things. When they come to a small stream, they allow the horses to drink, and they dismount to walk along the bank and across a small bridge, beautifully arched and linking the spot with Norman and Saxon history. They linger midway and look into the water. They fall into a brief silence, and there's not a sound to be heard, except the occasional snorting of the horses or the movement of the water.

"We've come this way before, haven't we?" Kit asks.

"A hundred years ago," says Tom.

"And the water that runs under this bridge is not the same water that passed this way before," says Kit.

"It never is."

Then Kit turns suddenly to face him. "You're going to marry Audrey Shelton, aren't you?"

"Probably," says Tom. "Does it really matter so much to you?"

"Of course not," says Kit. "A man in your position should marry. But—"

"But what, dear friend?"

"She's an odd sort of person, isn't she? Tell me about her."

"It's rather complicated," says Tom.

"I'm sure it is," says Kit. "Isn't almost everything?"

"It's not a question of love, God knows," he says. "Nor is it strictly a question of business. We get on quite well. She's probably one of the few women in the world with whom I could stand to live—assuming that marriage at this point is virtually a family obligation."

"Do you think she understands you?"

"As a matter of fact, I think she does, though it is not something we discuss very often. She has an uncanny sensitivity to certain things."

"And a shrewdness, I imagine."

"Oh, yes, there's that, too," says Tom. "But her shrewdness is not obnoxious. She can be very charming."

"I sense also in her a certain independence of nature," says Kit. "A certain *privacy*, as though she will always have her own life—perhaps her own secrets."

"We all have our secrets, don't we?" says Tom. "About some of hers, we have arrived at an understanding of sorts. And about some of mine. We will not be an ordinary husband and wife. Of that you can be sure. We will have to live together but apart, be intimate but independent, if you know what I mean."

"She seems on terribly good terms with Mrs. Thornborough," says Kit.

"They are the greatest of friends. Beyond that I think I need not go. What is between them is their business. She is also on very good terms with Robert Cecil."

"Oh?" says Kit. "What precisely do you mean by that?"

Tom hesitates, but only for a moment. "As a matter of fact, she's his mistress."

"Good Lord, Tom, I had no idea. And are you going to be able to live with that?"

"I've given it a lot of thought, naturally. And I really don't think I mind. I mean, we're all good friends. I wouldn't expect most people to understand, but I think you probably do. And you won't say anything, of course."

"It's not exactly the sort of thing one talks about," says Kit. He shakes his head and smiles as he digests the situation. "Sometimes, Tom, you fairly amaze me!"

"Do you think I'm doing the wrong thing?"

"I don't know," says Kit. "It sounds as though you may have struck an interesting bargain all around. Besides, every woman ought to have a lover. There's not an awful lot for them to do, and their lives can get very dull."

"I don't think Audrey's life will ever be dull."

"In that case, yours may be enriched, and you have my blessings."

"You're not jealous, then, or anything of that sort?"

"Not at all," says Kit, "providing she doesn't come between us."

"Oh, I'm sure the two of you will get on famously," says Tom. "She's very fond of poetry, you know. Quite remarkable in her own way."

They go on to St. Marye Cray, where they are given a warm welcome and a somewhat excessive lunch. The business of the pigs is accomplished, and by late afternoon they are on their way back to Scadbury.

They stop briefly to rest, and Kit brings up the delicate subject of Ingram Frizer. "When do you expect him back?" he says.

"I really don't know," says Tom. "He and Nicholas Skeres are in London or somewhere on business."

"What sort of business?"

"I think they have been assigned to a certain situation by Whitgift. I really don't know much about it."

"I have heard some odd things about this Nicholas Skeres," says Kit. "An unsavory sort, isn't he?"

"What exactly have you heard?"

"That he's not only been a bit of a petty cutpurse in his time, but perhaps also a professional cutthroat. I have it from certain fairly reliable disreputable types who knew him before he went to work for Frizer."

"I don't like the man much myself. He's a very ugly type, but Ingram assures me that he is extremely useful in certain ways."

"I can imagine."

"But let's not go on about it," says Tom. "There are all kinds of dirty jobs to be done in this world, and aren't we lucky that we don't have to do them. But, incidentally, Ingram is a man with considerably more substance. Give him half a chance when he comes back and I think you'll see what I mean. Oh, he's wily, all right, but he can also be quite interesting at times."

Kit doesn't answer. He stands up, looks at the sky, and says, "We'd better be on our way. It's getting rather late." They mount up and go the rest of the way at a good canter. The sun is in the west directly in front of them, so that at times they seem to be pursuing it.

ii

In his leisure time at Scadbury, after the confusions of London, Kit has turned to Ovid again and to some other old favorites out of the past. He is done, he says, with all that metaphysical nonsense and wants to write something simple and beautiful and unconnected with the present. He settles on the old story of Hero and Leander, treated by Ovid and, later, by Musaeus in Greek. He relies heavily on the Latin version of F. Paulinus, published in 1587 as part of a volume entitled *Centum Fabulae ex Antiquis*. Tom has a copy in his library, a gift from Tom Watson, affectionately inscribed.

At first Kit thinks he might amuse himself by merely translating the poem into English, but then, inspired by the narrative, the countryside, and his own recovered energies, he breaks away from the original and plunges into a poem of his own with freedom and feeling and a sense of exhilaration and joy that he has not known for some time.

He writes romantically, sensuously, and sometimes a bit cryptically, about two marvelous lovers, the beautiful Hero and the equally beautiful though masculine Leander. One lives at Sestos, the other at Abydos, two cities on opposite shores of the Hellespont. He mingles mythology and earthliness, dallies with his readers as his lovers dally with each other. As gorgeous as Hero is, Leander, though a lad, is more gorgeous still, and Kit cannot hide his leanings in these lines:

> His dangling tresses that were never shorn,
> Had they been cut, and unto Colchos borne,
> Would have allur'd the vent'rous youth of Greece
> To hazard more than for the golden Fleece.
> Fair Cynthia wish'd his arms might be her sphere;
> Grief makes her pale, because she moves not there.
> His body was as straight as Circe's wand;
> Jove might have sipt out nectar from his hand.
> Even as delicious meat is to the taste,
> So was his neck in touching, and surpast
> The white of Pelops' shoulder: I could tell ye,
> How smooth his breast was, and how white his belly,
> And whose immortal fingers did imprint
> That heavenly path with many a curious dint,
> That runs along his back; but my rude pen
> Can hardly blazon forth the loves of men,
> Much less of powerful gods: let it suffice
> That my slack muse sings of Leander's eyes,
> Those orient cheeks and lips, exceeding his
> That leapt into the water for a kiss
> Of his own shadow, and despising many,
> Died ere he could enjoy the love of any.

Christopher smiles at himself playfully, knowing that there are those who will find the double and triple meanings in his words.

Had wild Hippolytus Leander seen,
Enamoured of his beauty had he been:
His presence made the rudest peasant melt,
That in the vast uplandish country dwelt;
The barbarous Thracian soldier, mov'd with naught,
Was mov'd with him, and for his favor sought.
Some swore he was a maid in man's attire,
For in his looks were all that men desire,
A pleasant smiling cheek, a speaking eye,
A brow for love to banquet royally;
And such as knew he was a man would say,
"Leander, thou art made for amorous play:
Why art thou not in love, and lov'd of all?
Though thou be fair, yet be not thine own thrall."

They meet, of course, and love enters through the eyes and is
inevitable:

It lies not in our power to love or hate,
For will in us is over-rul'd by fate.

He weaves his poem out of the stuff of antiquity and decorates it
with high-sounding idealism—to please a patron or a personal
friend—but it is the memory of things quite physical and real that
gives the poem its seductive power:

He touch'd her hand; in touching it she trembled:
Love deeply grounded, hardly is dissembled.
These lovers parled by the touch of hands;
True love is mute, and oft amazed stands.

He describes Leander's hot innocence and Hero's female instinct
to lure, to lean, to hesitate, and then to flee, but not too far. How
much wiser women are than men! And what a dilemma love creates
for them. The jewel of chastity can only be kept to be given.
Guarded absolutely, it has no value. But once given, what then?

How Hero dreads (how all women dread) that after she has given
herself, the pursuit will end, and with it love.

　　In her legendary (natural) way, she imposes upon him a difficult
task—to steal a draught of the nectar of the gods—for which he is
punished and they are separated. But, undaunted and in the grip of
his mighty passion, he swims the turbulent Hellespont to be with
the woman he loves.

　　　　And now she lets him whisper in her ear,
　　　　Flatter, entreat, promise, protest, and swear,
　　　　Yet ever as he greedily assay'd
　　　　To touch those dainties, she the harpy play'd,
　　　　And every limb did as a soldier stout
　　　　Defend the fort, and keep the foeman out.
　　　　For though the rising ivory mount he scal'd,
　　　　Which is with azure circling lines empal'd,
　　　　Much like a globe (a globe may I term this,
　　　　By which Love sails to regions full of bliss),
　　　　Yet there with Sisyphus he toil'd in vain,
　　　　Till gentle parley did the truce obtain.
　　　　Wherewith Leander on her quivering breast,
　　　　Breathless spoke something, and sigh'd out the rest;
　　　　Which so prevail'd, as he with small ado
　　　　Enclos'd her in his arms, and kiss'd her too!
　　　　And every kiss to her was as a charm,
　　　　And to Leander as a fresh alarm;
　　　　So that the truce was broke, and she alas,
　　　　Poor silly maiden, at his mercy was.
　　　　Love is not full of pity, as men say,
　　　　But deaf and cruel where he means to prey.
　　　　Even as a bird, which in our hands we wring,
　　　　Forth plungeth, and oft flutters with her wing,
　　　　She trembling strove; this strife of hers (like that
　　　　Which made the world) another world begat
　　　　Of unknown joy. Treason was in her thought,
　　　　And cunningly to yield herself she sought.
　　　　Seeming not won, yet won she was at length.

In such wars women use but half their strength.
Leander now, like Theban Hercules,
Enter'd the orchard of th'Hesperides;
Whose fruit none rightly can describe but he
That pulls or shakes it from the golden tree.
And now she wish'd this night were never done,
And sigh'd to think upon th'approaching sun;
For much it grieved her that the bright daylight
Should know the pleasure of this blessed night,
And them like Mars and Erycine display
Both in each other's arms chain'd as they lay.

iii

The visit of Matthew Roydon on the twelfth of March should be a pure pleasure, but it is not. He brings his affectionate presence to Scadbury, but he brings also news of London, and the news is not good.

"The theatres are all closed again for the plague," he says. "But your *Massacre at Paris* was given several times in this abbreviated season, and, as you must have heard, it was a huge popular success."

"Oh, let's not talk about that rotten play," says Kit. "I can't imagine what made me stoop so low. As for the public, well, the public be damned. They have no literary judgment whatsoever."

The most disturbing news that Matthew brings with him is that a warrant has been issued for the arrest of John Penry. "The authorities are now thoroughly convinced that he is, in fact, Martin Marprelate," he says. "Too many people have known this for too long. It was bound to come out."

"I thought John had gone into Scotland," says Kit. Already a certain grayness begins to rival the bloom in his cheek. And he frowns as he tries to understand what the consequences of all this will be.

"The fool came back. He wanted to be closer to the scene," says Matthew. "Some say he was betrayed by a friend."

"Hasn't it always been that way?" says Kit. "Since Cain slew Abel and Brutus turned on Caesar."

"They say that Bancroft is on the warpath," says Matthew. "One way or another he'll have John Penry hanged."

"On what grounds?" says Tom. "His gadfly pamphlets hardly constitute a capital offense."

"I don't think it matters these days what's legal and what's not," says Matthew. "Bancroft will see him dead—and not only him. The city is a caldron of unrest, and the Council is in a panic to keep things under control. The other day they arrested a large group of Barrowists at a meeting in Islington. And there are rumors now that their leader, Henry Barrow, is in serious jeopardy."

"I'm afraid I don't have much sympathy for these Separatists," says Tom. "If everyone is allowed to go his separate way, it will mean the end of the Church of England."

"Nevertheless," says Matthew, "they have considerable sympathy for their views, especially for their attack on the abuses of the bishops and their ruthless inquisitions. And you must admit that they have a point when they claim that a secular government cannot rule in matters of religion. There are no grounds for this in the holy Scriptures, and it is a blatant violation of the whole spirit of Christianity to use the Church in such an obviously political manner. Mind you, I am not supporting the Barrowists or the Brownists or any of the Puritans, but how can any man in his right mind approve of the kind of religious and political persecution that we are now enduring in this country? If the Queen and the Council are not careful, they will push the people to desperate measures. Did you hear, for instance, that just a fortnight ago a plot to kill the Queen was uncovered? One of Parsons's men, a certain Gilbert Layton, confessed that he was sent by the Jesuits and Sir Francis Englefield and Don Juan de Idiaques to murder Elizabeth while she was on progress."

"Topcliffe can torture a man into confessing anything," says Kit.

"Granted there are abuses," says Tom, "but if any other sect or religious persuasion took hold of the reins of power, the situation would be no different. They would be as oppressive and as murderous as our own bishops. The Catholics were no better under Mary, were they? Worse, in fact. The Barrowists, I understand, would make it a capital offense to practice any but what they call the 'true faith.' Is that freedom?"

"I think you exaggerate the case against the Separatists and the Puritans," says Matthew. "That's the sort of thing that Archbishop Whitgift would have us all believe, because he is determined to put down all threats to the Established Church. For this he has the Queen's full support. But he has less support in other branches of the government than you might imagine. Burghley, for instance, has clearly tried to curb his attacks on religious deviations. And there are other members of the Council with certain Puritan leanings. The House of Commons, as you know, favors greater leniency in these matters. But what is the House of Commons, when the Queen repeatedly reminds them that the Parliament is merely her instrument for advice and has no power? When, just recently, Mr. Morris delivered a bill to the Speaker condemning the abuses of the bishops, he was severely rebuked, and the Speaker was informed by the Queen herself that the Parliament was not to meddle in the affairs of state or in matters ecclesiastical. And that was that!"

"The Queen's only concern is the stability and survial of the state," says Tom. "And to suggest, even for a moment, that civil power can be made subordinate to a handful of clergymen who imagine that they have a death grip on the real truth is sheer madness. I mean, that way lies absolute chaos."

"But damn it, Tom," says Matthew, "you cannot *use* religion for political ends. You cannot say that a man is a traitor to his country because he prays to God in his own way. And that is precisely what is happening right now. Any deviation from the official religion of the state is considered an act of treason, punishable by death. I know that's not exactly how the law reads, but that's how it's being arbitrarily interpreted."

"I still think that the government's primary duty is to keep the nation from falling apart," says Tom. "With the threat of Spain increasing again, and another invasion expected at any moment, we cannot afford internal dissension. Any display of weakness at this point is liable to prove disastrous."

"I don't consider such random murder a display of strength," says Kit.

"Oh, look who's talking about the use of force," says Tom.

"Sometimes the excessive use of force is a sign of weakness," says Kit. "A sign of lack of confidence. I agree that the people must be controlled, but there are more subtle ways. And a greater amount of freedom at this point, paradoxically enough, might prove to be a better form of control."

"I agree," says Matthew, taking from his pocket a folded piece of paper. "Here, look at this." He hands the paper to Tom. It is a printed broadside. "This is the sort of thing that is circulating all over London. When Roger Rippon, one of Barrow's followers, died in Newgate, his friends took his body, coffin and all, and laid it on the doorstep of Justice Young. Attached to it was this printed sheet, which was also distributed overnight to practically every tavern in the city. Read it. Read it aloud!"

Tom reads: " 'This is the corpse of Roger Rippon, a servant of Christ and Her Majesty's faithful subject, who is the last of sixteen or seventeen which that great enemy of God, the Archbishop of Canterbury, with his High Commissioners, has murdered in Newgate within these five years, manifestly for the testimony of Jesus Christ. His soul is now with the Lord; and his blood crieth for speedy vengeance against that great enemy of the saints and against Mr. Richard Young, who in this and many like points hath abused his power, for the upholding of the Romish Anti-Christ, Prelacy and priesthood.' "

Kit shakes his head in despair. "I knew this interlude was too good to last. The snake's in our garden again, Tom. Is there no way to escape all this dreary news?"

"I'm sorry," says Matthew. "I didn't mean to spoil your holiday in the country. I promise you that for the rest of the day we will put aside politics and talk about nothing but poetry and love and the swans in the Scadbury moat."

They laugh and go into the house, arm in arm, to see what they can find to eat and drink. "And after lunch," says Tom, "this moral monster here will read you a piece of his indecent new poem."

iv

On the thirtieth of March, George Chapman comes for a visit, and once again the bucolic pleasures of Scadbury are briefly spoiled. Actually, the cloud that was cast by Matthew Roydon has never quite been wafted away by the grazing sheep or the lazy breeze that ripples the waters of the lake.

Chapman's news only adds to their growing concern. "The Privy Council," he tells them, "has issued a warrant for the arrest of your friend Richard Chomley. And for Richard Stronge. But they say that Chomley won't be taken without a fight. He's got somewhere between sixty and eighty men with him, and they've gone into hiding."

"Good for him," says Kit. "He might as well die fighting as whimpering at the gallows."

"If they catch him and put him to the torture," says Tom, "do you think he'll say anything about Kit?"

"It's very difficult to tell about these things," says Chapman. "Chomley is a brazen sort. He could easily turn stubborn and tell them all to go to hell."

"It was foolish of me to even talk to the man," says Kit. "I gave him a few drunken lectures in a tavern and he took it for the atheistic gospel and went around boasting that he and I were the most intimate of friends and that I was the prophet of the new enlightenment. A mad adventurer—but amusing in his way. You know, when he was working for the government, apprehending papists, he'd take his pay from the Crown, and then, having captured his Catholics and recusants, he'd take their money too and let them go." Christopher laughs, but his amusement is mixed with bitterness.

"There was another disgraceful execution the other day," says Chapman. "It's talked about all over town. It seems there was a young man named James Bird of Winchester who had been in prison for some ten years for his stubborn refusal to go to church. He was arraigned for some reason, after all this time, and brought before the Lord Chief Justice Anderson, who was determined to see him hanged, having heard of his arrogance. So he put his case to the court in this ridiculous way. He said that a recusant is a man who refuses to go to church and that any man who refuses to go to church must be a papist, and since all papists are traitors, having pledged their allegiance to a foreign prince, then this James Bird must be a traitor, and so must be hanged. It took no time at all to bring the poor fellow to the gallows. But there, they say, he maintained his composure and forced the sheriff to admit that if he would only agree to go to church, he might beg the Queen's pardon. Having demonstrated in this fashion to the crowd that he was being put to death strictly for religious reasons, he said, 'I gladly die,' and was promptly pushed from the ladder."

"Must we talk about this gruesome stuff?" says Tom. "Tell us about the theatres. What news is there of plays and books?"

"Not much news at all of the theatres," says Chapman. "They've been closed since the end of January, and unless the plague eases considerably, they may be closed until next fall or winter. Still, Lord Strange remains optimistic and has set to work a group of writers to hack out a topical piece of stuff about the riots against the foreigners in our midst. He's found a neat parallel in the heroic efforts of Sir Thomas More, who, as Sheriff of London, put down the May Day riots of 1517 under Henry the Eighth. The situation in those days, apparently, was very similar to what we face today—at least in this respect. I mean, the times were bad, and people were pressed by poverty. At that time too, the influx of immigrants and refugees was a terrible threat. I think it was the Lombards mainly in those days, but now, of course, it's the Flemings and the Belgians and the French, looking for the protection of our Protestant Queen. She's been much too obliging, some people think. And I personally agree.

"At any rate, Tom Kyd has gotten himself involved, along with every other second-rate writer in London who has not been able to get out of the city. Lord Strange's Men are the only group left in London. The others have all taken to the provinces, and I hear that Ned Alleyn is considering the same course of action and urging Ferdinando to apply for a license to go on tour. But Ferdinando is still convinced that the theatres will open again, and, of course, should they do so, he will be in a good position to turn a shilling or two at The Rose. He wants to be ready with something new. I think he's hoping that by May first he can put on this *Sir Thomas More* play, since that would be the anniversary of that 'Evil May Day,' as they call it."

"Who else is involved in the writing of this so-called play?" Kit asks.

"Anthony Munday," he says, "and Henry Chettle, Tom Dekker, and Tom Heywood."

"Who in the world is Tom Dekker?" says Kit.

"A young fellow from London," says Chapman. "Can't be more than twenty-one or so, but I hear he shows some aptitude for this awful business. And since he's only getting his start, he's willing to work all kinds of hours, and for next to nothing."

"What a motley collection of scribbling idiots," says Kit.

"Except possibly for Tom Kyd," says Chapman.

"Oh, he's just as bad as the rest of them," says Kit. "Always moaning and groaning about how poor and neglected he is. He'd do a literary bend-over for a groat any day of the week."

"What's the play all about?" Tom asks.

"I gather it dramatizes the uprising of the apprentices," says Chapman, "and in language designed to please the angry rabble who are up in arms these days against those strangers who are taking the bread out of their mouths."

"Sounds as though it's liable to incite the audience to riot," says Kit. "It'll never pass Tilney. He'll censor it all to pieces."

"Well, of course," says Chapman, "technically the hero is Sir Thomas More, who quells the riot and restores law and order. Therefore, no one can really accuse the authors of anything but displaying the thing that they would refute. Surely you know how

that is, Kit. God, what atheistic speeches you put in the mouths of
Tamburlaine and Faustus and Barabbas. But it was all right, since
they were villains."

"I'm not sure it *was* all right," says Tom. "But tell me about this
Thomas More play. Who's really behind it? It wasn't just
Ferdinando's idea, was it? I wouldn't be at all surprised if Ralegh
had something to do with it. They are awfully good friends, you
know, and Sir Walter has been making speeches in Parliament for
some time now against these aliens."

"It's possible," says Chapman. "And there's no doubt that he's
looking for some popular support, in the hope of repairing his
influence, now that he's out of favor with Her Majesty. On the
other hand, it could also be the Earl of Essex."

"If it ever gets by the Master of Revels," says Tom, "it will no
doubt be a huge success. Maybe even more successful than *The
Massacre at Paris.*"

Kit glances at Tom and catches him concealing a smile. "I think
your leg is being pulled, Christopher," says Chapman.

"It's a play," Kit says, "for which my Catholic friends will never
forgive me." He is referring to the Catholic leanings of this branch
of the Walsinghams.

"Oh, a hit, a hit!" says Chapman.

v

During the month of April, visitors from London become more
and more frequent. Some come on legitimate business. Others
come only because the plague has driven them out and they must
move from friend to friend to while away the weeks. Frizer and
Skeres return at last, looking like a pair of cats who have swallowed
a dozen canaries. They offer conflicting accounts of where they
have been and what they have been doing, and it is quite obvious
that neither one of them is telling the truth.

To Kit, the most unexpected visit of all is from Robert Poley.
Oddly enough, though, Tom Walsingham seems to have expected
him, a fact which is confirmed the morning after his arrival when

Kit comes upon the two of them in intense and private conversation in the garden. They shift the subject deftly, but it's clear that they have been interrupted.

Before the day is out, Robert Poley has added considerably to the picture of a growing crisis in London. He says that on the last day of March, Henry Barrowe and John Greenwood, the Separatists, were brought in a cart to Tyburn to be hanged, having been condemned to death on the twenty-second of the month. "But just as they were about to be executed, with the crowd roaring and the victims in a fever of fear, they were granted a reprieve and taken back to prison."

"How horribly cruel!" says Tom.

"They say it was Lord Burghley who granted the reprieve," says Robert. "And that for this he had to contend with Whitgift. In any case, a few days later, on the sixth of April, apparently the bishops had their way, and Barrowe and Greenwood were suddenly hanged early in the morning."

"My God," says Kit, "what is the place coming to? Between the plague and this kind of senseless murder, London will soon be nothing but a huge graveyard."

"Oh, it's not all that bad," says Robert, in his cool way. "Life goes on, you know. A few disturbances here and there, a few hangings. But the shops are still open. On the surface, things look quite ordinary. Business as usual and all that. We're really quite a commercial country, you know. Not all that religiously fanatical. And there's still money to be made, if you've got the proper connections."

"And I suppose you think you've got those connections," says Kit.

"Why, Christopher," he says, "you *know* I do. I'm off for The Hague in a day or two."

"Oh, are you?" says Tom. "And how long will you be gone this time?"

"I plan to leave from Deptford, and I should be back there by the thirtieth of May—possibly a day or so earlier. I'll be staying over, as usual, at the house of Eleanor Bull. It will be perfectly safe for you to leave messages there for me. Old Mistress Bull is quite discreet in her ugly way."

"Being so well connected and all," Kit says, "you are quite aware of this play about Sir Thomas More, I suppose."

"As a matter of fact, I did hear something about that," he says. "It seems Mr. Edmund Tilney got very upset when it was submitted to him for his inspection."

"He rejected it, then?" says Tom.

"Well, not exactly," says Robert. "You might say he *castrated* it. I understand that he instructed the writers to leave out the entire insurrection on the part of the apprentices against the foreigners and to omit any discussion of the causes of that uprising. If the play is to be given at all, it will have to be limited, he says, to the good service done by the good Sheriff of London, namely, Sir Thomas More."

"There's no point, then, in putting it on at all, is there?" says Kit.

"I hardly think so," says Robert.

"Well, I think it's just as well," says Tom. "I've never thought much of the Master of Revels, but in this case I think he's absolutely right."

"I don't agree," says Kit. "I think his job ought to be to distinguish between good and bad taste and not to act as a censor for a certain political point of view."

"Don't be naïve, Christopher," says Robert. "Censorship is absolutely necessary, especially these days."

"Pretty soon," says Kit, "there won't be anything at all left to write about. We'll have to grind out little comedies about Mistress Titmouse and her ugly daughter Jane, making sure to omit anything whatsoever that might be misconstrued as an allegorical commentary on the state of the world. We might even have to remove the frogs from her stagnant pond, lest they be mistaken for Frenchmen."

"But, Christopher," says Robert, "there's always mythology. And I understand from Matthew Roydon that you've turned to it yourself—something about Hero and Leander."

"He has, as a matter of fact," says Tom, "and is off to a marvelous start."

"Which reminds me," says Robert. "I brought you a gift from London. Something I'm sure you would like to see."

"What is it?" says Kit.

From the leather bag beside his chair he takes a small volume and hands it to Kit. "It's a poem called *Venus and Adonis* by this fellow Shakespeare that everyone's talking about. I think you'll be particularly interested in the dedication."

Kit turns the pages and stops. A slow blush comes over his face. The others wait. "Well?" says Tom at last. "What is it? Read it to us."

Kit tosses the book in Tom's lap and stands up. "Read it yourself," he says, and stalks out of the room.

"What in the world's the matter with *him?*" says Robert.

"I really don't know," says Tom. He picks up the book and quietly, half to himself, half-aloud, reads the dedication: " 'To the Right Honorable Henry Wriothesley, Earl of Southampton, and Baron of Titchfield. . . . I know not how I shall offend in dedicating my unpolished lines to your Lordship, nor how the world will censure me for choosing so strong a prop to support so weak a burden, only if Your Honor seem but pleased, I account myself highly praised, and vow to take advantage of all idle hours, till I have honored you with some graver labor. But if the first heir of my invention prove deformed, I shall be sorry it had so noble a godfather: and never after ear so barren a land, for fear it yield me still so bad a harvest, I leave it to your Honorable survey, and your Honor to your heart's content which I wish may always answer your own wish, and the world's hopeful expectation.' "

"I think that's rather nice, don't you?" says Robert, not a hint of anything but innocence in his voice.

Tom does not seem to hear him. He is slowly discovering that the poem that he assumed Christopher was writing for him might actually have been written for someone else. But then he shakes away the suspicion and says, "Oh, yes. Yes. Very nice, indeed!"

vi

The news of Thomas Kyd's arrest and torture is brought to
Scadbury by Matthew Roydon. And when he says, "Unfortunately,
certain papers of yours were found mingled with his own; certain
rather embarrassing papers, I'm afraid," Kit is thrown into a
momentary panic.

Matthew has barely arrived and is still standing just inside the
door. His hair is damp with perspiration after his hard ride. He has
blurted out the barest essentials, and both Tom and Kit still do not
quite understand what has happened. "What papers?" shouts Kit.
"What papers are you talking about?"

"Stay calm, Christopher," says Tom. "Come, Matthew. Sit
down. Take off your coat. Peter! Peter! Some brandy, please. And
quickly." Ingram Frizer is suddenly in the room, though no one has
seen him come in. "Oh," says Tom. "It's you. Well, you might as
well hear this, too. Perhaps you'll be able to help."

There is a startled expression on Kit's face. Once again he asks
urgently, "What papers? I never gave him any papers."

Tom puts his hand on Kit's shoulder and says, "We'll sort this
out in a moment. Give Matthew a chance to catch his breath." The
butler comes in with a bottle and some glasses on a small silver tray.

"Things have been happening so fast I don't really know where
to begin," says Matthew. Tom and Kit and Frizer are gathered
around him in a small circle in front of the fireplace. But it is a
warm day, and there is no fire, nothing but a shallow, dark cave
framed in elaborate stone. It is late afternoon, and the sky is
overcast.

"The trouble began, I guess, with a series of very severe
demonstrations against the aliens two or three weeks ago. Slogans
and placards were put up all over the city, warning the foreigners to
leave England within ninety days or face dire consequences—calling them drones and parasites and cowards, accusing them of every
vice from drunkenness to hypocrisy. The Privy Council, afraid of a
full-scale uprising, held a special meeting and drafted special orders
for the Lord Mayor to root out the culprits by whatever means

necessary and to bring them to justice. They wanted action, and they wanted it quickly. They wanted to see a list of suspects. They wanted their houses and belongings thoroughly searched, and they wanted them questioned quickly and severely. Those who did not instantly confess were to be put to the torture in Bridewell.

"Apparently Tom Kyd's name was on that list as one of the authors of the play *Sir Thomas More*, which, as you must know by now, was severely criticized by Tilney as inflammatory. He was taken into custody, along with many others, the day after the Privy Council order was issued. Naturally he denied that he had anything to do with these libels against the aliens, which is perfectly true, but in the somewhat hysterical circumstances no one believed him and he was put to the torture. When his rooms were searched, they found there some papers which they labeled, '*12 May 1593: Vile Heretical Conceits, denying the Deity of Jesus Christ our Saviour, found among the papers of Thomas Kyd prisoner.*'"

"How did you find out these things?" says Tom.

"Through certain friends working as pursuivants," says Matthew, "but loyal to other causes." He glances at Frizer, who does not look away and whose face reveals nothing.

"Well," he goes on, "these atheistic papers were an even more serious matter. When Kyd was confronted with them he denied that they were his. He said they belonged to you, Kit. He said that some time ago you and he were working together in the same room and that apparently some of your papers got mixed up with his. He was very frightened. Perhaps he was put to the torture again. In any case, he described you as a thoroughly irreligious man, an atheist, in fact. He said you made fun of the Bible and that you denied that Christ was anything but an ordinary man. He accused you of terrible blasphemies and—oh, I don't know—numerous other things. I can't remember them all just now. Oh, yes, among other things, he said you were cruel-hearted, short-tempered and apt to be violent."

"The filthy, whimpering swine!" says Kit.

"Is it true about the papers?" Tom asks Kit.

"I don't know what he's talking about," says Kit. "From time to time I asked him to copy certain things out of books that I had borrowed. He has a professional hand, as you know, and my own handwriting is a bit less than legible at times. God knows what it is. It could be almost anything. I have collected a good deal of material of that sort."

"For what reason?" says Tom.

"Some of it background material for my plays," he says. "Some of it for our discussions at Durham House."

"But how could you be so careless as to leave such stuff lying about?" says Tom, obviously annoyed.

"How important can a few pages copied out of a book be?" says Kit. "Besides, I'm not even sure that it's true. For all I know, some papers were purposely mixed with his in order to incriminate me."

"I wouldn't be at all surprised," says Matthew. "There is no question now that there is considerable pressure to get at all of us."

"Who do you mean by 'all of us'?" Tom asks.

"Well, not you, of course," says Matthew, "though who knows! I mean Ralegh and his friends, the so-called School of Night, the Durham House crowd: Harriot, Warner, Kit, myself, and half a dozen others. Not to mention John Penry and his friends. The Puritan extremists. In short, all religious deviants. It's a general crackdown, a purge! And I, for one, am not going to stay around to get caught up in it."

"Where will you go?" says Tom.

"Scotland," he says. "I have good connections there. The climate is awful, but it's better than being dead."

"If you flee now, will you ever be able to come back?" Kit asks.

"There are no charges against me right now," says Matthew. "Perhaps there never will be. But I can't afford to gamble."

"Just what have you been involved in?" Frizer asks.

"I'm not sure that's any of your business," says Matthew.

Frizer lets the remark pass, and a moment of awkwardness is ended by Tom, who stands up and walks back and forth. "Well, now," he says. "Let's think about this situation. What shall we do? What shall we do?"

"Do you think I'll be arrested?" says Kit to Matthew.

"You almost certainly will be questioned," he says. "How far they will want to go with you, I don't know. However, if I were you, I'd get out now. I think Whitgift and Bancroft have gotten the upper hand on the Council. I don't think Lord Burghley and Robert Cecil can hold them in check. Things have gotten out of hand, and the Queen will back them all the way. I think they've got her completely convinced that severe measures are necessary at this point in the name of national defense. Why don't you come with me to Scotland? We can make a new start there. We have friends."

"We also have enemies there," says Kit. "My work with Robert Poley there put me in a very precarious position. It's possible that the Catholics already know that we betrayed them. And if they don't know, they are liable to find out. What then?"

"Assume a false name. Live quietly and discreetly," he says.

"And never come back to England?" says Kit.

"That remains to be seen," says Matthew. "After all, the Queen may die or something."

"But is my situation that desperate?" Kit asks. "Suppose they question me? Suppose they did, indeed, find a few sheets of paper, a few pages copied out of some book? In the first place, they wouldn't even be in my handwriting. I could deny that they were mine. It would be Tom Kyd's word against mine. Or even if I admitted they were mine, they might be easily explained. I'm on good terms with Robert Cecil—and his father. And some other people. And Ralegh is hardly powerless."

"He may be the one they are trying to get at through us," says Matthew.

"It will take quite a bit of doing to get that old fox," says Kit.

The windows grow dim as they continue to talk. Peter comes around and lights the candles. Tom tells him to bring in another bottle and to have the cook prepare some supper. Various suggestions are made and rejected, and nothing is clearly resolved, except that Matthew will leave in the morning for Dover, where he will make his arrangements to go by boat to Scotland. Kit decides that he will stay on at Scadbury and brazen it out. "That is, if you don't mind," he says to Tom.

"Not at all. Not at all," says Tom, but his tone is not entirely convincing.

Later, alone in his room, Kit cannot sleep. He is afraid to blow out the candle. He is too distracted to read. He does not even undress. He goes over and over the situation in his mind, until he is too weary to make any sensible predictions and is left merely with forebodings of disaster. Finally, shortly before dawn, he dozes for a while. The candle burns out. The crickets sing in the dampness and a gentle rain begins to fall.

vii

Almost a week goes by, and nothing happens, except that Audrey Shelton and her brother Ralph arrive for a brief visit. Kit's hopes begin to rise. "It's quite possible that our friends in London have taken care of the matter," says Tom. "Or perhaps the storm has passed. Having responded to the Privy Council with a series of arrests, perhaps the Lord Mayor and the aldermen feel they have done their duty and are relaxing their drive a bit. In any case, we've sent Nicholas Skeres up to London to make a few cautious inquiries. We ought to know a little more before long. In the meantime, I suggest you try to put it all out of your mind, if you can, and enjoy yourself a bit. Audrey and Ralph and I have organized an outing. I hope you'll join us."

"Make it an outing to the Outer Hebrides and I will be delighted to join you," he says.

"I see you're still inclined to run," says Tom. "Perhaps you should have gone with Matthew, after all."

"That would have simplified matters for you considerably, wouldn't it?" says Kit. "Then you and Audrey and Sir Ralph, surrounded by half a dozen servants, could go off into the country on a picnic—roughing it, so to speak. Back to nature and all that, portable wine cellar and all."

"Keep your temper, Christopher," says Tom. "You have no right to turn on me like this. I mean, after all, I'm doing what I can to help you out of this mess."

"And what exactly, may I ask, are you doing?" says Kit. "You're going on a picnic!"

"Among other things, if you must know," says Tom, "I have sent an urgent letter to Robert Cecil, through Nicholas Skeres. We should be hearing from him before long. In the meantime, I see no harm in enjoying these gorgeous days. You can't just sit around brooding and worrying all day. Come with us. Meet the Sheltons a bit more thoroughly. Audrey has seen most of your plays, you know. She's quite impressed."

"I suppose they're here to discuss marriage arrangements—or is it contracts?"

"Oh, no, we haven't come that far. Audrey and I still have a few things to resolve between us before we can go forward with the whole business."

"I thought Robert Cecil was going to handle your 'business,' as you so appropriately put it."

"Well," says Tom, keeping his composure, "I can see that there's no point in discussing anything with *you* today. But you're still welcome. We leave in about an hour."

Kit decides to go, after all, and the outing proves to be a fine distraction. The party includes just Kit and Tom and the Sheltons, plus two servants: Ralph Shelton's man Henry Whyte, and Tom Walsingham's head gamekeeper, John Harrison. They ride out to Footescray and picnic beside the pretty Cray River. It is a pleasant little affair, though hardly rustic in its equipment. There are some wooden utensils and containers, but there is also a sufficiency of silver to remind them all that there is an important distinction between men and beasts. En route, John Harrison provides a running commentary on such things as the nesting habits of pheasants, the terrain preferred by deer, and the elm blight of 1561. "Oh, but they've all come back," he says with a sweep of his hand in the direction of a fine stand of trees.

Ralph Shelton proves to be a very attractive and comfortable sort of person. He has the same fine features as his sister and the same dark hair, though with a premature touch of gray in it. He and Tom fall into a political discussion as they sit on the bank of the river. For a while, then, Kit and Audrey are thrown together. Apparently she and her brother know nothing of the Thomas Kyd affair. "I do like poetry," she says. "But I must admit that I've always thought of it more as an entertainment than as a full-time profession. It doesn't seem quite right to me that a man should spend his life merely making verses. I mean, there are so many other things that need doing. Don't you agree?"

"If you can possibly excuse the inexcusable brutality of my disagreeing with you, then, dear friend of my dear friend, allow me to explain to you just how important poetry really is." Kit says this with mock courtliness and elicits from Audrey an appreciative smile.

"You do that very well, Mr. Marlowe," she says. "You should have made it your business to be better born. You might have done well at court."

"Ah, it was an error in judgment for which I will never forgive myself," he says. "But about poetry—"

"Yes, please tell me about poetry," she says. "But allow me a tiny refutation, should you overstate the case."

"How shall I put it, then," he says, rubbing his chin and searching the gentle, narrow river for the proper words. A flight of crows bark in the distance on the other side, and Audrey's gaze moves in their direction. "Poetry is the longest arm of the human mind. As we strive for knowledge absolute, which is impossible, of course, everything eventually fails us: logic, science, and even words. The aspiration is our blessing and our curse. Our victories are brief but wonderful; our failures tragic, but still, in a way, wonderful. When we can no longer phrase in syllogisms what we feel we want to say, we turn to metaphors. Imagination leaps into the darkness beyond the small circle of logic's light and brings back sparkling fragments of truth. So you see, it is not for entertainment alone that I labor at my art and craft—though, God knows, I have entertained some several thousand people in my time. In the public theatres, I mean. No, it is for something far more ambitious, though far less nameable. And in any case, I have very little choice, being, like the nightingale, uncontrollably excited by the darkness to sing my song."

With her small white hands she applauds his performance. "You should be on the stage, not behind it," she says. "You are a marvelous actor."

"But aren't we all?" he says. "Aren't we all marvelous actors? Well, at any rate, actors."

"Why, Mr. Marlowe," she says, her coyness an irrepressible weapon, "whatever can you mean by that?"

"Nothing really. Nothing much. Except that we all, in a way, write our parts and then play them out. Now and then, of course, we forget our lines, and that's a bit awkward."

She's amused. She agrees. She asks him what part he has written for himself. He turns the conversation back to her, and she is not at all reluctant to talk about her family and her childhood and her circle of friends, including Mary Herbert, who "collects poets the way some people collect porcelain dolls." She is obviously envious of the woman, the Countess of Pembroke, and, hence, heaps upon her certain excessively flattering adjectives.

It is all very pleasant, and the food is good under the clear sky and warm sun, but the wheels have not stopped grinding in London, and the Privy Council has already taken the necessary steps to question Kit about the heretical papers attributed to him: "A warrant to Henry Maunder, one of the messengers of Her Majesty's Chamber, to repair to the house of Mr. Thomas Walsingham in Kent, or to any other place where he shall understand Christopher Marlowe to be remaining, and by virtue thereof to apprehend and bring him to the Court in his company. And in case of need, to require aid."

When they return from the picnic, they find Henry Maunder waiting for them. He sits stiffly outside the front door, his document in his hand. He is a sturdy, bearded man with eyes full of duty. He is properly impressed by the grandeur of the manor and a bit apprehensive about dealing with anyone who bears the name Walsingham. He is, therefore, exceedingly polite and apologetic.

He stands as they approach. He has heard them come across the drawbridge. He has seen them dismount and turn their horses over to the stableman. And he has watched them come up the path. He notices that they pause when they see him and that, after a brief conversation, they break into two couples. Audrey and her brother turn off and go to another part of the house. Christopher and Tom come forward to confront Her Majesty's messenger. They have guessed quite correctly what it is all about. While they are still out of earshot, Tom says, "Let me talk with him first. Keep your temper and don't say anything."

"I'm terribly sorry to inconvenience you, sir," says Maunder, "but I have this request, issued by the Privy Council, for one Christopher Marlowe, whose presence is urgently required."

"For what reason, may I ask?" says Tom.

"I am afraid, sir, that for me to discuss the matter would be to exceed my authority."

"Very well, then," says Tom. "Mr. Marlowe will get his things together and be with you shortly. In the meantime, make yourself comfortable and I will send my man out with some refreshments for you. You must be a bit dry after your journey."

Henry Maunder hesitates and looks from one man to the other and back again. He wants to suggest that perhaps he should accompany Marlowe to his room, but Tom quickly reassures him. "And don't worry about my good friend. He is a gentleman and a scholar and is not likely to disappear. I give you my word on that."

"Yes, sir," he says. "Very good, sir. But we will have to be on our way very soon if we are to have daylight enough for the ride back to London."

In Kit's room they confer quickly as they get together a few clothes and papers. "Only take what you think you will need," says Tom. "I would say it seems, at the moment, to be a routine matter of questioning. On the other hand, we can't take any chances. Where will you be staying in London?"

"I will go to Samuel Rowley's," says Kit. "He's a very good friend and a conventional sort. He works for Henslowe. He's put me up before. Or else, if the plague is too awful, I will go to my cousin in Deptford. If my attendance is expected for any length of time, I can easily travel the three miles into the city."

"Good," says Tom. "I will be in touch with Robert Cecil and some other people and should know very soon what this is all about. I want you to stay at Rowley's until you hear from me. If you should be forced to leave there, send word or leave word with him, with specific instructions as to where you can be found. As soon as I know the extent of the trouble, I will come myself or send someone. If it proves to be too much to cope with, I will make arrangements for you—of one sort or another. Trust me in this, Kit. I will manage it for you. Your part will be to make your appearance before the Council so as to avoid any charge of contempt, and to answer their questions as best you can. With luck, you will satisfy their curiosity and be licensed to move about freely again."

"You don't think they'll put me in prison, do you?" says Kit.

"No, no, I don't think there's too much likelihood of that," says Tom. "At least this warrant would indicate something much more routine. But come, we mustn't keep this fellow waiting too long. He's liable to wonder what we're up to."

They pause before the door and then embrace. "Thank you, Tom," says Kit. "You've been too kind to me. I don't deserve it."

"Oh, nonsense," says Tom. "It's not out of kindness but out of love, you fool. Now go, and compose yourself for your ordeal."

V

DEPTFORD

HAT very evening Kit is brought before the Privy Council, which is convened as a court in the Star Chamber. It is a brief appearance, and not all the members of the Council are present. Those who are there show the strain and weariness of excessive meetings and of such an accumulation of problems that they cannot always deal with them as fully and as carefully as they would like to. Kit is somewhat encouraged by the fact that not all of them seem to know why he is there and must be reminded. "It is, I understand," says Whitgift, "a matter of some papers found in the possession of one Thomas Kyd, whose rooms were searched in connection with the recent riots and demonstrations against the aliens. The papers seem to be of a heretical nature and, according to Mr. Kyd, are the property of Christopher Marlowe."

None of the Council members seem terribly impressed by this comparatively unimportant item of business, but they raise certain obvious questions and put them to Kit. Most of them know him or of him. Lord Burghley is there, and Robert Cecil. Also present are Charles Howard, the Lord Admiral of England and sponsor of the Admiral's Company, for which Kit has done such impressive work;

Sir Thomas Heneage, who has heard of Kit's service under Sir Francis Walsingham; and the young Earl of Essex, who knows only that Kit is associated with the Ralegh circle.

"Now, young man," says Sir Thomas Heneage, "what are these papers all about?"

"If I may be permitted to see them," says Kit, "perhaps I can be of some help."

Whitgift hands the three sheets to an assistant, who in turn hands them to Kit. It doesn't take him long to recognize the material. "Yes," he says, "I remember this passage. It is a summary of the Arian heresy, which I found in a certain book perhaps two or three years ago and which I asked Mr. Kyd to copy down for me. As you can see by the excellent italic script, he is a trained scrivener, as was his father."

"And why would you want a copy of such scandalous material?" says Whitgift.

"I am a scholar trained in divinity at Cambridge University," he says. "Though I have never taken holy orders, I have a continuing interest in theology. However, I should point out that the book from which it was copied was not a scandalous or heretical book at all. Quite the opposite. It was a book by one John Proctor, I think. And, if my memory serves me, its title was *The Fall of the Late Arian.* It must have been published at least forty years ago. Its purpose was to refute the Arian heresy. But how can one refute a position before that position is described? I thought Proctor's summary was very concise, and, since the book was only borrowed, I asked Kyd to copy it out for me, my own handwriting being a bit inadequate for these things."

"And to what specific use did you put the passage?" asks Lord Burghley.

"I intended to put it with some miscellaneous notes," says Kit, "but apparently it got misplaced among Kyd's papers. I might have intended to use it—again, for purposes of refutation—at certain discussions that some of us had from time to time at the home of Sir Walter Ralegh."

"In short," says Robert Cecil, "this document does not represent your personal views?"

"It most certainly does not," says Kit.

Archbishop Whitgift clears his throat and seems about to ask another question, but instead he merely stares at Kit, as though he is trying to look into him. "I don't think we have the time or the energy to carry this inquiry much further at this time. I would, however, like to see some verification, if possible, of the statements we have just heard."

"Since the hour is late," says Lord Burghley, "and the matter does not seem to be highly urgent, I suggest that we adjourn and take it under consideration another time. We ask you, therefore, Mr. Marlowe, to give us your daily attendance, and to make yourself available on short notice should further information be required of you."

As he walks away from the Star Chamber, a free man, bound only to hold himself ready to answer further questions, Kit feels that it has all been too simple, somehow. He wonders whether this is the end of the matter or only the beginning. That portrait gallery of Council faces lingers in his mind as he makes his way quickly toward more familiar neighborhoods. Is it possible, he wonders, that Robert Cecil and Lord Burghley have secretly come to his defense? Or is he, perhaps, less important than he imagines, just another scholar, another playwright, not nearly so notorious as Tom has led him to believe?

Some of the answers are in the hands of the informer Richard Baines, a somewhat disreputable lawyer who provides the Archbishop with confidential reports on numerous questionable individuals. Some of the material he gathers himself; some he has gathered for him and then assembles. At the very moment that Kit is crossing the river to get to Samuel Rowley's place in Southwark, Richard Baines is hard at work completing his reports on Christopher Marlowe and Richard Chomley. He is aware of the warrant issued for Marlowe and of the connection between the two. Chomley himself, though a wanted man, is still at large.

Baines's report on Kit is titled *A note Containing the Opinion of one Christopher Marlowe Concerning his Damnable Judgment of Religion, and Scorn of God's Word*. In it he mentions every damaging statement ever overheard by him or any of his colleagues or any of the dozens of people he has questioned. He includes everything from the opinion that Christ was a bastard to the drunken claim that St. John the Evangelist was his bedfellow and was used by him "as the sinners of Sodom."

He concludes in the following businesslike fashion: "These things, with many others, shall by good and honest witness be approved to be his opinions and common speeches and that this Marlowe doth not only hold them himself, but almost into every company he cometh he persuades men to atheism, willing them not to be afraid of bugbears and hobgoblins, and utterly scorning both God and his ministers as I, Richard Baines, will justify and approve both by my oath and by the testimony of many honest men, and almost all men with whom he hath conversed any time will testify the same, and as I think all men in Christianity ought to endeavor that the mouth of so dangerous a member may be stopped, he saith likewise that he hath quoted a number of contrarieties out of the Scripture which he hath given to some great men who in convenient time shall be named. When these things shall be called in question, the witnesses shall be produced."

His accusations against Richard Chomley are even more damning, because they are more political. He says that Chomley has called all the members of the Privy Council atheists and Machiavellians; that he hates the Lord Admiral Francis Drake and Justice Young; that he rails at Topcliffe; that he spreads libels and slanders about Robert Cecil; that he has praised the papists and seminary priests; that he has considered killing Lord Burghley; and that he has said "that one Marlowe is able to show more sound reasons for atheism than any divine in England is able to give to prove divinity, and that Marlowe told him that he hath read the atheist lecture to Sir Walter Ralegh and others."

ii

In the plague-infested city, Kit waits, day after day, hour after hour, for something to happen. He knows that he would be better off with his cousin in Deptford, but he is equally convinced that he would not find a very warm welcome there. He has not, in fact, heard from his own mother and father in a long time, and his last visit to Canterbury was awkward and even unpleasant. There are things that he cannot explain to them, and they seem content to treat him as a stranger. They are involved in their own middle-class affairs, growing old and fat and reasonably prosperous—at least, in their terms. And so he hesitates, dragging out the days in familiar taverns, haunting the bookshops of St. Paul's Churchyard, and trying, but failing, to do some work.

On the twenty-fourth of May he hears that John Penry has been convicted and sentenced to death. This news, coupled with the grim atmosphere and his own tension, throws him into a fit of depression. He takes to his room and stays there for several days. He is alone in the house, Samuel Rowley having found, at last, a way to escape to the country.

He plunges inward, into the bleak regions of his own soul. Has he been wrong, after all, about himself? he wonders. Has his reason and arrogance led him into the trap of eternal damnation? He closes his eyes to experience the darkness. He opens them only to stare at the stained white ceiling. What a ridiculous thing the human body is! Here he is, a man alone, lying on a bed in a small room in the middle of the day that might be his whole life. Is he any more divine or less ridiculous than an insect? Does the fruit fly complain about the brevity of his life? he wonders. Another time he watches for hours a spider working at his web in the corner of the window. How busy he is, spinning out his filaments, dropping nearly invisible threads, crawling up them again, crossing and recrossing, driven by some predatory instinct to make this ingenious trap. And all for what? To catch a fly, to devour him, to leave his crusty shell in the dusty cobwebs, and then, perhaps, to begin again in another corner, the pointless miracle repeated all over again, complete with dazzlements and disappointments, visions and revisions.

All the incidents of his life fall apart. His first day at the King's School. Hot wine with Master Rose. The endless years of Corpus Christi, undergraduates laughing in his ears. The sacred precincts of The Eagle, when everyone was still alive and his tongue first discovered the choirs of words that sang in his head. And young Tom Walsingham and raving Roberto. All the desperadoes of The Unicorn and The Bishop's Head. And William Bradley, clutching his chest as though he could stop the spurting blood with his hands, a look of disbelief on his face, before falling, falling, falling, so quickly, so slowly, into the dust of Hog Lane. And all those shadows that danced from his mind onto the stage to vent themselves upon the vulgar mob, to thrill them with obscenities and noise, to lure them into the web of truth, so that they, like the fly or the wasp, could be disemboweled and enlightened into skeletons, intelligence informing their bleached bones. And all the bodies of all the lads that ever lent themselves to him or sailed with Drake or died on foreign soil, their young blood sucked up by the bats of war or the jackals of hypocrisy.

How hopelessly muddled it all is! And now this waiting, as though it really matters, as though it hasn't already ended. "Why, this is hell, nor am I out of it." But no, the final thread of hope dangles him over the furnaces of this world. He would cut it if he could and stop caring altogether. But the force that has driven him all his life now prevents him from performing the one positive act that might truly make sense. His dagger is on his belt. His belt is on the floor beside the bed. It would be so simple. And yet—and yet! He cannot frame his refutation. Something in his body protests, something twitches to live. Buzz, buzz, goes the bluebottle fly! He has seen corpses with flies in their mouths and their dead eyes staring like slaughtered pigs in the butcher's shop. "See, see where Christ's blood streams in the firmament." But all he sees is the stained incoherence of the white ceiling, and all he hears is the grinding of wheels in the street below and the senseless babble of the human trade. He falls asleep with a dull throbbing in his head, like a drum slowly beating and beating and beating. . . .

iii

At Scadbury, things are thrown into confusion by an urgent letter from Robert Cecil that says that the situation has suddenly deteriorated. "I understand that Whitgift has gotten, through agents of his own, a very damaging report on Christopher's religious views and his attempts to influence others in ways that might prove dangerous to the stability of the Church and the state. There seem to be witnesses willing to testify that Kit is linked to Richard Chomley. I have also heard a rumor to the effect that he may once or twice have contributed to the Marprelate papers, and that also his friend Matthew Roydon may have had a hand in that business. Furthermore, they say that there is a movement building to undertake a thorough investigation into the affairs and beliefs of Sir Walter Ralegh and his friends. This business would seem to be spreading in ever-widening circles. Whitgift is determined to cut out the cancer that is destroying the Church. It has become a madness with him. He can talk about nothing but recusants, papists, Puritans, Separatists and atheists. He's got them queued up at Bridewell for the torture, with Richard Topcliffe working round the clock and enjoying every minute of it. The latest tavern joke, I understand, is that six minutes on the rack will wring more truth from you than six years at the University, and hence, the wits say, anyone put to the torture should be granted an automatic and honorary Master of Arts degree. What will happen next is difficult to say. My father and I are at odds with Whitgift and his faction. They are, therefore, somewhat secretive about their strategies. But we predict there will be another interrogation of Kit. And it is quite conceivable that he will be put in Topcliffe's hands, as Tom Kyd was. If this should happen, God only knows what will out. He is not the most stable or reliable person in the world. What he can be forced to say might be damaging to both of us. And my position right now is not as firm as I would like it to be. Besides, this same Richard Baines has apparently filed a separate report on Richard Chomley in which some reference is made to certain accusations of an indecent nature against me personally. The situation, as you can see, is drawing to a head. I urge you to do everything in your power to prevent any injury to our reputations. I can no longer afford to protect Christopher. I'm not sure you can afford to either. I trust you will look to the matter and send me word immediately by confidential messenger."

Tom Walsingham shows the letter to Audrey Shelton, in whom he has confided since the day Kit was taken off on a warrant by Henry Maunder. Her brother, however, remains completely unaware of the whole situation, and they agree not to involve him.

"What do you think I should do?" Tom asks her.

"It all depends," says Audrey, "on how far you are willing to go."

"What do you mean by that?"

"I am talking about your capacity for survival."

"You mean my capacity for ruthlessness."

"Call it what you will," she says. "In any case, the choice is yours, not mine. On the other hand, what I do may very well depend on what you do."

"Do I understand you properly?" he says. "Are you suggesting that you might reconsider our plans?"

"My dear Thomas," she says, "what sort of a future can I look forward to, married to a man who insists on protecting a condemned heretic and whose sexual life is a public scandal?"

Her bluntness shakes him and seems physically to force him into a chair. He sits there for a moment, staring into the empty fireplace. Then he buries his face in his hands and mutters, "Oh, my God!"

She softens and puts a comforting hand on his shoulder. "I know how you feel about him," she says, "but you have yourself to consider, Tom."

"But isn't there some other way? Can't we just get him out of the country—to Scotland, perhaps?"

"You will have to move very quickly to arrange that. And besides, there are no absolute guarantees that he will be safe there or that he will remain there. He may not even be willing to go."

He stands up and walks back and forth in front of the gaping fireplace. He is talking half to himself, half to her. "Robert Poley should be back in Deptford by tomorrow at the latest. He may be there already. We could send Ingram into London to talk to Kit. There are ways to arrange the papers, especially if they are done in the name of the 'service.' He could not easily be traced where Robert stays—at the house of Eleanor Bull. In any case, he would be traveling under a fictitious name. He's done that before. And Matthew is there now, and other friends."

"And what if it is already too late?" she says.

He stops and faces her. "It can't be too late," he says. "I'll call in Ingram right now. Say you'll agree."

They are face to face, negotiating silently for a moment. Her hard eyes are fixed on him. "On one condition only," she says.

He doesn't have to ask what it is but waits to let her speak.

"Should there be any difficulty about getting him securely out of the country, he must be silenced absolutely."

Tom hesitates, unable to agree.

"Not only for my sake," she says, "but for yours. You have a marvelous future, Tom. Don't jeopardize it for an infatuation."

Slowly he nods his agreement and says, with a sigh, "I suppose you're right."

"Will you call in Ingram now?" she says, her composure unshaken through this difficult conversation.

"Yes," he says, and walks across the room and through the door.

When the three of them are together, they go over the arrangements in great detail. "And you understand, of course," says Audrey, "that he *must* leave the country."

Frizer looks at Tom. "And if he refuses, sir?" he says.

"He must not be allowed to refuse," says Tom.

Frizer glances at Audrey and then turns back to Tom. "Do I understand you properly, sir?"

Tom nods, and there is nothing more to be said.

iv

Kit is disturbed shortly after dawn by Samuel Rowley's house-keeper, Mary Mott. He hears her moving in the next room, shuffling about, picking things up, opening and closing cupboards. Then she comes to the door and opens it slowly, quietly, to get a look inside at her little poet, as she calls him. She has been Kit's ragged old toothless guardian angel in these trying days. She comes by every day to clean a bit and to see to it that he takes some food. She knows he's not well, though she can't name his disease. He turns over on his back and opens his eyes. "Can I get you a bit of breakfast, sir?" says the old crone, her lips disappearing now and again into the cavity of her mouth.

She comes in and opens the shutters, letting in the soft morning sunlight. "Ah, 'tis a lovely day," she says. "A good day to be up and about and doin' things." Her sons are all dead, and she lives with her middle-aged daughter who never married and takes in laundry. She goes on about this and that, but Kit is not really listening.

She goes out again, and he can hear her fussing at the stove to get the fire started. Then there is the sound of pots and pans and the smell of bacon. As she works, she hums a tune to which Kit knows the words:

> Mother's wag, pretty boy,
> Father's sorrow, father's joy;
> When thy father first did see
> Such a boy by him and me,
> He was glad, I was woe;
> Fortune changed made him so,
> When he left his pretty boy,
> Last his sorrow, first his joy.

When she comes in again she has a tray of food, and he finds that he is actually hungry. And mere appetite is a pleasant sensation. He hasn't felt it for some time. He gets out of bed and pushes open the window to let in some air. "Feelin' a bit better today?" she asks him.

"Yes, I am," he says, "though God knows why."

"Well, things never stay the same, you know. They either get better or they get worse."

He feels himself give in to a smile and goes to the basin to wash his face before sitting down on the edge of the bed to eat his breakfast.

It's still quite early in the morning when there is a heavy knock at the door that makes his heart leap and startles even Mary Mott. "Now, who in heaven can that be at this hour?" she says. Kit is frozen in the doorway between the two rooms. "Who's there?" she calls out.

"Ingram Frizer for Mr. Marlowe," comes the voice from the other side of the door.

Mary Mott looks at Kit, who heaves a sigh of relief and rushes to let him in. It is not only Ingram Frizer, but Nicholas Skeres. The two of them have just ridden in from Chislehurst and step stiffly into the room, a bit damp from the morning, their boots spotted with mud.

"You'd better go now," says Kit to the housekeeper.

"But I haven't finished the—"

"Come back later," he says firmly.

When she's gone, the three men sit down at a small table to talk. Frizer tells him about Robert Cecil's letter and the Baines report. Kit's face grows tight. He pounds the table with his fist. He stands up and paces back and forth in the small room like a confined lion. "I suppose, then, they'll be coming for me any time now," he says.

"It's hard to tell," says Frizer. He seems oddly sympathetic. "But I wouldn't risk it, if I were you."

"But isn't running away more of a risk?" says Kit.

"It depends on what you're running away from," says Frizer. Nicholas Skeres, as though amused by the remark, chuckles quietly but says nothing.

"What exactly did Tom say?" says Kit.

"Mr. Walsingham says we should go to Deptford to talk with Robert Poley," says Frizer. "He's back from The Hague and staying at Mistress Bull's house. We've sent on word to him to wait for us there."

"And then what?"

"And then we will see what the alternatives are."

"Did Tom say anything about my going back to Scadbury?"

"There wouldn't be much point in that, would there?" says Frizer. "I mean, either you've got to make yourself available to the authorities or you've got to go somewhere where they can't find you."

"Why didn't he come himself?" says Kit. "I'd like to talk with him personally."

"I'm afraid he's the only one who can answer that question," says Frizer.

"Well, I suppose that doesn't leave me much choice, does it?" says Kit. "Either I go or I stay."

"You needn't make up your mind until you've talked to Robert," says Frizer.

"All right, then," he says. He gets up and goes into the next room to get ready for the trip. He is sitting on the edge of the bed, putting on his boots, when Frizer comes to the doorway and says, "I suppose you've heard about John Penry."

"What about him?"

"He was hanged yesterday not far from here. At St. Thomas à Watering on the Canterbury Road. All very sudden and simple to avoid any sort of demonstration. There were very few people there, and he wasn't allowed to speak."

Kit closes his eyes for a moment to contain this latest shock. And in the flashing lights of that brief darkness he sees the bright face of his Cambridge friend, blazing with enthusiasm, sitting across from him at The Cardinal's Hat, youthful and alive. Frizer is saying something about Bancroft and the Act of Uniformity, but his voice reaches Kit in undulating echoes that muffle the meaning.

They go on foot through the narrow streets of Southwark, cross The Borough, and wait for a boat on the other side of London Bridge near Tooley Street. "Too bad about the stinking plague," says Skeres. "It's a lovely day otherwise."

And on the water, it is indeed lovely. The river teems with commerce. Sails billow in the perfect breeze, and the shores are colorful clusters of buildings, their brown-red roof tiles drying in the late-May sunshine after the early-morning dew. The myriad spires of the city's churches reaching skyward, the massive bridge that recedes behind them a testament to man's aspiring ingenuity. From the little boat that carries them down the river, one cannot see the agonies in the labyrinth of streets, the nailing up of houses, the carting away of plague victims. And what one cannot see, in a sense, does not exist.

Kit leans against the low rail, almost enjoying the movement, the color, the noise of life. What difference does it make what it's all about? he thinks. It's all the same, in a way. The only true distinction is between seeing it and not seeing it, between being alive and being dead. And whatever eternal damnation is, perhaps it's better than death, after all. Even pain is better. And not so far from pleasure as most people think. Besides, there is a limit to torment, in spite of the sermons of the fire-and-brimstone preachers. If there is a hell, it may not be half bad. And besides, it is a kind of immortality—none of this scattering of one's elements back into Nature. Darkness. Oblivion. Flies in one's dead mouth. The crust of a wasp in a spider's web.

Eleanor Bull is a widow. Her tavern is located in Deptford Strand on the open square beside the Royal Shipyard. It is a pleasant place, all white with green shutters and a thatched roof. There are a few private rooms, and, for the good weather, there is a small garden in which one might take a meal or sit in the shade of an antique oak. Mistress Bull herself is a robust woman of fifty or so, all bosom and energy, eager to please, and proud of her ability to carry on the business after the death of her husband.

They arrive at the tavern about ten o'clock in the morning and find Robert Poley waiting for them in the garden. He greets them with exaggerated affection. "So good to see you again," he says to Kit. "Sorry to hear about this difficulty. You'll have to tell me all about it. I've arranged for a room where we can have some privacy. We can have our lunch there and sort this thing out leisurely. I'm sure that if we all put our heads together we can find a comfortable solution."

The room is in the rear of the tavern, overlooking the garden. It is small and rather sparsely furnished. There is a single bed against one wall and a dining table in the middle of the floor, with benches on either side—enough space to seat six or eight guests. The walls are bare, except for an embroidered motto and a small tapestry depicting a hunting scene with several men on horseback and a fatally wounded stag. There is a fireplace but no fire on such a day as this.

The men relax and take a bit of wine. Robert Poley listens carefully as Kit goes back over the events that have led to this conference. "Think very carefully," says Robert, "about your dealings with Tom Kyd. Are you sure there isn't something that you've failed to mention?"

"I said we worked on a play together," says Kit, "and that from time to time I asked him to copy down some things for me. We were, briefly, friends of sorts."

"Did he ever seem to be involved in anything political?" says Robert.

"Not that I know of," says Kit. "I think he was too much of a coward for that sort of thing. No, I think his weapon was the pen and not the sword, and not much of a weapon at that."

"And he was not privy to your conversations at Ralegh's house?" says Robert.

"Hardly!" says Kit. "I mean, he never came there, and I rarely discussed such things with him. He's not terribly well educated, though he has a certain literary facility."

They review the list of Marlowe's friends, searching for someone who might be interested in betraying him and weighing those who might now offer him assistance. "Every man has his Judas," says Robert.

Kit looks at Ingram Frizer, but he seems lost in concentration as he meticulously peels an orange with his dagger.

They drift into a discussion of Scotland and the circle of religious exiles who have started their lives anew there. "It's a complicated situation," says Robert. "Such a mixture of persuasions. And now, I understand Matthew's gone there, though God knows why. I don't think he was in any serious trouble."

"Perhaps he'll be back when things settle down," says Frizer. "This fuss can't go on forever."

"Do you think it will ever settle down?" Kit asks.

"Oh, yes," says Robert with his usual air of being well informed. "The Queen's in a bit of a panic, that's all. Things are not so serious as they seem. And the plague's got everyone on edge."

"Not to mention the war," says Frizer.

"Well, of course, there's that, too, isn't there?" says Robert. He yawns elaborately, as if the whole thing is a bore, and then says, "We could do with a bit of lunch and perhaps a little exercise afterward. Nothing like a little walk to help one think."

"I'll see about it," says Skeres.

"What news of your pigeon, Drew Woodleff?" says Poley, and suddenly the three of them—he, Frizer, and Skeres, who is halfway out the door—break into laughter.

"What's this all about?" says Kit.

"Oh, it's too complicated to go into," says Frizer.

But Poley insists on explaining how his friends have tricked a young gull into signing a bond for some cannons which Frizer had, by some mysterious means, stolen out of government supplies, and how Frizer then disposed of them for the poor fool for half of what he imagined he might get for them, except that he did not dispose of them at all. In any event, the upshot was that Ingram still had his stolen cannons and thirty pounds to boot. "There's more to it than that, but it's not even entirely clear to me."

During lunch they come back to the crucial questions. Kit is eager to know what Poley's estimate of the situation is, but this master of deception is rather evasive. "It's very difficult to tell," he says. "I mean, ordinarily a fellow in your position, with your sort of friends, would be fairly safe. After all, you're only a writer and not very politically inclined. Who would want to take the trouble to hang you? And yet, I suppose it could happen. I think I know this Baines fellow. Totally disreputable. He'll do anything for anybody for money. I'm sure he's told Whitgift precisely what he wants to hear. The question is, who will believe him?"

"I suppose those who want to believe him," says Frizer.

Poley rubs his chin. "You've got a point there, Ingram."

And once again they talk of Scotland. "I could probably arrange an assignment there for you that would cancel out this whole business," he says, "but it might not be the sort of thing you would enjoy."

"What sort of thing are you talking about?" says Kit, growing a bit impatient.

"I'd rather not go into particulars," says Poley, "but it would be what we call a *dirty* assignment. Its only advantage is that it might persuade the authorities that you are a thoroughly good fellow." He laughs at his own humor.

After lunch they walk in the garden awhile. Robert Poley seems to be enjoying his role as father confessor and practical adviser to this younger, handsomer, and more accomplished man. He can't entirely conceal a cruel streak. And Kit feels, after a while, that he's being toyed with.

Back in the room, they order more wine, loosen their clothes, and relax. By mid-afternoon it seems as though they have been over the same ground a thousand times and explored every possible avenue and backstreet of the situation. Kit is on the bed, leaning on one elbow, Roman-style, and holding a glass in his other hand. Poley, his Mephistophilis, is sitting on a chair near the foot of the bed, studying his man as a physician might study his patient. Frizer and Skeres have just finished a game of backgammon at the table, which has been cleared of lunch. Only the reckoning lies there, scribbled on a piece of paper by Eleanor Bull.

Kit feels the effects of the wine and raises his voice as he speaks. "I still don't understand why Tom didn't come," he says. "I want to see him first, damn it, before I decide what to do."

Frizer gets up suddenly from the table and turns to face him. "There is nothing left to decide," he says, unable to control his irritation. "It was all decided before we even came here."

"What are you talking about?" says Kit.

Skeres comes around from behind Frizer, until the two of them are standing just a few feet from the bed.

"Tom does not want you at Scadbury," says Frizer. "Don't you understand? He wants you out of the way."

"I'll believe that when I hear it from Tom himself, you lecherous bastard!" shouts Kit.

Poley stands up calmly and says, "I guess you're bound for Scotland whether you like it or not, Christopher."

But Kit does not take his eyes from Frizer. "It's not Tom at all," he says. "It's you, Ingram. It's you who wants to get rid of me. I knew it all along. And I'll be damned if I'm going to let you get away with it."

Kit springs to a sitting position and reaches for his dagger, but the three of them are by this time too close to him. Skeres knocks him backward with a blow across the chest, and Poley wrestles with his legs. Before he can utter another word or cry out, he sees the flashing blade of Frizer's dagger, but only for an instant.

He is blinded by a sky of blood. He rises. He falls. He rises again. Blood streams from the deep wound in his eye. He staggers against the wall, confused and angry. He wipes at his face as though he is trying to push aside a scarlet curtain. Profanities mushroom in his mind, but the floor is slipping away, and his speech is muddled. All that his "mouth of gold" can manage is an incoherent howl as he slides to the floor and then falls face down.

He hears the thud of his own flesh against the floor, but he cannot feel it. His eyes are open, but he cannot see. The drum of his life beats in his chest and throat. He cannot make the effort to rise, and, in the murky midnight of his mind, bells clang, and the little glass beads that were his life are broken apart and scattered like exploded diamonds or stars. Fractured form. A chaos of images that mingle with the last semblance of reality: the whispering men who stand and kneel over him. "He's still breathing. Shall we finish him off?" "No, leave him. Leave him . . ."

Cold wind rushing through damp caves. Hot wind sucking up the fire in his guts. "He's trying to say something. Stop his mouth." Time collapses. There is a foot near his face. He smells the leather

of the boot. He sees the scrap heap in his father's shop. Canterbury
in the rain. The Cathedral rising out of sight. In the wind he hears
the voices of a thousand boys and then the bells again. *It strikes, it
strikes! Now body turn to air.* . . . "Wash up the blood. Give
yourself a wound." *Adders and serpents.* Modo and Mahu! And
blasts of sunlight pulse through his inner eyes and fall on his
magnificent sword. He rises in a shaft of golden light *to be a king.* A
crown awaits him. He lifts his head. The ruby magic of his sceptre
transforms the world. He stretches out his arms. The tavern faces
roar. The galleries applaud. *And now we will to fair Persepolis.* "He
smiles in death. Why does he smile?" Trumpets and drums.
Trumpets and drums. "He cannot speak. He reaches out his hand."
The multitudes of the world have gathered at his gate. *Oh, my lord,
'tis sweet and full of pomp!* "His breath is stopped. Remember all
your lies and speak them well."

Lightning Source UK Ltd.
Milton Keynes UK
21 September 2009

143978UK00001B/128/A

9 780967 333458